Red
Ribbons
Louise Phillips

HACHETTE
BOOKS
IRELAND

First published in Ireland in 2012 by
HACHETTE BOOKS IRELAND
First published in paperback in 2013 by Hachette Books Ireland

1

Cataloguing in Publication Data is available from the British Library

ISBN 978 14447 4303 6

Typeset in AGaramond, Gill Sans and Pragmata by Bookends Publishing Services.
Printed and bound in Great Britain by Clays Ltd, St Ives plc

Hachette Books Ireland policy is to use papers that are natural, renewable and
recyclable products and made from wood grown in sustainable forests. The logging
and manufacturing processes are expected to conform to the environmental
regulations of the country of origin.

Hachette Books Ireland
8 Castlecourt Centre
Castleknock
Dublin 15, Ireland

A division of Hachette UK Ltd
338 Euston Road, London NW1 3BH

www.hachette.ie

For Robert

In the dark, all he could hear was the flow of the water. The ground underfoot was a mix of scrub and barren soil; he made no sound as he moved. They were now in a place without shadows.

Her breathing had been deep, her chest moving in and out, her body trembling.

'Let's play a game,' he had said, and in his mind he had heard the old clock ticking – tick tock, tick tock – followed by its familiar elongated pause: everything in perfect rhythm.

He had left the duct tape across her mouth to keep her silent. The skin on her lovely face now, blotchy, bruised and wet from tears. Her arms and legs tied securely.

He wanted it to be quick.

Tick tock, tick tock.

He pulled the electric cable tight around her neck, closing off her oxygen, trapping the blood vessels. This time, expediency was all that mattered, although he did not want her to suffer.

He prepared her body properly – brushing her hair and tying both plaits neatly with the ribbons. Her lips had reminded him of a painting by Vermeer, the deep shades of cherries over-ripening on the canvas. He laid out her body, as if she were a young girl sleeping, before gently kissing her forehead. She hadn't understood, but then, why should she?

She was never good enough.

Tuscany, Italy

HE COULD HAVE TAKEN A DIRECT FLIGHT FROM DUBLIN TO Galileo Galilei airport in Pisa. Instead he chose a Dutch airline with connecting flights first to Paris and then on to Florence. Examining his boarding pass, he double-checked the date and times on the overhead monitor, 10-03-2011 – departure 06.20. If all went according to plan, he had plenty of time to catch the connecting flight to Florence at 11.05 a.m. He cared little about losing a few more hours; it meant nothing. The only important thing was his intention and the knowledge that this trip, well overdue, was finally coming to pass.

Once safely on the plane, he smiled affectionately at the stewardesses, sitting back with ease, enjoying the sound of English, French and Dutch instructions coming from the cockpit just like he had as a boy, when his curiosity about language had first been aroused.

He was now three months into his leave of absence from Newell Design and he missed developing architectural plans and elevations. Still, looking after his deranged mother had had some advantages. For one thing, it meant he didn't have to listen to the continuous whining of the imbeciles with whom he worked. He prided himself on being a good listener, for, these days, far too many people spent far too long talking rather than thinking. Of course, the upside of being a good listener was that he found out most things he needed to know, in the end.

Studying people was one of his pet pastimes – working out exactly what made them tick and why. He liked to categorise them, something that had been easy at Newell Design, given how transparent his colleagues had been.

There was Jackie, who had done numerous courses – 'up-skilling' was what she called it, but he had another name for it, 'jack of all trades and master of none'. It was the mark of a woman who longed to be someone different, but who didn't have the imagination to achieve any real change. Then there was snivelling Susan, who had buried her husband last year and was looking to 'start over', which entailed a lot of blathering about inner peace and a new penchant for Tarot cards. And 'young cool guy' David; oh yes, the boss definitely liked him. The others didn't particularly interest him either – Karla from Scotland, Daniel with a face like a bulldog and reliable Henry, who had worked at the company for so long that everyone kept a keen eye on his desk in the hope that one day he might not be there. They were a tedious bunch, only Jarlath offered any sense of intrigue. Jarlath shared his admiration for seventeenth-century French philosophers and mathematicians, which meant talking to him was at least tolerable. In appearance, however, Jarlath disappointed. He was in his early thirties and scrawny, a man who would benefit from some building up and taking more care of himself. Despite being twenty years Jarlath's senior, he felt physically superior. He suspected Jarlath was an only child, just like he was. This was indicated by some of his more obvious qualities: self-obsession, a loner, happier burying his head in a book rather than watching television, a keen appreciation of music – good music, that is, not the rubbish variety that seemed to be played in every home, office and coffee shop.

'Would you like some tea or coffee, Sir?' The stewardess had such a lovely smile.

'Any herbal tea, my dear?'

'Of course,' she said and smiled again.

Jarlath and he had often discussed Blaise Pascal, a pure intellectual in the truest sense, combining a love of mathematics and logical reasoning with an insatiable desire to understand mankind.

When he had told them he needed a leave of absence from work, snivelling Susan had been the worst. Still lamenting her late husband, when she had found out he had an ailing mother she had stupidly thought he could share her pain. Jarlath had displayed heightened levels of discomfort at Susan's overkill of empathy. It was the kind of emotional display that never sat easily on the shoulders of the young.

Choosing a window seat, he was relieved that both seats to his right remained empty, and he was free to enjoy the clear blue sky above the clouds, losing himself in thought. It was often difficult keeping up the façade of being nice, and he had no doubt that if any of his colleagues had been asked about him, their opinions would be completely flawed. This was of his own making, of course, as generally he made a point of only presenting a two-dimensional aspect of himself to the world. Accordingly, he had dished out his usual round of pleasantries before leaving, promising Jackie he would consider her suggestion to examine all forms of 'up-skilling' while he was away.

'Oh, such a lovely man,' he had heard Susan say as he'd closed the office door behind him.

He smiled grimly at the memory of being out of their company and able to breathe in fresh air.

Yes, he had earned his break, and not just from them but from the old bag too. He knew tongues would wag in the village about him taking a trip to Tuscany while her ladyship was on her last legs, but a week's respite was what he needed. Let the local rumour mill churn out whatever it chose, it would never be any more than speculation.

≈

Standing in the elegant foyer of the Hotel de Tucci, he stood back and admired the black-and-white chequered floor. Across this enormous chessboard, guests, hotel staff, and overly pampered dogs and cats scuffled nosily. He would not stay long in Florence. One night's rest was all that was required, then he would be ready to start the drive to Livorno. Choosing to take the stairs rather than the lift to his room on the first floor, he thought again about how his mother's unintentional trips down memory lane had awakened feelings he had suppressed for far too long, and how it was with a mix of anticipation and trepidation that he planned the next leg on his journey. In many ways, his life was now echoing the words of Pascal: 'Let each one examine his thoughts. He will find them all occupied with the past and the future.' This empathy of thought pleased him.

≈

The drive to Livorno was a pleasant one, with russet-coloured rooftops dotting the landscape. The road eventually led into the lovely seaside town he remembered so well from his youth. The distance was short, a little over twenty kilometres, and he had switched cars at Pisa, enjoying the covert aspect of it all. Much time had passed since that old business, so there was really no cause for any concern, but being careful added a certain excitement to the proceedings. With the car window rolled down, he took in the familiar smells of a place to which he had always known he would return.

Mother hadn't meant to resurrect the old wounds, but years of keeping her trap shut had been undone by the garbled workings of a decaying brain, and once resurrected, it had changed everything. It started harmlessly enough, but then, it usually did.

'Do I look different today?' she had purred, deluding herself that her beauty had returned.

'No. Not particularly.' The air in her bedroom had been dry, stifling.

'But you are looking at me, staring the way you like to. You always liked looking at your mother, didn't you?'

'I was just looking, nothing more.'

'You shouldn't stare at me that way, people might talk.'

He had turned his back to her, but the idiotic bitch had continued.

'But who cares about them? We don't, my darling, do we? We never did. None of them understand. Jealously is a dreadful affliction, don't you think?'

'No one is jealous. You are rambling.'

'Don't lie, little boy. I can see right through you.'

Standing at her sick bed, he had breathed in the stench of her old age.

'I am not a little boy any more.'

'You are staring again.'

'Am I?'

'You know you are, and don't lean on my shoulders so hard. It hurts. You think I'm weak-minded don't you, but I have the measure of you.'

'Just checking your reflexes, Mother. They are as sharp as ever I see.'

'You were the same with that young tramp, staring at her too, following her like some demented lapdog.'

'Why don't you take your pills, Mother? You know how you like to lose yourself.'

'She was a tramp, you know. Antonio liked tramps – young ones, especially. Don't you remember? Don't you? Oh, but you must.'

He'd felt his spine tighten as he clenched his fists. He'd remembered Tuscany, and the room with the long windows. 'Shut up.'

'Tickle, tickle, tickle,' her claw-like fingers had reached out, touching his chest. 'Remember how you liked this, little boy?'

'I never liked it.'

He'd stood back farther, because the desire to punch her had suddenly become so strong, throbbing through him like a sharp pain. It would be a mercy, some might think, to finish off the old bitch. He'd taken a long, measured breath, letting her ramble, as he'd listened.

In the end, he was glad he had. It had been so long since he had allowed himself to remember any of it.

≈

Arriving at the outskirts of Livorno, he felt relief at being far away from her. He could almost taste the treasures that Suvereto would unfold. His intentions and aspirations had been clear from the beginning: the trip was simply a way of rekindling the more positive aspects of the past. Sometimes, though, life sends you an added bonus and the course changes, taking you somewhere unexpected.

As he walked across the paving stones in Suvereto's ancient town centre, its narrow alleyways and broad squares captivating him, he saw Bishop Antonio Peri. At first, he had thought his mind was playing tricks, that it was just a stooped, overweight old man who resembled Antonio. When he looked again, it was undeniably him, even without the pomp and glamour of his ornate bishop's robes. The last he had heard, the poisonous bishop had been relocated to Florence, but it seemed he too had been compelled to return, and there he was, drifting easily with the locals, none of them knowing the kind of monster he was.

It took some time to secure a private audience with him. In the end, just like the old bitch, the once-arrogant pig shared far more than he had intended; words crawling through old wounds. The fall from the cliff edge some days later would have been attributed to his fragility and stupidity – what was a frail old man thinking, walking on such a dangerous cliff edge? The sea had been so blue, the sun blinding on the water, the fat bastard whining like an abandoned baby, tasting fear, begging for clemency with his pathetic babbling.

He had smiled to himself as he heard the bishop's scream curling through the air, his death resonating a new beginning.

NUI Maynooth, Renehan Hall
Saturday, 12 March 2011

HEAVY RAIN CLOUDS WERE BEARING DOWN ON YET another dark afternoon when Dr Kate Pearson finally reached the car park. She had spent over an hour negotiating her way through bumper-to-bumper traffic coming out of Dublin, and was hoping to get a shot of caffeine before the talk began. The conference at the university had been booked to capacity over a month in advance, which meant a packed room of people, all waiting for Kate's talk. It seemed that understanding the psychology behind crime and criminal profiling was the latest buzz and fascination for the masses.

It was the first time Kate had given a lecture at Maynooth and the line-up was impressive, featuring some of the best crime writers and criminology academics in the country. Since returning from London to Ireland after Charlie was born, she'd spent the last few years working with young offenders – a far cry from her tenure with criminal psychologist Professor Henry Bloom. Her current work was aimed at the prevention of criminal acts, rather than identifying key aspects of them. Henry, who was well respected and held in high regard by Scotland Yard, had taught her a great deal about getting inside the mind of an offender, but, despite the positive attributes of her current role, a part of her still pined to unravel a profiling puzzle.

Before entering Renehan Hall, she looked at the whiteboard erected outside:

CRIME AND CONTEMPORARY IRELAND –
NUI MAYNOOTH PRESENTS
'THE TRUTH BEHIND CRIMINAL PROFILING'
An illustrated talk by Dr KATE PEARSON
– Criminal Psychologist
2.00 p.m.–3.00 p.m.
Sold Out

Kate had prepared her notes the week before, but had revised them earlier that morning. It was important to strike the correct balance when presenting a talk to both students and members of the public, breaking it down over general profiling headings and actual case studies. It was usually best to choose one main case for deep analysis, and she had deliberately chosen a case that would underline the most frightening aspect of most criminal studies – the ordinariness of the offender.

Walking to the top table from the back of the conference hall, Kate deliberately avoided eye contact with members of the audience. She always felt a degree of apprehension about talking in public, but, despite the butterflies in her stomach, past experience told her that once she was up there, she would be fine. Nonetheless, Niall King's enthusiastic face seemed like a double-edged sword. As head of the Humanities Department, he had chosen all the speakers for the day with care, and she knew his expectations of her were high.

'Hi, Niall.'

'Ready to be fed to the lions, Kate?'

'Thanks for putting me at my ease,' she laughed.

'Don't worry, they've all had their lunch, so they should go easy on you.'

'Can I upload my file here?' Kate pointed to the laptop connected to the overhead screen.

'I'll load it for you – it's being temperamental today.'

'Thanks.'

'Whenever you're ready, Kate, I'll do the intro.'

Kate handed Niall her memory stick, and removed her notes from her briefcase. She took her seat, still avoiding eye contact with the audience, and waited for Niall to begin his introduction.

'Well, everyone, we are in for a treat this afternoon. I'm delighted to introduce Dr Kate Pearson, a lady whom I admire greatly. As some of you might be aware, along with my keen interest in studying criminology, like many of you here, I'm a firm believer in examining and questioning the social, economic and cultural aspects of Ireland today. It was through this interest that I met Kate, who is currently working with the Counselling and Young Offenders Reintegration Programme at Ocean House. However, it is not her work with probation services that she will speak about today, but rather her extensive experience of criminal profiling from her time in the UK. Kate holds a first-class honours degree in Psychology from Trinity College, a Master's in Criminology from University College London and a Doctorate in Forensic Psychology from the University of Nottingham. She has vast experience in the area of criminal profiling, having worked with Professor Henry Bloom, one of the leading psychologists in the UK. Since her return to Ireland, she has also given some help to An Garda Síochána. Ladies and gentlemen, please give a warm welcome to Dr Kate Pearson.'

As Niall stood back, Kate took her position at the podium, looking directly at the audience.

'First, I would like to thank Niall for organising this event and to thank you all for coming here today to listen to my talk on the truth behind profiling. Let's begin by exposing some of the myths behind criminal profiling. Many people think of profiling as conforming to what they have seen on television, showing an entire crime solved within an hour-long programme. Sadly, the reality is very far from this, not just in the length of time it takes to apply profiling correctly but also regarding some of the methods used by profilers. The first question we must ask, therefore, is: what exactly is criminal profiling?'

Turning away from the audience, Kate looked up at the screen and read the definition written there.

'"Criminal Profiling is the process of identifying personality traits, behavioural tendencies, possible biographical maps, or even geographical locations of an offender based on characteristics and evidence found at the crime scene, whether that crime scene is a primary or secondary one." I will explain the difference between primary and secondary crime scenes later in our discussion. For now, crime scene characteristics are a good place to start.'

As the dark clouds started to shift and the long windows of Renehan Hall admitted thin streams of afternoon sunlight, Kate could tell she already had most of the audience's undivided attention.

'Let's look at how we would pull together the various factors from a crime scene.' Kate flicked onto the next slide. 'The three key things we must look at are the important *behavioural aspects* of the crime, what *inferences or probabilities* we can deduce about the perpetrator based on these and, finally, what *other crimes* the offender is likely to have committed.'

Kate was glad she had chosen the Dunmore case to discuss. It displayed all the aspects of what is typically described as a disorganised crime scene, where often an offender has committed a crime spontaneously. One of the important factors that Kate wanted to stress about spontaneous crimes was that although they can happen from a spur of the moment decision, they do not necessarily occur out of the blue.

'Okay, now I'd like to move to discuss one case in particular, where we can see the work of the profiler on the ground. The case I've chosen is the Dunmore case, in which I was personally involved. I worked with members of An Garda Síochána to piece together a profile of the attacker who committed his crime in a frenzied manner.

'The attack on Noelle Dunmore was sexually motivated, but the motivational needs of her assailant had built up over a period of time. The severity of the attack, including the level of violent force used, was in itself a reflection of the need, anger and compulsion of her attacker. Many of the characteristics of the particular crime scene – the violence, the choice of a public park as the location for the attack and the risks her assailant had been prepared to take both in his choice of location and in leaving his victim at the scene – helped me to form a number of conclusions about him.

'In cases of angry, sexual and violent assaults, the psychological condition of an attacker is frequently at the point where they have the ability to depersonalise their victim, seeing him or her solely as a means of fulfilling their own needs and fantasy, often without any of the guilt. Noelle's attacker left her for dead. Thankfully, she survived, but as she had been blindfolded, she could not provide any description of the offender. However, certain aspects of his behaviour, including his incorrect assumption that he had killed his victim, indicated someone who was not just impetuous, but someone who did not have the maturity or intelligence to take his intentions to their conclusion. Even without making the mistake of thinking his victim was dead, he knew Noelle would be found. This told me that his needs and heightened desires were such that fulfilling them was far more important to him than the risk of being caught.'

There was a perfect silence among her audience as Kate delineated the key points of the case. It was almost like they were all holding their breaths, waiting for the revelation that was coming.

'I was working on the case with Detective Inspector O'Connor. As most of you no doubt know, profilers are not welcome in every police station' – there was a ripple of muted laughter at this, and Kate knew she must have a garda or two in the audience – 'but O'Connor and his team were willing to bring me in on this case. It paid off. I was able to tell them that the attacker was immature, probably a young male between eighteen and twenty-five, and that he was someone whose anger had built up over time, possibly as a result of seeking relationships, but because of inadequate social or communication skills, had failed. This profile helped narrow the list of suspects. The investigation team had plenty of forensics from the crime scene, but had been unable to find a match against known offenders, or anyone else who would have been considered high risk. As I had told them the possible age of the perpetrator and the extremities of psychosis he displayed, further questioning within the local community very quickly led to the arrest of nineteen-year-old Jonathan Kinsella. He had been interviewed by police during their house-to-house enquiries, but his shy and backward behaviour, living at home with his parents, with no previous record, meant he had been overlooked. Kinsella was subsequently convicted of the assault and attempted murder of Noelle Dunmore and sentenced to fifteen years.'

Kate smiled at her audience. 'I'm almost ready to finish up. I hope that you found today's discussion helpful in eradicating some of the scepticism around criminal profiling, and the assistance it can bring to bear on criminal cases. It's very easy to be sidetracked by assumptions and presumptions – the aim of profiling is to work with the available details, however small those might be. It is a far more pragmatic science than its detractors give it credit for and, of course, it's a fascinating area of criminal work. So, to conclude, let us put the base elements of good profiling in a nutshell, if we can.'

Kate clicked up her final slide of the afternoon, which covered methods of operation and key signatures left at a crime scene.

'The one thing we should always keep in mind when examining any case is that despite obvious indicators of a particular form of operation, or signature, perpetrators very often do similar things for very different reasons. So along with finding the signals, we must also be mindful not to be led in the wrong direction.'

Cronly Lodge

HIS FLIGHT FROM FLORENCE LANDED BACK IN DUBLIN airport at 4.15 p.m., so it was late evening by the time he got back to Cronly Lodge. Instead of going up directly to see the old witch, he chose to walk the beach instead. The spring and summer crowds had not yet begun to arrive for their annual land grab of the sunny southeast but, at this hour, either way, the strand was deserted.

He walked slowly on the sand, near the water's edge, not wanting to rush his next move. Mrs Flood, their housekeeper, had been given the thankless task of minding his mother while he was away. She had left moments earlier, when he had called to confirm he was near at hand. Everything was at long last firmly crystallised in his mind. He knew what he needed to do. Once the bishop had filled in the missing pieces, all other plans had changed. It was strange how that one part of the jigsaw had escaped him for so long. The truth was, he had not thought even his vile mother could sink so low. The only reason he was now delaying the inevitable was his desire to hear it all from the bitch herself.

Leaving the beach, he walked up to the house and let himself in. He locked the door behind him, then drew the curtains downstairs before making his way up the old staircase. When he reached the landing, her roars told him she knew he was there well before he opened her bedroom door.

'Is that you, you selfish little shit? Back to mind your ailing mother? Not before time. The prodigal son returns, let's all thank the heavens.'

Part of him didn't even want to look at her, wanted to just shut her up once and for all – but he knew that it was at testing times that a person's true character proved itself.

'I see you haven't lost any of your charm while I was away, Mother.'

'No thanks to you. Off on your little holiday while I'm cooped up in this hellhole like some bloody prisoner. Is that stupid cow gone?'

'Mrs Flood?'

'Of course Mrs Flood, how many stupid cows are there? Nobody gives a shit about me, not you, not anyone – least of all that awful bloody woman. Give me my pills. The cow hates me, you know. Hates me, hates me, hates me. Are you listening? I'm telling you, they're all the same, bastards, fucking bastards the lot of them. Do you hear me?'

'I hear you.'

'They're all swine, worse than swine, and you're no better. Give me my pills.'

'Not just yet.'

'I haven't had any. I don't care what the old bat said. I remember more than she does, you know.'

'I don't doubt it.'

'Where did you sneak off to anyway while I was dying in my bed? Give me the pills, will you? Come on, there's a good boy.'

'I was meeting old friends.'

'Lucky you. Friends? What friends? Some cheap tart was it? Is that cow still here?'

'Mrs Flood left an hour ago. It's just you and me now, Mother.'

'Good, good, that's good. We were always good together, you and I, blood is thicker than water, a cut above the rest of them, we always were.

'I met an old friend of yours. Bishop Antonio.'

'I don't know any Bishop Antonio. Why won't you give me my pills?'

'You don't need them. Not yet. We don't want to blur the mind too soon, do we?'

'I'm tired, why are you talking about that damned man?'

'You brought him up.'

'No I didn't … I don't remember.'

'Two weeks ago, before I left.'

'Two weeks is a lifetime when you're dying. Give me the pills, will you? Don't be cruel.' Her eyes were pleading, narrowing into slits. 'Oh, but I forgot, you like being cruel, don't you? Makes you feel big, doesn't it, picking on an old, defenceless woman? You're no better than the rest of them, taking advantage. Some loving son you are.'

'He was asking for you, Antonio, wanting to know how my mother, the old hag, was getting along.'

'There's a place in hell for people like him, and you.'

He watched, disgusted, as a line of spittle settled on her top lip. 'Fancy visiting it?'

He crossed the room to her swiftly and she gasped at the sudden pain. 'Stop pulling my hair. It hurts. Get away!'

'It's supposed to hurt. Antonio was very generous with his information, Mother, filled me in on a lot of missing gaps.'

'He was always a mouth, the slimy bastard. Stop at my hair, stop this instant! You can't make me say anything. I'm not afraid of the likes of you.'

'Can't I? How's this?' Grabbing her dried-out grey ponytail, he pulled her head so far back, the bones in her neck creaked in response. 'Here, look in the mirror, Mother, see how ugly you are.' He took up her hand mirror with the ivory handle from the side table and turned it towards her.

'He told me a little story, Mother. It was all about you. You like being the centre of the story, don't you? You always did. You're not looking, Mother, open your eyes. Not a pretty picture, is it? They say a mirror cannot lie, but you can. Can't you? You lie better than anyone.'

Letting go of her hair, he walked over to the window and yanked up the bottom sash so he could breathe in the evening air. The outside seemed as humid as her bedroom, a heavy veil of smothering. He watched shadows engulf the garden, thinking he could hear the leaves of the elderberry trees swaying. His indignation rose as she continued to chide.

Out of nowhere, she began to laugh, loudly and hysterically. 'Got you all riled up, son, has it? All excited about your young tramp? Or maybe you liked Antonio more? He always said there was something not right about you, silly sneaky little boy. You are a sneak, aren't you? Like a snake crawling around in the dark, slither, slither, slither, snake, snake, snake.'

'Shut your mouth or I'll shut it for you.'

'Not with your back to me you won't. Go on you idiot, keep looking out that window – dreamer – loser. All that money for your education, and for what? Do you think you would have had any of it, if it hadn't been for me?'

He pulled the window down, clicked the latch over and closed both curtains. Turning, he waited in the dark, listening to her chiding him, the room becoming clammier with the passing of time. She never stopped, it was relentless. It had always been relentless, for as long as he could remember. He walked over to her bed once more and stood over her, smelling the sweat from her body, her hair wet with moisture, her breath foul. Inside him, a savage mixture of old memories and hate churned.

'Why don't you tell me your side of the story, Mother? I am sure it will be very insightful.'

'Tell you what, you little shit?'

'Come on, you know you want to. Let's hear it from the whore's mouth.'

She stared at him, eyes wide open, her hands balled up into useless fists. 'You're mad.'

'I guess that makes two of us.'

'I want my pills. Give me my pills.'

'Not in the storytelling mood, are we?' He had left the bedroom door open so he could hear the sound of the Napoleon clock from downstairs. It swooned up the stairwell, the way low sounds can move in near silence. Tick tock, tick tock.

Her arms were already badly bruised from injections and blood tests, a few more marks from tying up her hands would go unseen. He knew now that she might never tell him, just as he knew everything the old bishop had said was true. He had wasted enough time – a lifetime – trying to get her to explain things. No more.

She screeched like a wounded animal before he pressed the pillow down hard, but he held firm. Beneath his hands her frail body resisted, thrashed and writhed with a strength he hadn't expected. He viewed it all clinically, objectively, like he wasn't even involved. He was glad she put up a good fight, though. The kill, in the end, was all the better for it.

Six Months Later ...

Ellie

I KNOCK ON THE DOOR. WELL, ISN'T THAT WHAT YOU'RE supposed to do with doors? That, and open and shut them. I hear a man inside the room cough, the sound muffled by the wooden divide. Maybe if I stand here long enough, I can disappear, sink into the ground or evaporate into the air. I wouldn't mind that. I am wearing some other person's clothes, an unbecoming grey blouse and faded jeans. By now, I am used to these things. Everything I have belonged to someone else at one time or another, everything, that is, except the bits that matter. Sadly, the bits that matter are all mine. My short, brown hair is washed and tucked, childlike, behind my ears. I wear neither make-up nor jewellery. There is no need for such things here. I have no need for such things.

Moments earlier, on the way to this door, I had caught sight of myself in the gold ornate mirror in the corridor. Unlike me, it is beautiful. It has an intricate frame and hangs on the wall past the sign for Female Rooms. The mirror does not discriminate. It welcomes all of us on our daily walkabouts. Of course, there are those of us who have looked in the mirror who are no longer here – some of us are no longer alive. Apart from the tiny black spots around the glass edges, it is perfect, and never fails to greet us. We cannot avoid it as it hangs in the walkway leading to the kitchen and Living Room 1 and Living Room 2. I wonder which genius decided on that: to hang a large mirror where we are forced to look into it, and be looked at by it; confirming the *nothings* we have all become.

Why today, of all the days, did I stop and allow my image to puzzle me? It certainly wasn't because I expected to see the vibrant Ellie Brady who used to live in my body. I had expected someone else, the grey ghost she has become. For a time I stood there, staring. In this place, you do a lot of that kind of thing, 'nothing things'. There is no pressure to be anywhere else, to do anything other than the daily routine, which is so embedded in your mind that you can catch yourself doing things without remembering how you got to the place in which you are doing them.

At the mirror, I tilted my head as if the woman in the glass would become more recognisable. It wasn't just the shabby clothes or the childish hairstyle, it was her face. For it was in this that my truth was hidden, buried beneath skin, behind eyes and burrowed into the wrinkled stress lines that cover my brow. My shoulders leaned inwards, stooping my back as if every part of me was worn down. I took a second to stand up straight, fixing my clothes as best I could. I had never done that before, and again I asked myself why I felt so differently today. I even opened my eyes wide, staring, daring me to see the person I remembered from so long before. But all I saw was a ragged person, in matching ragged clothes.

I think all this as I stand at the door waiting for the good doctor to answer my knock. I knock again, harder. The sound of his footsteps tells me my peace will now be broken.

'Ellie, please come in.'

His cheerful voice says this like he's an old friend, an acquaintance from the past, from a happy time. But I don't know him, I only know of him. He is the new doctor, the one who is reviewing my file. This I understand, because this much, at least, they have told me.

I sit on the patient side of the desk. I don't mind being the patient; the chair is comfortable enough. I have sat in it many times before. I am happy to say nothing, might as well enjoy it while I can. He is sure to intrude soon, sure to ask his questions and try to get a response

– that is what they do, that is what they all do. But I don't have a response, I have nothing. In nothing I feel safe, for now.

The doctor is tall and graceful in his movements. I notice this as he walks across the room, but I can tell this even when he is seated. The elegant way his arms move as he turns over the case notes, the slow, delicate indentation of forehead lines as he concentrates. When I walked in, he held the door open for me, as if I was some kind of lady. He has an air of gentle confidence, which must help him to control proceedings. I wonder if he is this way out in the real world. Does his disposition change when he is not dealing with lunatics like me? There is already a wooden plaque on the desk with his name on it: 'Dr Samuel Ebbs'. It is followed by a string of letters. I have learned that the number of letters adds to their importance, but importance to whom? Certainly not to me. To me, he is of no importance; to me, he is simply here.

To the side of the case notes lies a jotter and he writes in it from time to time, even before we start to talk properly. His head is bent and his eyes move constantly from the case notes to his jotter, looking up briefly to smile every now and then. I notice the beginning of baldness, just a slight thinning out in the centre of the crown. His hair is black and his suit expensive, neat. The skin on his face and hands tanned, as if painted by a different climate. He has a sharp nose, but it suits him, gives him an air of intelligence. The wedding band on his finger tells me he is married. His enthusiastic scribbling confirms to me that he is new.

Raising his head, he lays the pen down on the desk without making a sound. These are all indicators that he is now ready to move our proceedings forward.

'Well, Ellie, thank you for seeing me today.'

Stupid statement – like I have a choice. I say nothing. He looks at me, my silence causing an upward movement of his right eyebrow.

'You've been here a long time?' He knows this from my file. 'I would like to help you, Ellie, if I can.'

He waits. So do I.

'Perhaps we could spend some time together over the next while. I am here to listen and of course to help you any way I can.'

He pauses then, like I'm going to respond. I don't, not even a blink.

'Maybe, Ellie, we could aim to have our chats in the afternoon? How would you feel about that?'

'Fine.'

He can have as many chats as he likes, but I won't be saying anything. It has all been said before, dragged up and dissected, mulled backwards and forwards. It doesn't change anything, nothing can.

I lean farther back in my chair and he stares at me like he knows I am about to say something. I suddenly like this about him, noticing the small things probably makes him a good judge of people.

'Do you have children, Dr Ebbs?' I ask this as I turn away from the framed photograph of his children on the desk. They look about eight and ten years old. The girl is the younger one. I know he has caught me looking. I don't care.

'Yes. I have two, a boy and a girl.'

'A gentleman's family. You should mind them well, they won't always be around, you know.'

'Indeed.'

I can tell he feels uncomfortable with someone else setting the agenda. He says nothing about me looking at the photograph. He is being polite, no point in upsetting the lunatic too soon. Perhaps I should feel guilty about taking advantage of our meeting, of him wanting to put me at my ease, but there are always pros and cons on both sides. I know the protocol better than most. He will talk to *me* on first name terms, but if I were to call him Samuel, it would be overly familiar. He knows he is in charge of the questions and that it is my expected duty to answer them. He will try to make me *better*, but I don't want to be *better*. I am fine as I am, history-less.

'Your bouts of depression, it says here, Ellie, they started not long into your marriage?'

Picking up his pen, he clicks down the top, like he's pressing the Play button on a tape recorder, as if now I should open my mouth and speak so that he, being the good doctor, can write it all down diligently. The fact that I remain silent does not unnerve him, merely initiates a change of tactics.

'Ellie, I know this will be slow. It will take time for you to learn to trust me, but I do intend to help you. Little by little, we will work through things together.'

All this is said with sincerity, the lines on his forehead deepening, his eyes looking straight at me as he leans back in his chair, every movement designed to put me at my ease. If I cared enough, I could humour him, give him some encouragement, but I don't care. Soon, he won't either.

'I want to go.'

'But, Ellie, you've only just arrived.'

'So?'

'So now that you are here, it might be good to talk a little longer. I won't delay you, Ellie, just a few more moments of your time.'

I almost laugh out loud, to hear him talking to me like I'm some busy person. 'Do I have a choice?'

He leans forward again, his physical proximity requesting a more intimate response.

'Didn't think so,' I say under my breath. I can see my smart remark is a disappointment to him.

'Ellie, I'm going to talk straight with you. I'm new here at St Michael's, but I've been involved in psychiatric care for a very long time.'

This is supposed to make me feel confident, happy to spill the beans, to trust him. But I am too long at this game for stupidity like that.

'You look tired. How have you been finding the medication?'

'Fine, tired is good.'

'You enjoy sleeping?'

'It passes the time.'

'Which is a good thing?'

He is starting to annoy me now, bad enough sitting here answering his questions without them being completely stupid. I say nothing. He'll learn.

'For now, let's say we keep you on the same medication but that we can review it later.'

Again he plays the game. We both know he decides on the medication, it is not and never will be a joint decision.

'Ellie, I've been looking forward to meeting you, to putting a face to the file, as they say.'

He laughs at this. I don't. My lack of reaction does not unnerve him. The good doctor is showing distinct possibilities.

'Next time we meet, Ellie, we can really get things rolling, how does that sound to you?'

'Just dandy.'

Standing up, he walks me to the door, guiding my movements with his extended arm as if somehow I might have forgotten my way out.

'Till next time, Ellie.' He shakes my hand like I'm a normal person. It surprises me. I don't expect touch. I don't expect anything. Not any more.

Dublin Mountains
Friday, 7 October 2011, 8.00 a.m.

DETECTIVE INSPECTOR O'CONNOR WAS ONLY moments away from an early-morning meeting in the squad room at Rathfarnham Garda Station when he got the call about the missing girl. She hadn't been seen for two full days – never a good sign for a Category 1 high-risk disappearance. Although O'Connor's district was based in Rathfarnham, it also covered Templeogue, Firhouse and had jurisdiction over the southwestern side of the Dublin Mountain zone. O'Connor had investigated his fair share of murders and missing persons over the years, and he knew more than anyone that for every case solved, many others remained open.

The C1 disappearance had been the talk of the Dublin district. That morning, when Chief Superintendent Nolan's number lit up his hands-free set, O'Connor took the call and listened, grim-faced.

A sheep farmer had found freshly dug up soil. The storm from the previous night had brought down a fence on his land, and caused his sheep to ramble. When his dog refused to leave the area where the stray animals had been retrieved, he was forced to walk farther in. It was then, just as dawn was breaking over the sprawling city of Dublin, that the grave – suspected to be of Caroline Devine – had been discovered.

O'Connor turned his car around and headed straight to the location of the suspected burial site. Driving towards the mountain road, O'Connor rapped the steering wheel in frustration. He was only too aware that the first forty-eight hours of an investigation were critical. One of the first pieces of information his team sought to establish in any missing person case was the last known sighting of the subject. Caroline Devine had last been seen after finishing school, waving goodbye to her friend Jessica Barry on Rathmines Bridge at the canal. Her family in Harold's Cross had expected her home shortly afterwards. All the potential routes Caroline could have taken home had been examined, but nothing had turned up so far. A diving team from the Underwater Unit had already dragged the base of the canal, from both the Rathmines and Harold's Cross ends. The canal didn't have a major water flow. If the girl had fallen in, accidentally or otherwise, they would have found her.

Nolan had told him that he had already advised Mick Rohan, the Chief Press Officer at Garda HQ, about the site location and possible finding, but no official statement had yet been released. O'Connor knew he had a number of calls to make, one of which would be to DI Frank Gunning, who had been heading up the missing person's enquiry from Rathmines. Gunning wouldn't be happy about O'Connor taking over the case, but if it was Caroline Devine's body up in the mountains, it was O'Connor's murder now and not Gunning's – the investigation always follows the corpse.

'Hiya, Frank, it's O'Connor here.'

'I'm on my way up there. Where are you?'

'At Bohernabreena Cemetery,' O'Connor replied. 'I should be there in less than ten. A couple of uniforms are already in situ from the first call in.'

'Right, I'll see you shortly, turning at Kiltipper now.'

'Frank, just to tell you, Nolan has already advised Rohan about the possible outcome, but nothing official is going out until we know what we're dealing with. I'm getting a full squad in place, and I have Morrison on standby in case we find anything.'

'Where *is* our talented state pathologist today?' Frank asked.

'Golfing in Blessington, it will take him no time to get over.'

'How much of an area are you going to cordon off? It's a bitch of a place.'

'As much as I have to – I'm not about to lose a step in this investigation and not be able to recover it.'

'I'll make a call to Shelley Canter,' Frank offered. 'She's assigned as the family liaison officer.'

'Good – just tell her to keep the family calm and informed. As of now, this could turn out to be nothing. There is no point in upsetting them unnecessarily.'

'She knows that, and she also knows what the parents will be thinking no matter how this ends up.'

'Just once we're all working from the same sheet, Gunning.'

O'Connor hung up and made his next call – to Robert Hanley. Hanley would be heading up the technical team and he had a reputation, even by techie standards, of having something of a Midas touch.

'Hanley?'

'Good morning, Detective Inspector.'

'Are you on your way?'

'Yes.'

'Me, too. First priority will be cordoning off the area. I'll have a better idea of just how much when I've seen it, but it could be large.'

'Nothing I can't handle.'

'You know the drill, Hanley, if it does turn out to be the missing girl up there, I may be the one in charge, but as far as protection of the crime scene goes, you are God Almighty.'

'Rest assured, Inspector. I won't even let Nolan pass if it risks compromising things.'

'Right, let's get digging so.'

Turning up the mountain road, O'Connor's Avensis negotiated the steep climb on the narrow winding road that was barely able to take one vehicle. He took all the bends at speed. O'Connor knew this area like he knew its surrounding suburbs and as he reached the point on the road where the city was behind him, he got that familiar sense of being right smack in the middle of nowhere.

≈

Once the decision on the size of the area to be cordoned off had been made, a slow and methodical extraction of the ground began. There was no guarantee they would find Caroline's body, but based on the knowledge of her disappearance, the proximity of the location to the centre of the city and the remoteness of the site where the recently dug soil had been found, there were enough things telling O'Connor that they were dealing with either a secondary or primary crime scene. Search teams were on hand to sweep the area, together with the community police and the guys from Tallaght, who often worked side by side with the Rathfarnham squad. Although Gunning was someone O'Connor neither liked nor had much time for, right now he was the man with most of the information, and O'Connor wasted no time getting as much as possible out of him.

'Okay, Frank, fill me in. The dig will be slow, so we'll be here for a while.'

'Missing Persons were notified two days ago. Right now, they are just monitoring the information as we feed it to them.'

'Go on.'

'We've pulled the girl's PC and mobile phone. She wasn't allowed take her phone to school, so both it and her laptop were still at home. The IT guys are combing through them now. We have a number of contact points/sites being examined, but it's too early to tell if they'll be of any use. Buccal swabs have been taken from all members of the close family, along with the girl's toothbrush and hairbrush, both bagged and tagged. If it is Caroline down there and the body isn't clearly recognisable, we can check the DNA comparisons with what we have already.'

'What about the house-to-house?'

'It's been intensive around the area she lived in – her school, local swimming pool and the last sighting. We have CCTV footage from some of the local businesses, quite a lot down from where she waved goodbye to her friend. Checkpoints monitoring movements around the area have been constant since she was first reported missing. Teachers, friends and family members have all been interviewed. The parents and family are finding it tough, needless to say, but at the moment the girl's father seems to be the one with the cool head. Shelley Canter has been working with both the parents, and the girl's only sibling, a sister.'

'Right,' O'Connor said, taking charge, 'assuming it is Caroline down there, I want a complete list of everyone who's been interviewed. I presume you have pulled listings from everywhere.'

'Of course, and cross-checked with the names we have from the house-to-house.'

'Anything on known paedophiles close by?'

'Nothing yet, but I got a call just before I headed up here. We might have a possible sighting of someone interesting from a checkpoint set up the day after she went missing. I'll know more soon.'

O'Connor looked at his watch. 'I'll want it for our first briefing at 10.30. Nolan's been in touch again. He says you're to stay involved. As of now, you are the man with most of the information, so stay close.'

Frank Gunning raised an eyebrow, but O'Connor couldn't tell what he was thinking. Probably delighted to be considered important, arrogant bastard.

'Don't worry, O'Connor, I've no intention of going anywhere.'

Ellie

I WATCH THE SUN CREEP THROUGH THE SMALL
window in my room. There's just a hint of it now, catching the bottom
of the sill. It enters the darkness as it does every day, climbing grey
walls and pink chipped window frames; revealing itself discreetly, like
some virginal bride. It has a confidence in the unveiling, a confidence
that, day after day, says it can be renewed. If it could be amazed, it
would be amazed by its own wonder, the determination to come back
again and again, with little in the day changed from what went before.

Soon the sunshine will reflect on objects that through the night
had no life at all. The twelve-inch square mirror I use when washing
my face is alight with sun spots and dust particles drifting in and
out of its delicate world. The light blasts against the metal door lock,
shooting rays across the room so vibrantly it's as if they could break
open a hole in the opposite wall. I, too, feel amazed; amazed that the
sun is here again, touching, reaching all parts of everything that is dull
or half-deadened, bringing its teasing presence to rest and slide along
the floor beneath my bed.

It moves as it does most mornings, tentatively at first, testing and
finding resting places in all that was once in darkness. Today the sky
is cloudless, so the sun is free to dazzle my face with a white brilliance
that should please me. If I was another person, a person out in the real
world, someone filled with hopes and dreams, it would be enough to
make me wake and rise and go visit the sunlight and explore all its
wondrous temptations. But I am not out in the real world, and I have

little desire for its teasing. It belongs to memory, a time long past. Now the darkness suits me better.

This afternoon I am to visit Dr Ebbs again. What will he ask me today? What will I answer? Being sunny, he will probably be even chirpier than he was yesterday, more enthused. He thinks he can help, but what is there to help? I have nothing left. He will ask about the fire, of course, that is usually where they start. As if the fire has answers, as if unravelling the truth about it will give them some magical key that will open doors. But the answers are not in the fire, they never were. When I think about it now, I see it like an ending in a film. Sometimes I can even hear music while I see it played out in my mind's eye. Another confirmation that my time spent in a lunatic asylum has worked well. The melody is slow, sounding like waves drifting in and out, taking stories out to the vast oceans. The music takes my life with it, or rather, what was once my life.

When I think of the fire, the first thing I see is the dark, dirty, grey smoke rising, bellowing like angry clouds cascading into one another. At first there is silence, then the crackling, the fire exploding within itself as if on a wild and dangerous dance. I hear glass smashing, things falling, plates coming off shelves, furniture crumbling and then nothing. A black silence. I remember being dragged out. I remember the smell. I had not expected that. I had surely not expected that.

But what had I expected? In truth, little, for even now when I look back, the madness of it all fills me with nothing other than my wrenching feeling of loss, a loss that came in waves, like a separation of self, of Amy, my daughter, of life, a separation from everything that counted.

I do wonder why I had ever agreed to go on holiday to that place to begin with. Why I didn't just say no. I hadn't wanted to go, that much I am sure of. Joe knew this, of course, but he insisted on the trip, over and over. Such a trifling thing really, the repeated monotones of another, but I just couldn't listen to his harping on any more. It was easier to agree. He never told me his brother would be there. If he had, I would not have gone. That much I do know.

I hear sounds outside, the morning trolleys being pushed up and down corridors. Bridget will be in soon, and she will expect me to swallow my tablets, she will expect me to get up and wash and go down to Living Room 1, where we will all have breakfast and clear our plates. I will do all this, I always do. Bridget will say something like, 'Beautiful day' or 'How are we today?' or 'Look at you still in bed, while I have half the day behind me.' Bridget likes to talk about the day, she feels comfortable talking about it; to her, it is safe territory. To Bridget, the day is innocent, normal, new. To me, the day is the same as it was yesterday; it just surprises me that it keeps coming back.

Right on cue, she opens the door. She is quiet for a change. I want to ask her if the cat has caught her tongue, but I don't. She might think I want to talk; no point encouraging her.

It doesn't take her long. It never does.

'Morning, Ellie, how are we today?'

'Fine.'

She has a kind face, non-offensive. Her brown hair is the colour of mine, but soft, short and curly. The rest of her is much the same, ordinary, not fat, not tall. Bridget has green eyes, 'cats' eyes' she calls them. She must be sixty. She wears regular clothes, nothing too fancy. Bridget has been a cleaner all her adult life. Her children are well grown up now. I know this because she talks about them endlessly. She tells me about each one of them with pride. They've all 'flown the nest' as she puts it, looking upwards to some imaginary sky as if by chance she might see them somewhere up there, for when she talks about them 'flying the nest', it's as if they have all joined the imaginary birds within it. She still has her husband. She calls him 'himself'. 'Himself was watching the football yesterday', 'Himself cut the grass', 'Himself doesn't want to get out of his armchair', 'Himself knows everything.'

Bridget is like the sun, she keeps coming back, even though she makes no difference.

'Nice bit of sunshine.'

'Mmm.'

'Makes a change, cheers you up.'

'Do you think?'

She's not impressed. Bridget doesn't like it when she's challenged, she likes to keep things simple.

'The weather man predicted rain, heard him on the telly last night, should have known. They always get it wrong.'

She looks out the window. 'A great day for drying.'

It is not a comment she expects an answer to. I sit up in bed. She hands me my tablets and I swallow them with a glass of water. It tastes of metal. Of course, most cleaners would not be trusted to give out medication, but with Bridget, they all turn a blind eye. In truth, she is probably more familiar with the routine than a lot of the nurses. She's only allowed to do this with the long-term patients, the ones on medications that are as predictable as the hours in the day.

'Believe you've met the new doctor.'

'Indeed.'

'He's supposed to be very experienced, worked all over the world, I understand. But, then, you can tell that about him, he looks like a man of the world.'

'Are all men not of this world?'

'Now, Ellie, you know what I mean. Don't go taking advantage of me being less educated than you.'

Again she says this without expecting a response. We have over time developed an acceptable banter between us. She knows I don't mind her talking about her grown-up children or 'himself', and she turns a blind eye to my indifference. For Bridget, her family give her an identity, something that comforts her, protects her. When she talks about them, part of her lights up, although it's different when she talks about 'himself'. When she talks about 'himself', it's as if she is talking about a broken-down washing machine.

I never get dressed while Bridget is in the room; she respects my privacy, but she does expect me to get dressed soon after she leaves. If I didn't, I would let her down and she might lose some of her bonus hierarchical duties, so I always comply. Part of our understanding is in the repetition of our encounters. She always arrives on time, and always with a cheery disposition. She talks to me as she keeps herself busy emptying the bin, sweeping under the bed, dusting down the chipped window panes, making conversation that is neutral but upbeat, then standing like some wise old woman at the doorway saying her few words before she leaves. She always says these words in a tone that is slower and softer than any previous conversation, and today is no exception.

'Dr Ebbs, he called me by my name this morning. Only in the door and he knows my name is Bridget, would you credit that?'

I smile because I know she wants me to. Bridget always has hope, which is what I like and dislike about her.

I wait until I hear her farther up the corridor before getting out of bed. When I do, I cannot avoid the tiny mirror. It is in shade now, the sun has passed on its way. I need to look at it to clean my face. I use a small pink facecloth that is the same shade of pink as the window frames. Practically everything in here is either pink or grey. I brush my teeth using water from the sink. Once I am done, I stand looking for just a second and again I see that person looking back at me, the lost person. I cannot look for long, but I look, I cannot help myself.

Once done, I know I have but the briefest of moments before I must head down to Living Room 1. I use this time differently each day. Sometimes I just sit on the bed and try to manage all my 'non-thoughts', piecing them together until I am as close to nothing as I can possibly be. Some days this causes me little pain; other days are different. Today is going to be one of those different days. I don't know why, but I feel uneasy, agitated. Perhaps it's the new doctor. Perhaps it's my latest habit of staring into mirrors. All the days here have been a chore in different ways, but if I am being truthful, for the most part I like knowing what to expect. Today I don't know what to expect and the lack of predictability unsettles me.

I chastise myself. There is no point worrying about the good doctor. I have met his type many times before. But there is something new hovering. It is only when I dress and walk over to the window that I know for sure what it is, and that it has bothered me since yesterday.

The leaves are falling from the trees, some of them have already become that dry, crisp texture that makes them crunch underfoot. It has been a mild autumn. By now I am an expert on such things. As I stand here I think about the previous day, how I was caught unawares when I found myself smiling. To most that would be nothing, but to me, it is disturbing, because smiling is not something that I do.

It does not bother me that it is a long time since I have had a happy memory. Happy memories are not part of the game. In certain ways yesterday was of no real consequence, a harmless childhood recall, nothing more. I was running through the dry leaves of autumn. In the memory the colours of the leaves are as they are today, beautiful shades of orange, red and yellow, a spectacular flight falling from lines of trees. As a child I was amazed by their falling, creating a sea of crunch and colour that I could almost glide through. It was just a silly memory, but it had made me smile, and I had not expected that.

Now when I look at the trees, I think about how they have the strength to survive the harshest of winters, the short days and the long nights, and how, unlike me, they will be reborn again. Could I be like the trees? Could I, after such a long, cold winter, re-form again? Is it the question that unsettles me or the fact that I have thought of it at all? For the thinking of it makes me wonder if I might once again fall victim to that thing I've long since given up on: hope.

This afternoon, if Dr Ebbs asks me about the fire, I will let his questions fall away like the leaves are doing now. I will say I don't remember; he cannot make me talk. The sooner he realises how empty I am, that he is wasting his time and mine, the better it will be for everyone. Then I can go back to just being my old self. It is easier that way. It is what I do best.

As I walk down towards Living Room 1, I pay a visit to the Female Toilets. In here, the tiles are a lighter powder pink and cover the walls and floors. The tiles on the floor are different from the ones on the wall, they are larger and less shiny. In the Female Toilets, there are four cubicles. I can tell Bridget has already been in because each one smells of cleaning fluid and every toilet roll holder is full. The others have already made their way down to breakfast.

I savour my final minutes alone, collecting my thoughts. Breakfast is the worst chore of the day because at breakfast, I will meet everyone for the first time all over again – and, today, I feel nervous. I worry that I might not be able to hide my feelings the way I usually do. The silent, polite exterior of my protective shell feels less sure. Whether it is because of the good doctor or the memory of the fallen leaves, I do not know, but I have the sense that today, despite my desire to remain steadfast, my protection might slip.

WALKING OUT OF HER OFFICE AT OCEAN HOUSE ON Arran Quay, Kate Pearson planned to grab some lunch at the Legal Eagle pub nearby, before picking up Charlie from school straight afterwards. It was still hard to think of him being in 'big school', but as her mother had said to her at his birth, four years earlier, time flies quicker than anyone can possibly imagine. Out in the fresh air, the last person she expected to see leaning against the Liffey wall opposite was DI O'Connor. He was lighting a cigarette, his hands cupped around to avoid the breeze. Tall and bulky, he was a man who'd have looked more at home in a traditional pub, with his short auburn hair and curls to the front that never knew which way they wanted to settle. As always, his beard stubble was only a hair's-breadth from looking unruly. He had shared very little with her about his personal life during the Dunmore case, other than his confirmed bachelor status and what seemed like an avoidance to reveal his first name. Crossing over as soon as he saw her, his blue eyes smiled in that cheeky way of his.

'Those things will kill you, O'Connor,' she said lightly.

He grinned at her. 'Sure, something has to, Kate, might as well be something enjoyable.'

'Stalking me now, are you?'

'Now, now, less of the ego, it doesn't suit you.'

'Is the pleasure mine or someone else's?'

'It's your lucky day. Tried to get you on your mobile. I had to ring Probation and Welfare to find you.'

'Consultations all morning, mobile off, you know the way it is.'

'Lunch?'

'You're a mind-reader, O'Connor. I'm heading for the Legal Eagle.'

'Mind if I join you?'

'I assume there is more to this than lunch?'

'You assume right.'

Lunchtime at the Legal Eagle was always hectic, but they got lucky – a corner table came free as they arrived. The pub smelled of roast beef and strong coffee. It was dark coming in from outside, the place packed with city workers amidst the clatter of trays and easy conversation. Once the preliminaries of ordering lunch were dispensed with, O'Connor set about his real task.

The contents of the envelope he handed to Kate were stark. All the images, except for one – a school photograph of the victim – had been taken at the mountain burial site where the young girl's body had been found. Working her way through the photographs, Kate was immediately gripped by what she saw. As each of the images revealed itself, she got the sense that everything about her first introduction to this young girl would remain with her, like a recurring bad dream.

'Not pretty,' he remarked drily.

'They never are, O'Connor.'

'Well, what do you think?'

'I'm guessing this is unofficial?'

'It is for now.'

'These things take time to assess, O'Connor, you know that.'

'Yeah, well, sadly we don't always have the luxury of time. Rohan is doing his best, but the press is going mad with this thing, even bloody Twitter has gone crazy with it, trending top of the Irish tweets, whatever the hell that means.'

'As I say, there are never any quick answers, Detective Inspector.'

'I know, I know, but gut reaction.'

'Gut reactions can mean jumping to wrong conclusions. Leading you down the garden path isn't going to help anyone.'

'Kate, I'm asking you off the record. What do you think?'

Just as she was about to share her thoughts, O'Connor's mobile rang.

'Sorry, I have to take this. I've been waiting for this call.'

'Sure, go right ahead.'

O'Connor stepped outside, giving her the opportunity to study the images alone. The light in the pub was dull, but the more she looked at the photographs, the more her eyes became accustomed to it. The shots were taken from different angles and at varying ranges: the girl's body seemed tiny, black clay beneath her nails, her fingers long, wrists narrow, almost doll-like. The tech guys looked to have done their job well. Every square inch of what could have been the victim's final resting place was covered with white chalk marks and numbered flags. All potential pieces of evidence were noted in the shots, ranging from close-ups to wide angles of the surrounding area – and it would seem O'Connor, as the Senior Investigating Officer, had pushed the boundaries out pretty far when cordoning off the area.

The terrain was certainly challenging. In the images, she could see the uniformed guards posted at various points to protect the site and the tech guys at work, including Hanley, whom she had met on the Dunmore case. Gone were the days when members of the force could enter a site uninvited, high ranking or not. Now when it came to protection of a crime scene, there was no doubt who called the shots, and Hanley wouldn't be backward about reminding people.

In the grave, the girl was still wearing her school uniform – sky-blue cardigan and shirt with a navy pinafore and tie – which Kate recognised from a local school near where she lived. The girl's body was lying sideways in the foetal position, her hands joined to the front, each of the fingers intertwined, almost as if they were clasped in prayer. The right side of her head, which received the blows, had been placed downwards into the soil, the hardened blood matted into her hair, protecting it initially from view. It would have been an arduous process, but photographs of every movement of the body at the 'seat' of the find had been taken, and meticulously recorded.

She looked again at the images taken before the girl's body had been removed from the burial area. Other than the speckled black clay covering her body like an extra layer, the child gave the appearance of being in a deep sleep, one from which, like in a fairytale, she might suddenly awake. Kate was lost in thought when O'Connor resumed his seat heavily.

'What age was she, O'Connor?'

'Twelve, last year at national school.'

'Her name?'

'Caroline Devine.'

Looking at a photograph, Kate asked, 'I see Morrison. Does he have any idea how long she was down there?'

'Well, he was clear on a number of points. There is, as you can see, little sign of decomposition. Although earthworms had begun proliferating some of the open orifices, they were in the early stages. Plus there's minimal skin blistering, so the body hadn't been down there long. With no external protection, even with the low temperatures in the mountains, Morrison believes she couldn't have been below ground for much more than twenty-four hours, and probably a whole lot less.'

'At the very least, I guess it means it'll be less horrific for the parents to identify her body than it might have been.'

'For sure.' O'Connor paused, both of them taking in the last piece of information before he continued with Morrison's assessment. 'Rigor mortis, which normally sets in within one to six hours of death, had already relaxed, so she'd been dead for some time before burial. Morrison has his suspicions about the positioning of the corpse, he thinks it might have been forced prior to the relaxation of the rigor.'

'So how the girl was lying was intentional?'

'We'll know more once the postmortem is complete. I'm due to see him later this evening.'

'Anything else?'

'Yeah, neither Hanley nor the other techs have found any blood splatters in the area, despite the severity of the blows to the girl's head. The heavy rainfall during the storm the other night might have washed away a lot of the trace evidence, but the complete lack of blood deposits other than those found on the corpse means the girl was killed someplace else, according to Hanley.'

Despite the subject matter of their conversation, the arrival of food didn't stop O'Connor tucking in like a famished adolescent. Kate, on the other hand, had lost her appetite. She continued to examine the photographs while the DI ate his lunch.

The girl's strawberry-blonde hair had been arranged in two long plaits, both tied with red ribbons. Her white knee socks looked like crumpled layers above a pair of black leather school shoes, everything now looking too large for the girl's narrow frame. The ground, murky and damp from the heavy rain, was rugged. Fragments of stone, granite for the most part, meant it wasn't an easy terrain to carry out a burial. The grave area was deep. She looked up at O'Connor again.

'The grave, O'Connor, it's not shallow.'

'Over three feet. The killer may not have acted alone – either way, he came equipped.'

'Or, if alone, he would have to be physically fit.' Kate looked at the images again. 'If what Morrison says is true, about the short time the corpse was below ground, then the killer waited for nightfall to bury his victim.'

'And he chose a bitch of a night to do it.' O'Connor raised his fork, as if to give emphasis to his last remark.

'Her hair – is that the way she normally wore it?'

'Good question, Kate, why do you ask?'

'The ribbons, I don't know, they look wrong, nearly old-fashioned. The bows are too large, like the way kids wore them years ago.'

'You're spot-on. According to her friend, Jessica Barry, who was the last one to see her, Caroline wasn't wearing her hair in plaits that day. Rarely did.'

'And the ribbons?'

'Parents know nothing about them. They *are* unusual, though. You might not be able to see it in the images, but they have a perforated edge running along the side, a kind of herringbone pattern.'

'What else was picked up at the scene?'

'Despite Hanley's best efforts, apart from the victim herself, there's a partial boot print from the side of the ditch, that's all. Of course, the heavy rain could well have put paid to any skid or drag marks left by the killer getting the body down there.'

'So not much really?'

'No, not yet. But you and I both know you can't exclude evidence just because it isn't there.'

Kate looked down at the images again. There were also some black-and-whites photographs and they reminded her of another murder she'd been involved with during her placement with Henry Bloom. That had also been of a young female victim, a teenager named Rachel Mellows. Rachel had been viciously attacked in a laneway on her way home no more than a hundred yards away from where she lived. On that occasion, they'd arrested the killer, a psychopath called Paul Whitney. When Whitney was asked why he had chosen Rachel, he told the investigation officers that on the night he killed her, he had picked her out for no other reason than he'd been attracted to her white scarf. Whitney said it had reminded him of a sail blowing in the wind. It taught Kate one indisputable lesson: whatever brings a murderer to a location, the choice of victim could be determined by the smallest of details.

'So, Kate, now that I have finished my lunch, what do you think we have here?'

'The killer was careful, O'Connor. Notwithstanding the storm and possible erosion of evidence, whoever killed Caroline Devine buried her in challenging terrain, but he took his time and was calm. It all looks too organised for any other interpretation.'

'Go on.'

'The crime scene – the secondary crime scene if Hanley is right – is far too neat. Typically, organised crime scenes are planned, but we have to remember this is probably a secondary scene. It may mean the killer simply put extra thought into the burial, but, in so doing, it shows him – or her – to be very particular and specific. Look at the way the child is positioned, everything seems very exact, almost like a picture. It is not unusual when a murder has been committed for the perpetrator to hide the body, but this is different. This body wasn't just dumped and hidden. Everything about the site says there is a high level of intimacy here.'

'Intimacy?'

'Look at the girl, her hands, the way they are joined, the plaiting, how each ribbon is resting neatly on her shoulders.'

'I'm listening.'

'The killer was careful. It must have taken him some time to dig out that grave, yet if Morrison is correct, he made a point of preparing the corpse, positioning the girl in a very specific way. Did Morrison say whether the hair was plaited before or after the head injuries?'

'After, he thinks, but the postmortem will firm that up.'

'Perhaps the killer was familiar with the area. It's not an easy area to get around.'

'Or perhaps, Kate, our *pal* likes to take his time burying innocent young girls?'

'Guilt makes people sloppy. This guy was anything but.'

'Great, a neat killer, exactly what I wanted to hear.'

'You asked for it.'

'Anything else?'

'The blows to the head, they look severe.'

'They were. Morrison says both blows came from behind. Although the injuries to the head were deep, they're not the likely cause of death. We should know more later on, but according to him, the most likely cause was asphyxiation.'

'I can see the marks and bruising on the neck.'

'Yeah and the spotting around the eyes, another tell-tale sign.'

'What was used?'

'Hands probably.'

'The two indentations at the front?'

'Pressure thumb marks most likely.'

'Was she conscious?'

'Too early to tell, but Morrison thinks the blows may have knocked her out.'

'A small mercy.'

'What's that?'

'Nothing, I was just thinking out loud. No sign of any sexual assault?'

'No, if there was, we might have something on the bastard.'

'Yeah but …'

'I know. You don't have to spell it out for me. We're all feeling the heat on this one, and for obvious reasons. Who knows what the hell was on this sicko's mind. I've run checks on known offenders in the area, and some farther afield. You know how these things spread out, those bastards like to share things with their friends.'

'What have you released to the press?'

'The bare minimum. Rohan's in charge of all press communication. You need a bloody degree in the thing these days to deal with those guys.'

'Nothing about the plaiting or the ribbons?'

'Not yet, but we may have to give something out. The type of ribbon could turn out to be useful in a public appeal.'

'I see.'

'By the way, we haven't made an official statement yet, confirming the body is that of the missing girl, not until after the postmortem. Anyhow, I need to be getting back, we've another briefing in half an hour – you know how these things go, by the time I get any sleep tonight, I'll have at least three of them under my belt.'

'Where's the briefing?'

'We're working out of the Incident Room in Tallaght. The next meeting is a biggie. Everyone will be there. Do you remember Gunning from the Dunmore case?'

'How could I forget?'

'Well he's mighty pissed off that the investigation has moved from his territory to mine.'

'So he's no longer involved?'

'The chief wants him to stay in, but only to assist, along with some extra detectives from Harcourt Square, criminal bureau guys. Don't get me wrong, I'm glad of the extra support, but some of those DI's are right elitist bastards.'

'Not behaving, are they?'

'They'll do their job. I'll make sure of it.'

'I know you will.'

'Just one other thing, Kate.'

'Go on.'

'Caroline, she was wearing a pair of small stud earrings.'

'Like the ones in the school photograph?'

'Yeah, the thing is, they're missing.'

'You're thinking a memento, souvenir?'

'They could be. But listen, Kate, I don't need to spell out what I came here to ask you.'

'Will he reoffend?'

'Yeah.'

'Hanley is sure the girl wasn't killed where she was found?'

'The site's too clean, although we're not ruling out the surrounding area. The tech guys are still there, and I've given instructions to move the search area out farther, but it's a hell of a place to find anything. Chances are he brought the victim there, but he certainly found himself a nice secluded spot.'

'We know he is organised, O'Connor, and specific in how he handled the body. He didn't seem to panic in the terrain, and although he had no way of knowing that the victim would ever be found, putting her, as you say, in a nice secluded spot, there is no argument that a lot of care went into her burial. Your killer went to huge lengths for a body he didn't want found. She meant something to him. If he is not connected with her directly, then chances are he might have chosen her. This doesn't look random.'

'So he could strike again?'

'If he does, I doubt he'll do it in a hurry.'

'Why do you say that?'

'He is, as I said, particular, probably a man who likes to take his time. Something about this girl drew him to her. My guess is he didn't reach his decision quickly.'

'So we have time?'

'I think so, but he didn't arrive at this juncture overnight.'

'I know that, Kate, but having time on our hands is exactly what I want to hear right now. I don't need to tell you,' he paused, 'every parent, granny and bloody tabloid newspaper out there are all asking the same thing.'

'What's that?'

'When the hell are we going to catch this fucker?'

St Michael's Psychiatric Hospital, Dr Samuel Ebbs' office

SAMUEL HAD A LARGE NUMBER OF PATIENTS UNDER his care, all of whom needed different things. Ellie Brady might have been considered one of the least optimistic cases at St Michael's, but after meeting with her the previous day, hers was certainly one of the cases that intrigued him most.

He had reflected long and hard about their first encounter and was quite sure, irrespective of what his prior expectations had been, that he had been very much surprised by Ellie Brady. Sedatives used in institutional care were not uncommon – the majority of his patients were on benzodiazepines, and night sedation ran to about 65 per cent of the patients at the hospital. But he sensed a spark about Ellie yesterday, bubbling just below the surface, a kind of feistiness that gave him hope. He was glad he had made the decision to tweak her medication. The alteration would have gone unnoticed, other than by those in the hospital pharmacy. He had not mentioned it to Ellie purposely. It wasn't always a good thing to advise a patient of such a change, especially a long-term patient who might fret, impacting on any benefit there might be.

Although at first glance Ellie's appearance had been drab, as was the case with most of the inmates of the institution, and she undoubtedly looked every bit her forty-seven years when she walked into the room, the remnants of her youthful beauty were still apparent to him within moments of meeting her. It was one of the first things that had struck him about the old photograph in her file – how attractive she was, and how alive and vibrant she seemed. He had been taken aback by her remarkable bone structure, both in the photograph and then in real life. But there was something else. It was in the way she looked at him, how she seemed to lock onto his face, unusual for someone of her condition, leaving the distinct impression that when she stared at him, she did so with the knowledge that she had seen a great many things which he had not.

Re-examining the case notes, he went to the last entry written by his predecessor, Dr Norris.

Ellie Brady (née Thompson, born 20/10/1963)
Patient displays no change in condition since last review.

Based on her prolonged period at St Michael's, it would seem unlikely that any improvement in her mental state is envisaged in the short or medium term.

Memory of events leading up to and after the fire are still sporadic.

Patient still seems capable of only minimal recall.

Continues to demonstrate behaviour of withdrawal and a reluctance to engage in any activity other than the basic interaction with others.

As symptoms and behaviour show no signs of alteration, for the short term, I recommend continuance on existing medication and set review date for six months from today.

Signed: Dr G Norris

His predecessor's assessment confirmed Samuel's suspicions about the entire file: many of the reviews of the past few years had achieved little more than repeating the same things that had been stated previously.

If anything, the assessments were nothing more than a recording of what seems to have been accepted as the status quo when it came to handling Ellie's case.

The only reviews of any difference were those recorded when Ellie was first admitted to St Michael's. She was undoubtedly a very sick woman from the outset, willing to take her own life by whatever means had been open to her. Once the initial danger Ellie posed to herself had passed, it seemed that what had been adopted was little more than a desire to keep her condition stable.

Samuel had been struck by something else during his encounter with Ellie, apart from her feistiness. There was no denying that she had made direct eye contact with him, in fact she had no problem on numerous occasions attempting to outstare him. This was unusual for someone who supposedly had withdrawn inside themselves, even given the slight adjustment to her medication. More importantly, it caused him to question if Ellie Brady had not been leading them all a merry dance.

Flicking through the file, he picked up the photograph of Ellie with her daughter. When he had studied it before, he had wondered about how both mother and child had looked at the camera, smiling in great amusement. The girl's smile was not unusual, but there was something about Ellie, as if she displayed more than the normal level of affection one might have expected when someone was posing for a photograph, almost as if Ellie's smile was for the photographer alone. The photograph was taken before she had arrived at the hospital. The girl was probably about ten at the time. She had the same hair as Ellie, only longer and it was tied in two plaits. On first reading the file, he had been rather taken by the case, not just because all his predecessors had seemed to fail in its regard, but also because there were a great many aspects to it that didn't make sense – and it was Samuel's experience that if something didn't make sense, there was usually a very good reason for it.

Incident Room, Tallaght Garda Station
Friday, 7 October 2011, 2.30 p.m.

THE INCIDENT ROOM IN TALLAGHT WAS FULL TO capacity, every stacked black plastic chair had been taken down and occupied. The atmosphere felt tight; a cauldron of manpower and resources that could tip at any moment, depending on what fresh information was fired into the mix.

The occupants of the top table were already seated, except for O'Connor, who took his seat to the right of Chief Superintendent Brian Nolan, whispering, 'Hiya, Boss', before nodding at the bookman, James Donoghue.

As was customary at this point in the investigation, all key posts had been allocated and although these had been made primarily by O'Connor as the Senior Investigating Officer, others had had their say too. DS Dermot O'Brien had been put in charge of CCTV footage, Tom Byrne was the DS for records on preservation of the crime scene and protection of evidence, DS Brian McCann was heading up the house-to-house enquiries and DS Martin Pringle had been made overseer of witness statements.

When it came to the multiple interactions within the Incident Room, the engine of any investigation was the bookman. In this case, it was James Donoghue who would call the shots. There was never any doubt about who would be appointed. Donoghue was at the height of his career, he knew more about many members of the district than Nolan, and had more experience behind him than half the people in the room. It was his job to see links or inconsistencies within the information collected, and it was up to the detective sergeants, detective inspectors and everyone else to get that information filtered through the tried and tested hierarchical system, a system to which every single one of the fifty-plus people in the room would strictly adhere. The bookman was the one person who saw everything worth seeing, and by noticing an association that might otherwise have been missed, he could change the course of a case in an instant.

O'Connor had already mentioned to Donoghue that he was not happy with DI Gunning remaining as part of the team, but Donoghue, had agreed with Nolan. Gunning may have been a thorn in O'Connor's side, but Donoghue knew that if you wanted someone to play hardball then Gunning was the man, and it was better to have him in rather than out.

Having got everyone's attention, Donoghue set about his task like the seasoned master of proceedings that he was.

'Job 11. O'Brien, what's the update on CCTV?'

'We're still going through everything sent over from Rathmines. We've new tapes just in from Gunning, along with fresh local stuff.'

'From where?'

'Shops and businesses down at the main junction, security footage from the GAA club and church grounds, and a couple of the bigger houses on the way up the hill have their own CCTV cameras.'

'Right, I want a complete overview by tonight's meeting for O'Connor here. McCann, you're next: house-to-house, who saw or heard anything out of the ordinary?'

'First-round statements taken, all given over to Pringle, but we still need to catch up with a couple of stragglers, especially Matt Long, owner of the land where the girl was found.'

O'Connor nearly jumped from the top table in frustration. 'Why? Where is he? What's the delay?'

'The man is nearly a hundred. He's been unwell, bedridden.'

'But he's at home?'

'Yeah.'

'Send Hyland up there immediately. We need a statement from him, and with Hyland's medical background it should be a doer. Just make sure he takes it nice and slow.'

Donoghue, who was busy recording the next job number to Hyland, looked to Pringle. 'What's the story with the statement from the woman who saw the car at the canal?'

'Statement says she remembers being annoyed when she had to walk out on the road in order to pass a navy Toyota Carina parked on the footpath. It was parked on one of the smaller roads off the canal, around the time the girl was last seen. She'd noticed it on another occasion, earlier that same week, but hadn't seen anyone in it. She was positive it was a Carina because she used to drive the same model, but hadn't taken note of the registration plate.'

'Anyone else notice it?' Donoghue looked out over his glasses.

'No.'

'What, is she the only person with eyes?' He turned from Pringle to McCann. 'Look at the times when she saw it, we need to know who was at home, who else could have seen it. Maybe someone else might remember more.'

'Before you do, McCann, let me have another look at that house-to-house sheet.' O'Connor looked over at Donoghue, who noted the request. 'We'll need to put something more specific in there about unfamiliar cars parked in the area.'

Chief Superintendent Nolan turned to O'Connor. 'Right, bring us up to date before we start the visuals.'

'Okay,' O'Connor said, standing up so everyone could hear him. 'We've extended the search area, but it's still too early to send in the tracker dogs. Hanley and the tech team need time to make sure they've picked up everything. The photographs, which will come up now in the visuals, reflect the general terrain, access roads to and from the area, Montpelier, Glenasmole, all the way up to Military Road.

We are concentrating the search in the area to the left of the main Bohernabreena Road, the side the girl's body was found.

'A cast impression has been made of the boot print found at the scene, using the usual Crownstone. The size of the boot is between a nine and a ten and, judging by the depth of the impression, our guy is in and around the twelve stone mark, certainly not too heavy on his feet. Other points about it – tiny particles of gravel, more than likely built up over time, were found in the indentions or grooves on the sole of the boot. We've checked with the sheep farmer, Murphy, the only other person who walked in the vicinity, and the print is not his. The impression is from a left boot, showing excessive wear on the left-hand side, meaning the wearer had an inclination to lean more on the far left of his left foot. Pattern not unusual, could be found in many makes of hiking boots, but based on the cast taken it is likely that this boot was put to frequent use.'

'Update on forensics?'

O'Connor turned to Nolan. 'Yeah, sorry, Boss. Hanley has confirmed that we are probably dealing with a secondary crime scene, no blood splatters found. As of right now, the body is giving us very little. We'll know more when Morrison does the postmortem this evening, and we have a better handle on the whole thing.'

'O'Connor, put pressure on the labs if you have to,' Nolan ordered. 'We'll need those toxicology reports pronto, you know how they like to take their time.'

O'Connor turned to Gunning. 'Caroline's friend, Jessica Barry – what's the story with her?'

'I interviewed her when the initial missing person's report came in, and she's been interviewed again today by one of McCann's team, both times with mother present. So far, she knows nothing other than the details of the last sighting.'

Nolan pushed his chair back and the castors creaked into motion. 'This is starting to sound like an investigation where nobody knows anything. We have to get the information in guys, pull the people, neighbours, the postman, anyone on that CCTV footage, get talking to them all, we need to ask the right people the right questions before the Chinese whispers start taking hold. O'Connor, are you listening?'

'One hundred per cent.'

'What's the story on known paedophiles?'

'I'm going to handle that line myself.'

'Good. Now, Matthews, pull those blinds down and let's look at these visuals. O'Connor, you have a captive audience.'

When the room darkened, everyone knew what to expect. Ordinarily the slide show would start with images and data from the main crime scene. But with no primary crime scene, the first of the images came from the burial site, taken at bird's-eye-view level, including mapping and markings done by the forensic team. This would create a three-dimensional reproduction of the crime area – in this case, the burial site. This was O'Connor's starting point.

'Hanley examined a number of ways of gaining access to this area. It's open terrain and the bad weather has probably eroded any clues that could have led us to the likely entry point the killer used. In the final analysis, Hanley concluded that there was no way to establish with certainty where the perpetrator gained access to the site. This had delayed things considerably, as his team had to use galvanised steps to examine the area, minimising any potential damage to possible entry points.'

'Who was deployed to examine the roads leading to the scene – the main roads and walking tracks?' Nolan looked to O'Connor, but Donoghue already had it covered.

'Burke, anything of interest turn up there?'

'No CCTV up that far. You reach a point halfway between the turn off for Friarstown and the climb towards the Military Road, and there isn't even any road lighting. There was a guy hanging out at one of the lay-bys, sleeping rough in a car for a time earlier in the year, but he's well gone.'

O'Connor moved on to the next set of images, those taken from the grave area, with the young girl still lying in it. There was a concentrated silence as everyone in the Incident Room maintained what might appear to others as a cold, clinical approach to the evidence, but it was an approach that they had been trained to apply. O'Connor paused for a couple of seconds before continuing, knowing everyone was taking in the image of the schoolgirl dressed in her uniform. In death, her slim arms and tiny legs made her look even younger than she had been.

O'Connor cleared his throat. 'I don't need to remind anyone here that even though the general public will never see these images, they will be imagining them, and I cannot overemphasise how high the stakes are. The abduction and murder of this young girl has understandably generated a huge outcry from the public. It has also brought an enormous interest from abroad, including a very high media presence, which is growing by the day.' O'Connor looked over at Rohan, and got a nod back. 'Just to say here, there is absolutely no direct evidence of any sexual assault on the young girl, but I don't have to tell you, the jury is still out as to what the killer's real intentions were.'

When O'Connor had finished, Donoghue, as bookman, had the last word. 'You don't have to have a young family to think about how this girl will never get a chance to grow up, or how she might have suffered. We are at the height of this investigation, guys, and everyone in this room, including the much-appreciated support from Harcourt Square' – he nodded to the guys from the National Bureau of Criminal Investigation in the corner – 'knows what's needed. Now, let's get some answers, before there are too many more bloody questions.'

Meadow View

IT HAD BEEN SIX MONTHS SINCE HIS MOTHER'S DEATH, and he had returned to work at Newell Design, and the stupidity of his co-workers was now a constant irritant to him. He felt relief each evening when he finally turned the key in the lock of his two-up, two-down townhouse and closed the door on the world.

The house was small and of little consequence. Looking at it from the outside, one might consider it bleak, situated as it was at the end of the street, with none of the decorative frivolity of many of the others. He detested the exterior of the neighbouring houses, having no time for window boxes, door knockers with the face of lions or the diverse range of window dressings on display, from cheap lace to every variation of bobble and blind, including the latest addition of the wooden Venetian kind. He liked things to be uncluttered, hygienic and, at the very least, purposeful. Nothing existed in his house outside these guidelines. Ornaments were something he had a specific disdain for, being of no value other than to gather dust, along with his fervent aversion to fine bone china and a complete loathing of any form of waste. Olive oil bottles were turned upside-down, jars and tins cleared out with methodical knife-scraping, and tubes, especially toothpaste tubes, were flattened to perfection.

He had decided to buy Number 15 Meadow View four months previously. He had made up his mind that his childhood home at Cronly Lodge would never be suitable as a permanent residence. He didn't care much for the name of the street; he failed to understand why it held the title when no meadow, or view of one, existed. Perhaps at some point the square patch the house was built on had been part of a meadow, but if that were true, he felt a terrific irony in the fact that none of the houses on the street possessed so much as a front garden.

Once inside the house, with the door shut firmly behind him, he relaxed. He was still getting used to the liberating feeling of living in his own place, with the freedom to have things just as he wanted them. He had rented since starting work in Dublin, but it had been tiresome, always having to be concerned about how the landlord felt regarding arrangement of furniture or decorative changes. It had limited him. Sometimes, like now, he would walk around in the dark, remembering being a boy, roaming the corridors of Cronly at night, or those warm clammy evenings at the castello. It was important to remember the past. When he did turn on the light, he took solace from everything being just as he had left it. In fact, he never left without preparing the house for his return. If, for example, he left the house in daylight but knew he would not return until late evening, he would close the curtains. If, on the other hand, he left the house at night and knew he would not be back until morning, he would do the opposite. He had no time for people who didn't prepare or plan. After all, most things in life were predictable and capable of being forecast, if you put your mind to it.

Although visitors to Number 15 were very few indeed, the house was at all times impeccably clean and tidy. Opening the kitchen cupboards, he noted the consumables sorted into their relevant categories, the earliest sell-by dates to the front. Taking down the small tin chest of Mokalbari tea, he felt an immediate sense of pride, delighted with this little find from the nearby Indian shop. The tea not only tasted of malt but had a very distinct and splendid hint of elderberry.

The house was quiet, other than the low hiss from the boiling kettle. Being situated at the end of the street meant very few people ventured all the way up to the top of the cul-de-sac. The only living thing other than himself in the house was Tabs, the cat. Tabs was the last in a long line of cats called Tabs from Cronly, an unwanted but necessary bequest from the big house. Despite having no particular affection for the animal, it was nonetheless a tolerable pet. The cat demonstrated traits that he found matched his own – predatory by nature, incredibly selfish and, for the most part, kept himself to himself. As well, of course, as being impeccably clean.

As he poured the just-boiled water over his tea leaves, he watched with amusement as the cat cleared his bowl of milk. Tabs reminded him of Jarlath, both of them had skeletal-like frames. Indeed, on closer examination even their eyes looked similar – strained and watery, with a keen sharpness about them. Jarlath looked liked someone in need of a good meal, or at the very least some physical exercise to build him up a bit. He himself enjoyed his keep-fit routine, believing it was an essential part of a good life balance. He knew many viewed him as something of an intellectual, but that didn't mean he shouldn't take care of his body too.

Of course, this had not always been the case. When he was younger, like Jarlath, he too could have been thought of as sickly. If he had had siblings, he most probably would have been described as 'the runt' or 'the weakling', something that in another species of animal would be considered for extermination. It was only after finishing his studies at college that he set about improving himself physically; a change of image part of his fresh start. Most exercises he did alone, like walking, running, hill climbing. He enjoyed swimming too, usually early morning or late evening, times when most people would be someplace else.

He emptied his cup of Mokalbari as diligently as Tabs cleared his bowl, and his mind wandered to events earlier in the day. At work, little had changed from before: Susan was still there with her sniffles, and Jarlath was just as enthused about Pascal's unfinished work on the Pensées.

He had wondered if any of them would have guessed at his little secret, or did his quiet disposition still fool them into thinking he was harmless? The thought brought a smile to his face. In part, he liked being a man of mystery, it allowed him to deflect questions, surprisingly enough, rather than answer them. No, he was quite certain that none of them thought there was anything unduly strange about him – even of late, when life had proved so challenging. After all, he didn't look like the type of man to do anything out of the ordinary. Even his ongoing, uninvited visits to other people's homes would be laughed at as ridiculous. Visualising him going into places he was not supposed to was not an image that would spring immediately to mind.

The first place he'd broken into was the sacristy of the local church. Not that he considered it breaking in, more childish curiosity than anything else. He had obsessed for a long time about the place where the priest prepared himself for mass, wondering what rituals and mysteries would be involved. Was there a mirror in which the priest could admire himself in his colourful robes? Were there treasures hidden in this priestly place, things specifically for the ordained and not for mere mortals? He took his opportunity one Sunday after mass. His mother had engaged Fr Mahon in the type of conversation that didn't allow interruption, making it easy for him to slip away unnoticed. His curiosity about religious customs was aroused well before his and his mother's trip to Suvereto later that same year.

The moment he was inside the sacristy, his excitement rose. He had stood leaning with his back against the door, taking in all around him, as if he'd just entered a cave full of treasure. The room had smelled of candle grease and incense and was filled with heavy, dark furniture, which he had suspected had been there long before Fr

Mahon. There had been old papers too, hardback books, mostly of a religious nature, and a tall mahogany unit in the corner with carvings on the front depicting a scene from the Garden of Eden. The unit had been locked, but the key was in the door. He'd turned it, forcing it a little, his nervous excitement rising as he'd felt the bolt release itself, and the door opened.

Inside, the vestments had hung like a line of coloured soldiers. He'd moved his hand along the top, stroking the embroidered garb, like he might have touched a painting in an art gallery that he had been forbidden to lay a finger on. At first, he'd worried that someone might come in and find him, or that the heavens would strike and punish him for committing such a sin. His palms had felt sweaty as he'd looked all around him, thinking the very walls could alert others to his misbehaviour and, just for a moment, he had been sure he'd be paralysed to the spot. It was then that he'd noticed the large crucifix hanging above the doorway. The sight of the crucifix should have scared him more, but it had encouraged him, as he'd realised that neither the walls nor the crucifix had any power over him. Alone, he'd been free to move at will, so when he'd found the biscuit tin with the altar bread inside, he had not hesitated to pick up the wafer bread, place it high above his head and, facing Jesus on the cross, say, 'Hoc est enim Corpus meum, quod pro vobis tradetur' –'This is my body, which will be given up for you.' At no point had he felt any guilt – even afterwards when his mind had rambled now and then and he'd worried about being punished. Those feelings had soon passed; the lack of retribution had strengthened his delight that he had got away with it. After that, he often broke into places – after all, it was perfectly natural to be inquisitive, even if he carried out his curiosity in a way others would not have done.

He still had a few minutes before the six o'clock news, which he planned to watch upstairs. He had heard the headlines during work at lunchtime; they had all been about the missing girl. He looked forward to listening to the news with no distractions, reading his notes, and his copy of Pensées. In his rush to get upstairs, he tripped on the second step. Falling forward, he dropped the book, his notes scattering on the staircase just as Tabs attempted to slip past. He turned, a blow from his left hand sending the cat flying backwards through the air. Tabs was lucky, having nine lives. Picking up the notes one sheet at a time, he placed them back in the book at exactly the same page, which now had a dirty crease down the centre. The mark would be permanent.

Straightening his back, he walked back down into the kitchen. The cat was nowhere to be found. Taking down a drinking glass, he wrapped a tea towel around it before hammering a meat mallet down hard, smashing it into tiny pieces. With protective gloves on, he opened a tin of cat food, mixing the smaller pieces of glass in with the food, then filled Tabs' bowl to the brim. By the time he left the kitchen, everything had been tidied away and looked exactly as it had done before. Tabs would have an uncomfortable night. His mood shifted again. He smiled, knowing he would still make it upstairs in time for the news. He expected the main story to give more details on the missing girl, and he was keen to keep abreast of all developments – but the headlines were not as he expected.

> *Gardai are this evening examining remains found in the Dublin Mountains. It is feared they may be that of missing twelve-year-old schoolgirl, Caroline Devine. The identity of the body has not yet been confirmed, but it is understood that her family have been informed, and an autopsy is due to be carried out by state pathologist Donal Morrison later this evening.*

He stood in front of the television screen, not quite believing what he was seeing, as a reporter from the scene reiterated the meagre information. Garda cars were parked up on a ditch at the side of the road, yellow tape running for as far as he could see. He saw men dressed in white boiler suits, their faces looking downwards, wooden sticks in each of their right hands, breath billowing from their uncovered faces.

He had left her near perfect. He had wanted everything to be as it should be, not just for him, but for her too. Whilst staring at the television screen, he felt the intrusion of those unknown men, messing things up, a sense of violation rushing through him.

He replayed the broadcast, looking at the police in their white boiler suits, mucky tyre marks on the road with the onslaught of their cars, the black of the tall spruce trees shadowing the foreground, turning everything in their path to miniature. He paced around the room, with a multitude of thoughts flooding him all at once. There was no time for regret; he had to think, and think clearly. The finding of the girl's body brought new difficulties, loose ends that would have to be dealt with. They had forced his hand, and he now needed to be one step ahead of them. The distance would not prove a problem. He still had another couple of hours before dark.

Ellie

IT IS LATE IN THE AFTERNOON BY THE TIME I MEET Dr Ebbs. I've had a bad feeling about today since I woke. I sense change and change isn't a good thing, it's unpredictable.

When I arrive, he has my case notes closed. On top of them is his jotter from yesterday, but that, too, is closed. I assume talking will be the order of the day, but it surprises me that he doesn't want to write anything down.

'Hello, Ellie.'

'Hello.'

I sit down, join my hands and I wait. He smiles and draws in a deep breath to initiate conversation.

'How are you today?'

'Fine.'

He smiles again.

'You look tired.'

I don't answer him.

'Ellie, I have been going over some of the background history here in the file.' He makes a hand gesture towards the closed case notes.

My blank stare does not unsettle him.

'You were committed to St Michael's in 1995.'

He coughs.

'At that point you had been married to Joe for, what, almost ten years?'

'Sounds right.'

'How would you describe your relationship? After all, ten years is a long time.'

'I'm here longer. That time has flown.'

He ignores my sarcasm. 'It says here that it was Joe who signed the committal papers.'

'That's correct.'

'And how did that make you feel?'

'I felt nothing, he did the right thing.'

'No anger towards him, disappointment even?'

'No, all the anger and disappointment was for him alone. I understood that.'

'Ellie, if I am being completely honest with you, my main concern here is that you have made very little real progress since you arrived here. Do you feel we might have let you down?'

'Perhaps I don't want to make progress.'

He leans back in the chair like he did the day before. It is one of those reclining types. My chair does not recline, it suits me fine and reflects how I feel, rigid.

'Why not?'

'Because.'

'Because what?'

'Because I don't, didn't—'

'Didn't?'

'Don't.'

'I want you to be truthful.'

'What is the truth, Dr Ebbs? Sometimes we think we know the truth, but we don't. One man's truth is another man's lie. I'm sure you've heard that one before.'

'Well, yes, the truth is subjective but, for now, what I want to know is your truth.'

'Ah, my truth, now that is a little bit tricky.'

'Why's that?'

'Because, Doctor, I haven't worked that particular part out yet.'

'Well, let me ask you something else then.' He can tell I'm irritated. He's playing his cards carefully. 'How have you found your time here at St Michael's?'

In truth, his question isn't any different from any other question I have been asked in the past. So I'm surprised at my outburst.

'Well, let me see. Initially, when I wanted to kill myself, I found it most annoying, awkward even. Later it became quite acceptable, more suited to my needs. And now? Well, now I am used to it and it's just fine.'

I knew my big mouth would get me into trouble.

'And why does it suit you just fine?'

'Fine, like truth, is subjective, Dr Ebbs. One man's fine is another man's hell.'

'Indeed.' He thinks long and hard on this, as if he respects what I have to say.

'You went missing for some time before the fire?'

The fire again. I close my eyes, more out of frustration than anything else. He picks up on this immediately.

'Is your distress because of the fire or because we are talking about it?'

'The fire means nothing.'

'Nothing?'

This surprises him. I wait. I have already said too much. He leans forward again.

'Do you know, Ellie, there is a saying I learned a long time ago, it has always stuck with me.'

I hold my stare. This gives him encouragement, it seems.

'It says the mad are more sane than you think, and the sane are more mad than you know.'

'Do you think I'm mad?'

'Do you?'

I don't answer. He raises his eyebrow, but it does not deter him.

'I suppose it tells us, Ellie, that people are not always what they seem.'

'People are seldom what they seem.'

'Indeed, you're right. People are seldom what they seem.'

He pauses again.

'Would it be fair to say, Ellie, that your marriage was an unhappy one?'

'Not always.' I am surprised at my honesty.

'You and Joe, you came from very different backgrounds?'

'He was a good man, but I wasn't good for him.'

'The circumstances before you came here to St Michael's, they must have been difficult for you both.' He says this more as a confirmation than a question. 'It is a hard thing losing a child, a hard thing for anyone.'

'Yes.' The fact that I have answered surprises me. I feel uncomfortable, out of my depth.

'Ellie.'

'Yes.'

'I want to help you.' His words are said softly, but with directness. It feels unnerving. I don't answer, I don't want to.

'I would like you to try something for me. Would you be willing?'

'I don't know.'

'I would like you to try and go back to the point that you, Ellie, see as the beginning. Maybe write down a few short lines about it.'

'Now?'

He senses the panic in my voice.

'No, no, over the next few days is fine. You don't have to do it, of course. But think about it, and depending on how you feel, if and when you do write things down, you might wish to share your thoughts with me. Either way, I would like you to at least consider doing the exercise. If afterwards you prefer to keep your thoughts to yourself, that would be fine.'

'I don't have to show or tell you anything?'

'Nothing, if that is what you want.'

'Okay, I'll think about it.'

'Good. That pleases me, Ellie.' He smiles.

I say nothing, but I sense I am only buying time.

'So maybe we could meet again in a few days, just to give you time to think about what we have discussed?' He smiles again, the type of smile that doctors use to put you at your ease.

'All right.'

Just like yesterday, he stands up and gestures me with arm movements to the door and I, like a well-trained dog, stand up and move forward, doing exactly what is expected of me.

O'CONNOR WASN'T LOOKING FORWARD TO HIS VISIT to Morrison. Tallaght Hospital may have been a very different building from the old city morgue at Marino, but the slick lines of modern design and shiny floors were purely cosmetic when it came to the stench of death. He passed the visiting smokers and patients in their dressing gowns congregated outside; he was dying for a cigarette, but had no intention of lighting up with them. Once through the revolving doors, he entered the main hospital, busy with visitors, patients and hospital staff, all criss-crossing each other within their business of recovery, and the reality that for some of them anyway the fight might soon be over.

He had been just a rookie guard when he'd attended his first postmortem, but some things have a habit of never leaving you. He had expected similar smells to a hospital – clinical, sterile. What he hadn't expected was the smell of decomposition, and that unforgettable feeling of everything being slowed down. The male victim had been in his late teens and had been discovered in an alleyway down from a popular nightclub. Laid out on the steel slab mortuary table, he'd been photographed fully clothed, the images taken at various angles. As the pieces of his clothing had been removed, the delayering process, the clothes, and any of the items found in them, were photographed in turn, forming separate links in the chain. The naked body was then photographed, again at varying angles, paying particular attention to any markings, some of which had occurred prior to his killing, but every single mark was photographed and referenced.

During the process, O'Connor had been surprised by the simplest of things: how the small metal rulers used for measuring and illustrating the size of body parts, wounds and abrasions had been the same type as the one he had used at school. Each of the metal rulers was disposed of at the end of the autopsy, a new one for every corpse. The chrome scales used to weigh the individual organs looked similar to those he remembered from old-style butchers, and the plastic buckets to hold organs were not unlike the kind you would find in any hardware store. All of this activity happened within a bubble of time slowed down, everyone speaking in the same calm monotone, sometimes reduced to a whisper, as if the guy on the slab might somehow hear and answer back.

O'Connor had learned something that day. He had learned that when it came to autopsies, you needed to think, and not let your feelings get in the way. You had to take in the angle of the knife, the potential size of the weapon, the penetration of entry wounds to the torso, and anything else that might help solve the crime. Nobody was a spectator at an autopsy, everyone had a purpose, and he wasn't going to let anything get in the way of him doing his job, no matter how difficult it might be.

Even before O'Connor entered the mortuary section of the hospital, he had imagined Caroline's grey statuette form lying waste on the steel trolley, the squeak of metal wheels against the shiny, spotless floors, Morrison carrying out his task with the precision of a master, everyone suited up in their surgical gowns. The girl's body held answers, and he hoped the state pathologist would find them. If the autopsy was still in progress, experience told O'Connor that he needed to prepare for what he was about to see.

As he walked through the corridors, he took in all the sounds around him: the shuffle of slippered feet, machines bleeping, steel metal bins being flipped open, lift doors opening and closing shut. O'Connor only looked far enough ahead to follow the signs, despite it being a well-worn path. The farther he walked, the more the human traffic around him reduced, till the only person he could see was the uniformed guard stationed outside the double doors. O'Connor engaged the young guard in conversation and introduced himself, then asked the young man his name and where he was based. They talked for no more than a minute, but it was enough to cement the feeling that they were in this together.

When he saw Morrison walking towards him, he knew the autopsy was over. O'Connor was relieved that the last memory he would have of the girl would be the one from the grave, and not on a stainless steel slab.

'Good evening, O'Connor.' Morrison had already changed out of his autopsy garb.

'So what do you have?'

Morrison eyed him the way you might an impatient schoolboy, assessing whether or not he was worthy of being given a speedy response. Morrison chose to be accommodating.

'Well, Detective Inspector, what we have is an adolescent female, probably less than a year into pubertal period. There is very little fat tissue on the body, practically skeletal in certain areas, could be part of accelerated growth or an aggressive diet regime.'

'Meaning?' O'Connor looked up from writing in his notebook.

'Meaning exactly what I just said.'

'Fine. Go on. Sorry.'

'The plaiting of the hair happened after the blows to the head, heavy matting within the hair follicles, broken in parts to achieve the tying of the plaits, along with cotton fibre interspersed, perhaps a cloth used to clear away some of the blood, of which there would have been plenty. No fresh blood on the outer layers. I believe some time had passed from the blows being given to the hair being plaited.'

O'Connor continued to write in his notebook. He knew he would get a full report from Morrison in time, but at such an early stage in the investigation everything moved fast, and it was good to have certain things close at hand.

'Also, Detective, there were bite marks inside the victim's mouth. Judging by the size of the teeth marks, most likely belonged to the victim herself. The blows to the head came from behind, a narrow steel implement; the first blow did the most damage, after that it was just repeated force.'

'But the blows didn't kill her?'

'No, asphyxiation is still the most likely cause.'

'And how the body was placed?'

'That's the interesting part. As you know, a body will automatically curl into the foetal position, but we are dealing with something very different here. When the girl's body was placed underground, rigor mortis was in the latter stages, so a considerable number of hours had passed since her death.'

'How many?'

'Well, Detective, I normally avoid giving in-depth science lessons, but when the victim's body was exhumed, a relaxed body state had already occurred. Therefore, in my opinion, the girl was killed shortly after she went missing.'

'What makes you so sure?'

'Rigor sets in within a couple of hours after death – you say the girl went missing around 4 p.m. on Wednesday? If the girl was killed a couple of hours later, rigor mortis could have begun to take hold by 8 p.m. The entire contracting process is completed within eight to twelve hours. So, using ten hours as an acceptable mid-ground, that means that the entire rigor would have been completed ten hours after death, or around 6 a.m. Thursday morning. The body then remains fixed for another eighteen hours in a state known as the rigid stage, which would bring us up to around midnight, and that's important.'

'Why exactly?'

'After that point, the reversal of rigor occurs, but at some juncture after rigor began, the rigor was forced.'

'Forced?'

'He broke her bones, Inspector, at the knee joints, elbow joints, fingers ... do I need to go on?'

'No, I get your drift.'

'Which is why the positioning is important. As I said, the way the body lay could be construed as a fairly natural position for a corpse, but this time nature had a helping hand.'

'So what happens after the rigor reverses?'

'To fully relax takes a further twelve hours. The body was exhumed around midday on the Friday, and at that point the body was practically in a fully relaxed state. Mind you, rigor can be variable based on conditions, but considering the girl went missing at 4 p.m. on Wednesday and the relaxed body state had already occurred when she was found, she had to have been killed within a few hours of going missing.'

'Is that the end of the science lesson?'

'Not quite. Do you want to hear this or not?'

'I'm all ears. I'd never dream of rushing you.'

'Correct answer, Inspector – any more room in that notebook of yours?'

'Plenty.'

'The tissue decomposition is important too. It wasn't advanced. Therefore it was delayed in some way.'

'How?'

'Any number of reasons or conditions, but I'm talking about the time before burial.'

'When it was probably kept somewhere else?'

'Yes, Detective Inspector, and considering the rate of decomposition, it wasn't kept anywhere warm.'

'Do you mean it was kept outdoors?'

Morrison gave O'Connor one of his judgemental stares. 'Unlikely, Detective Inspector, there are no traces of any protection being put on the body. In weather like this, a body exposed to the elements, even in cold temperatures, would have had more advanced decomposition. Most likely the body was kept indoors, but, as I said, somewhere cold.'

'We're not talking a fridge here?'

'You've watched too many *CSI* programmes, O'Connor. If the body was in a damn fridge, I'd have told you.'

'Okay, okay, just trying to get a handle on things – and, just for the record, I don't watch that crap. Now, can we get back to the cause of death?'

'As I said, asphyxia caused by strangulation. She has bruising to her face and body, possibly from a fall and/or as a result of the initial attack, but specifically there is acute bruising and injuries to the neck. There are external and internal signs of strangulation present – fracture of the hyoid bone and thyroid cartilage, the two structures making up the voice box, plus the haemorrhaging, spotting around the eyelids, meaning sufficient pressure and time had been applied to her neck. There is also major bruising to the side of the trachea.'

'Trachea?'

'Windpipe. There's bruising on the back of the victim's neck, meaning the assailant was facing the victim. She was still alive after the blows to the head, Detective, and no sign of anything else used on the neck, other than the killer's own hands.'

'Was she conscious?'

'I doubt it. The markings are consistent with her being in a sedentary or lying down position, the killer leaning over her. If she'd been conscious, and despite the slightness of her frame, she would have attempted to fight back. There was nothing found under her nails, no skin deposits or any other indicators that she'd put up a struggle.'

'Is that it?'

'Why, is your notebook full?'

'Not yet.'

'Good. Well then, one last detail.'

'Go on.'

'There was blood pooling down the right side, consistent with how the body was found. The body's position didn't alter in any significant manner once the pooling occurred.'

'What's the story on the toxicology findings?'

'You know how long they take, Detective Inspector.'

'I'll apply some pressure.'

'I'm sure you will.'

'You said steel implement, Morrison, any theories?'

'A steel bar of some kind, Detective, round and narrow, might even be a household poker. Not my area of expertise, though, I'll leave the *CSI* stuff to you.'

O'Connor left Morrison's last comment unanswered, but it didn't help his mood as he exited the revolving doors at the front of the hospital. Pulling the collar of his jacket up, he checked his phone for messages before crossing the main road to the station. As the beginning of another gale began to take hold, he stopped before entering the Incident Room to light up, standing on the exterior steel steps, wondering what kind of sick weirdo would break the bones of a young girl into place.

Crumlin village

HE SAT IN THE DRIVER'S SEAT, THE CAR RADIO TURNED down, not hearing the young teenagers' conversation but watching everything. His head barely moved, fixated on the girl laughing with the others, tossing back her waist-length, strawberry-blonde hair that curled at the end, as if it kept the best bit till last. Her hair was darker now, the summer brightening almost faded. Out of nervous habit, she twirled the front strands around her right index finger; teasing. There were four of them huddled at the side of the shops, all girls, swapping their silly stories.

He followed her from the house, knowing her routine. She would spend some time here, while her friends sneaked their cigarettes, before moving on. Amelia was popular. She liked to spread herself around.

His eyes moved to the other side of the road and spotted a young guy in a black hoodie who started to run over. One of the local studs, strutting up to them, they laughed in unison, delighted for him to be part of their little group. Such is their girlish silliness, elevating the stupid asshole to something important.

His gloved hands slid around the steering wheel and he stretched out his fingers on reaching the top. It wasn't yet dark. He looked at the scarf on the dashboard, and read 19.45 on the clock. She wouldn't be expected home until ten. He had everything he needed; preparation and good timing were an essential part of his success.

He waited, watching her pull away from the group, reaching into the pocket of her denim jacket, answering her mobile phone. The annoyed look on her face telling him the call is unwanted, probably her awful mother. He would need to take care of that phone; no loose ends.

She crossed at the traffic lights, obeying the green man like a good little girl, then turned down the road towards the sports centre. He followed, pulling in on the left-hand side ahead of her and checking the rear-view mirror to make sure it was only her he saw. Leaning over, he rolled down the passenger window, before calling out to her.

'Hi there.'

'Ah, hiya.' A nice big smile.

'No swimming this evening?'

'What?'

'No kit bag …' He points to her left shoulder.

'Oh yeah – no, not tonight, just heading up to see some of the others.'

'Hop in. I'll give you a lift. I'm going there myself.' She hesitates. 'You can tell me all about your new medals, you must have more.'

'Only one.' She laughs.

'Slacking on the training, are you? Come on, get in.'

'They don't come easy, you know,' she says, sitting in beside him.

'Nothing worthwhile ever does, Amelia. Roll up that window. We don't want you catching a cold.'

He knew panic would set in once he passed the sports centre, so before reaching it he said, 'Mind if I pick up someone else, they are just around the corner?'

'Sure, no problem.'

'Turn on the radio if you like.'

'Cool,' she bent her head down to flick around the stations.

The entrance to the back lane was on his left. As he turned the car she looked up, almost instinctively trying to get her bearings.

The punch to her face hit the underside of her chin. Dazed, her head hit the passenger side window, and for an instant she stared back at him before lunging for the door handle. He had the large kitchen knife to her throat before she could reach it, pulling her back by the hair.

'Now, Amelia, let's be calm. If you are a good girl, I promise I'll make this easy for both of us. Do you understand me?'

She nodded.

'Good, now sit back down, nice and easy.' A trickle of blood crept down her neckline, like a jagged teardrop. 'We don't want anything nasty to happen, do we?' She didn't answer. 'No words? That's not like you.' He smiled before indicating to the scarf on the dashboard. 'Tie that around your eyes, good and tight now, double knots, no peeping.'

She did exactly as she was told.

'You're doing great, now arms down, join your hands together so I can put this knife away.'

The next three punches knocked her unconscious. A quick check up and down the lane, then he opened the car boot. Once he had shoved her inside it, he tied her hands and feet quickly and taped her mouth. He was about to shut the boot down when he remembered the mobile phone. He pulled it out of her jacket pocket, smashed it under his boot and kicked the broken pieces to the side. The next part would take longer, but the hard bit was over. From here on, it would just be the two of them, and the dark.

≈

He pulled the car into an inlet to the left of the mountain road, the Special Area of Conservation to his right, the city behind him. He turned off the headlights. The road back down to the city was winding, and from his location he could see as far as the old bridge. He timed it, confirming that he had at least two minutes from when he spotted a car, to hearing it pass him. His own car was parked well in off the road, out of sight. The important part was getting the girl down into the ditch unseen. The drop on the far side would be steep, but that did not concern him.

Opening the car boot, her breathing was deep, her chest moving in and out, her body trembling.

'Let's play a game,' he said, and in his mind he heard the old clock ticking – tick tock, tick tock – followed by its familiar elongated pause: everything in perfect rhythm.

He left the duct tape across her mouth to keep her silent. The skin on her lovely face was blotchy, bruised and wet from tears. Her arms and legs still tied securely.

He wanted it to be quick.

Tick tock, tick tock.

He pulled the electric cable tight around her neck, closing off her oxygen, trapping the blood vessels. This time, expediency was all that mattered, although he did not want her to suffer.

He could still picture her from months earlier, placing those small toes in to test the water, pulling her hair back behind her ears before the dive. He had watched as the long strands of her hair had become immersed, floating to the top like seaweed. He had listened attentively as he heard someone call out her name: Amelia. It was such a pretty name for a young girl. He had thought she would be perfect.

In the dark, all he could hear was the flow of the water. Despite the lightness of the girl's frame, she felt heavy on his shoulders. The ground underfoot was a mix of scrub and barren soil; he made no sound as he moved. They were now in a place without shadows. He had a long way to go. The farther he walked, the more he became part of the night. Past the gorse patches, where groundwater seeped through sand and gravel, the ground then hardening, before turning into the chalky bedrock he required.

For the first time since he left the mountain road, he turned and looked behind him. The vast, darkened wilderness brought him peace. Dumping the bag containing her body to the side, he stretched upwards, allowing his own breathing to settle. This was the place. The grave would not have to be deep.

Even though she had been such a disappointment, he still prepared her body properly – brushing her hair and tying both plaits neatly with the ribbons. Her lips had reminded him of a painting by Vermeer, the deep shades of cherries over-ripening on the canvas. He laid out her body, as if she were a young girl sleeping, before gently kissing her forehead. She hadn't understood, but then, why should she?

She was never good enough.

Mervin Road, Rathmines
Friday, 7 October 2011, 6.30 p.m.

KATE WALKED DOWN THE LONG HALLWAY OF NUMBER 34 Mervin Road and pulled the bright yellow Georgian door firmly behind her. With at least another hour before Charlie and Declan were due back from the cinema, she had decided to get out of their apartment and go for a run. The three-storey building was divided into apartments, each occupied by a small family, but it was all quiet as she stood on the doorstep, pulling her jet-black hair into a tight ponytail. To Kate, changing into her running gear was like putting on a new skin, but tonight she knew she couldn't outrun the images in her mind – she would end up thinking about the photographs O'Connor had shown her over lunch.

O'Connor had a good success rate, but that in itself was no guarantee that they would find out who killed the girl. But there was another thought niggling at the back of her mind. She had been surprised at how pleased she'd been to see O'Connor again, and couldn't help wondering if the difficulties she and Declan had been experiencing lately had anything to do with it. She didn't like the way that last thought made her feel, so she struck out along the path, determined to run it and all the other thoughts out of her system.

As she made her way out of Ranelagh village, past the small line of bijou shops and bars, she let the breeze consume her as she instinctively ran faster. Her feet sent her on the usual route: rounding the corner at the top of Appian Way, past the road leading to the Royal Hospital and farther on towards Donnybrook. Turning left towards Herbert

Park, she felt her body get into a more uplifting rhythm; she could hear the swish of her ponytail and the repetitive sound of her runners hitting the footpath, feeling the bounce as the ground resonated from the soles of her feet up through her body.

The faster she ran, the faster the questions about the murder came. What had led to the event? Why this victim? What had motivated the killer? She thought back to the images from the burial site, how murky everything had looked, alternating shades of grey and black. In the images, it looked as if the soil had eaten into the girl's body, layering it, creating a sort of uniformity with the land, except for the small glint that one of the cameras had picked up – a silver crucifix around the victim's neck, reflecting splintered light when all else was dark.

Entering the gates of Herbert Park, she took in the smell of recently cut grass, probably the last cut of autumn. Other than the odd rook and jackdaw cawing from the trees above, the park was empty, and as she made her way past the old stone water fountain, the cascading water blended with the sounds of the tall rustling trees.

The image Kate couldn't get out of her mind was the school photograph of Caroline Devine, the photograph her parents had given to the gardaí. What struck Kate most was the girl's smile. It was one of those large, unthinking smiles that children gave and it was, according to O'Connor, the clearest image Caroline's parents had of her. They must have prayed someone would recognise their bright shining daughter and bring her back, but Caroline had not come back, at least not in the way her parents had hoped.

In the photograph, the girl's blonde curls were held back by a narrow hairband, revealing tiny stud earrings, which reminded Kate of a pair she'd worn at that age. She could still remember being twelve, self-conscious, aware of her body changing, her parents not quite knowing what to do with her any more. Had Caroline felt self-conscious, no longer a child but not yet a woman? The few months since that school photograph must have changed things. The development of her body, visible in the mountain grave, meant Caroline had begun adolescence, newly formed sexuality like an undercurrent waiting to settle.

What had happened to her in the hours before her death? What, other than terror, had gone through her mind? Kate was familiar with the area, it was remote and if the burial had happened at night, considering the heavy rain and cloud cover at the time, visibility would have been difficult, giving all the privacy needed. The killer had taken great care to bury his victim, and she wondered whether it was an area he, too, was familiar with. She knew the age of the girl was going to make this case more difficult than most. The death of a young victim had a habit of elevating emotions. No matter what had led the killer to this point, Kate hoped she was right in her prediction to O'Connor. Either way, Caroline's killer had crossed a line, and was only too capable of killing again.

≈

When she turned the key in the front door, Kate was surprised that Declan and Charlie still weren't home. She checked her phone for messages. Just one, from Declan: 'Got delayed, we're grabbing McDonald's.' She managed to smile at this. If nothing else, her preference for correct spelling in text messages had finally rubbed off on her husband. As she showered, her mind went back to the murder. What if the girl's body had never been found? Had that been the killer's intention? If so, why take so much care to position a corpse he didn't want to be discovered? She thought about the close-up shots of the girl in the grave. Her hands with all her fingers interlinked, clasped together, her hair braided carefully into two plaits lying neatly on her chest. The plaited hair, just like the body, seemed to be placed in a very particular way. Everything about the girl looking tidy, arranged.

Getting dressed after her shower, she thought about something else that had been bothering her. The stud earrings Caroline had worn to school that morning. According to O'Connor, they had been removed, yet her silver chain with the cross on it hadn't. Why? Had the killer wanted to keep something of her, a memento of sorts? Why take the earrings and not the silver cross? Then there were the ribbons, tied in two large bows, old-fashioned as she had mentioned to O'Connor. If Caroline was unconscious from the blows, the killer had plaited her hair, and if the ribbons were left with the victim, then just like the positioning of the body, there was a reason for them looking the way they did. The more Kate thought about the images, the stronger her belief became that whoever buried Caroline Devine had demonstrated an unusual level of care and detail towards his victim. The girl herself was important, and how she lay and every detail about it meant something too, even if the killer hadn't wanted her to be found.

There was the click of a key turning in a lock and her son's excited voice ended her thoughts about Caroline Devine.

'Mom, Mom, where are you?'

He burst into the room and raced over to her. She smiled the first genuine smile of the day.

'Look, Mom,' he beamed, holding up a miniature Gutsy Smurf toy. 'Daddy got me a Happy Meal.'

'I can see that.'

Declan looked tired, his face strained – a look she had become all too familiar with recently. He smiled at Charlie, then glanced at her, before turning away again. Was he purposely avoiding eye contact with her? She hadn't meant to appear angry, but she must have done.

'There's no need to look like that Kate, we were both starving.'

Charlie bounced up and down on the couch, delighted with life.

'Anyhow, I don't smell any home cooking.' The tone in Declan's voice was as strained as his expression.

Why the hell, in the twenty-first century, do men still think it's a woman's duty to make the bloody dinner? She knew it was a jibe at her, just like most of their conversations seemed to be these days. But it was easier to let it go, for Charlie's sake.

'I know, Dec, I just got tied up with things.'

'Nothing new there.'

She wanted to snap back at him, but there was no point. It would only end up the way all their arguments had ended up over the past six months, right back at the beginning. Ever since he missed out on that promotion, it was as if everything that went wrong was her fault. Although all the extra hours she was putting in with her new responsibilities heading up the project team hadn't helped.

'I was worried about you both, that's all.'

A look of disbelief crossed his face as he picked up the remote control. 'Well no need, we're here now.'

She tried to make light of it. 'I guess I'm the only one going hungry, so.'

'I have some chips.' Charlie shook his Happy Meal box.

'At least someone loves me.' Kate attempted a laugh, but when she looked across at Declan, he had already stopped listening.

'Come on, buster, it's late, time to get ready for bed.'

'Ah, Mom, but—'

'No buts, Charlie. Look, Dad's watching his boring programme.' Again Declan ignored her. 'While you're getting into your pyjamas, you can tell me all about your day, and I promise to read you the longest story.'

'How long a story?' He squinted his face tight.

She smiled back. 'Really long.'

'How long is really long?'

'Until you're asleep.'

'Promise?'

'Of course. Come on, up you get. Last one to the bathroom is a slowcoach.'

≈

When Charlie was in his pyjamas, with his face cleaned and teeth brushed, he picked up the biggest book he could find for her to read.

'Mom, I beat Daddy running from the top of the street.'

'Did you? I wish I'd seen that.'

'Why didn't you come to the cinema, Mom? Gutsy was brilliant. He's the bravest Smurf ever.'

'I'm sure he was brilliant – but he's not as brilliant as you.'

'Dad says you're always busy.'

'Does he now?'

'It's Mikey's birthday next week. He'll be five, and I'll be still four. It's not fair.'

'You'll be five soon enough.' Kate looked at the size of the weighty storybook he had picked out for bedtime and smiled, pulling the covers up and giving him a big hug before getting started. No matter how tired she was, she always enjoyed their special time alone at night.

It never took Charlie long to fall asleep. After he dozed off, instead of leaving the room, Kate stayed back awhile to watch him sleep, his mouth slightly ajar as the pillow soaked up his dribbles. His jet-black hair, even darker than hers, stuck up like tiny spikes on his head. Charlie had his father's eyes, sea-green. When he was born, they had thought his eyes would be deep blue, like Kate's, but they'd changed. She placed her hand gently on his forehead, loving the softness of his skin. She tried to hold on to the moment, thinking only of her and Charlie, but instead her mind drifted to Caroline's parents. What sort of nightmare must they be living through? It was too awful to contemplate something like that ever happening to her beautiful Charlie. As for her and Declan, she couldn't help but wonder if Charlie was the only reason they were still together.

She moved Charlie's favourite teddy in close and pulled the duvet up tighter underneath his chin. One last look, then she knew it was time to go down to the living room and be with Declan. She sighed, before switching off Charlie's bedside lamp and walking out into the hallway. She eased his bedroom door over, leaving a slight gap, so that he wouldn't be in complete darkness if he woke during the night.

In the living room, Declan already looked like part of the furniture, slouched on the couch wearing one of his favourite old T-shirts and tracksuit bottoms, the television still on.

'He's asleep then?'

'Yeah, out for the count.' Still Declan didn't look at her. It was as if she was invisible. When did they stop making an effort to look well for each other? When was the last time they had sex? Not remembering wasn't a good sign. One of them needed to make an effort.

'How was work, Dec?'

His expression told her it wasn't the best choice of conversation. 'The same as always.'

He turned back to the television screen, ramping up the volume.

≈

By midnight, Kate couldn't stay awake any longer.

'I'm going to bed, Dec.'

'I'll be there in a minute.'

Kate doubted it.

When her mobile rang, it was almost a relief. She grabbed it on the second ring, and was surprised to hear O'Connor's voice. Even over the noise of the television, Declan raised his eyebrows at the loudness of the inspector's voice.

'O'Connor, calm down, what's happened?'

'Another Category 1, that's what's happened. Thirteen-year-old girl, Amelia Spain, hasn't returned home. Her mobile was pinged by the guys at HQ, last time it was active was a call from her mother about two hours ago, when she was with friends. Turns out she has a second mobile on a separate network for her close pals. Boyfriend texted her at 8.15 p.m. We picked the signal up at the Military Road, Kate. Looks like you might have called this one wrong by a mile.'

'But she's still only missing, you could still find her.'

'She isn't up at Military Road for any good fucking reason, Kate. He's taken her, I know it.' There was a fury in his voice that she hadn't heard before. O'Connor hung up the phone before she got a chance to say anything else.

For once, she was pleased Declan kept his silence. She needed to think. Her professional pride was hurt. Damn O'Connor for hanging up on her. Egotistical shit – but what if he was right? What if she had called this one wrong? She walked into the kitchen, automatically flicking on the kettle, even though she had no intention of using it.

Picking up her mobile, she rang O'Connor back. She expected it to go to his voicemail and was surprised when he answered.

'O'Connor, if it turns out bad and you do find Amelia Spain up there, I know why he moved quickly.'

He held his silence. She heard him sighing, then speaking. 'Kate, you better have something good to tell me.'

'He'd already groomed her, maybe even disregarded her.' Another silence. Kate continued. 'For whatever reason he moved on, but the finding of Caroline's body must have spooked him. If I'm right, Amelia may turn out to be the one who got away who became a complication he needed to get rid of.'

'Jesus Christ, Kate, we're talking serial killer territory here.'

'And I want to be part of finding him.'

Declan entered the kitchen, catching her last words, muttering under his breath, 'Saint Kate, wants to save the world.' His sarcasm was not lost on her, but O'Connor was her focus now.

'Kate, you know what the force feels about using outsiders. And you've fucked up on this already, don't forget.'

She wanted to scream at him but instead she held back, although the angry tone in her voice was undeniable. 'I don't give a damn, O'Connor, officially or unofficially I can help you. I want to be involved.'

Ellie

WHEN DARKNESS COMES, I FIND SOME PEACE LISTENING
to the sounds of the familiar – the creaking of beds in the other rooms,
the rattling gutter that has needed to be repaired since the storms last
winter. Even the sound of my own breath as my face burrows into the
pillow has become a form of practised regularity. How long have I felt
security in predictability?

When the lights outside the door go out, I know I will suffer a
long night. Since meeting Dr Ebbs earlier, my mind has been rattled
– but I had felt rattled even before I saw him. Maybe it is yet another
aspect to my life of nothingness, how I can sense even the slightest
shifts in mood. I did well enough today, shielding it from the others,
those lonely women who share my time in here. Some of my fellow
patrons have come and gone a long time back, some more like visitors
to a mad house than anything else. I guess for them, those who stay
only a short while, their real place in life is outside of here. Others,
like me, have been here so long we have drifted into the soul of this
Godforsaken place. In here, you get used to sharing your thoughts
with just yourself. It feeds into the madness of it all.

I haven't decided if I am going to write anything. In fact, the very
thought of it sends chills through me, as if someone has opened a door
and a gale is blowing through it. It bashes the door of memory back
and forth, and the very thought of it causes a banging inside my head.
What does he mean by 'the beginning'? Beginning of what? Of when
I started to feel crazy or of when I stopped caring?

I think back to the affair, as if it might provide a beginning of sorts. It was so long ago – can I really remember it as it was then?

He was different to Joe, that was for sure. Even though they were brothers, they had nothing in common, either with each other or how they were with me. When Joe looked at me, it was almost as if he was apologising for being there – but Andrew wasn't like that. He looked me straight in the eye, as if no one else existed. When I think about it now, a part of me wonders if he was the only man I've ever loved. Afterwards, just like the others, he didn't believe me. I held no grudge. Afterwards, I held nothing.

My pregnancy had not been planned; it wasn't something I had even thought about. In the beginning, I wasn't even going to tell Joe. It happened at the end of my first year at college, and it certainly wasn't the news my mother had expected.

Going to college was something that hadn't been within her reach. She was so proud of me. As things turned out, her dying before Amy's death was a blessing. At least she didn't have to face that final heartbreak. If my father had been alive, things might have been different. He was always the one I was closest to and he taught me everything, from how to fish to how to fire his hunting gun. I remember my mother being cross when I told her about the gun. I couldn't have been more than eleven when I shot at my first hare. Funny the things you remember years after.

Joe had wanted to marry me when he heard about the baby. And what had I wanted? I look back at that young woman and I see a head filled with silly notions. I took the easy choice I guess, there's a laugh. Ignorance, I've learned, fashions its own crosses.

At the beginning, the pregnancy made me feel trapped, I remember that. Up until then everything had been fine with Joe. Expecting a baby changed the agenda completely. If anything, I felt like a mouse caught in a maze that had no exits, only dead ends. Of course, it wasn't as if I had to marry him. My mother would have understood; I know that now. But it was never about her understanding. It was about disappointment, about feeling that I had let her down.

I never finished college, but I suppose by then I was happily married, or so my mother thought. In those early days of pregnancy, I should have known that I didn't love Joe. If I had loved him, I wouldn't have felt so trapped.

When Joe and I were first married, it was like playing a game of happy families. It made Joe happy, the idea that we were going to have a child, and he became even more attentive than before. He was kind and funny – all the things that made Joe who he was. I suppose they all got exaggerated, hyped, tricking us both into believing the world would be a better place because of the baby.

I closed my eyes to all the danger signs; I didn't want to see them. And then there was the biggest one of all, the one that I only recognised later. It was the way Joe never held too high an opinion of himself, the way he'd put himself down. It wasn't obvious at first. He hid it well with others and, to an extent, with me. He used his exterior good humour and bravado to overcompensate for his low self-esteem. I understood later, though too late, how this made him hold such an exalted opinion of me. My stupidity and Joe's delusion tricked us both. *Two blind mice … see how they run …*

DRIVING OUT OF RATHMINES, KATE'S MIND WAS churning with questions about the case. She needed to find out who Caroline Devine was, the kind of person she had been, and if Amelia Spain turned out to be the next victim, what links there were, if any, between the two girls. Understanding the victim, or victims, would give her a better grasp of how each of them would have behaved given a particular set of circumstances.

If they came across as confident but somewhat distant, the perpetrator may have taken their behaviour as an insult and been angered by it. In both cases, the girls were on the brink of adulthood; many of their values would not yet have been fully formed. Adolescence was a time when things changed, when what had gone before was not always indicative of what would follow. If she was right and Caroline hadn't been chosen at random, the girl could have inadvertently encouraged her abductor. There had to be a reason why she'd been taken. If Kate could work out what that reason was, it would give her a clearer picture of the killer.

Heading up the mountain road, she thought again about the argument she'd had with Declan the previous night about looking after Charlie on Saturday. He'd agreed in the end to mind Charlie – something he never usually minded doing – but she knew that wasn't the real reason for his anger. 'We all have choices,' he had told her. But in her mind right now the death of a young girl and the possible killing of another took precedence. Kate thought of Charlie. She had checked in on him before she'd left. He had been deep in sleep, one hand resting on his pillow, the other clenched across his chest.

As she drove, she also thought of her own mother. It had been days since she had visited her at Sweetmount, something else for her to feel guilty about, and something else she would have to put to the back of her mind for now. She knew from the text she got from O'Connor earlier that Amelia still hadn't returned home. Army helicopters would begin roaming the area from first light, and a full-scale search operation would soon be underway. One of her first starting points in this case would have to be the area where Caroline had been buried – the grave was the last connection to the killer.

≈

The road from Bohernabreena towards the Military Road had varying levels of steepness, the landscape opening out to a vastness of lush green fields and mountains capped with dense forests. Small cottages and larger homes dotted the road either side until Piperstown, where civilisation in the domestic sense ended and the barrage of police entourage began.

Kate pulled her car in tight to the side of the ditch; even from a distance she could see O'Connor's agitation. Things were moving fast, faster than he would have wanted, but the look on his face said he had every intention of moving with it, and all around him better keep up or get the hell out of there.

'O'Connor.'

'Right, you're in for now. Nolan was sceptical, but even he knows this thing is shaping up a whole lot differently from anything we've dealt with before.'

'Any more from the phone signal?'

'No. The battery's probably down at this point. We're concentrating the search where Caroline's body was found, over to the left and all the way up to the Military Road.'

'What about over there?' Kate looked out to the barren landscape on the opposite side of the road.'

'What about it?'

'It's an area of special conservation, runs for miles, nothing but flora and fauna.'

'Kate, talk sense will you.'

'The SAC is protected, which means no one is allowed to live, farm or even so much as turn a sod of turf on it. He isn't stupid, O'Connor. The phone was a mistake, but if he took her up here, he wouldn't go back to the same place and take a risk on some nosy sheep farmer spoiling his plans again. If he has taken her and buried her, the SAC makes sense.'

O'Connor gazed out on the landscape stretching as far as the eye could see, sighing. 'That's some amount of land, Kate.'

'All the more reason he would pick it.'

Kate could tell O'Connor had his doubts, he was probably still thinking about the conversation they'd had about the timing of the next abduction and killing.

'Listen, this guy is a planner. He didn't abduct a young girl in broad daylight without thinking things through. If he has taken Amelia, it means, somehow, he is able to gain his victim's trust. He will know you'll look where Caroline was found. If he did see Amelia as a loose end needing to be tidied up, and so brought her out here, he'd bring her somewhere nobody would find her. Had it not been for the second phone, O'Connor, none of us would be standing here even asking this question.'

≈

The army aerial search continued, but it was the tracker dogs working the ground that picked up Amelia's scent. The dogs led them to an area of raised soil, which answered their questions immediately.

Even before it was confirmed that there was a body, both Kate and O'Connor knew to expect the worst. O'Connor pulled out his phone and called in Morrison. It was time for him to be involved.

Amelia's body had been laid out in the same way as Caroline's – hair plaited and tied with red ribbons, both hands joined at the front and the body positioned sideways and in the foetal position. This time her limbs had not been forced into position, probably unnecessary because of the speed with which he'd buried her. Morrison noted that the markings on her neck meant Amelia's death was most probably caused by asphyxiation, just like Caroline. However, there had been no blows to the head, although the face was badly bruised.

'Kate, what sort of mindless fucker is doing this?'

'The kind who doesn't think like you or me, O'Connor.'

'Don't give me any sympathetic psychological crap about fucked-up bastards.'

'I've no intention of it,' she retorted.

'Whoever did this knew exactly what they were doing, Kate, and from what you've already told me, he takes great care in getting the thing done exactly right.'

'No argument on that score, but there are differences.'

'The terrain, you've already covered that.'

'I'll want to see the other site first hand. Even if Amelia was a complication to be dealt with, both logic and intimacy played a role in how this man thought about his victims. There's a lot more to this.'

'What do you mean?'

'Look around you, O'Connor. The place is barren. It's like Amelia was less worthy. You can't deny the similarity between both girls. I mean, they look almost like twins. He obviously has a fit he's trying to achieve.'

'Jesus Christ, Kate. Whatever about the public outcry and the shit we've been dealing with up until now, it will be nothing compared to the fucking mayhem this is going to cause.'

'I know that.'

'Rohan is going to buy us time with the second burial site, Kate, but it will have to be announced soon.'

'The ribbons, the plaiting, the positioning of the body, it's all part of his signature, but with Amelia, apart from the choice of burial site, there is another important difference. She's not wearing a silver cross.'

O'Connor threw his hands up. 'Thank heavens for small mercies. Nolan hates all that religious shit raising its head.'

'Caroline's parents, what did they say about the one she was wearing?'

'It was just a cheap thing, like you'd find in any pound shop.'

'But he left it on her, although the earrings were missing. This guy does things for a reason. If he left the cross on Caroline, he deliberately wanted it there.'

'We can't be sure he took the earrings. They could have fallen out.'

'Maybe, but the crucifix is an iconic symbol, he didn't leave it there unless it pleased him. People do similar things for different reasons.'

'Talk English, Kate.' O'Connor sounded tired.

'Okay, listen. We have to look at each girl, then compare them to establish what they have in common and what makes them different from each other. If Amelia was a threat he needed to get her out of the way, his intention was to kill her from the moment the abduction took place. Caroline's death was different. The blows to the head don't fit, too messy for him, unless, of course, they were the result of things not going according plan.'

'Meaning?'

'Meaning, maybe he hadn't intended to kill Caroline to begin with. But the positioning makes sense to him. He was able to dispose of Amelia quickly, indicationg he felt very little guilt, if any. He is a killer capable of compartmentalising events, O'Connor. Killing Amelia has proved that beyond doubt, and killers who are capable of that are the most dangerous kind.'

O'Connor turned away to answer his phone. He spoke briefly, then ended the call abruptly.

'Leave your car here, Kate. That was Dermot O'Brien. They've picked up a well-known bastard on the CCTV footage from the canal where Caroline went missing, and we're both about to pay him a visit.'

Meadow View

HE HAD SET THE ALARM FOR 5.30 A.M. GETTING UP early was something he did whether it was a work day or not. The Cronly family had an ancestry of army men known for their discipline, and despite his aversion to joining such a hideous profession, he was more than willing to churn out the family history at times of convenience, especially when such information could put him in good stature. In truth, the surname and the army ancestry came from his mother's side, but he wasn't going to share incidentals like that with anyone if he didn't have to.

Irrespective of the previous night's events, continuing his daily routine was important. Teeth brushing for a minimum of ten minutes, using the 'firm' toothbrush variety with a designated life span of no more than two weeks. Weighing was another part of his routine. He had kept his BMI at twenty-four for the past five years; with a height of five foot ten inches and a waist of thirty-four inches, maintaining a body weight of no more than twelve stone was imperative.

It was still dark when he finished showering. Down in the kitchen, the kettle was full from the night before. His routine had changed since he moved out of Cronly, but of course the schedule would have been different either way in the big house. Tasks such as lighting the morning fire, turning on the immersion and looking after the old hag would have delayed things considerably.

Porridge made with water was a sturdy start to the day. By the time he sat at his kitchen table for breakfast, he felt a soothing sense of equilibrium return, already looking forward to browsing the newspapers online.

Exactly ten minutes later, he switched on his computer in the living room, ready to pick up whatever details were available. He was intrigued when he read the term 'Mr Invisible' used in one of the lower-grade publications to describe the abductor and killer of Caroline Devine. It sounded to him like a superhero character from a comic. Had he entered the world of superhero status? Of course, it wasn't with candid admiration that the media referred to him that way, but, nonetheless, the inference was there and the language was, at the very least, dramatic.

Unsurprisingly, the story was the lead item on the news when he turned on the radio. 'Gardaí are appealing for witnesses who may have travelled through the Dublin Mountains area over the course of the past few days.'

Going back to the internet again, it pleased him to find that the term 'Mr Invisible' also appeared in one of the more respectable publications. It seemed the use of the term had stemmed from the lack of concrete details about Caroline's disappearance and murder.

There was no mention of Amelia. No surprise there. It was still early days.

Ellie

IT IS NOT YET SIX WHEN I HEAR THE BIRDS. THEY SWOOP between dark and light while others sleep. Each morning they are my first connection to the living. In the same way as everything about being here is safe in its predictability, so too are they. I don't envy them their energy, although the night has exhausted me. I envy them their delight.

Soon, I hear Bridget. She is putting her things away in the closet at the end of the corridor. She will hang up her coat on one of the iron hooks, take off her outdoor shoes and put on her slip-ons. Then she will clear her throat. Bridget is the first sound I hear after the birds. The long night is over, and with this the knowledge that I must now face another day.

Was Andrew the beginning of my madness? Would I have done things differently if I had known? All those years ago, yet I still remember how I loved him, how every inconsequential detail of my life revolved around the two of us being together. The fact that we became lovers was inevitable. But now when I think of him, I think beyond our time of secrets, beyond our passion, I think of how, even back then, somewhere in the back of my mind, I had a deep-rooted sense that in the end what we had together would be tinged with regret.

Before Bridget arrives into my room, I make the decision to ask her for a pen and paper. No harm to have it, just in case. I know this will surprise her, but I have no intention of asking her until just before she leaves. I am not ready to have my motives questioned, not just yet.

If I am to write, what will I write about? Will I write about how I got here? How Ellie Thompson became the shadowy figure that I am today. Could this draw a line under all that has happened, something that I have failed to do for the past fifteen years? We are all products of our past I suppose; none of us is born the person we ultimately become. I have long since stopped feeling shame about the affair – though it was not because of shame that I denied myself absolution. If it was just that, some lover's cruel recall, I would not be haunted as I am haunted now.

House of Charles Innes
Saturday, 8 October 2011, 10.30 a.m.

KATE HAD NO IDEA WHAT TO EXPECT WHEN THEY turned into the narrow street where Innes lived. O'Connor stopped the car slowly, pulling in like someone who knew he wasn't going to be welcome and with no desire to warn anyone of his arrival.

Terraced houses crept along on both sides of the road. In some ways, they reminded Kate of the house on Landscape Avenue where she grew up, although they were a lot smaller. There, too, the houses followed each other in orderly fashion, regardless of whatever notions the owners held about individuality. But whatever similarities existed between the two streets, one difference was quite apparent: Landscape Avenue was upper-middle class; this place most certainly was not. The discreet movement of curtains in each of the windows they passed didn't do anything to settle her, although O'Connor, if he noticed them, didn't comment. His mind was focused on Charles Innes.

The front door of the house had glass panels on either side at the top half. Kate could see the dark shape walking from the back of the house to the front, and braced herself for the encounter.

Maybe Innes had expected someone friendly, but the original smile that greeted them when he opened the door vanished quickly, replaced by one of utter disdain. He may not have met O'Connor before, but Innes knew he was a copper even before he opened his mouth and asked to have a chat with him.

'I don't have time for chats. Now bugger off while I'm still being polite.'

'Your car went through a checkpoint near Rathmines canal yesterday, and a couple of days before that.'

'Is it a crime to drive? Last I heard we live in a free country.'

'Suppose you've heard about the murder of Caroline Devine?' O'Connor moved in closer to him, but Innes wasn't shifting.

If she had to guess an age, Kate would have put him in his late forties, small, overweight and balding. He wore pyjama bottoms with navy stripes and a white sleeveless vest that had seen better days and was nearly as grimy looking as what was left of his thinning fair hair. She didn't know what Innes worked at, but his tanned arms to below his armpits and rugged face told her he wasn't the kind of man who sat in an office.

'I've got nothing to do with it, so get the hell out of here.'

O'Connor eyed him coolly, but Kate could sense the tension in his body as he tried to keep his feelings in check. 'Listen, Innes, we can keep shooting the breeze out here on the doorstep or go inside. I don't much care either way, but maybe your neighbours might get a little jittery if we continue the party out here and I have to send a couple of squad cars around.'

Innes looked at O'Connor sulkily, but Kate could see him weighing up what had been said. 'You have a warrant?'

'I'm not looking to search the place, just talk. But I'd have no problem getting one if you want. Mind you, it'd be easier to drag your fat arse in for questioning, so why don't you just invite us in, like nice civilised folks.'

Innes stood back to allow both of them to pass. 'Kitchen's straight ahead,' he said off-handedly.

O'Connor allowed Kate walk in through the narrow doorway ahead of him. Innes smiled at her as she passed. Once inside, she took in the various rooms – the whole place looked like someone had just done it over. In the kitchen, dishes were piled high in the sink, the bin stank to high heaven and there were bits of rubbish on every surface

– empty drinks cans, cardboard takeaway packaging, newspapers, and the remains of, most likely, this morning's breakfast, a plate with hardened egg yoke and the remains of a burned sausage.

'The cleaning lady not working today?' O'Connor asked sarcastically.

Innes shot him a dark look, then knocked some clothes off a kitchen chair, and newspapers off the next, indicating they should both sit down. Kate was fascinated to see that once they were in his house, his manner changed markedly, switching from open hostility to a tone that approached friendliness.

'Cup of tea anyone?' he offered.

'Not for me,' snapped O'Connor.

'No thank you,' Kate followed.

'I see the lady has manners.'

'Listen, you little shit, I don't have time to play tea parties with you. Tell me why you were in Rathmines, and what you were doing three days ago, at four o'clock in the afternoon.'

'Suit yourself,' Innes replied, smirking at them. 'For your information, Detective, I needed to pass that area for work, and as for three days ago? Hmm, well, let me see, that would be Wednesday. Oh yes, I remember now. I was visiting an old friend at the Welfare Office, Jimmy Deavy, lovely man, has a nice warm heart, does his best for people down on their luck.'

'Down on your luck, are you?' O'Connor didn't even try to hide his disgust.

'We can't all have fat salaries, you know. Times are tough. You lot have no idea what it's like for ordinary folk to try and make ends meet.'

'My heart bleeds for you.'

Recognising that O'Connor's tactics weren't getting a whole lot of information out of Innes, Kate decided to weigh in.

'Mr Innes, a young girl has been murdered. If you were in the area, you might have seen something?'

When he smiled at her again, it took a lot for her to return the compliment. She had a sick feeling about him, even without knowing his back story. Everything about him felt rotten, and she had to suppress the memories that were threatening to surface whenever he looked directly at her.

'Miss, I really wish I could help you.'

'Kate. My name's Kate.'

'Nice name. Kate.' He smiled again. 'I've seen a picture of the girl, very sweet, but not my sort I'm afraid.' He gave Kate a leering smile, then added, 'A little old for me.'

Kate held his stare, her face a mask. O'Connor had heard enough, though. He snapped, grabbing Innes by the front of his vest and slamming him back against the kitchen sink. Innes wasn't rattled at all. O'Connor's outburst brought another smirk to his face.

'Quite the temper, Detective. Did I hit a sore spot?'

'You are a piece of filth, Innes,' O'Connor said in a quiet voice. 'I'm going to check out your alibi and if there's any holes in it, I'll be back to pay another social call. In the meantime, I suggest you keep your fat arse at home. I'll have guys watching you. One slip and I'll nail you. Any questions shithead?'

'You're the one with the questions; me, I'm just your average law-abiding citizen.'

'Really, well then you won't mind if we borrow your PC?'

'Do I have a choice?'

'You're quick, I'll give you that.' O'Connor took the warrant he wasn't supposed to have from his jacket pocket and handed it to Innes. 'A surprise for you, Mr Law-Abiding. I like to be a man of surprises, sort of adds a little extra spice. We'll have this piece of junk back to you before you know it.'

They made their way out of the house, with O'Connor carrying the hard-drive of Innes' PC. As he put it into the boot, Kate sat into the front seat, glad to be out of Innes' house and company. O'Connor snapped open the driver's door, hurling himself into the front seat before slamming the door shut. It was obvious he was in no mood for talking, but Kate risked it anyway.

'He's not our man, O'Connor.'

His hand stopped halfway to the ignition and he turned to look at her. 'Maybe not, but I still need to check out his alibi. The bastard's sick enough, that's for sure.'

'Creepy, yes, but the killer, no.'

'You can't rule him out just like that, Kate,' O'Connor said, unable to hide the impatience in his voice.

'I can,' Kate replied evenly. 'Everything about Innes, even his house, is wrong. The place is a pit, everything is way too messy. And he's not exactly fit. If he was involved with Caroline's death, he'd have to have been working with someone else, and somehow Charles Innes doesn't strike me as the sharing type.'

'Fucking creep,' O'Connor muttered, his shoulders still tense with anger.

'Not a nice man, for sure.'

'I'll tell you something, Kate. I'm very glad I'm not the one who'll be looking through that fucking computer of his. The likes of him make my skin crawl.'

Kate needed to pull his mind back onto the case. 'I still want to visit the first burial site, O'Connor. I've been thinking about the blood pooling down the right-hand side of Caroline's body. If Morrison is right that Caroline's body wasn't moved once the pooling occurred, then the killer did more than force the rigor, he maintained the position of the body the way he wanted it to be, not just within the burial but prior to it, as she lay waiting for him to bury her. Choosing that particular place to bury her was another layer of importance to him.'

'You'll have to go alone, so. I've another briefing in half an hour.'

'That's fine. Can you drop me back up to my car?'

'Sure, I want to check in with Hanley and everyone before the next conference.' He flicked a glance in her direction. 'Kate, you seem distracted, something else on your mind?'

She shrugged. 'It's just a theory, nothing concrete.'

'Go on.'

'I don't think our guy is sexually motivated.'

'You can't be sure.'

'We can't be sure of anything yet, but there are lots of reasons, other than sexual ones, why an adult male can be drawn to a child or, as in this case, a pre-teen girl. He may find it difficult to relate to other adults, for example. Children don't pose the same threat. There is every possibility that he had the highest respect for Caroline, may have found her company more comfortable and interesting than many of the adults he encounters. Also, if he was sexually motivated and Amelia was a loose end he needed to get out of the way, then he would have taken his opportunity with her. The place couldn't have been more isolated.' She paused. 'There's something else, too.'

'I'm listening.'

'He was particular with both girls – the ribbons, the plaiting, the joining of the hands, the positioning of the bodies. It's almost like he was preparing them for something, but what?'

'If you don't mind me saying so, Kate,' O'Connor attempted to soften his tone, 'you look a little pale.'

'No, I'm fine. It's just, well, creeps like Innes can get to me too, you know.'

He nodded. 'They're part of the territory, but none of us likes it.'

'Do you remember being young, O'Connor?'

'I'm not exactly old, thanks very much.'

Kate smiled. 'No, I don't mean that. Do you remember being their age?'

'Like the two girls? Of course I do.'

'Were you ever afraid of anything?'

'I think all kids are, but I'm figuring your answer might be a whole lot more interesting than mine.'

'I don't know why, but this case has me thinking about when I was that age.'

'Go on.'

'Let's just say my memories aren't the stuff fairytales are made of.'

O'Connor was unusually quiet, and, just for a moment, Kate thought he was going to reach over to touch her. She held her breath, surprised to realise that she'd like it if he did. She could feel the heat creeping up from her chest onto her face, like some wayward teenager. She felt a stab of sadness too: it seemed like an eternity since anyone had held her, touched her. The distance between her and Declan was growing wider by the day. Mostly, it was like she didn't have a husband any more; she certainly didn't have a lover.

O'Connor shifted in his seat, rolling down the car window, looking away from her instead, before turning to smile back at her. 'I don't know, Kate; some of them so-called fairytales are pretty scary.'

Despite herself, she laughed. 'Start the car, O'Connor, before you begin reciting some of them to me.'

'You could be missing out on a whole lot of entertainment.'

'Maybe, but I think we both have enough on our plate right now, don't you?'

This time when O'Connor pulled his car out, he didn't care who saw him.

Meadow View

HE WAS RELIEVED NOT TO BE GOING INTO NEWELL DESIGN, it being Saturday, especially considering the events of the night before. Had it not been for all their vulgar interference, disturbing Caroline from her place of rest, things could have been very different, with no necessity to address the complication of Amelia. It had been a mistake to mention Cronly Lodge to her, trying to impress her with his joy of swimming along the Wexford coast. He had been much more discreet with Caroline, wanting to surprise her with it all.

It would be too risky to take his usual walk up the mountains, so he decided to stay closer to home, opting for a walk in the nearby park instead, planning to pick up a newspaper at the local kiosk on the way. He wanted to keep abreast of events and figured that compiling newspaper cuttings of developments would be a good place to start. Now that he was something of a celebrity, he may as well enjoy and record his elevated status.

Although he enjoyed his walks in the mountains, as he entered Herbert Park he reflected on the niceties of a more structured planting environment. The gardens at Cronly were designed with orderly structure in mind – circular bedding areas, shaped hedges, clipped camellias – with all the elements orchestrated to create the perfect balance between control and beauty. Even the wild flowering areas were set within definitive borders and sub-borders to ensure that whilst they displayed all that was good and wonderful about their softness, they were maintained and trimmed to ensure the garden was always the farthest thing from wilderness.

Herbert Park still boasted the vibrant reds and pinks of late flowering, along with some winter bedding still in its infancy. The farther he walked, the more energised he felt, and he began to look forward to things to come. He managed to pick up a couple of papers at the kiosk. Initially he thought he might stop and have a good read whilst he was out, seeing as both papers had headlines covering the murder, but, on reflection, he kept them under his arm, deciding it would be much better to investigate everything when he got home.

As he strolled along the pathway through the trees, he picked up the loud voices of a couple arguing. Although, he hadn't needed to hear them shouting to realise what they were at. His study of people had made him quick to detect any changes of body posture or facial expression. Most people could be rather stupid, tending to fall into the trap of thinking that just because they didn't hear or see you, then you couldn't see or hear them.

The young girl near them was very pretty, with waist-length sandy hair and an innocent face. As he watched, he could tell her parents were paying no heed to her whatsoever. He sat down on a park bench and held one of the newspapers below eye level and watched. Immediately, he noticed how sad the young girl looked. He could tell that about her straight away. The family had a dog with them, a large black Labrador. The girl was fond of the dog – and why not? It wasn't as if her parents were giving her any attention.

He was patient, watching the scene unfold. The mother was attractive, and the type of woman who knew it. It was in the way she flicked her hair, held her shoulders back. The man was clean-shaven and dressed well. His style was not exactly to his way of dress, but it was classy nonetheless. Studying the father, he suspected him to be one of those get-rich-fast types, someone who, perhaps by virtue of the current climate, had fallen on harder times. Maybe they were arguing about money. That was a popular one these days.

He hadn't expected the girl to come over, but the dog played a part in their chance conversation. He despaired sometimes at how negligent parents could be.

The dog's name was Woody. He heard the girl repeat it a number of times, so by the time Woody flew past him into the bushes, the young girl racing behind him, he was able to join in and help her try to call the dog back. Perhaps it was the smell of Tabs, but Woody came to him immediately.

The girl was younger than Caroline, but equally as friendly. He could tell she was lonely because of the way she displayed such affection for the animal. That was the thing about children – by and large, they were far more trusting and good-natured than adults. It never ceased to amaze him how adults failed to understand the way children thought. He understood it, but it seemed he had a rare gift. Then again, other adults didn't study children the way he did. He watched and listened carefully, and, in so doing, made numerous helpful observations, including how children made friends quickly and easily – two seconds and you might as well have known them their entire life.

'Woody's very obedient,' he remarked lightly.

She was delighted with this compliment of her pet. 'He tries to be a good dog, but he can be tricky.'

'Well, he seems like a very good dog to me. It's hard for dogs, not speaking our language.' He smiled, hoping she would smile back.

'He likes you,' she said, bestowing a small smile on him.

He patted Woody on the head. 'Do you think so? I used to have a dog, but sadly I don't have him any more.'

'Did he die?'

'Afraid so, but then he was a bit like me, not so young.' He smiled again.

'My granddad's old.'

'I bet you and him are great friends.'

'Mam says Granddad spoils me. He calls me a chatterbox.'

'Does he? Is that because you're so quiet?'

'No, silly, it's because I talk too much.'

'My name is William by the way.'

'Mine's Melanie.'

'Hmm, a lovely name.'

'I'm called after my grandmother. She's dead now, like your dog.'

'Oh dear.' He looked at her with deep appreciation.

'Melanie, come over here.'

'Okay, Mam, coming. I'd better go. Nice to meet you …'

'William.'

'Woody, leave William alone now. We have to go home.'

'Good dog,' he said, ruffling the dog's head, 'off you go now. Be good for Melanie and next time I might have a treat for you.'

'He loves bones,' she said quickly, almost conspiratorially.

'Does he now? Well, I'll have to bring one so.'

'Melanie, hurry up, we have to go.'

'See ya, don't forget the bone.'

He watched the girl as she ran back towards her parents, Woody at her heels. He smiled to himself. Yes, he had sized up the mother exactly. She didn't even look at the child when Melanie went over, simply turned away from her and walked out of the park, with the father and child in tow. As they went through the park gates, he could see Melanie dragging her heels, holding herself back from both parents. He thought again about how sad her parents must be making her feel. He remained seated on the park bench until the family were no longer in sight. Folding his newspaper, he placed it under his arm and started to make his way out of the park. Perhaps they would be back again. The park was a great favourite with families.

Dublin Mountains
Saturday, 8 October 2011, 11.45 a.m.

KATE SAT IN HER CAR WHILE O'CONNOR GOT HIS update from Hanley, lifting her head up from her notes to wave to him before he sped off downhill. When he was gone, she checked her phone – nothing yet from Declan. She thought about ringing to find out how he and Charlie were getting on, but if she did, she'd probably feel even worse about deserting the two of them on a Saturday.

She sent Declan a text – 'I shouldn't be long' – and regretted sending it as soon as it was gone. She had no idea how damn long she was going to be. Who was she fooling? Maybe it was her unwillingness to talk to Declan, or feeling vulnerable during the conversation with Innes and that unexpected reaction to O'Connor, but she suddenly decided to ring Sweetmount. Whatever the reason, she couldn't deny the feeling of wanting to talk to someone she felt close to. It was coming up to lunchtime and if she was lucky, she could have a quick word with her mother before they all gathered to eat.

The call was answered quickly by the receptionist, but then it felt like an age passed before she heard her mother picking up the phone. When she did, the signal in the mountains was awful, the sound of her mother's voice coming in and out. Her mother got more and more confused the longer the call continued, so she ended the call. It had been a mistake to phone her in the first place, but a part of Kate wanted to hear her mother's voice, remember a time when she depended on her not only as a listening ear, but someone who showed love and support to her.

She grabbed the camera from the car boot and walked uphill to the first location that was still cordoned off. Her gut was telling her that the first burial site would hold different, and perhaps more important, answers from the second one. Although it was sometimes a very harrowing part of her job, it was always imperative to see a crime scene first-hand. Everything about it was important – what you saw within the surroundings, what you heard, smelled, how isolated it was, how busy, who you would expect to see there, the level of exposure, anything that made it different or unique and, most importantly, what it was that had brought the perpetrator there. Photographs could tell you a lot, but they didn't relate everything.

Despite the large garda presence, Kate tried to imagine the area as it would normally be – deserted. During the day, the mountains were tranquil, but once night fell, it was a lonely place. Kate walked farther up the mountain road, keeping a slow pace, taking it all in. She tried to imagine the terrain in complete darkness, listening to the sound of water flowing down from Montpelier Hill. Kate had passed the last street light a hundred yards back. Without a torch or the lights of a car, this area would be densely black at night.

The road got steeper the farther up she went. She passed furze bushes on either side, the last yellow flowers of the year just about hanging on. Kate knew she wasn't there for the beauty of the landscape, but there was still something purifying about leaving the city behind and breathing in the crisp, pure air, so different from the suburban madness below.

When she reached the area marked off by the yellow and black tape, the drop down to the burial site was steep, and the ground was still soft after the rain from a couple of nights before. From where she stood, she could see granite stones and boulders embedded into the soil, as well as smaller stones which probably came from the old granite wall bordering one side of the site. She saw the remnants of an old cottage, almost lost, as if it had been eaten by the earth. Just before the drop levelled, there was a narrow stream. The water flowed fast, rippling along a stony path, in a hurry to move on. At first, the noise of the stream was all she heard, but as Kate moved nearer to the spot where Caroline's body had been found, she could hear the birds singing. Like the water, they seemed rushed. Chaffinches and greenfinches flew excitedly through the undergrowth, their birdsong falling like raindrops.

From the roadside, she could see how the lower branches on the trees were barren, dark brown, because they were hidden from the light. To her right, beyond the trees, a carpet of heathers and bilberry bushes spread wide, still in full colour. She could smell the sap from the fir trees and in the distance, farther up the mountain, she saw spruce trees of giant proportions, almost touching the practically clear-blue sky. The place was tranquil, filled with the sounds of nature. She had to shake herself free from its seduction and refocus on the task in hand.

She continued along the path, meeting more squad cars parked like unwanted visitors, with uniformed guards positioned as sentries along the taped-off terrain. She signed in with one of the guards, who looked fresh out of training college. There was no point engaging the officer in conversation. Once she had clearance, she continued down to the centre of the site, where the burial had taken place beneath an enormous elderberry tree. The tree reached up to at least twenty feet from ground level and much of the upper foliage was still intact because of the shelter afforded by the fir trees beyond. As a result, the berries on it were plentiful.

The steep drop down to the open grave was full of twigs, pine cones and mossy stones. The landscape was as difficult as it had looked in the photographs O'Connor had shown her. In the dark, it would be tricky to negotiate. Whoever brought Caroline's body down here must have been agile and fit. She thought about how secluded the area was. Unless you knew where to look, the drop down to the level of the burial could not have been spotted from the road. Cars would have passed by and seen nothing. Whoever the killer was, he knew this area, and was comfortable even in the dark, to make his way around it.

When she reached the grave, the whole atmosphere changed immediately. This was a place that felt totally cut off from the outside world. What struck Kate most, however, was the beauty of it all: the rambling stream, the birds fleeting in and out of the trees, the elderberry tree and the almost seductive smell of mossy earth, more potent the farther down you went. It felt like a special place, almost private, forgotten. The killer had to have known about this spot beforehand – it seemed highly unlikely that he had stumbled on it in the dark. The intimacy with which he'd arranged certain things about both girls now made sense to Kate in terms of the place he'd chosen for Caroline's final resting spot. This secluded area was as private as he might have imagined his relationship with her to have been. The more she looked around her, the more convinced she became that this place had been chosen very specifically. If she was right, then like every other component of the burial, there had to be a good reason for it.

She took her own photographs of the site, first kneeling down to take shots of the immediate area: the ground underfoot, the dugout grave, the view above her, the foliage, the berries on the elderberry tree, the steep drop down – everything was important in order to imagine the killer working his way within it. Standing up, again she used the lens at different angles, close-ups and wider shots, stopping to speak into the small Dictaphone machine she always carried with her, noting the various senses: the sounds, the light touch of a breeze on her cheeks, the smells, the remoteness, the feeling of privacy. She attempted to re-imagine the night of the burial: the blackness, the time it would have taken the killer to prepare the grave, the physical act of burying the girl, yet he had been calm, specific, displaying a detachment from the victim within his own personal sense of intimacy, and probably deep-rooted need.

Caroline's body was no longer there, but to Kate, the memory of the burial being re-enacted in her mind brought the girl so close it was almost as if the landscape and Kate had just witnessed the burial all over again.

It didn't take Kate long to drive back up the mountain road to the next crime scene, which was still under the supervision of Hanley himself. Although less than a mile farther up, the difference in the landscape was remarkable. To the left, the lush green hedgerows led upwards to forest and mountain peaks, while to the right, where the second burial took place, the land was flatter, more barren, seeming to run for miles with little change in the contour.

She parked well down from the cordoned area and took some general shots of the terrain. The burial site was farther in than she was allowed to go. Currently, no one other than Hanley and his team would get anywhere near it. Zooming in and out with her camera lens, she could see the line of white bodysuits moving across the area, tech guys walking in slow motion, every piece of the landscape under their intense focus. They looked at odds with the place, reminding Kate that this was another tranquil setting that would be marked forever as the burial ground of an innocent young girl.

One thing was for certain, taking both burial sites into consideration, it hadn't been the killer's intention that either victim would ever be found. Kate was worried about what would happen next: if he had been spooked by the finding of Caroline's body, how would he react to the discovery of Amelia? Kate believed he would react in one of two ways. He might lie low, take his time – as she had thought he would do in the first instance. Equally, he might do the very opposite. It could trigger a new phase and God only knew where that would lead, and to whom. The only thing she was sure of was that once he knew that they had found Amelia, he would be thinking about his next move.

As she walked back to the car, some brittle branches snapped under her foot. Looking over her shoulder, she caught the light shimmering in and out between the hedgerows, just like in her old memory. She thought about Caroline and Amelia being scared, like she had been all those years ago. He had grabbed her from behind and the feeling of hopelessness had been immediate. No one had realised she'd been missing. The whole world had seemed a lifetime away, and she had been powerless to reach it. In those moments of adrenaline and terror, she had felt forcibly that her life was in his hands – he hadn't cared if he hurt her or took everything away from her.

Kate stopped walking and willed herself to breathe deeply, to be aware of the here and now. She hated when the past crept up on her like that, taking her out of herself for whole minutes at a time. It was like a sick joke he was still able to play on her. She couldn't save Caroline or Amelia, but she would do her best to ensure that their tormentor didn't get to anyone else.

Ellie

ANDREW AND I WOULD MEET IN THE AFTERNOON, twice a week, when Amy had music practice. The clandestine nature of that escape, the duplicity, aroused feelings I had long since forgotten. I would drive so far and then abandon the car, walking the remaining half-mile to where he lived. His house had a rear entrance through the back garden, a black wooden door he had given me the key to. If I met anyone as I walked the laneway past the other back doors, I just kept on walking to the end. Once inside the garden, no matter what the weather, I would stop and take out the small compact from my bag to examine my face, fix my hair. Sometimes I would feel as if I was being sucked into my own reflection, as if someone else, a piece of me I hadn't known existed, was going to meet him. Even on days when there was no need to reapply lipstick, I would do so. I always wanted to look my best.

Usually, he would be in the upstairs back bedroom, where he painted. Unlike him, I would feel awkward at first. He never did. He would stop painting when I walked into the room – I would tell him to continue, but it didn't work that way. Andrew painted alone.

Almost at once he became a different person. The expression of anguish he wore on his face as he worked on the canvas would evaporate, and all he would seem to want was me. He could be flippant about things and yet completely in earnest, such was the complexity of his nature. Each time we were together, I knew what would happen. If I felt guilty about our meeting, he would charm it all away; in truth, he had no time for such nonsense. With him, it was all about the living, the moment, the experience; few rules applied. Sometimes I would feel overdressed, too prepared, as if I should have been brave enough not to worry about lipstick or powder or any of that nonsense. I would feel that I should have been more like him, and have abandoned the complicated frivolities that seemed to feature so prominently in my life back then.

His place was different from where I lived with Joe. He cared little for all the things that Joe felt were important. Possessions were simply items of necessity. What obsessed him was his art and, for a time, me.

Sex was always immediate, as if the two of us had been starved. He had confident hands and his lips were gentle, sensual, before becoming harsh and needy. When his desire was at its most selfish, he felt both shocking and delightful. Afterwards, he would hold me, sometimes make fun of me, but then he would change again and become serious, talking to me in the softest tone, the one that utterly consumed me, the one I could not live without. From those early, intimate days, the one thing I remember most vividly was how he looked at me, as if I was some wonderful stranger who, having entered his life, would not be allowed to leave.

I cared little, at times, what he talked about, whether it was his art or his time in Canada, the land, the people. It was in Canada, far away from the confines of Dublin, that he had finally made the decision to study art. It was while away in a foreign place that he learned to appreciate the colours and textures of home, so that when he returned, it was as if he saw it all for the very first time. But for that decision – to return – our paths would never have crossed. My only connection to him would have been nothing more than Joe's references to his 'good-for-nothing brother'.

Meadow View

AS HE OPENED THE FRONT DOOR OF 15 MEADOW VIEW, he made a mental checklist of everything. Before leaving, he had gone through the same routine, checking the windows and doors last. One could never be too careful – breaking and entering was far easier than most people imagined and being familiar with the many tricks of the trade, he never took any chances. He combed the rooms thoroughly, ensuring that all was as it should be.

With everything to his satisfaction, he examined the reflection of his face in the hall mirror, fiddling with his shirt collar. Then he stood back and took in his full appearance. Sliding his fingers through his hair, which in the past number of years had developed slight tinges of grey on either side, a development he approved of, he couldn't help but feel pleased about his overall look. He had no intention, at the age of fifty-two, of looking like some old fuddy-duddy, happy to wear smart jumpers and nondescript jeans when not in work. After all, he was physically fit, a non-smoker, a moderate drinker and he had a good eye for design and style. There was no reason he couldn't continue to look this good for at least another fifteen years, once he adhered strictly to his regimes. He reached under the stairs and put away his walking boots, feeling quite the 'frontier man' – a description upon which he had moulded his appearance for a very long time, since childhood in fact.

At Cronly, the solitary framed photograph of his father had sat on the piano in the music room. He'd never met his father, but he had made up many stories about him. The image in the silver frame was of a tall, handsome man with arms wrapped around a white husky dog. Behind the man and his dog were mountains with snowy tips. He remembered how pleased he felt about this man behind the glass, this man who was his unknown father.

When he got older, around the age of eleven, he'd become suspicious of the picture in the frame. He had waited and chosen an afternoon when he knew Mother would be 'otherwise occupied' – that was how Mother referred to the times she'd go missing without explanation – to remove the image from the frame. When he released it from the outer casing, he discovered at the bottom of the image the words 'Frontier Man'. It didn't take long for him to work out that the picture was a cutting from a copy of National Geographic, for on the reverse of the image was an article about Tibetan monks. He never did find out any other information about the man in the picture, other than the simple truth that he was certainly not his father. This lie told to him by his mother would lead, over time, to the uncovering of many others.

He felt particularly energised after his early-morning stroll in the park, so he switched on his PC before he even started on lunch. Sometimes the darn thing took ages to crank up, but he had no intention of changing it unless he had to.

A police press conference was due to be held later, but there had been early-morning reports about a second girl who had gone missing. One report even noted that 'criminal profiling' was being carried out as part of the ongoing investigation. There was a reference to Kate Pearson in a couple of the articles, listing her training in the UK with prominent criminal psychologist Professor Henry Bloom.

'Good, that's very good indeed,' he noted out loud. He could hear rumbling from next door; the house attached to his was often louder with its weekend domesticity.

Running another search through Google, there were any number of hits, but one in particular attracted his attention, covering Kate Pearson's work with the professor. He saved it into Favorites, then went to the kitchen to make a bowl of pasta for lunch. His next trip wouldn't take long. The bus stop was less than a five-minute walk from the house. He had the choice of any number of buses, which was partly the reason he had chosen 15 Meadow View because it meant that, despite the unreliability of the bus services in the city, the abundance of routes would ensure being late for work, or anything else, was not a problem he would encounter.

Locking his car in the Terenure garage the night before had been a rather rushed affair, and although he'd been careful that there was no mess this time, he would feel happier once he had double-checked that everything was as it should be. Things must always be as they should be.

He arrived at the bus stop ten minutes after finishing his lunch. A group of old ladies were waiting, and a teenage boy – a good sign, another bus would be along soon. It was an excellent day, with lots of sunlight, although chilly. He was glad he'd worn a warm jacket. The bus arrived empty except for a couple of passengers, so he stood back and allowed the others to go ahead of him. This generated smiles all round from everyone except the teenager, who stood back awkwardly.

Once on the bus, he chose a window seat. As he sat down, one of the old ladies smiled at him again. It was amazing how a small gesture could bring you close to people. If he wanted to, he knew he could be on first-name terms with the woman before either of them got off the bus. Instead, he decided to look out the window, allowing his mind drift to Blake's *Songs of Innocence and Experience*, a masterful collection that explored the contrary states of the human soul. Blake saw childhood as a state of protected innocence although, importantly, it was not immune to the immoral world and its sometimes dreadful institutions.

At the stop before his, the old lady with the eager smile got off. He purposely nodded goodbye to her. She looked even happier than before. He didn't wave to her as the bus pulled out, although he noticed she waited on the footpath for him to do so. There was no point getting too friendly, that was something he kept for people who could be either useful or of interest. He closed his eyes and waited until the woman was no longer in view before returning to watch the rest of the passengers. He liked to watch how people moved, listen to how they talked and take in every little thing about their appearance and that way, bit by bit, he could build up an exact picture of every person he encountered. It felt like a stolen intimacy, and that notion pleased him immensely.

Devine Family Home, Harold's Cross
Saturday, 8 October 2011, 1.15 p.m.

KATE RECEIVED O'CONNOR'S TEXT BEFORE SHE reached the end of the mountain road. She had no doubt that the last meeting at the Incident Room would have been a difficult one. Two young girls had been murdered, and O'Connor and his colleagues were under serious pressure to deliver the culprit. The text said: 'Canter's set up meeting with Caroline's parents, see you there in twenty.' Kate sighed – any thoughts of getting back to Declan and Charlie early in the day were lost now.

From the moment of Caroline Devine's disappearance, the feeling of unrest in the city had been rising. Kate knew there had been editorials on the Devine case and numerous calls to various radio chat show programmes, with callers complaining bitterly about government cutbacks in policing, the dangers to children in today's society and the seeming inability of the police to find the killer. Any sort of crime concerning children upset people hugely, and attacking the police seemed a kneejerk reaction.

Once confirmation of the second killing was released at a press conference later that afternoon, Kate was well aware that panic would take hold quickly. By the end of her first day on the case, she would have to attempt a detailed profile of the killer, but she knew more than anyone that an accurate profile never happened overnight. Nonetheless, she was going to have to draw on every resource she had to help her figure out what she could about this particular killer. She had learned a lot from Henry about solving the puzzle, questioning everything, probing and exploring all possibilities then back-tracking to confirm conclusions. The only thing that mattered was getting it right, but with time in such short supply, she knew that any protests she might care to make would fall on deaf ears: O'Connor would expect her to help them narrow down the lines of inquiry, and he would expect her to do it fast.

Leaving the mountain road behind her, Kate made her way across the city to Harold's Cross. The traffic was hectic, but she still made good time, arriving there seconds before O'Connor, whom she could see was talking intently into his mobile. Caroline's family had been interviewed already, by Gunning, and O'Connor had spoken with them yesterday, but with Amelia's killing it was essential that they talked to both families, to try to establish any correlation between the girls. Amelia lived nearby in Crumlin and like Caroline she was an active swimmer, another thing apart from age and general appearance the two girls had in common. O'Connor wanted Kate there so they could both get a feel for the girls' backgrounds and, hopefully, their similarities. Kate knew that in the absence of both victims, the only people who could identify similar or disparaging traits about the girls were their family and friends.

While O'Connor finished his call, Kate got out of her car, locked it and focused on the external surroundings of the Devines' house. Their semi-d overlooked the canal and was one of a half-dozen houses that were stepped back ten metres from the rest of the buildings on the street. She looked at the canal waters in which, a few days earlier, it was thought Caroline might be found. Crossing over to the canal side, she viewed the house from a distance.

As Kate stood there, thinking about Caroline, she heard a car door slam. O'Connor was crossing the road towards her, striding with purpose. He looked to be still riled from the Incident Room briefing. His manner was brisk and businesslike.

'Right, Kate, we've security in place on Jessica Barry. Viewing the killing of Amelia as a means of tidying things up has really upset Nolan, even more than her obvious physical similarities to the first victim. None of us likes the idea of a tidy killer out there. Jessica and Caroline went swimming together, so if swimming pools are the connection, she might know something the killer doesn't want anyone else to know. We'll be paying a visit to her after this. There's something about that girl's statement that's been bothering me.'

'What's that?' Kate asked.

'It's too bloody short.'

≈

When Peter Devine opened the front door, Kate could see that he and O'Connor already had respect for each other – the way O'Connor shook Peter Devine's hand firmly, holding on to it for longer than was really necessary, and how Peter, in turn, looked directly at O'Connor, his eyes asking all the questions he could no longer put into words. Not for the first time, Kate thought about how tragedy had a habit of turning people into fast learners, how victims and their families quickly became fluent in a whole new language of grief.

O'Connor had given her a copy of the report from Shelley Canter, the liaison officer, and so she knew the family's back-story. At the beginning, when there was still hope for Caroline, Peter and Lilli Devine had been keen to do whatever was necessary to get their daughter back. They gave the gardaí every possible help – the school photograph and the public appeal had all been a means by which their energies could be channelled, in order to avoid that inevitable sense of helplessness that engulfs those left behind.

From the outset, Peter Devine had been the more proactive of the two parents, not only keen to give the police any information that could help but also being the one family member who had fought back emotions in an effort to keep together whatever fragments of normality remained. From what Canter had seen of the father prior to the finding of Caroline's body, he came across as a serious and quiet man and one who, although inwardly anxious, had been determined to maintain a strong stance under pressure. Lilli Devine, on the other hand, had completely caved in after the girl's disappearance, becoming far too distraught to converse or engage with the case in any meaningful way. Although, like Peter, she would have done anything to help find her daughter, her distressed state meant a large burden of responsibility had been placed on Peter in the early stages of the investigation. It was he who became the lynchpin that held the family together. However, when O'Connor met the parents after Caroline's body had been found, it was obvious their roles had changed dramatically. It was now Lilli who was taking the leading role.

This had come as no surprise to Kate as she had seen this type of alternating reaction before. The man, brought up with the emphasis on being the 'strong' one, very often held things together at the beginning. It was his coping mechanism, a means of finding respite and even comfort in being busy and proactive. The woman was often far more instinctual in her reactions, displaying the obvious outward signs of desperation after the initial disappearance. When the prospect of a solution to the status quo was no longer an option, Peter Devine hit a brick wall, no longer able to physically change things, the scale and acceptance of his loss finally registered, leaving Lilli Devine, who to some extent had already begun the devastating process, to become the stronger outwardly of the two.

Peter Devine held open the sitting room door and stood aside to let Kate and O'Connor enter. He didn't ask who Kate was and didn't seem to care. He shuffled after them into the sitting room where his wife and daughter were sitting with Shelley Canter. Emily, Caroline's sister, was seventeen – five years older than Caroline, an age her sister would never reach. The atmosphere in the room was quiet and strained – like

everyone was holding their breath so they wouldn't scream. Kate felt
the emotions rising inside her in the face of their grief.

Once seated, O'Connor introduced Kate, who took the armchair
opposite Lilli Devine. Emily remained standing by the door, never
taking her eyes off Kate. It was Lilli Devine, though, who was the first
to openly acknowledge Kate.

'What's she here for exactly? What's a psychologist have to do with
anything?'

Shelley Canter was quick to respond. 'Lilli, Kate is here to help
work out the type of person we're looking for.'

'Is she going to help find him, Shelley?'

'We hope so. Kate brings a huge amount of profiling experience to
the table, and has previously helped police solve other murders, both
here and in the UK. It's important that you talk to her as honestly as
you can, Lilli, okay?'

Lilli stared at Kate with the kind of look that seemed to fight back
any hope she might have that Kate could actually help.

'I keep looking for him, you know, searching people's faces, anyone
I can remember, or anyone we met, even vaguely. All those faces, they
keep going over and over in my mind like a revolving nightmare. Part
of me wants to see him. I want to have him stare straight at me, so I
can tear the bastard's eyes out.'

'Mrs Devine—' O'Connor cut in, anxious to calm the situation.

'Lilli, you might as well call me Lilli. It's a bit late for social niceties,
Inspector.'

'Lilli,' O'Connor said gently, 'if you and Peter could answer a few
more questions about Caroline for Kate, it could help us a lot.'

Kate took their lack of response as agreement. She looked over at
Emily first. 'Is it okay with you too, Emily?'

The girl shrugged her shoulders, whilst tensing her facial features.
'Sure, whatever.'

There was no doubting the feelings of bitterness in the room, and

Kate knew Caroline's mother and sister were not going to be easy to deal with, but she pushed on, deciding to start with Lilli Devine.

'Lilli, I think your instinct regarding trying to remember everyone who Caroline came in contact with is a good one. From what we have so far, there's a strong possibility that whoever abducted Caroline may have met her before.'

'What do you mean?' Peter interrupted, his voice sounding anxious.

'Well,' Kate said carefully, 'it may well be that Caroline wasn't chosen at random.'

'Sorry?' Lilli looked at Kate, her face displaying hostility.

'Lilli, whoever abducted your daughter could have planned it, and for reasons that could have meant absolutely nothing to Caroline, but a lot to her abductor.'

'But she … she was only *twelve*. How would Caroline have known anyone who would do something like this?' Peter Devine looked devastated.

O'Connor was quick to put him at his ease. 'Peter, Kate's not saying Caroline necessarily knew him, for all we know she might not have even spoken to him.'

Both parents looked distraught at what Kate was suggesting, but she knew she had to keep going. She held her gaze on Lilli. 'The important thing here is that we explore all angles. If Caroline did meet him at some point, there's every chance she may have viewed their encounters as completely innocent. Your daughter was a clever girl by all accounts, but unfortunately that was not enough to protect her.'

'Ask me whatever you want to know,' Lilli replied, her voice stronger now. 'I know nothing's going to bring her back, but I want you to get him. I need to know he'll pay for what he's done.'

'Lilli, tell me what type of things Caroline liked to do.'

The woman's demeanour changed perceptibly, almost as if revisiting her daughter's memory somehow took away the pain.

'She liked to read. When she wasn't at school or swimming, her head was constantly stuck in a book. She thought about being a teacher. She was good with little ones.'

Lilli Devine closed her eyes, knowing that teaching was yet another thing Caroline would never do.

'What else, Lilli?' Kate said, trying to keep Lilli's mind on her daughter.

Lilli sighed and started again. 'She loved swimming and it was a great way to use up her energy – even from a small tot she was always full of beans. You could never keep her easy for long. She'd go to the Rathmines pool, the one nearest her school, at the weekends with her friend, Jessica. Sometimes she'd even go to the pool before school.'

'So she was happy?'

'Yes, of course, she was perfect.'

'And what about her computer, did she spend a lot of time on that?'

'Ah, you know what kids are like.'

Kate looked over at O'Connor. She knew the Computer Crime Investigation Unit, CCIU, hadn't turned up anything of value on it.

'And her friend, Jessica, they were close?'

'They were always together.'

Lillie paused, and when she spoke again her voice was hard, the anger that had been hovering underneath rose to the surface. 'She called in here with her mother when they heard the news. I couldn't look at the girl.'

'Go on.'

'I couldn't look at her mother either for that matter. I just kept thinking, you're so lucky, so lucky to still have her. Almost as soon as they arrived, I wanted them both to leave. I kept thinking, what if it was the other way around, what if it had been Jessica who'd been taken? All I wanted to do was turn the tables, tell her she'd got it wrong, that it was her daughter and not mine who'd been buried in that hole up there.'

Kate watched Lilli's hands as she twisted them in her lap. She spoke as softly as she could. 'Lilli, I know how hard this is.'

'Do you?' Lilli shot back at her. 'Do you really know? Have you lost a child, Ms Pearson? Are you experienced in these matters?'

'No, Lilli, I'm not, and please don't think that I'm trying to undermine how you feel in any way. I'm just trying to put all the pieces together, to find something that might stop something like this happening again.'

'It won't bring her back,' Lilli said in a dead voice.

'No it won't, I know that.'

Lilli looked at Kate, and then nodded. 'Go on, ask your questions.'

'Was there anything about Caroline's behaviour that had changed over the last while?'

'No, not really, other than—'

'Other than what?'

'Well, you know, it was nothing really. She was never overweight. I mean, she was a fit girl, what with the swimming and everything. But lately she'd started to go on about the types of food she wanted to eat – no carbohydrates, no bread, wouldn't touch chocolate or any of "that rubbish", as she called it.'

Kate remembered how thin Caroline had looked, and what Morrison had told O'Connor about there being very little fatty tissue on the body, that it was practically skeletal-like in certain areas.

'Do you think she felt under pressure to lose weight?'

'No, no, I mean she wanted to be healthier, that's all.'

Kate could tell there was an element of doubt in Lilli's last sentence, an anxiety that, as a mother, she might have missed something.

'She'd lost lots of weight.'

All four of them turned to the teenager standing by the door, surprised by her sudden contribution to the conversation.

Kate didn't waste any time. 'Why do you think that was, Emily?'

'Same reason as most, I suppose.'

'And what's that?'

'To be like everyone else.'

'Do you think Caroline worried about being like everyone else?'

'Listen …'

'Kate, call me Kate.'

'I don't see the point in all this. We're not going to be able to ask her now, are we?'

Peter Devine looked over at his daughter and then to O'Connor. 'That's the hardest part, Inspector, we all feel it, just the three of us here, it's all wrong. Caroline should be with us, bounding in through that doorway. There's always been the four of us and now she's not here, she's gone, and we can't ask her anything, we can't bring her back, no matter what we do.' He broke off, crying, his shoulders shaking.

'Peter, please stop.' The softness had returned to his wife's voice.

Kate purposely avoided looking at either Peter or Lilli, and instead kept eye contact with Emily. 'Emily, did Caroline say something to you about it?'

'About what?'

'About why she was losing weight?'

'No, not about that exactly, but I knew she wasn't happy.'

'How?'

'Emily, if you have something to say, then for God's sake just say it.' The softness had left Lilli's voice and she was looking at her eldest daughter with a look that was somewhere between fear and frustration.

'She got fucked up. There, satisfied now?'

Kate kept looking steadily at Emily. 'And how did that happen, Emily?'

Emily shrugged. 'She started to think the way she looked was more important than all the other stuff. I told her she was being stupid. I mean, in a way I understood, it *is* hard.' Emily looked over at her parents. 'I'd talked to her a couple of times about it, nothing too heavy, just sister stuff. I kept telling her how great she was at the swimming and how I'd love to be as smart as her at school. I felt she was getting sense. I mean, the things she told me about what she was thinking were just daft.'

Other than Kate and Emily, everyone else kept their silence. 'And what were they, Emily, the things going on inside her head?'

'Look, she thought lots of fucked-up stuff.'

'But what specifically do you remember? It's important.'

'I can't say it.'

'It's all right, Emily.' Lilli looked at her daughter. 'You don't have to worry about your father and me.'

'What does it matter now?' Emily demanded, the rawness of her emotions clear in her voice.

It was Kate's turn to give support. 'Well, it may not matter a whole lot, but, then again, it could help us find whoever did this.'

Emily chewed a fingernail. 'As I said, it was stupid. I kept telling her she was gorgeous, that she was wrong to think the way she did.'

'And …'

'And, well, it's hard when someone doesn't want to listen. No matter what I said to her, she kept thinking the same bloody thing.'

'And what was that?'

'Emily, just spit it out, please.'

'I'm trying to, Mom.' She stared hard at Kate. 'If you must know, ever since she started changing, becoming aware of her body, well she talked rubbish about how her body was ugly, that she hated it. She didn't want to grow up. It scared her.'

'And what did you say to her?'

'I told her that it would be okay, that I'd felt like that too at her age, and that she'd feel differently.'

'Why do you think it scared her so much?'

'Caroline was different.'

'What do you mean?'

'Well, Mom and Dad will tell you. Caroline cared too much about everything, always did. I mean, half the time I wouldn't even notice things Caroline would pick up on as quick as anything.'

'Like what?'

'Like anything. If someone was upset, or if a person needed help or something, Caroline was always the first to notice.'

'She was sensitive, is that what you mean?'

'Maybe. But lately when she was down and all, thinking those awful things about herself, no matter what I said, none of it made any difference.'

'Emily, thank you. What you've said may help a great deal.'

'She was very pretty, even if she didn't know it.'

'I know, and it sounds like she had a great sister, too.'

'Not great enough.' Emily's eyes looked glassy, and it was obvious she was struggling to hold back tears.

Lilli Devine walked over to her daughter, cradling her like you might a younger child. Peter Devine looked at both of them, a man in total despair. The viciousness of their loss was palpable, like a vacuum sucking them down, beyond reach.

'Lilli,' Kate asked quietly, 'would it be okay if Detective O'Connor and I had another look at Caroline's bedroom?'

'Of course,' Lilli answered, her voice weak and brittle.

As Kate and O'Connor walked upstairs, Kate looked back down at Shelley Canter and the family, all of them looking like seasoned performers in the final act of some Greek tragedy.

≈

When Kate and O'Connor entered Caroline's bedroom, the first thing Kate noticed was the view of the canal through the window. The room was exactly as you'd expect any young girl's bedroom to be – cheerful, bright bedcovers with matching purple curtains, an array of items on her dressing table from tweezers to a small heart-shaped frame with a smiling Caroline and another young girl. There was a portable television on a high bracket in the corner opposite her bed, and a white wickerwork laundry basket. To the right of the bed, there was a tower of schoolbooks, behind which stood a low wooden bookcase filled with books. The room smelled of freshly washed sheets and looked like a room the young girl might step back into at any moment.

'I assume your guys have already examined this place from top to bottom?'

O'Connor raised an eyebrow, as if her question was ridiculous. 'You assume right, Kate.'

'Nice view of the canal. I'll want to step outside again after we're finished here.'

'Sure. But what are you looking for?'

'I don't know, at least not yet.' She nodded at the heart-shaped photo frame. 'Who's that in the photograph with Caroline?'

'Jessica Barry, I think.'

'Makes sense.'

O'Connor was looking at the bookcase. 'She certainly was a reader,' he remarked.

Kate knelt down to read the titles. 'She liked to keep her books, look at the variety, probably every book she's read in the last year or two.'

'Can't say I'm an expert on young girl fiction.'

'It changes, O'Connor. There is a big leap at that age, moving from easy reading to young adult. Caroline has everything here from *Anne of Green Gables* to *Pretty Little Liars*.'

'So?'

'So, they all make sense, except for this one,' she said, pointing at a particular book.

O'Connor knelt down beside her to see. '*The Complete Works of Edgar Allan Poe*? What don't you like about that one?'

'Apart from it being unusual reading these days for a young girl?'

'I'm listening.'

'Edgar Allan Poe married his first cousin, a thirteen-year-old girl called Virginia Clemm. Some people believe the couple's relationship was more like brother and sister than husband and wife, although he was fourteen years her senior when they married.'

'Did he not write about a detective?'

'He did, a character called Dupin, but he wrote many things, including poetry. If this is a full collection, it will include his famous poem 'Eulalie', which was about his wife.'

'I thought you said her name was Virginia?'

'I did, but he liked the 'l' sound.'

'Anything else about it?'

'Well, Poe had a recurring theme in his poetry – the death of a beautiful woman. He believed that was the most poetic topic in the world. Perhaps if Caroline had started to believe she wasn't attractive, it could be that her killer sensed her anxieties, might even have used them to his advantage to gain her trust. Perhaps this was his way of reaching out to her.'

'And what about the wife? What happened to her?'

'Died of TB in her early twenties.'

'Cheerful fellow, no doubt.'

'Well he may not have been cheerful, but if Caroline had a copy of his work then there is a strong possibility our killer gave it to her.'

Was Kate kidding herself or did O'Connor actually look slightly impressed?

'Right, don't touch it. I'll get Hanley to go over it again, page by page. Are you finished here?'

Kate took a last look around Caroline's room. 'Think so. Let's step outside.'

'You go on. I need to have a quick word with Canter before I leave.'

≈

From the footpath on the canal side, Kate took in the view of what she now knew was Caroline's bedroom. Stepping over the low wall running along the canal bank, she stood on the grass verge facing the house, her back to the water, then walked farther along the bank until she stood directly under the bridge. As the grass verge neared the canal bridge, it lowered by about a metre and a half, which meant Kate could still see the Devines' house while being all but completely out of view from above.

When O'Connor crossed over to join her, she realised that at first he couldn't see her. Eventually he spotted her under the bridge and came down. He looked around the spot where she was standing. 'What are you thinking?' he asked.

'I can't think of a better viewing point than right here,' Kate replied. 'If he stalked her, O'Connor, he got to know her movements, followed her home. What better vantage point could there be than watching her in the safety of her own home?'

O'Connor looked up at the bedroom window, just like her abductor might have done. 'So, Kate, if he was stalking her, why take her now?'

'That I don't know. He could have felt it was time to move their relationship to another level. Fantasising about Caroline, watching her, following her home, they all fed into some need he had, but it's a bit like an addiction, it doesn't remain stationary. He wanted more.'

'This grass verge gets plenty of traffic, Kate. Look at it.' The verge was littered with cigarette butts, sweet papers, even a couple of empty vodka bottles. 'It could have been used by under-aged drinkers, someone homeless looking for shelter, even lovers. But if our Peeping Tom did use this area to keep an eye on Caroline Devine, then Hanley will be kept busy when he gets here. I'm not sure what he's going to find after so much time, but if there's something here, I'll be damned if we're going to miss it.'

Ellie

I THOUGHT OF WEXFORD THIS MORNING. THAT LONG, hot summer in 1995 – the last year I considered myself a free woman. The good weather was part of the reason why Joe had pestered me for so long: 'It would do us all the world of good,' he kept saying, 'especially Amy.' But what he really meant was that it would do *me* the world of good.

Joe, I realise now, was handicapped when it came to dealing with his feelings towards me, especially where my bouts of depression were concerned, being a man with a mind that never entertained self-indulgent notions. With Joe, it was always about finding solutions, moving forward, no need to dwell on anything for too long, too much thinking can cloud your brain, no point in letting all that 'overanalysing malarkey', as he called it, get in the way of things. At times, especially near the end, he became more like a surrogate father than a husband. I guess, though, that was as much my fault as his. By the time of Amy's last birthday, our daily conversations had slid into the type of exchanges you would normally have with neighbours or mild acquaintances. But, in fairness, I should shoulder most of the blame. I was the one who married him on false pretences. At least at the time, Joe was honest in his belief about loving me.

The drive down to Wexford was tedious. I felt locked in – with my own husband and daughter. What kind of person feels that way about her own family? Joe's positivity irritated me, too. The music was loud, him singing at the top of his voice, getting Amy to join in from the back seat whenever a song came on they both knew. Now, when I remember back then, I know if I had the ability to turn back time I would go back to that very moment, stop it right there and ask both of them what they were thinking. I could probably guess at Joe's thoughts, but Amy's thoughts – what were they?

The pretence we were somehow a normal family going away on holiday irked me as well. I allowed my annoyance with Joe to get in the way of any link I might have had with Amy. I never got to the point where I asked, or wondered, what her thoughts were. But if I'm being brutally honest, I'd have to admit that I barely thought about her on that drive down to Wexford. I'm not the first parent to fool themselves into thinking their children will always be around, that we can pick up wherever we left off, whenever we want to. We forget – I forgot – that life doesn't work that way, that things happen that we cannot know about, unless we ask.

Apart from the singing and the humidity in the car, when I try to remember that drive I do recall that Amy's mood was more subdued than normal. At the time, I had taken it as a blessing. She'd made the effort to join in with the singing when her father prompted her, but it must have been just pretence. Was it a pretence for Joe, or for me, or for both of us? Either way, I made no effort to join in with them. I was like some closed-up machine, thinking only about how much I missed Andrew. It had been seven months since our affair had ended and although there were times, thanks to the antidepressants and the alcohol, that I managed to shelve the hurt, I had never got him completely out of my head. I became like some silly adolescent with exaggerated notions of obsession, imagining ways we might meet up, or how it would feel to talk to him again, to be able to share the silliest of things, to have him back in my life.

I must have appeared quite alien to both of them, doing nothing other than staring out the car window as they sang summer songs at the tops of their voices, a wife and a mother who paid more attention to the landscape than to the people who shared her life. In a way, I think I looked on both of them as the enemy, because they were the reason I had to pretend, to take part, to behave as normal. I remember wondering what Joe's expectations were – just because I'd reluctantly agreed to go didn't mean I was going to magically transform into a happy-clappy red coat. And again, I made the mistake of putting Joe and Amy together, as if they were both the one person and should be treated as such. Wasn't that what I did? Hadn't I let the distance between Joe and me forge a distance between me and Amy? I should have tried. I should have done that much at least.

How many times have I thought about that since I've come here? The sin of self-obsession. If my regret began anywhere, it began on that sunny drive to Wexford, my husband and daughter estranged to me, as I behaved like someone who cared for no one other than herself. In a way, that is why I accept my punishment so readily – 'What goes around comes around', another one of Joe's favourite affirmations. If only I'd realised that chances don't come by too often, that in that drive to Wexford I had at least a chance. I could have made things different. I could have simply turned to Amy and given her a smile, the smallest of gestures, just to let her know that I was there, that her mother cared about her.

If I had my way now, I would stop that car. I would stand right in front of it and when it was still, I would reach inside and give that lost woman in the front seat a good shake. Then I'd look to my daughter and take her by the hand. I'd bring Amy out of there to someplace safe, to me. I could give her one of those long hugs that don't require words, like the ones I gave her afterwards, when it was too late. I would tell Amy I love her more than anything, more than life.

If I could go back, I would not go to Wexford. I would obliterate it from my memory and live a different life, a life with my daughter still in it.

Rose Lane

HE MADE GOOD TIME GETTING TO TERENURE, THEN HE waited patiently at the top of Rose Lane until he was sure no one would see him slipping down to the garage. Even garage space was expensive to rent around here, but he had no choice after buying the terraced house in Rathmines. He needed to keep the old car parked safely, and this was the best option available.

When the garage door was shut tight behind him, he switched on the mahogany floor lamp he'd taken from Cronly, its bare hundred-watt bulb giving out plenty of light. Part of the reason he had chosen the garage was because of its mains electricity, and checking the coin meter before starting up the vacuum cleaner in the corner, he was pleased that there was still plenty of credit left. While vacuuming the car, he hummed to the familiar rhythm of an old church hymn, 'Be Not Afraid', putting a more upbeat slant on its normal rendition.

There was still some red ribbon left in the glove compartment. He sat in the passenger seat, where Amelia had sat the night before, and felt the coolness of the ribbon as he twined it between his fingers. He made a mental note to put the ribbon cutting away in the top drawer of his bedside locker when he got back to Meadow View. Continuing to caress the smoothness of the ribbon, he felt that same sense of wonder he had felt all those years ago.

He remembered the day he first found the ribbon, two days after his eleventh birthday, standing at the large sideboard on the upper landing of Cronly. He'd been angry with his mother, who'd once again done one of her disappearing acts, and so soon after his birthday. She had left him alone before, but that was the first time she'd been gone overnight.

She'd told him he was old enough to look after himself. After sulking for most of the first day, he'd decided he would turn the next morning into an adventure, using his time usefully to make discoveries. He had always been partial to touching things, using the sensation to explore aspects of his surroundings that vision alone could not conjure. The sideboard on the upper landing was a favourite place, primarily because he'd enjoyed running his fingers along the intricate wooden detail across the top, allowing his fingertips to go in and out of the bevelled grooves. It had three top drawers, side by side across the top, drawers that were always locked. Underneath each one of them were three separate sections used to hold extra sheets and pillowcases. The reclaimed wood in the sideboard was the same type as the mirror he now had in the hall at Meadow View. It smelled of beeswax and age.

He'd opened the middle drawer first. Even though he'd been the only person at home, he'd felt nervous using the small screwdriver to prise it open. It took a while, fiddling with the lock, and there was no way he would have succeeded unnoticed if anyone else had been there.

The first thing that had struck him about the contents was the diversity of colours and then, on closer examination, the patterns. They'd reminded him of a kaleidoscope with its mix of different shapes – spools of thread in every shade, thimbles and cushions with pins of varying size, yarn for darning and odd ends of wool. When his hands had brushed across the contents, he'd been instantly excited, but it was in the small wooden case at the back that he'd found the fabric cuttings, cottons, velvets and silks. When he'd placed it against his face, the silk felt soft and cold, almost as if it was a trickling stream. He'd known all these items had belonged to his late grandmother –

his mother was not the type of woman who entertained knitting or sewing of any kind.

He'd found the ribbons caught behind the wooden box. The colour – cherry red – caught his eye instantly. One inch wide, larger than the others, the ribbon had a perforated pattern running along both sides, which he would later discover was called a herringbone weave. It was the feel of it against his skin that he'd liked the most, not just the silk-like quality, which felt cool and smooth, but the herringbone edges, which delicately, but undeniably slowed the movement down, allowing for a more intense experience.

Now he rolled up the small cutting of ribbon and carefully placed it deep inside the pocket of his jeans. The ribbon was the first thing he had ever stolen, and it gave him a sense of power, just like that day in the sacristy. He hadn't felt any guilt on either occasion. Even the fear of being caught became, eventually, part of the allure.

Once the Carina was as clean as it could be, he tidied everything away before switching off the floor lamp. The garage was trapped in darkness. He would need to return tomorrow – he had more plans for the car. It was a number of days since he'd visited Cronly, and it didn't do to allow these things go unattended for too long. The time would soon come when he would have to consider selling the old place. He had already made discreet enquiries in the town. After all, even in today's market, it would fetch a decent sum. For now, though, it would remain as it always was, except for one small detail – his late mother no longer lived there.

O'CONNOR'S MOOD HAD NOSE-DIVED AFTER THEIR visit to Innes, and as they pulled away from the Devines', Kate could see it had deteriorated even further. His shoulders were tense and he relieved his obvious stress by driving far too fast, his use of foul language upped a hundred-fold the more other people got in his way. She was about to say something when his mobile rang. He barked into it, 'What?' He listened for a second and then hung up.

'Gunning,' he said. 'He says Jessica and her mother are ready to see us.'

Kate looked at the dashboard clock wondering what Declan and Charlie were up to. She had already been gone most of the day, a point which would be regurgitated by Declan when she got back. She jumped as O'Connor suddenly thumped the steering wheel, obviously caught up in negative thoughts of his own.

'It would help everyone, O'Connor, if you would calm down.' Kate's voice was tense.

He glanced at her. 'Yeah, well, let me clarify some things for you, Kate. I *am* calm, but I'm also fucking livid. Gunning should have picked up that scene from the girl's window. She was abducted less than a mile from her house, for fuck's sake, bleeding sick bastard.'

'I assume you're referring to the killer and not Gunning,' she said, raising her eyebrows.

'You assume right,' he snapped back.

'No need to take it out on me, O'Connor. My job is to analyse the killer and his actions. It's your job to find him. Killers are just like the rest of the human race, they rationalise their behaviour to make excuses for what they've done. We need to work out what he's thinking, and why.'

'Well, Kate, most of the human race don't do fucked-up things like this.'

'Look, I'm just making a point. Whether we like it or not, the way his mind works is important if we have any chance of working out what he's going to do next.'

'The only thing I'm thinking right now is that two young girls are dead, and back there in that house there are three people trying to pick up the pieces because of someone else's messed-up head.'

'Which is exactly why we need to calm down and shelve the angry outbursts.'

O'Connor let Kate's last sentence stew for a while before grabbing his phone again and calling CCIU to check for updates on Innes' computer and confirmation, or not, of his alibi.

'Right,' he said, throwing the phone onto the dashboard, 'Innes' alibi looks rock solid, but the files on his hard drive were another story. Do you know Manning?'

'No.'

'He's the top man in CCIU. He wants me to back off. It seems Innes didn't like to do everything alone and he's sharing images. The CCIU team are watching him closely, but there's no clear link to either Caroline or Amelia.'

'You don't sound happy.'

'I guess it was a long shot. I just hope CCIU nail the bastard when they're ready to make their move.' He took a deep breath. 'What's your take on what Emily had to say about Caroline losing weight, not thinking she was pretty?'

'It's not uncommon for girls to over-obsess about weight. Practically any young girl you meet on the street would have an opinion on their weight, good or bad, but probably bad.'

'You don't think it's an issue, then?'

'I said it's not unusual, but it could well be an issue. Her sister obviously believed it to be a problem, otherwise why mention it?'

'The mother, Lilli, seemed to think differently, though. According to her, she just wanted to eat healthily.'

'We all see what we want to see, O'Connor, or rather don't see.'

'You think she's keeping something back?'

Kate thought about her own mother, how even before the Alzheimer's took hold, in so many different ways she never looked at life full on.

'Kate?'

'Sorry. What were you asking?'

'I was asking if you thought Lilli Devine was holding something back.'

'We all have secrets, O'Connor, but she's just lost a daughter. She's hardly in a position to welcome any criticism of Caroline.'

'What's your call on it, then?'

'Well, considering the information Emily gave us about Caroline's body image, it gives us an insight into how Caroline thought about herself. What Emily said went beyond Caroline thinking she wasn't pretty. She said Caroline thought her body was ugly. That's a strong word for a young girl to use, especially when you take it in the context that it was a big enough problem for her to share it with her sister.'

'But isn't all that looking cool crap just something every kid frets about these days?'

'Maybe, but combining it with the weight loss, it means Caroline was going through more than the normal level of pre-teen doubts. It could be the weight loss was less to do with wanting to look like Kate Moss and more to do with not wanting to develop physically. Either way, she seemed to feel vulnerable.'

'What are you getting at?' O'Connor asked.

'Pre-teen is a turbulent time, and how we develop during that period forms the adults we become. If there are problems, it's not unusual for them to manifest themselves at that particular time. Feelings of low self-esteem, becoming overly self-conscious, thinking you're different from everyone else, they all raise their ugly heads in any number of ways, not least of which is a feeling of vulnerability and a desire to be accepted.'

'And the book of poetry, what do you make of that?'

'If our killer was the one who gave it to her, it means he befriended her in some way. It confirms she didn't perceive him as a threat, probably the very opposite.'

'Just as well we're visiting Jessica Barry next,' O'Connor said, turning the car a sharp left, 'she might have some idea what new friends Caroline was keeping in the last while. It's a little over twenty-four hours since we've found her friend's body, hopefully it will concentrate her mind, and not do the very opposite.'

'She's another link all right,' Kate agreed. 'If Caroline did obsess about her weight and appearance to the degree that there were fundamental changes physically, then her vulnerability may have been something the killer was attracted to, may even have manipulated.'

'And how would he have done that?'

'Well, any number of ways.'

'Give me one.'

'For a start, if he recognised her vulnerability, the simplest way to gain her trust would be to display his own.'

O'Connor slid the car into a parking space and turned off the engine before turning to her. 'Like what?'

Kate pushed her hair back from her face. 'Okay, this is just complete conjecture, but let's say he came across as someone kind, someone the rest of the world had been unfair to, a person on the margins even. Well, that might have appealed to Caroline's own sense of perceived isolation. She could have seen some of her own pain in him, and therefore considered him harmless. He wouldn't necessarily have needed to have a lot in common with her. In fact, the more outside her realm of experience he was, the less able she would have been to recognise any of the normal warning signs. If our man targeted Caroline, there is every chance she wouldn't have seen the danger signs until it was much too late.'

O'Connor looked like he was mulling this over. 'For what it's worth, Kate, if they did meet somewhere, my money's on the swimming pool in Rathmines. This little lady we're about to meet might just shed a whole lot more light on things.'

Kate nodded. 'Before we go inside, would you mind giving me a minute? I just need to make a phone call.'

'Sure, no problem. I could do with some air. I won't go far.' He got out of the car and headed off down the street.

Kate tried Declan's mobile three times, but each time it rang out. That meant it was on, but he wasn't answering – or was he choosing not to answer? As the ringing tone reverberated in her ear, her mind drifted back to the black-and-white image of Caroline in the grave, the clay covering her body like an extra layer of skin. Down the street, she could see that O'Connor was taking sneaky glances at the car, obviously hoping her call was finished and she was ready to get on the job again. *A body in a makeshift grave.* She felt the anxiety rising up through her and kept the unanswered phone tight to her ear, stealing a few more seconds to compose herself. It could have been her, in a grave like that. She could still feel his hands, grabbing her, the intensity of his intent. The memory was never far away from her, still raw even after all these years.

≈

Jessica Barry was the same age as Caroline Devine, but as far as her appearance went, she presented herself as an entirely different girl. Her eyes were circled with heavy black eyeliner and her hair, obviously dyed blonde, was backcombed, making her look taller than she actually was. She oozed confidence, despite the police presence stationed twenty-four/seven outside her house. Her lipstick was bright red, her jeans tight, and tucked into biker boots, while her designer white T-shirt with 'Attitude – What Attitude?' stamped across the front hung seductively off her right shoulder.

Kate could see O'Connor's disapproval of Jessica Barry from the moment he walked into the sitting room and laid eyes on the girl. She smiled to herself at his old-fashioned notion of youth. To her, it was a fascinating contrast: Caroline had wanted to stem the oncoming tide of adulthood, while her friend seemed to have big ideas in the opposite direction.

Sitting in a large armchair, Jessica looked like a cross between a contestant from a beauty pageant and some out-of-her-head rocker. Her mother, on the other hand, was dressed conservatively in cream-tailored trousers and matching long-sleeved blouse, fading into the background in comparison to her daughter. The Barry house was also very different from the Devines', more stylish with its wooden floors, large plush couches and decor that wouldn't have looked out of place in an interior design magazine. If Jessica's mother designed and created the interior, thought Kate, then she had a good eye for detail. Maybe when she'd been younger, she had applied this skill to her personal appearance, like Jessica did now. Even behind her now somewhat bland cream attire, you could tell she was once a 'looker'. Was she happy to be eclipsed by her daughter? Did it create tension between them?

Mrs Barry waited until Kate and O'Connor were seated before taking her own seat on the armrest of her daughter's chair. Jessica's mother may have dressed like someone more comfortable in the background, but with her straightened back and head held high, there was no doubt that any questions O'Connor or anyone else might have for her daughter, she would be very much part of the process.

'Mrs Barry,' O'Connor began.

'Pauline, please.'

Kate watched Pauline Barry shift slightly on the armrest, dragging her fingers through her pageboy-style brown hair, pulling it back off her face in response to O'Connor's words. Maybe Pauline Barry wasn't such a shrinking violet after all. The officer on duty had already introduced both O'Connor and Kate when they arrived, filling Pauline Barry in with the barest of detail.

'Jessica, this is Detective Inspector O'Connor, and Kate Pearson. They have some questions for you. Are you okay with that, darling?' She looked at her daughter.

'Sure, why not?' Jessica's answer seemed tense, nervous, but was delivered emphatically.

'She's still very upset, you know. Jessica and Caroline were very close – such an awful tragedy.' The mother, thought Kate, was either trying to add a greater impression of upset than her daughter was prepared to display or was intent on being Jessica's spokesperson. Either way, this would take a lot longer if Pauline Barry remained the main mouthpiece.

'It certainly is a tragedy,' O'Connor said, giving Mrs Barry a reassuring smile. He looked over at Kate before directing his first question to Jessica. Gunning had interviewed the girl already, but that was before Caroline's body had been discovered, and before they had a second murder on their hands.

'Jessica, I know this is difficult,' he began, 'but it is important that you try and remember everything you can about the past few days, weeks, even months – before Caroline's abduction.'

Kate knew O'Connor's use of the word 'abduction', instead of 'murder', was a means to keep things calm. Whatever reservations he might have about Jessica Barry, he needed her on his side.

'I'll do my best.' Her answer was a little softer this time.

'Okay, well what I'm going to do is this, I'm going to ask you some questions and all you have to do is answer them. If you find any of them confusing, just ask me to clarify. Take as long as you like, it's important that we do this right.'

'Okay.' Jessica took in a deep breath, tensing her body, as if she was about to sit an impromptu exam.

Looking across at Jessica, Kate could see some of the girl's mask was dropping already. There was a reason she was best friends with Caroline, there had to be more there than the exterior image she was projecting. Looking at the emotions playing across her face, Kate knew the two of them must have been close.

'Jessica, you and Caroline were best friends, right?' O'Connor continued.

'Yeah, since our first day at school.'

'You two have been through a lot together, so?'

The young girl nodded at O'Connor.

'So you would know if there was anything troubling her, things she mightn't have shared with other people?'

'I guess.'

Kate watched Jessica curl her knees up to her chest, an almost instinctual protection exercise.

'So you would know if Caroline had any issues about her body weight or anything like that?'

'She wasn't anorexic, if that's what you mean,' Jessica said defensively.

'But she did discuss her weight with you?'

'We both talked about it – not just her, me too.'

Jessica's mother put her hand on her daughter's arm in support, but the girl wasn't having any of it and pulled away roughly. It could have been just a teenage rebellion thing, but Kate wondered about the reason behind the underlying hostility.

'Did you discuss losing weight?' It was Kate's turn to ask the questions.

'A bit – I mean, the weight bothered Caroline more than it did me. I like being curvy, not being big or anything but, you know, normal.'

'Caroline had lost a lot of weight. Why do you think that was?' Kate held the girl's gaze.

'She had her reasons.'

'Jessica, if you know her reasons,' Kate's tone was gentle, 'it would help if you told us.'

Whatever difficulties existed between Jessica and her mother, the girl still looked up to her to check if it was okay to talk.

'Go ahead, darling. I am sure it is nothing Ms Pearson hasn't heard before.'

'She didn't like her body. At first, it was all about her changing shape, she said it interfered with the swimming, reduced her speed or something daft like that.'

'And then?'

'When she got, you know—'

'When she developed breasts?'

'Yeah, she had a bit of a freak out, made me rent out that movie, *Black Swan*.'

'The one with Natalie Portman?'

Kate felt the girl was more comfortable with her asking the questions rather than O'Connor.

'Yeah. I thought it was crap, but Caroline didn't. She thought your woman, Natalie, was great.'

'Would you say Caroline was self-conscious? Embarrassed even?'

'She just didn't like changing, none of it.'

'So she didn't have a boyfriend?'

Jessica gave her a look, the kind of one that said: if you think I'm going to answer that, you need your head examined.

'Jessica, it's important.' O'Connor leaned forward, using his bulk to add weight to the question.

'No. She didn't.'

'Okay.' O'Connor remained sitting forward. 'I want you to think long and hard before answering the next question. Did anyone try to get friendly with Caroline, you know guys, younger, older, anyone hanging around the pool or anything like that?'

'There was this one guy, he was a bit weird.'

'Why didn't you mention him before?'

Jessica looked back at O'Connor. 'I didn't think he was important.'

'Did he talk to you both?'

'More to Caroline than me.'

'Why's that?' asked Kate.

'I don't know. I only saw him the once at the swimming pool, but he talked to other kids too. He was friendly I suppose, harmless.'

Jessica Barry's use of the word 'harmless' to describe the friendly man at the swimming pool put both Kate and O'Connor on alert. They exchanged a look, but tried not to let their body language show the girl or her mother how eager they were to get more information.

'Go on, Jessica, tell us what you remember about him,' O'Connor said, knowing when to give a witness space.

'I think Caroline felt sorry for him,' Jessica replied with a shrug, 'that's why she stopped to talk to him. He gave me the creeps, though. I mean, he was ancient. Caroline said you shouldn't judge a book by its cover.'

'What did they talk about?'

'I dunno. I only remember seeing her talk to him, I wasn't listening to them. Like I said, he talked to others too. It wasn't just Caroline.'

'Was she friendly towards him?' O'Connor looked from Kate to Jessica.

'She wasn't anything – she was just, you know, normal. That was Caroline's way, friendly. Me, I just blanked him.'

Kate needed to get a few more answers. 'Jessica, if you didn't hear what they said to each other, could you make out how he spoke? Did you hear an accent or anything?'

'Nah.'

'Did he talk fast or slow?'

'Slow, I think, just, I dunno. He talked well.'

'Confident?'

'Yeah, but not cocky; relaxed, I guess, like an old guy.'

'Old – what age would you say?'

'Mom's age, I guess.'

'Did he smile at you or at Caroline?'

'I think he knew I didn't like him. Yeah, he smiled at Caroline, but, as I said, I only remember seeing him there once.'

'And did Caroline smile back?'

'Well, she wasn't going to be rude or anything.' Jessica's forehead was creased and Kate could tell she was afraid of misrepresenting her friend. Even though Caroline was gone, Jessica didn't want to 'tell' on her friend. Like all kids, the code of friendship was stronger than anything else.

O'Connor was watching Jessica's face intently. 'Did you two ever see him anywhere other than the swimming pool?'

It was the subtle movements in Jessica's posture – straightening her back up, her head slightly raised from her shoulders, her facial features tightening – before she delivered her emphatic 'No' to O'Connor which told Kate the girl was hiding something. O'Connor obviously got the same impression.

'Are you sure, Jessica?' he asked quickly.

'I said so, didn't I?' Jessica looked to her mother.

'Inspector, my daughter has been through a lot, and now to add to everything, we have police protection outside our door. Believe me, we want to be as helpful as possible, but my priority right now is Jessica, and you can see how upset she is.'

Pushing a witness, particularly one who was a minor, was tricky and O'Connor knew when to back off, but he had no intention of leaving without getting something concrete from the girl.

'Jessica, do you think you could give a visual description, help one of my guys put together a photofit of this man?'

'I suppose so, yeah.'

'Good girl.' Jessica's mother put her arm around her daughter. The girl leaned in willingly, looking less like a contestant in a beauty contest and more like a young girl on the brink of tears.

Ellie

BRIDGET MUST HAVE SENSED MY MOOD TODAY; SHE
is quiet during the usual morning routine. Like I planned, I say nothing
to her about the pen and paper. I wait until I know she is about to leave.
She reacts according to form, open-faced, followed by a narrowing of
the eyes, as she tries to fathom a motive. But she doesn't go on about it,
just says, 'No problem', as if I'd just asked her for an extra bar of soap.

I trust Bridget. I trust that she will come back with what I've asked
for. Funny when you think about it, that the one person I trust in here
is someone I've spoken to about little more than the weather.

She came back to me just before lunch was being served in Living
Room 1, before the end of her rounds. The copybook she handed me
was like the type Amy used at school, small and chunky. She also gave
me two ballpoint pens in blue. I looked up at her questioningly.

'Can't trust those blasted things, they always stop writing just when
you're in the middle of something important.'

I smiled at her, and I could tell she was pleased.

I place the pens and the copybook at the end of my bed before I go
to lunch. As I walk down the corridor, I can smell the scrambled eggs
on toast. I know I will force myself to eat it. I have no time for any
remarks from anyone today. As I eat, I think only about the copybook
and the pens waiting for me, knowing that shortly I will have to return
to my room and face them.

≈

I sit on the bed, me, copybook and blue ballpoint pens – quite the little threesome we are. When I was younger, I used to enjoy writing. That was partly why I'd chosen an arts degree at college. I had only just started my first year when I met Joe.

I had been working the Friday-night shift at the cinema. I was pleased when I was told about the extra shift, one of the girls was out sick and more hours meant more money. If not for that, I might not have met him.

At the cinema you met many different sorts. When I met Joe I remember thinking, this guy is some kind of chatterbox. I liked meeting chatty people then, it made the night go in quicker. He had two tickets for *Rocky IV* and apparently his friend hadn't shown up. Whether the friend was male or female I never found out. I was behind the popcorn counter when it was his turn to be served and as cheeky as anything, he asked me if I wanted to watch the film with him.

I couldn't because I was working for another couple of hours and, besides, I wasn't in the habit of going to movies with strange men. The first part of my reasoning I shared with him, doing my own bit of chatty tease – he was, after all, handsome. I don't know what I expected really. I didn't think he would come back again. But he did, right after the movie. I guess I admired his persistence as well as his good looks because the following week we met up in town. He was working as a mechanic, which meant his money was good and he got plenty of cash jobs on the side. We went out any night I wasn't working. He was fun to be with and, for the most part, his positive attitude was contagious.

I have no intention of writing any of this in my copybook. As I think about what I am going to write, I stare at the cover of the copy. It's dark green, the kind of green you see when mould has had a chance to develop on food. Written across the front of it, in black print, it states that it has '120 ruled pages'. Bridget must have been feeling particularly optimistic when she picked out this one.

Finally, I open it. I fold back the front cover as if I mean business. I have already counted that there are twenty-two lines on each page, so taking into account the front and back of each sheet, that makes 5,280 lines in total. I know all this because I have multiplied it out on the inside cover, using one of my blue ballpoint pens.

As I sit there, I think again about what would have happened if I'd stopped being so selfish and thought about Joe, and particularly Amy, during that last drive. What if I'd turned around to her and said, 'How are you?' What would she have answered? Would it have made any difference? Of course, the chance of me doing that was remote. It would have meant clearing my head of all the nonsense and picking myself up out of the dark hole I had decided to occupy with such determination for the previous six months. If there had been any prospect that I might actually do that, it was completely shattered the moment Joe told me Andrew would be meeting us there. After that, the only thoughts in my brain were thoughts of him.

When I finally write in the copybook, I write three words: 'Wexford' – 'Amy' – 'Dead.' I give each of them their own individual line, leaving 5,277 lines empty. An odd form of clarity creeps over me as I stare down at each one of those words. I understand only too clearly the strength behind each one.

I don't expect tears, because they are something I haven't experienced for a very long time. When they come, creeping stealthily up on me, they don't feel like relief, they feel like pain. It's like an overwhelming pressure behind my eyes from a place deep inside that I don't want to feel any more. My vision blurs, trying to focus on the middle word: 'Amy'. The evening sunlight is almost gone and the three letters making up her name burn into my brain. I know that even when the light goes and I'm sitting in the dark, I will still see them. The ache I feel is primal – rooted in the very reason for my madness.

When I hear the weeping, it seems as if it belongs to someone else, someone more deserving than me. I ask myself the question that has recently begun to weaken my resolve: *What form of man or woman would seek to live when the world they live in is no longer a world they care for or want?*

Meadow View

HAVING CLEANED THE CAR, HE PLANNED TO TAKE ANOTHER bus into town, pick up some books and, depending on how the afternoon went, be back at Meadow View by evening. Maybe it was the delight of being considered 'Mr Invisible' that gave him the inclination towards taking risks, but instead of going into town, he took a bus to the outskirts of Tallaght. He got off the bus at the Old Mill pub and started walking up towards Bohernabreena and farther on towards Glencree.

He was halfway up the mountain road when he spotted two short legs with ankle socks and runners sticking out from the hedge. The boy who owned the short legs fired a tennis ball across the road to the other side, forcing him to duck quickly out of the way. He looked surprised, then smiled in a friendly way at the boy, who watched him the way children watch strangers, with that 'should I talk to him?' question on his face. He nodded at the boy and walked on.

He was a good two miles up the road when he spotted the police cars, and made the decision. 'Mr Invisible' or not, the risks of being seen were just too great. No matter. It was a lovely day, and although he was anxious to get back and check on developments, he was glad he had avoided the pollution of town when fresher air was to be had.

On his way back down the road, he met the boy again, only this time he had a friend with him, another boy of the same age, about seven or so.

'Are you the boy who nearly killed me with the tennis ball?' he asked, pretending to scold.

'No, mister, it was Jack,' pointing to his friend, 'he sent it over first.'

'Shut up, Tommy.'

'You both friends?'

'I live up there.' Tommy pointed across the field, feeling more confident than before. 'Jack lives at the end of the hill.'

'Do you only attack strangers, or do you fight with each other as well?'

'Sometimes,' they both answered, and then laughed.

He smiled back at them. 'With tennis balls?'

'Nah, I kill him at Xbox,' Tommy replied.

'I wouldn't know anything about that.'

'That's because you're old. You like walking, mister?' Jack squinted as the sun shone down on him.

'Oh, yes, I love it. You two boys keep out of trouble now, do you hear?'

'We will, mister,' they chimed in unison.

He could hear the two boys still giggling even after he turned the bend. Smiling to himself, he mused about how children were, by and large, much more trusting and open than adults. It was such an attractive quality.

≈

By the time he reached Meadow View, he was peckish again. The last week had seen a further shortening of the days, with the change in the evenings giving the air an extra bite. Soon it would be Hallowe'en. That wasn't something he had ever engaged in as a boy. At Cronly, the gates were usually locked early in the day, preventing children from calling. He had no memory of ever dressing up, but, then again, who would he have called to even if he had? Meadow View was different. The proximity of the houses meant that strangers might be tempted to visit, looking for their 'trick or treats'. Another pagan festival commercialised for all the wrong reasons. He had every intention of keeping the house in complete darkness that night, discouraging any neighbourly interactions.

After feeding Tabs and boiling water for his Mokalbari tea, there was still some late-afternoon light in the kitchen. He felt positively elated at the prospect of checking the internet again. He thought about the website he'd looked at earlier that morning, the one he'd saved in Favorites for reviewing later. His intention was to spend the remainder of the afternoon finding out as much information as possible about the investigation. He took his filled teacup into the living room and switched on the computer, logging on and checking the breaking news first.

It didn't take long to find out about Amelia.

Pacing up and down the floor, he was damned if he could work out how they had found her, and so quickly. He didn't like it when things didn't go according to plan. He took several deep breaths to still himself. The most important thing was that she was of no use to them. A dead girl couldn't talk. He had handled things expediently and, irrespective of developments, everything was still under control.

Wondering whether the answer to the success of the police investigation had anything to do with the new criminal psychologist attached to the case, he decided to turn his attention to Kate Pearson. He found plenty of helpful information about her and the whole area of criminal profiling. The champion of this work in the UK was Professor Henry Bloom, under whose tutelage Kate had emerged as something of a star pupil. She had been involved in a dozen cases with him, some of them very high profile, and scored a success rate of over ninety per cent.

He Googled images of Kate, wanting to see what his new adversary looked like. When he saw her, he was completely taken aback, sitting upright in his chair before smiling back at the screen. Once the initial shock had passed, he laughed to himself. Sensing his master's good mood, Tabs jumped onto his lap and was rewarded with some rare gentle petting.

'Well, Tabs, isn't life full of the nicest little coincidences?'

Deciding it was time for a second cup of tea, he went back into the kitchen. The house was silent other than the hissing of the kettle coming to the boil. He searched for something nice to have as a treat. A packet of plain digestives would do the trick. He took his cup of tea and biscuit back to the computer, rejuvenated now, eager to find out more.

According to the biography he found on Kate, she had an impeccable educational background. Further searches revealed her late father had been an English literary professor, and had turned into something of a recluse in his later years. Kate was currently working with young offenders as part of the Counselling and Offenders Re-Integration Programme.

'Well, well, well. Who would have guessed? Quite the do-gooder by the look of things, and intelligent, Tabs, don't you agree?' The cat looked up at him expectantly.

NEITHER O'CONNOR NOR KATE SPOKE UNTIL THEY were safely away from Jessica Barry's house and driving back to where Kate had parked her car, outside the Devines'.

'She's lying, O'Connor.'

He turned to her. 'Too right she is. But if she can put together a good photofit, it could be the best lead we have to date. There is only so far we can push her, but I've a feeling it won't be the last tête-à-tête we'll be having with young Jessica. I'm going to assign a female officer to stay inside the house as extra security. It might spook the family even more, but that mightn't be a bad thing. If there are more answers to be had, we might as well shake them out of her sooner rather than later. What do you think about what she said, about the guy?'

'If it is him,' Kate said thoughtfully, 'he came across as calm, relaxed enough with Caroline not to worry Jessica unduly, even if he did, as she says, give her the creeps. Caroline was a quiet girl, sensitive, wouldn't have created a scene, happy to be polite. If he is our guy and he is the one who gave her the book, he would have spent some time watching her, testing her with brief interactions before he made his move. He wouldn't have been just grooming her, he would have been courting her as well.'

'Go on.'

'My guess is he watched Caroline, followed her home, studied her. Whatever about Amelia, I don't think his plan was to kill Caroline. I think she was special to him in some way. The burials, the killings of

Amelia and Caroline are at odds. There would have been a lot of blood caused by the blows to Caroline's head. After the second hit, the place would have looked like an abattoir. Far too messy. He's a planner, he wouldn't have meant things to turn out the way they did. You only have to look at Amelia's killing for that. If he wanted someone dead, he would plan it to be neat and controlled. The blows to Caroline's head were frenzied, which means more than likely he reacted to things not going his way. If he is the guy at the swimming pool, then what he wanted from Caroline was some form of relationship, a closeness of sorts.'

'But not necessarily sexual, right?'

'No. He might be naturally drawn towards younger females, even children. Jessica did say she remembers him talking to other children, so perhaps he doesn't find adult relationships easy to form and is emotionally attracted to or stuck within a particular type. He could be isolated, a loner, damaged – and if he is, he probably has been so for some time.'

'So why act now? That's what I keep asking myself.'

'Damage never remains stagnant, O'Connor, it's a bit like an addiction, and the fallout increases over time. He may have been happy for a while, indulging his fantasy, developing what he perceived to be a close relationship with Caroline, but then something must have acted as a trigger. It wouldn't necessarily take a lot to make him cross the line, maybe a need to know more or wanting a bigger reaction from her, or even a specific reaction. The trouble is, we know it didn't end there. Caroline didn't work out, so she ended up dead, and now Amelia, sadly the same.' She looked at O'Connor, wondering how he'd react to her next sentence, 'The thing about him, though, is that he will look for his fulfilment elsewhere. He won't stop. For him, the challenge is working out the best candidate, and the best time to make his move. That's probably what he loves most of all – when he's caught up in all that planning and potential.'

O'Connor sighed and rubbed his eyes. 'Christ, I already feel I've been on this case too long.' He looked at Kate. 'So I'm up against a guy who's already choosing number three?'

Kate shrugged. 'I think so. So what's next, O'Connor?'

He looked at his watch. 'I'll get on to Morrison now, and about two million other people I need to check in with. The next meeting in the Incident Room is scheduled for 5.15, and Nolan will be looking for concrete progress. Fuck!'

'I'll start working on my report as soon as I get back home.' She smiled back at him, despite knowing it wouldn't change his mood. 'I'll need you to send over the images from both burials. Can you do that quickly?'

'Will do.'

'Thanks for the lift.'

'Anytime, Kate. You all right now?'

She stopped, her hand on the door handle. 'What do you mean?'

'Earlier today, after that thing with Innes, you seemed a little shook up. I don't want to pry, but—'

'I'm okay, just a couple of things on my mind.'

'Well, you know where I am if you need me. We're not strangers.'

'Yeah, me and the two million other people,' she said, smiling at him again. 'Thanks for the offer, though.'

Kate got out of his car and walked over to her own. It was time to go home, to Charlie and Declan.

Ellie

THE NIGHTS ARE ALWAYS LONG HERE. AT LEAST DURING the day there is the routine, things to do, even if they are of little importance. I'm angry at myself for my change of mood. That's the thing about moods, the way they often take you as they see fit. Maybe over the course of time, these shifts happen to everyone, but in the happening you can lose heart, because the inner core of you, the part that knows you best, knows when the mood is not for turning.

I kick the blankets down, leaving just the sheet over me. It feels clammy in here, although the night outside is anything but. The heating has been on all night and with the small rooms and lack of ventilation, it makes the air unbearable. It feels stale and sparse, as if at any moment I might lose the ability to breathe. I can hear a dog barking outside, it sounds as lonely as I feel. There is no breeze, the rattling gutter is silent, and if the branches on the trees sway, they do so without sound. It's too early for the birds; perhaps the dog is barking because, like me, he's unsettled by the silence.

I have felt lonely on many occasions during my time here, but I have for the most part been able to find solace in that form of loneliness. I have seen it as a type of life penance that is, at the very least, deserved. That was something I worked out a long time ago. What had I been trying to achieve yesterday, writing in that copybook? What possible outcome do I hope to gain from it? Why would thinking achieve anything? It's nearly funny, after all the years of being here I've adopted an approach from Joe's old book of wisdom – don't think too much.

Pathetic. Dr Ebbs asked me to write about the beginning, yet in truth all I found were endings.

By the time I hear the others rising, flushing toilets, the water tank overhead filling, making its gurgling sounds, I've made up my mind what to do next. Today when I meet the good doctor, I will tell him he was wrong to ask me about beginnings, because in the beginning I understood nothing. The understanding came later and, when it came, it was like a slow wind that swept up everything in its path, until what was left held a very different answer from the one which I had sought at the beginning.

You think when you lose someone certain memories will come flooding back. But it's not like that at all. Memories are like life, they don't obediently do your bidding. Still, even when you know you can't control them, you keep trying. You reach in and seek them out, as if you were a child going into a sweetshop to pick out sweets.

Immediately after the fire, I wasn't capable of remembering anything. When the first glimpses came back, I fought hard against them. In part, they were too painful; in part, I felt unworthy. Now, knowing my mood has changed, I equally know I'm not prepared for the change.

I remember the first thing that struck me about memories was how different they were from their reality, how each one possesses a layer that might have been missed first time around. Like how I used to hold Amy in my arms when she was little, sitting her on my lap. In my head, I thought the memory was about the actual holding, the many nights I sat there with Amy when she was small, small enough to be in need of her mother's arms. But that wasn't exactly what I remembered. What I remembered were other, less obvious details. How when she left my embrace, a feeling of tension returned to my body. I found myself remembering the ease and joy her weight and warmth had brought me, and how when they left, I felt less whole and, at times, almost abandoned. Layer by layer the memories came back. More often than not, they were just tiny flickers, igniting the months of darkness. After Amy died, the loss was so great it was bigger than anything I believed any human being could bear.

That alone might have been enough to send me to this dismal place. I guess very soon after the real sense of loss took hold of me, after all the dreams and even the guilt were cast away like scattered nothings, they were replaced by something else, a deep and seething anger that was all-consuming. In time, even that passed, and the disbelief over everything became of no consequence. It was all my destiny. That was when I'd given up completely, when I was at my most hopeless. Then I realised the truth – what was left behind, along with all the things I couldn't change, was my future.

ON HER WAY BACK TO THE APARTMENT, KATE'S MIND was preoccupied with both the investigation and all the other things she needed to organise so that she could devote her time to it. Rescheduling work commitments at Ocean House wouldn't be a problem – her next court appearance wasn't for another two weeks – but until she knew how much time this investigation was going to take, she would have to ask Sophie to do after-school care for Charlie. He wouldn't be happy about it, but there wasn't any other way.

She parked the car on the street outside the house and gave herself a few seconds before stepping out and clicking open the small wrought-iron gate. She made her way up the stone steps to face Declan and a little boy who would have spent the day wondering where she had gone. She gave herself another few seconds at the front door before sliding her key into the lock and turning it. She found them in the living room.

'Hi, you two. Sorry, Declan, things took longer than I thought.'

'Banned the use of phones, have they?'

'Mom, look what I did.' Charlie held up an A3 sheet covered in black paint.

'Let me see, sweetheart.'

'Dad said I could draw any superhero I wanted, so I picked Batman.'

'He looks amazing.'

'Batman *is* amazing, Mom. He fights baddies and he has a special car that can fly.'

'I wouldn't mind one of those.' She attempted a laugh, looking over at Declan. His face remained set in a hard stare.

'Charlie and I are heading out to the park,' he said, more like a statement than a request for her to join them.

'But I've only just got back.' Kate was dismayed by his coldness. All she wanted was to be near Charlie for a while.

'Maybe next time you'll phone and we'll know when to expect you. Charlie, off you go, wash your face and hands.'

'Your painting is brilliant, Charlie. You go clean up like Dad says, and I'll put your paints away.'

'Mom?'

'Yes, honey.'

'Do you know what else is special about Batman?'

'Go on, tell me.'

'No one knows who he is because he wears a mask and a cloak when he's helping people.'

'He sounds really great.'

'Charlie, hurry up, you do want to go to the park, don't you?'

'Dad, can Mom come, too? Please, please.'

'That's up to her.'

Kate looked at Declan and for a brief second she felt a surge of hate that took her by surprise. He was challenging her – challenging her to be a good mother. She knew he'd probably enjoy the moment when she failed. 'Next time, Charlie. Mom has some work she needs to get out of the way. Here, come on. I'll race you to the bathroom.'

She purposely avoided looking at Declan as she bounced Charlie down to the floor and the two of them ran out of the room. She couldn't cope with Declan's righteousness.

In the bathroom, she stood Charlie on a low stool and they watched the white sink become a black mess within seconds.

'Are you like Batman, Mom, helping good people?' His hands flapped in the blackened sink.

'Who told you that?'

'Dad told me.' At least Declan was seeing her in a positive light, she thought, even if she couldn't remember the last time he had given her a direct compliment.

'Well, yeah, I suppose I do in a way. But I don't get to wear a cool costume like he does.' She flicked some water into Charlie's face.

'Ah, Mom, stop it. You're not like Batman, he needs his disguise. When he's not dressed up, he's just ordinary, like everybody else.'

Leaning down, Kate kissed him on the forehead. 'You're my superhero, Charlie.'

'Cool. What superhero do you think I am?'

'Oh I don't know. Mr Super.'

'Mr Super?' He gave her a doubtful look.

'Yeah, sort of a mix between Superman and Batman, but you're extra special.'

'Why am I extra special?' he asked, his eyes widening.

'Well, at first people think you're just a regular superhero, but you're not, because even though you're a very young superhero, you have lots of different powers.'

'Like what?' He jumped down from the stool, as Kate handed him a towel.

'Like the way you think about others, making sure they are okay.'

'So what do I have to do? What's my mission?'

'It's simple. You just have to be yourself.'

'That doesn't sound like much of a mission.' Wrapping the towel around his shoulders like a superhero cape, he puffed his lips out.

'Oh, but it is. Like the other week when we were in the park, and you ran and caught the ball for the little boy who fell over.'

'Yeah.'

'Well you were his superhero then.'

'I was?' She watched the beginning of a smile on his face.

'Yes, of course you were. Do you not remember how he stopped crying when you gave him back the ball?'

'Yeah, but I didn't do anything *special*.'

'To him, you did.'

'Mom?'

'Hmmm?'

'I missed you today.'

Kate wanted to scream inside. 'I missed you, too.'

'Mom?'

'Yeah?'

'Will you be here tomorrow?'

Maybe Declan was right. Maybe she was an awful mother. Not that he used those words exactly, but she knew he thought them, and the irksome bit was that the more she thought about it, the more convinced she was that he was right.

'I'll have to see, honey. Hopefully, I'll get through my work in a jiffy and we can do lots together really soon.'

'Mrs Evans says a jiffy is a hundredth of a second.'

'Your teacher is very clever. Now come on, Dad will be wondering if I ate you.' Kate made a face like a scary monster, then scooped him up before chasing him back out to the living room, where Declan was waiting, holding Charlie's coat and hat.

'Enjoy yourselves. Bash some leaves for me, Charlie,' she said, giving him a final hug.

'I will, Mom.'

Declan pulled Charlie's woollen hat down as Charlie struggled into his coat. He looked up at Kate and his face looked softer. She tried to smile at him.

'I could get a takeaway, Kate, open a bottle of wine when we get back?'

In one way, Kate wanted to say 'yes, let's do that, let's spend time together the way we used to,' but something held her back, and she wasn't altogether sure it was just her looming report.

'No drink for me, I'm afraid, I've a report to do.'

'Suit yourself.' She winced at the harshness of his tone.

'Declan, I'm just—'

'Busy. Yeah, I know.'

Turning his back to her, Declan took Charlie by the hand, pulling the apartment door shut behind him with a firm bang. Kate cursed under her breath. She knew she'd just missed an opportunity she would most probably regret, but there wasn't anything she could do about it now. Heading down the hallway towards the door of her study, the primary task ahead of her was focusing her mind on the report for O'Connor.

Ellie

AS I TAKE MY SEAT IN HIS OFFICE, DR EBBS IS HIS USUAL cheery self. The fact that I have brought the copybook hasn't gone unnoticed. He tries to disguise his interest by looking the other way, but I'm as good at picking up small details as he is. I notice the slight rise in the right side of his forehead, replaced quickly by a blank expression. He might be worried I didn't write anything down, or perhaps he's concerned that what I've written in the copybook is something for which he is ill-prepared. Either way, he has chosen to look again at something in my file, apologising, asking me if I could bear with him for a few more moments. I decide to distract myself.

I imagine the two of us swapping chairs: him sitting on the patient's chair and being just that, patient. I would think the good doctor would be very good at this. If I were sitting in his chair, would I be trying to look intelligent like him? Perhaps if I were looking at him across the desk as my patient, I would be trying to figure out the emotions on his face. Maybe I could work it out from how he sits, how he holds himself, figure out what truth is hidden behind his calm exterior. Perhaps he is able to do all of this with me. He looks up, closes my file. It didn't take the good doctor long.

'Well, Ellie, sorry for keeping you there. I just wanted to check a couple of things, hope you didn't mind.'

I say nothing. I suppose I could smile, but then that might give him the wrong impression.

'I see you have a copybook with you.'

I could be smart and say, 'Very observant of you', but I choose not to.

'Yes.'

'And how did you get on? Did you find the process difficult?'

'Surprising.'

'Surprising? In what way?'

'That I wrote anything at all.'

'And what did you write about?'

'An ending.'

'An ending? Not a beginning?'

'No, not a beginning. You asked me to write about the wrong thing.'

'Did I?'

'Yes, you asked me to write about the beginning, but the only things that matter are the endings.'

'Endings?'

'Yes, there were two. The first when I killed my daughter, the second when I stopped wanting to kill myself.' His facial expression is one of discomfort, but he retrieves himself well.

'So what did you write?'

'Three words.'

'Three words?'

'Yes.'

I hand him the copybook. In truth, I don't want to take responsibility for it anymore. I can see him look over the words, taking plenty of time to allow their impact sink in. I don't know what I feel now, but it's a bit like I'm forming a distance between the words in that copybook and the person who sits in this chair.

'Your words here – "Wexford, Amy, Dead"—'

'Important three words, don't you think?'

'Yes, Ellie, very important. Can you tell me why you chose those three specifically?'

'Isn't it obvious?'

'Well all three are, as you say, extremely important. But Wexford – even though it is the place your daughter, sorry, Amy, died – is still simply a place. I would not imagine it holds the same weight as the other two.'

'You underestimate its importance.'

'Do I?'

'Yes, because if we hadn't gone there, she might still be alive.'

I can tell he is mulling over this, trying to work out his next question. Perhaps my response was not what he expected. I could help the good doctor here, say something else, but I'm curious which way he is going to turn next.

'Ellie, I'm confused.'

'Confused?'

'Yes. Perhaps I had expected some kind of remorse.'

'I do feel remorse. If I feel anything, it is remorse. I feel it every living, breathing second of this thing called my life. Remorse and loss are the two things that haunt me most.'

'But your words, "Wexford, Amy, Dead", they are so factual, no emotion.'

'Well she is dead, isn't she?' I snap at him.

'Yes, of course.'

'So what's the point in writing anything else down? Other than those three words, nothing else is important.'

'But what about the fire?'

'What about it?' I lessen the anger in my voice, tired of the same old questions.

'Well it would seem to me to be extremely important.'

'The fire meant nothing.'

'Nothing?'

'Nothing.'

'It says here,' he flicks through the pages, 'that when they took you in for questioning, you displayed no outward signs of either upset or regret. An unusual response from a mother who says she has always felt remorse.'

'I told you the fire meant nothing.'

'But your daughter died in the fire.'

I want to explode. 'She was dead before the fire. Listen, I've said all of this before. You don't believe me, the others didn't believe me, so why don't we just drop it. I'm sure you have more pressing things to do.'

'You're talking about the mystery man you saw with Amy?'

'Yes.' I want to leave, I'm sick of playing this game. My thoughts drift inwards. He interrupts again.

'The man no one else remembers?'

I've spent so long inside my own head, if I try hard enough I can shut his words out completely. I'm not bothered by any of them. What I remember is that summer: the light winds scattering grains of sand, families chattering, children running in swimming suits, towels across their shoulders, wet hair mangled, queuing up for ice-cream cones. I can still hear the music from the carousel, over and over, above the noise of slot machines, and in the middle of it all I remember *him*. He looked out of place, as if somewhere deep inside, some warning stirred.

'Ellie, are you listening to me? We were talking about the man.'

'Do I need to go over it all again? It didn't matter then, it's hardly going to matter now.'

'But you've just admitted, by your own words, that you killed your daughter, not to mention the statement in your file.'

'Oh, yes, the file – everything is in the file.'

'It's not that I want to labour the point, Ellie, but part of moving forward is accepting the truth. What you say doesn't add up.'

'Not neat enough, you mean.'

'Things are seldom neat. That much I certainly do understand.'

'Well if you understand so much, Dr Ebbs, why do you waste your time with me? I am what I am, and for the most part, that does me just fine.'

'You say you killed your daughter, you've signed a statement saying the same thing, yet you still talk about this mystery man.'

'I'm not talking about him, *you are*.'

'The report in the file says the fire killed Amy.'

'The report in the file?'

'Yes.'

'Well that's just dandy so.'

'Ellie, you're not helping.'

'I thought that was your job.'

'Okay, let's start over. If Amy was dead before the fire, how come you said – and in fact still say now – that you killed her?'

'I did kill her.'

I can tell he's agitated, not angry agitated, more confused. I don't blame him.

'How?'

'How what?'

'How did you kill her, if not by the fire?'

'I killed my daughter, Dr Ebbs, when I stopped being her mother.'

Incident Room, Tallaght Garda Station
Saturday, 8 October 2011, 5.00 p.m.

O'CONNOR REACHED TALLAGHT GARDA STATION AT exactly five o'clock, just as the early evening news came on his car radio.

> *The Garda Press Office has just released a statement. A second young girl, Amelia Spain, who was reported missing by her parents late last night, has been found dead. State pathologist Donal Morrison is currently carrying out a postmortem at Tallaght Hospital. The area in the Dublin Mountains where the thirteen-year-old was found is some distance from the site of the burial of Caroline Devine, who was found early Friday morning, although police believe both deaths could be connected. Chief Superintendent Brian Nolan has asked the public to remain calm, saying they are doing everything in their power to track down those responsible. Any information the public may have to help with inquiries can be given through the designated helplines or directly to Tallaght Garda Station, where the main Incident Room has been set up.*

'Shit, shit and more shit.' O'Connor knew that whatever about asking the public to remain calm, that was one thing Nolan was not going to be. He was going to be dragged over hot coals, there was no two ways about it. He needed a cigarette before going in. He lit up, sucking the nicotine in hard and quickly, without pleasure, before finally stumping it out and heading reluctantly inside.

The Incident Room was even more packed than the last time –
after the discovery of Amelia Spain's body, the guys from Crumlin
were now involved. At the top table, Nolan looked like a man who was
ready to commit murder himself and Donoghue, seated to his right,
looked equally as pissed off.

Donoghue got the session underway. 'Right, starting with you
Pringle, any more on that car from the canal? Our killer needs to be
getting from A to B, and he ain't flying.'

'We have a second witness who saw the Carina, didn't get registration
number either, but we have a year – 1994. We're running checks on
tyre markings and paint used on that particular year and model.'

'Good, let's go with it. Get a picture of the make and model out, who
knows what it might bring in. No county details for the registration?'

'No, just the year.'

'Right, McCann, I want everybody interviewed on the estate where
Amelia Spain lived, or anywhere that young girl went. The guys from
Crumlin will work with you,' he nodded to the crew seated up the
front. 'If you need DI Hyland or any of the others from Harcourt
Square to row in, just ask O'Connor.'

'On it,' McCann said with a curt nod.

'Now, O'Connor, what had Morrison to say about the second girl?'

'He's doing the postmortem now, but preliminary examination
shows the killing was similar but different. The rigor wasn't forced this
time, but that was most probably because of the speed of the burial.
The girl was killed by asphyxiation most likely, same as Caroline, but
this time a ligature was used, looks like a narrow cable of some kind,
no rope marks. No blows to the head, but bruising to face and wrists.'

'And your profiler, what's she come up with?'

'The killer is a watcher. Hanley's working on an area under the
bridge in Harold's Cross, opposite the first girl's family home. Looks
like he may have been friendly with her beforehand, the techs are
looking for prints from a book of poetry he could have given her.'

'Poetry? A cultured killer. Fucking fantastic. Just what I wanted to hear.'

'We'll run whatever prints we get through AFIS and, if there's a match, we'll find it.' O'Connor hoped that the Automatic Fingerprint Identification system would find a match – they needed a break, and quickly. He continued, 'Also Jessica Barry has opened up. She's putting a photofit together with DS Campbell.'

'Good, glad the security's been increased on the girl. I want that photofit as of yesterday.' Donoghue put O'Connor's name down against that particular task as well. 'Anything else?'

'McCann and Hyland have spoken to Matt Long, the farmer who owns the site where the first girl was found.'

Chief Superintendent Nolan looked around the room for Hyland and found him at the back. 'Well, Hyland, what stories did the old man have from his sick bed?'

'Said he saw a guy hanging around his old family place, the ruins near the burial site.'

'And that was okay with him, an obliging farmer, is he?'

'He thought he was one of those hillwalkers. Both times he saw him was over the weekend, says the guy was very smart looking, not the kind you'd find milking cows.'

'Age?'

'Couldn't be sure, his sight isn't too great.'

'Brilliant. Right, get what you can out of him and if it bears any resemblance to the fit Jessica Barry is putting together, I want to know about it. O'Connor, I assume you're running a check on all hillwalking clubs.'

'Yes, and on the second swimming pool in Crumlin where Amelia went swimming. Both girls were excellent swimmers.'

'Grand,' Nolan said, nodding, 'this web is getting itself a lot of legs, but I don't want anything missed. DI Donoghue was asking you about your profiler; other than the leads picked up at Caroline's home, what else?'

'Kate narrowed the search area for the second missing girl, which saved us a shitload of time.'

'Good, you know how I hate to waste taxpayers' money.'

'She believes him to be a loner, very particular, capable of keeping a calm head. Someone who can gain people's trust easily, he won't appear threatening. The ritual burials are personal to him, but she thinks the disparity between the two locations and the speed by which he made his move on Amelia means, as I said before, that he considered her a loose end. Either way, bottom line, he is capable of killing again, so he'll look elsewhere now.'

'When do we get her first report?'

'This evening.'

'Right, make sure Donoghue and I see it the moment you have it. And that Innes guy, what's the story with him?'

'Rock solid alibi for both abductions. CCIU have asked us to back off, they have their own operation running on him, and some of his friends.'

'And other sex offenders in the Dublin area and beyond?'

'I have the list, but none of them operate anyting like this guy. Dr Pearson doesn't think his motivation is sexual.'

'No? What's her theory then?'

'Probably best to wait for her report, but our man would have had ample opportunity with Amelia, if that had been his intention.'

'I thought you said Ms Pearson figured Amelia to be a loose end? Maybe he was, as she said, particular? Gunning, where are you?'

'Here, sir.' Gunning put his hand up from the side.

'I want more pressure applied outside. If there's no match against the ribbons and everything else at home, we'll need to push on Interpol searches.'

'I'm on it, Boss, they'll be getting a reality check from me no matter what their preferred language might be.'

'Good – that okay with you, O'Connor?'

'Sure.' O'Connor wanted to punch DI Gunning in the face and remove any notion he had of being the star pupil. He should have got the boot in earlier about him missing the site opposite Caroline Devine's house. He wouldn't make the same mistake twice.

Nolan was still on a roll. 'I assume you've run checks on any possible visiting paedophiles O'Connor?'

O'Connor was even quicker to respond this time. 'Yes, Boss, nothing concrete in as yet, but we're pressing every possibility; any link or potential link, we'll see it.'

'Toxicology reports on the first girl back in yet?'

This time O'Connor was pleased to have a definitive answer. 'No drugs or any other substances were found in the victim's system. If Caroline got into a car with someone, she did so of her own free will. That would back up Dr Pearson's assessment that he gains their trust. All other trace evidence was in line with deposits from the burial site, nothing more.'

'Right, while I think of it, O'Connor, get Rohan to tell those press guys to back off. If I see 'Mr *goddamn* Invisible' in print one more time, I'll be even more bloody annoyed than I am already.'

Donoghue did the wrap up. 'Right, you heard the boss. Gunning, push the Interpol searches, you know how slow they can be to come in. O'Connor, I'll want to know what Hanley comes up with from the canal, that book of poetry, and Ms Pearson's report when you get it. We'll run a public appeal later this evening with the photofit from the Barry girl, and a visual of the Carina. It may not be his, but he's getting from place to place, meaning he can move anywhere countywide, and if Dr Pearson is correct, this guy isn't waiting on us for his next move. I don't need to remind you all, there's a computer in every police station in the country connected to the Pulse database. I want everyone out there using it. This place is filling up in here, and there's only one of him. I don't need to state the obvious.'

Ellie

I CAN TELL DR EBBS IS TAKEN ABACK, AS IF HE NEEDS time to digest what I've just said. It's in the way his head moves and his fingers tighten on his pen. He stares at me as if he might get some answers from my silence. Getting up from his chair, he walks around the room, slowly at first, then with more vigour.

'So, if Amy was dead before you set fire to the caravan, why did you do it?'

'Set the caravan on fire?'

'Yes.'

'I would think that's obvious.'

'Not really.'

'Because, Dr Ebbs, I saw no point in living.'

He opens the file, flicks back through the case notes again.

'You were dragged from the fire by an Oliver Gilmartin?'

'Yes, the caretaker of the caravan park.' I remember Gilmartin, and his big mouth. All bravado he was, talking about how he thought at first the fire was set by vandals, looking at me, all smug that he was some kind of hero of the hour. I'd only seen his caravan once. The day we arrived at the site, Joe had dragged me in to sign some goddamn registration book.

'Ellie, are you listening to me?'

'What?'

'Ellie, the morning of the fire, it says here Oliver Gilmartin tried to get Amy out as well, but he couldn't reach her after the gas explosion.'

'People said a lot of things.'

'Like what?'

'Like I was depressed, like I was crazy, that I'd wanted to end my own life, wanted to take my child with me.'

'And why would they say all that if it isn't true?'

'I don't know, all I know is I'm the only one who saw him, the man who killed my daughter. No one believed me about him. There was nothing of Amy left after the fire, nothing but her bones, and they said very little.'

'Ellie, according to the file *you* said a lot of things afterwards, much of which proved incorrect.'

'There are still bits I can't remember clearly.' My voice sounds weak.

'Well there would have been trauma, there is no denying that.'

I wish he would stop flicking through that file.

'I don't know what I was back then.'

'You say when you got back to the caravan, Amy was already dead.'

'Yes.'

'So how do you know this mystery man killed her?'

'She spoke about him.'

'What did she say?'

'I didn't think anything of it. I thought he was just one of the kids from the caravan park. But afterwards, I remembered her telling me about how the two of them had gone exploring. She even tried to show me where.'

'And you thought of this when you found Amy?'

'No, not immediately. Immediately, I had other things on my mind.'

I feel annoyed. I know I should put an end to this.

'Ellie?'

'Can I go now? I don't want to talk any more.'

'Sorry, just bear with me a little longer. I know it's difficult.'

'It's all in the file, why don't you just read it again and let me go.'

'When you found her, you said that you thought she was sleeping?'

'Yes, she looked so calm, innocent. Everything about her seemed perfect. I had only opened the bedroom door to make sure she was still asleep. It was then I noticed them.'

'What?'

'At first I thought they were of no importance.'

'What were of no importance?'

'The ribbons, the ones on her plaits.'

'What about them?'

'They were wrong, they weren't the way she wore them. It was because of the ribbons that I looked closer; if not, I might have closed the door and just assumed she was asleep.'

'So you went over to her.'

'Yes, that's when I knew. When I touched her, her face was cold. Have you ever seen a dead person, Dr Ebbs?'

'Yes, Ellie, I have.'

'Her face was that grey colour of death.'

'And you were absolutely sure she was dead?'

'Yes.'

'But you didn't think to raise the alarm?'

'What for? I just wanted to be with her. Maybe I wasn't thinking straight.' I pause. 'But I do remember how she was lying.'

'How was she lying?'

'It was so strange. It took me a while to work out why.'

'Why did you think it was strange, Ellie?'

'Because she looked like a statue.'

'A statue?'

'Yeah, a statue of an angel.'

'Why do you say that?'

'It was her hands, they were joined as if she was praying and her body was all curled up, her knees looked like she was kneeling.'

'What you've just said about the ribbons, and how Amy was lying, you've never mentioned this before?'

'I had my reasons.' He flicks through the file again and my head starts to ache. 'Don't you get it, Dr Ebbs? None of it matters. She's dead. My daughter is dead. Those words on the page, 'AMY' – 'DEAD' – 'WEXFORD', that's all that matters.'

He stops, and when he speaks his voice is gentle. 'Nor have you mentioned anything since.'

'Since?'

He looks straight at me. 'Since you've been here.'

I hold his gaze. 'No one else has ever asked.'

Meadow View

HIS BEDROOM IN MEADOW VIEW WAS SPARSE: A SINGLE BED, a solid-oak two-drawer locker picked up at an auction in Rathmines, a portable television, a music centre at the wall opposite the end of the bed, and one small window looking out onto the street. It was a place to sleep and unwind; taking time out was important to him. Everyone needed to close the door at some point, mentally shut out the world.

He could hear mumbling from the neighbours, more prominent during times of his silent solitude. Pressing the play button on the music centre, the sound of early-morning birdsong filled the room. With the curtains pulled, he felt content in the dark. Sunlight was for outdoor pursuits, now he needed everything to slow down.

The cherry-red ribbon was still inside his jeans pocket. Lying back on the bed, he removed it and let it run through his fingers before placing it on the bedside locker. He would be back at Cronly soon, where he could put it away safely. As he closed his eyes, he thought about his battered attaché case underneath the old metal-framed bed in the big house, a suitcase that had travelled with him to Suvereto when he was twelve years old. He remembered feeling excited about the trip and thought about the boyhood stickers he had applied to the case so diligently, most of which were still intact. It was always a treat opening the attaché case, just like the drawers in the old sideboard, with all its treasures. To him, everything in it, from the dull to the glittering, meant something, providing a window to the past.

He would need to buy another crucifix to replace the one he'd given Caroline. Amelia's one had gone missing long before, another tell-tale sign of her inadequacy. They weren't expensive, so he didn't mind.

Caroline had been such a sweet girl. He had told her how the crucifix would keep her safe. She liked the idea. She was even wearing it the afternoon he picked her up for their trip to Cronly. He was glad he was going back there soon. He wanted to look at the photographs of Caroline again, now that they were all he had left of her. They were at the bottom of the attaché case, taken with his Polaroid camera, the one he had bought to replace the now-broken one he had received on his eleventh birthday.

He'd been on a high when the two of them had left Dublin, telling Caroline how important she was, how special. She had been taken aback at first, upset. That had been quite disconcerting, not at all what he had expected. She was concerned, obviously, but he had told her there was no need to fret. He would look after everything.

She hadn't liked the house. He could see that from the beginning, the way her eyes had peered all around her, the rest of her body still. He'd put so much time and effort into taking her there, only for her to let him down. He knew it had been difficult for her to understand. Of course, he hadn't let her response deter him. After all, if there was one thing he prided himself on, it was his determination and resolve.

Like Amelia, he had put her at her ease, explained everything would work out once she remained calm. All she needed to do was trust him. She did trust him. She'd told him she did when he'd asked her. A girl with such appreciation of emotion understands these things very well. Even when she'd cried, he hadn't lost heart. His thoughts and feelings had been tested in the past, but he had never faltered. She must have felt a chill, shaking the way she did. He had even lit a small fire to ward off the old house's draughts and made her cocoa, but instead of drinking it she'd just sat there, her face red and puffy, her eyes wild. The more upset she'd got, the more he'd started to question if he'd been right to take her there in the first place. The last thing he'd wanted was for her to think badly of him or, even worse, think he was one of those lowlifes who sought out innocent young girls for their own enjoyment.

If only she had understood. He had tried to explain things – but the more he'd explained, the more melodramatic she'd become, and the distress became so unsettling to him. He had no illusions about Amelia, but Caroline had been different. He'd had such high hopes for her. But in the end, it seemed, she had wanted to spoil everything too. What choice had he – the way she ran to the door like that? He'd had to stop her. Uncanny the way the hands on the Napoleon clock had struck six when she'd gone quiet, a straight line pointing north and south, cutting the white clock-face in two.

It was when she'd stopped that she'd been at her most beautiful. He'd already had the red ribbons in his pocket as a surprise for her, just like before. She hadn't minded him plaiting her hair then. In fact, he'd got the sense of her smiling while he'd done it, and this had pleased him more than anything. When her body had hardened, he'd needed to fix her – she wouldn't have felt anything at that point, her peaceful expression had remained constant throughout.

He regretted taking her to Cronly. It was wrong of him. The size of the house, not having told her about it, must have frightened her. More than most, he understood how someone so young could be in awe of such a strange place. But she'd had to be stopped once she'd started screaming. The second blow to the head had produced such a profusion of blood, but he was sure she hadn't felt anything after that.

In his bedroom, the gentle sound of birdsong and the darkness eased his body and mind. What he regretted most of all was that he hadn't had the chance to take Caroline to his hideout, down by the wonderful elderberry trees.

Ellie

DR EBBS IS LOOKING AT ME LIKE I'M A COMPLICATED puzzle he needs to solve. His elbows are resting on the desk, the fingers of his hands joined at the fingertips. There is a smudge on his glasses, and I have the strangest urge to take them from the end of his nose and clean them. Maybe my mind is playing tricks, drifting from the past to the here and now. I could get up and leave, tell him I no longer want to answer his questions. It wouldn't be a lie. Re-living everything brings a clarity that has a habit of making tiny moments last forever.

'You were undoubtedly in shock, Ellie. Perhaps at the time, when you were asked about how you found her, your shock prevented you giving the information correctly?'

'Maybe.'

'But later, why didn't you mention it then – the ribbons, the way you found Amy? I find it incredible that no one asked you before this, or if they did and you've forgotten, that this is the first time it has fully come to light.'

'Maybe I had my reasons for not clarifying things. Maybe I still do.'

'You lost your daughter, Ellie. It must have been difficult.'

'"Difficult" – that's a handy word. Yes, difficult. It was difficult to accept my daughter was dead, it was even more *difficult* to know her killer was still out there.'

'Had you ever spoken to this man?'

'No, but I saw him.'

'When?'

'Soon after we arrived.'

'At the caravan park in Wexford?'

'Yes, near the beach.'

My mind drifts again to the road at the back of the sand dunes, the wild grasses, the smell of recently cut hay, a dirt track opening to a clearing.

'And you said this to the police at the time?'

'Yes. As I said, no one listened.'

'I'm listening now.'

'It's not important now, not any more.'

'Why do you think that?'

'Death has a way of focusing the mind, Dr Ebbs. My world fell apart, but I learned one thing fast.'

'And what was that?'

'The truth.'

'The truth?'

'Yes. Amy was dead, and the reason for it was clear. It wasn't just leaving her that night, the night she was killed, it was the fact that I'd been missing all the time beforehand. I failed her, Dr Ebbs.'

'You blamed yourself?'

'Wouldn't you?' He ignores this. I must learn to take a leaf out of his book.

'It must be hard, Dr Ebbs, to put yourself in the shoes of a mad person.'

'I don't think you're mad, Ellie.'

'Don't you?'

'I think you could be quite sane, which in many ways, if what you say is true, makes this a whole lot worse.'

'I'm not asking you to believe me.'

He sighs. 'Perhaps we should finish for today, Ellie.'

'Have you ever felt lost, Dr Ebbs? The kind of lost that stops you wanting to be found.'

'No, Ellie, I can't say I have.'

'You're lucky.'

'I guess I am.'

'When I found Amy, in a weird way she looked more beautiful than ever. Uncanny really, how calm I was. I even shocked myself.' I manage to smile at this. 'I sat talking to her, you know, stupid things, like how much she loved school, how kind she was. I didn't say anything about being sorry, letting her down, none of that. We both knew, you see, without words. I tried to remember the last time I'd looked at her properly, made eye contact. I'd forgotten how lovely she was. How can a mother forget such things? I undid the red ribbons in her hair, they didn't belong to her, brushed her hair out, and all the time while I was doing it, I knew.'

'Knew what?'

'That losing her meant that nothing else mattered.'

'You had no inclination to tell Joe what had happened?'

'No.'

'I find that surprising.'

'We were beyond words, Joe and I, even from before I found Amy.'

'So you decided to set fire to the caravan?'

'Yes. I waited until Joe left. He had no idea she was dead. I let him think everything was as it should be. It was better that way.'

'But when you were taken from the fire, what did you tell him then?'

'Nothing. Not at first. He thought the worst, they all did. Words seemed pointless.'

'And the man, did you tell Joe about him?'

'Eventually.'

'And?'

'And nothing. Like the others, he'd already made up his mind.'

'And this man you think killed Amy?'

'What about him?'

'You can't be completely sure he killed her?'

'No, but when I found her, I remembered things, things I should have paid more attention to.'

'Like what?'

'She said she thought he was real clever, just like me. I paid no attention to it. As I said, I guess I thought he was just one of the kids at the holiday park.'

'That hardly makes him a killer.'

'No. But I'd seen her with him. I mean, I didn't know for sure it was him, but I'd seen him twice.'

'And you didn't think it strange? Unusual?'

'Well no, not the first time. I figured he was one of the dads. I didn't know his name. The first time I saw them, Amy was petting his cat.'

'And the second time?'

'The second time she was heading for the beach. She had just come off the pathway at the back of the sand dunes, the place she tried to show me once. I could tell they had been talking. She waved goodbye to him. I did think it odd. I mean, a grown man taking time to talk to a young girl. I'd meant to say something to her. I'd definitely meant to ask her about him. Tell her to be careful.'

'And?'

'I never got a chance, or never made one, I guess.' Again my voice lowers.

'And these things make you think he was the killer?'

'You don't believe me either,' I snap back.

He ignores my last remark.

'This man, could you recognise him now?'

'I don't know. It was a long time ago. But sometimes I'm surprised by what I remember and by what I forget.'

'Shock can be indiscriminate, Ellie. It affects everyone differently.'

'Do you know what I think about when I think about back then? I think about how numb I felt – shocked, as you say. I thought there could be nothing worse than finding Amy the way I did. Then afterwards, when the real pain came, when the shock finally wore off, I wished I could have the shock back again, for what followed, Dr Ebbs, was a whole lot worse.'

'Ellie, do you realise the importance of what you're saying?'

'Dr Ebbs, don't you get it?'

'What?'

'None of it matters.'

'But you're saying you're innocent of the very thing that brought you here.'

'I didn't use the word innocent. I was never that. All the time we were in Wexford, I left her vulnerable. I wasn't brought here because of what happened. I was brought here because they thought I was mad. Don't waste your time, Dr Ebbs, the life I have now is my life. I've learned to accept it, that's all.'

'Ellie, why did you tell me all of this if it's of no consequence?'

'Lately, I've started to feel different. The change scares me.'

'Change can be a good thing.'

'It won't bring her back.'

'No it won't, but at least you are talking about it.'

'Talk is cheap.'

'It can be, but not this time I don't think.'

He hands me a plastic cup of water from the dispenser over by the window.

'Ellie, you said about the ribbons, the ribbons in her hair, that when you found her, they didn't look the way Amy would wear them, that the ribbons weren't hers.'

He walks back to his desk and rummages through the file. He takes out an old photograph of me and Amy.

'You said that when you found her, her hair was in plaits.'

'Yes.'

'But they looked different.'

'They were tied with perfect red bows.'

My head throbs. I want the ground to swallow me up. I look into the plastic cup filled with water and I can see the sea, puddles building up in the sand, the past swirling around my feet like quicksand. That familiar sinking feeling, knowing this time if I go down, I might never get back up again.

Dr Ebbs picks up the copybook and rereads the words. He seems distant, as if his frame is closing in on me. Small details overlap each other, his shape appears loose, his voice farther away. I try to get him back into focus, but it's like I'm wearing glasses that no longer suit my eyes. Everything around me darkens. I put my head in my hands, and the pain begins to settle. It takes all my strength to look back up.

'The fire, Dr Ebbs.'

'What about the fire, Ellie?'

I'm back there again, being dragged out, the cracking of the windows, the flames as they roared, the stench of rubber, and then that smell, the one I least expected.

'I had not expected it.'

'Had not expected what?'

'The smell of burned flesh, Dr Ebbs, I had not expected that.'

'Ellie, I'm so sorry.'

He unlocks the bottom drawer in his desk and gives me two white tablets, gesturing for me to drink my water again. I swallow both straight down.

I trust him. I now have two people in this hospital to trust. He waits. I can't tell how long it is before I raise my head and finally look at him.

'Just one other thing, Ellie.'

'Yes.' I feel the tablets kicking in quickly.

'In this photograph ...' He holds up the one of me and Amy, the one taken the year before we went to Wexford. 'You look happy in this picture, Ellie.'

I look at the woman in the photograph, and again I wonder where she has gone. I don't know who she is any more.

'Yes.'

'Who took the photograph, Ellie?'

'Andrew.'

'Joe's brother?'

'Yes.'

'Did you love him?'

'I thought I did.'

Dr Ebbs hands me the copybook, this time holding my left elbow as he leads me to the door. He calls one of the new nurses. She tells me her name is Sinead, like it should make a difference. She seems kind. I don't mind her taking me to my room. At least now, I know I will sleep.

Mervin Road
Saturday, 8 October 2011, 5.30 p.m.

IT HAD BEEN OVER AN HOUR SINCE THE BULKY
motorbike courier with his glistening black helmet had pounded up
the pebbled pathway of Kate's home, a large brown parcel covered in
protective plastic under his arm. Kate had spread the photographs
out like a mismatched carpet across the study floor, grabbing the
desklight down beside her as she knelt to examine each one in detail.
The images revealed themselves like an old movie playing out slowly,
each of them somehow intimate in their silence. She checked again
that the study door was locked, shutting out the world outside and
keeping the horror within, safe from her son.

As she studied both sets of photographs, it was clear that the
girls' similarities were more glaring than their differences: both were
beautiful, both young adolescents, both covered with a sprinkled layer
of clay, like a second skin. Kate went back to the photograph with the
gleaming crucifix. There was something about it that bothered her:
what was it? The clothes – Caroline's school uniform and Amelia's
jeans and tracksuit top – although at odds, could be distanced from
how both girls looked, but the crucifix on Caroline, being so close to
the plaiting and the ribbons, didn't make sense. He was crafting them,
she was sure of it, turning them into an image that was important to
him. So why leave one with a crucifix, and one without?

Kate looked down to both girls' hands, their small, delicate fingers
intermingled, looking almost like stone. Standing back from the
photographs, something else struck her. It was as if both girls were

kneeling, reminding Kate of stone guardian angels you would see in a graveyard, erected in memory of the dead. Once the connection was made, each time she looked at the images, Kate kept seeing the very same thing.

When she heard Declan putting his key in the door, she opened the door of the study and went out to them. Charlie was asleep on his dad's shoulders, exhausted from the park. Declan put his index finger up to his lips, signalling for her to keep quiet. As she still hadn't finished her report, Kate was relieved to see her son asleep. Declan went in the direction of Charlie's bedroom and she left him to it, slipping back into her study to finish the report.

≈

It was past nine o'clock by the time she was ready to phone O'Connor. Everything in the report had been composed based on logical reasoning, but there were other elements that had crept into her mind over the course of the evening, elements she couldn't include, not yet.

Report on the Murders of Caroline Devine and Amelia Spain

Compiled by Dr Kate Pearson

Crime scene characteristics:
- Organised.
- Secondary crime scenes.
- Both burials detailed.
- High level of intimacy demonstrated (perceived or otherwise) with victims.
- Minimal trace evidence gathered from secondary crime scenes.
- No sign of sexual assault. (See cause of death and body markings below.)

- Difficult terrain.

Location: Dublin Mountain Zone.

- Large stone deposits both locations.
- Remote.
- Ease of access to city.

Contrasting site characteristics:

(Site A)

- Area of natural beauty, stream, views of surrounding forests, heather, large elderberry tree, abundance of birdlife, green and luscious.

(Site B)

- Special Area of Conservation - grave area particularly barren, little or no natural greenery, flatter land contours, calcareous bedrock.

Cause of death:

- Asphyxiation, in both cases.

Injuries to victims:

(Caroline Devine)

- Pressure markings on victim's neck - manual strangulation.
- Multiple blows to head. Blunt force trauma, causing large loss of blood.

(Amelia Spain)

- Ligature markings on victim's neck, strangulation by form of cable/cord.
- Bruising to face - no blood loss.

Positioning and observation of victims:

- Preadolescent females.
- Similarity of build/facial features and hair colouring.
- Both girls physically fit: swimmers.
- Both put in foetal position (rigor forced with first burial).
- Hair plaited.
- Hair tied with red ribbons (identical ribbon used).
- Hands joined together (fingers intermingled as if in prayer).

- Earrings missing from Caroline Devine.
- Cross/Crucifix on silver-plated chain left with Caroline Devine, around her neck.
- Clothing - School Uniform (Caroline) versus jeans and tracksuit top (Amelia).

Abduction:
- Caroline Devine - Victim last seen mid-afternoon.
- Amelia Spain - Victim last seen early evening.

Inferences (behavioural factors):
- Killer may have certain specifications that his victims needed to fulfil (physical similarities), and perhaps personality traits.
- Killer wasn't sloppy, demonstrating a high level of intelligence. (Research has established that the more organised and methodical a killer, the more intelligent he is likely to be.)
- Tidiness of crime scenes consistent with ability to desensitise, compartmentalise events, perhaps to the extent of externalising blame. Psychopathic reasoning - may believe his victims have let him down.
- Could be familiar with the area or, in Caroline Devine's case, may have an attachment to it, other than the privacy offered.
- Both burials occurred during hours of darkness. This and the physical act of burying victims mean, if he acted alone, the killer was physically fit, male most likely, and capable of managing a difficult terrain. Possibly someone at ease with the outdoors.
- Blows to the head in the case of Caroline Devine, at odds with second murder - could be the result of the killer becoming panicked or angry.
- Ability to strangle defenceless victims, capable of disconnection.
- Ribbons/plaiting/positioning of victims - aspects of burials giving value to him.
- Details of first postmortem - killer prepared body elsewhere, someplace he felt safe.

- Blows to the head of Caroline Devine frenzied as noted above, could have been reactionary. Bruising and killing of Amelia most likely planned.
- No indicators that either attack was sexually motivated.
- Attention to detail – burial crafted.
- Risk-taker within controlled parameters. Abduction of Caroline Devine in broad daylight. Likely to have taken risks before – burglary or other similar offences.
- Calmness, planning, attention to detail, ability to develop trust with victim, indicating older/mature person, and someone not perceived as a threat.

Conclusions:
- Male
- Physically fit
- Outdoor recreational interests
- Age profile 30 +
- Intelligent
- Educated
- Working in professional environment
- Planner
- Repeats behaviour
- Lives alone
- Risk-taker – history of burglary/similar offences
- Attention to detail – high
- Level of control – high
- Ability to disconnect and compartmentalise events – high
- Capable of establishing trust/building rapport
- Ribbons/plaiting/positioning of body of personal relevance
- Choice of victims based on physical and personality traits.
- Stalks, and seeks relationship – murder may not be main motivation for subsequent killings.
- Similarities in age and physical characteristics of victims – early basic pattern.
- Selection of burial sites unlikely random – first site may be of greater significance.

    Likelihood of repeat killing – HIGH

≈

The phone only rang twice before O'Connor picked up.

'O'Connor, Kate here.'

'Just about to phone you.'

'The report's ready.'

'Good, Nolan's been on my case.'

'Can we meet? There are a couple of things I'd prefer to talk through with you face to face.'

'Sure. Where?'

'Near here, if possible.'

'I could call up.'

'No don't do that. Charlie's asleep. I'll meet you in Slattery's.'

'Give me ten minutes.

Meadow View

HE FOUND THE HOUSE EASILY USING GOOGLE MAPS. He was already familiar with the street, having passed through it many times before. Research was vital. Getting to grips with the exterior, grounds front and back, connection and proximity to surrounding dwellings, streets and laneways, were all part of the preparation process. He was pleased the rear of the house had a large garden, with access to a laneway running along the back of the houses, and those opposite. Each house had a side entrance, connecting front and back of the property accessible at ground level. So much could be done from the comfort of your own home, and he wanted to get all the external factors about her location firmly in his mind before making his next move.

It was dark by the time he left Meadow View, but the darkness always pleased him. He loved the night, drifting through it, almost invisible in his black running gear, avoiding streetlights, slipping easily around corners, sliding from one street to the next. There was a special hum tonight, cars passing, making a swishing sound as their tyres embraced the damp tarmac, raised voices from a basement flat causing his head to turn, a cat rummaging in a bin. They all converged in the symmetry of the night. The roads became quieter as he neared her street. He moved with ease, having learned over time the art of being unseen.

The streetlights bounced off the wet concrete, showing the tentative beginnings of black ice. As a boy, he had found the dark to be an adventure, offering him insights into many things that daylight could not. He had a natural boyhood curiosity, often going from place to place unnoticed, well after he'd been sent upstairs. 'Go along up, darling, and read some of your books', 'William, it's time for you to go upstairs', 'Mommy is entertaining, run along now'. He was something to be dismissed, the list of prompts as endless as the nights. He didn't mind going upstairs, preferring his room to spending time with her and whatever male companion she'd chosen to replace him. Most of them let him be, but those who didn't, with their pathetic efforts at being friendly, irritated him more. When it came to the many male guests his mother entertained, he was well aware that neither they nor his mother wanted him as part of their enjoyment.

He was glad he'd decided to go out running. Running wasn't normally one of his night-time pursuits, but he'd made an exception because of the necessary timing of events. When he left Meadow View, he did so with two destinations in mind, and neither had a lot to do with healthy exercise.

≈

The first thing he noticed was the open window on the first floor, at the side of the house. There was a light on in the room, but the blind was down. He wasn't sure which level she lived on, but it wouldn't take him long to find out. The small gate was ajar, so he moved quickly into the front garden. There were lights on in the top-floor apartment, too, so he stood back in the shadows, a large laurel hedge giving him all the protection he needed. He looked at the windows in the basement apartment; a latch hadn't been pulled over on one of them. Some people were far too trusting. It often surprised him that others didn't think the way he did. He'd been amazed at the number of times he had found it nearly too easy to break into places. Often, there would be an open or an unlocked window, or the occupants might leave a door ajar while they put out their rubbish, or went to talk to a neighbour.

Sometimes, as was the case with the Devines, the lights would be left on upstairs when the curtains weren't pulled. The second time he'd seen Caroline, he had made the decision to follow her home, knowing he could check everything out on Google Maps once he had an address. Her home wasn't far from the swimming pool. It took him no time to return later that night, in the dark. The Devines never left unlocked windows or doors, but by leaving their curtains open upstairs he could watch and wait. He was a patient man. Caroline would do her homework each night by the bedroom window, looking out onto the canal. Sometimes, if he got lucky, while she was there she would call a friend on her mobile or she'd go on the internet with her laptop, all of which meant he could watch her for longer. He had watched people like this before, all sorts. Once, he'd watched a family for months. They'd intrigued him, they'd always seemed so happy. In the end, he had tired of them and moved on to more interesting subjects. When it came to peeping into windows at night, the early dark evenings proved very handy.

The act of breaking in still excited him as much as it had always done, and that night was no exception. He knew this was her place, he had seen her coming out of it before. All he needed to do was establish which floor she lived on. It wouldn't take him long to check out the intercom system and get his bearings before making his house call later.

The name Cassidy on the middle buzzer threw him initially, before remembering her husband's surname, proving once again how vital research was in these matters. The fact that Kate lived on the first floor meant an opportunity to demonstrate his dexterity and agility, which was at its peak from summer months spent hiking and hill climbing. Although keeping agile and being fit were important, ensuring swift and easy movements meant success wasn't just in the agility, but in the keenness of the eye.

Pulling back into the shadows behind the deep laurel hedge, he made his final appraisal of the building. The sudden click of the garden gate was unexpected, but he remained calm. The little boy, wearing his woolly hat, rested his head in sleep on his father's shoulders. Lucky Charlie, he thought, having a father to love him.

Ellie

IT'S THE MIDDLE OF THE NIGHT BEFORE I WAKE. THE medication Dr Ebbs gave me rendered me unconscious from the moment I got back to my room. Now my mouth feels dry and my tongue enormous, like some savage beast wanting to choke me. It's hard to believe, but I feel even more lethargic than normal.

I almost want to laugh out loud when I think about the woman I used to be, the one who ran so quickly through her thoughts in her eager effort to avoid them. I stumble out of bed and drink some water from the tap. It doesn't take long for my eyes to grow accustomed to the dark. I wash my face, and the water chills from the outside in. When I sit back down on the bed, my knees curl instinctively tight into my chest. I wrap my arms around them.

The weather has changed. The wind is rising. It sounds as wild as the one from a few nights back. The pelting rain hits the small window panes in an attempt to bring freshness, fast and heavy, the wind carrying it in sheets of water, with barely time to stay on the glass. I watch the rainwater flow down in large puddles, mushrooming into one another. It's as if the water wants to clear everything in its path, wipe away all that is no longer necessary.

Who had I dreamed about – Amy, Andrew, Joe? Yes, they'd all been part of it, all part of the nightmare that creeps into my subconscious, clawing to be realised. In the dream, I was trying to sort things out, fix things, but I couldn't manage it no matter how hard I tried. Even in sleep, the answers to old questions still escape me.

Today with Dr Ebbs had been difficult. In many ways, once I had written in that copybook, I should have known my change of mood would precipitate such things. Over time I've learned to recognise these shifts. Like most things, they have a habit of creeping up on you, disguised in subtle ways, until finally you reach the point where you have gone too far to ever go back again.

Up until now, I've been able to keep these changes to myself, to such an extent that no one other than me would have been aware that anything had altered. The good doctor had been surprised by what I'd told him. At the start he was sceptical, I could see that, but I'm used to their scepticism. It's their belief I have a problem with, no longer used to such a thing.

I think Dr Ebbs thinks my whole time here has been some kind of travesty. It would be normal, I suppose, for people to think that way. Some, if they knew the truth, might even call it unjust. But I care little for injustice, at least not the injustice that has been done to me.

Today surprised me all the same. Not so much by what I'd said, more that I'd said it at all. Yes, before the meeting I'd been anxious, and I'd certainly never revealed so much before. If it had rested there, in my one act of revelation, perhaps sleep would have granted me some release. I would not have woken more distressed than ever, as I am now.

I'd been surprised by my words, taken aback by my own honesty. My voice had felt like the voice of someone else, a stranger, someone far stronger than I could ever be – someone capable of shocking me nearly as much as I might have shocked Dr Ebbs.

Fifteen years is a long time to maintain your silence. At the beginning, I'd tried to tell my story, but it isn't easy when people don't want to listen. I was angry, so angry, the rage inside me was black and choking. But in the end, I think the sadness won out over that.

I was taken aback by other things today, such as the strength of resolution I heard in my voice, something that seemed to have eluded me for a long time. There was a strange security to be found within it. Then later, I had been surprised again, when Dr Ebbs asked his last question. By then I'd already felt the medication kicking in, relieved by its irresistible exhaustion. Perhaps it was because the good doctor had taken me unawares, perhaps the exposure of myself had left me raw, unravelling the layers to the point where anything other than honesty was impossible. But I'd been shocked by my answer all the same, because I had forgotten how much I loved him.

Andrew had come to me immediately after the fire. He'd been distraught, loud and accusing, shouting at me. I remember looking at him, staring him blankly in the face, all the while thinking how different he'd been only hours before.

I knew that by going to see him that night I had taken a chance. I had tried to see him the night before, but that caretaker, Gilmartin, the one who dragged me from the fire, had spotted me. He was out doing his own bit of night roaming, poaching most like. Up until that summer, and even now, I still believe Joe had no idea about Andrew and me. If Joe had woken up on either occasion, he would have been suspicious straight away, wondered where I had gone and come out looking for me. But I'd no choice but to talk to Andrew. I'd spent days trying to find time alone with him, without success, so I chose when everyone else was sleeping, I was like a ghost who was most at home in the dark.

When he opened the door to his caravan, Andrew had not even looked surprised. It was as if he had expected me all the time. I loved him and hated him for that. There were times in the months before that summer, especially when I'd got deeper and deeper into my depression, that I'd wondered if I'd loved him at all. And yet, when he looked at me, I knew. It was in the way the words between us never mattered. The way I could feel him without touch. The way I knew he felt the very same things.

He was the first to speak. He'd asked me if I was cold. It was just a small thing, something of no relevance really, but it was enough to soften my original intentions. In my head I had planned to argue with him, to ask him why he hadn't been in touch, why he cared so little, rally my anger against the foolishness that I had once believed in him, thinking he felt the same about me. As on so many occasions before, he sat back and waited. It didn't take long for me to run out of steam. While he listened, part of him was shaded by the dark. I could see only half of his face. The outside lights from the caravan park lit the seating area, as if the light was with me and the dark with him. Finally I went over and sat beside him, a willing audience. My silence lasted only a few seconds before he spoke.

He told me he had never stopped loving me all the time we'd been apart. He had felt a void in his life like nothing he had ever felt before. He admitted it was he who had suggested the holiday to Joe. A friend had owed him a favour and said he could use both the caravans if he wanted to. Almost immediately he'd jumped at the idea, knowing full well it would be an easy way for us to meet. He said all this as if everything that had happened over the previous months could be brushed aside, as if none of it mattered.

I remember wondering even then if I was mad. All those months of torment, when I believed I was losing my mind, when every waking hour was spent thinking about him, when missing him became my whole existence. Perhaps that's the good and bad thing about love, the way you have no control over how you feel. Elation and desperation come hand in hand. In truth, even when I look back, I never had any doubt that I loved him. Or as near as anyone can feel for someone who is not their flesh and blood.

Our time apart was supposed to be temporary. It was his idea to take it 'easy'. Over the seven months, he had thought about making contact but had held back, thinking that the more time we were apart, the easier it would be for him, for us both, to forget and move on.

He had thrown himself completely into work, painting with more zeal than he'd painted his whole life. But what he saw staring back at him from the canvas told him everything he needed to know. And the more he painted, the more he knew he would see me again.

That morning when I left Andrew and went back to our caravan, I was happier than I had been in months. I had no idea where the rekindling of our relationship would lead us, but one thing I knew for certain: I wanted to be with Andrew more than anything else I could imagine.

But that was then.

I realise now that people think differently when real suffering visits their door. In my head, I suppose I thought that I had suffered over the previous six months, that those black days before we got back together were the worst thing possible. I had so much still to learn about suffering.

If I had the energy now, I'd laugh out loud at the person I used to be. Blind ignorance allows such flights of fancy. On that walk back to the caravan, when others, including Joe, were still fast asleep, I thought about how I would have done almost anything to keep Andrew in my life. I would have told any number of lies to be with him. Although I wasn't altogether sure how I was going to make that happen, I was resolute in my thinking that we would never be apart again.

Like the light touch of rain, cold, sharp and pure against my skin, I felt our love alive. How was I to know that within moments those thoughts would be gone, replaced by something completely different.

Ludicrous when I think about it now, how I once believed the world spun around me. Maybe the emotions I felt for Andrew fooled me into thinking they would be strong enough, deep enough, to withstand so much. But afterwards, when I found Amy, my love for him drifted to a place kept for history, of little or no relevance any more.

When Andrew arrived after the fire, I wasn't surprised by his anger. Joe told him how withdrawn I'd been, how dependent I had become on antidepressants, how he should have seen this coming. Andrew had never witnessed any of these things about me, but he knew enough about his brother to know he was not a man to lie. I hadn't helped matters. When he looked for an explanation, I gave him little in return.

Maybe Dr Ebbs was right and it had been shock. But all of them, Andrew, Joe, the rest of the world, meant little when the sheer horror of real loss hit me. I know I could have tried more, but there was so little of me left to fight, and what little there was didn't want to. When I think about the person I was that day, the day I found my Amy, I see a woman lost, a woman who was not only beyond saving but who held no desire for it either.

I have no idea what I will say to Dr Ebbs the next time I meet him. As I sit here with my arms wrapped around my knees, my future feels emptier than before, a gaping abyss, a vast nothingness.

I don't want to cry. I fight hard against it. The copybook and pens are down by the side of my bed, waiting for me to revisit them. I listen to the rain as it sweeps across the landscape and I wonder if it could carry me. If I could abandon this earthly body and be no more. When I was a child, I used to listen to the howl of the banshees in the night. I used to think I had something to fear from things I didn't understand, that the unknown was the scariest thing. Now I've learned differently, it is the things I know that I am scared of most. And again I ask myself the question I've asked so many times before: *What form of man or woman would seek to live, when the world they live in is no longer a world they either care about or want?*

Slattery's public house
Saturday, 8 October 2011, 9.00 p.m.

'WE'RE STARTING TO MAKE A HABIT OF MEETING IN dark pubs.' O'Connor stood up for Kate to take a seat.

'Yeah, well, rumour has it they need the business,' Kate responded, with a smile. O'Connor looked tired and crumpled, but he still managed to smile warmly at her. She reckoned he was happy to be away from the focal point of the investigation, even if only for a short while.

'You want a drink, Kate?'

'Water is fine, thanks.'

'That's not going to do a lot for their trade figures.'

'Okay, I'll be wild, get me an orange juice.'

While O'Connor went to the bar, Kate took both copies of her report out of her leather satchel. Despite everyone having less money in their pocket, the place was busy, with singletons and couples starting out on their Saturday night on the town. There was a good-humoured atmosphere that was a million miles from how Kate was feeling. She looked at the people around her, and everyone looked so free and unworried. She found herself thinking that they mustn't have children – or lukewarm marriages, or any of the other concerns that seemed to be taking residence in her brain these days. She shook her head, pulling her mind back from self-pity. This was work time, that was all.

'Right, Kate, I'm all ears.'

'Just read through the report first.'

O'Connor took a gulp out of his large brandy, picking up his copy of the report and studying it. 'You have him at thirty plus? But the guy at the swimming pool is probably older.'

'I know, it's just a guide. It doesn't rule out the swimming pool guy, far from it.'

'It also says that murder is not his main motivation?'

'He's looking for something, O'Connor. If he did court Caroline, he was looking for something from her and if it isn't sexual or motivated by a desire to kill, then it has to be some kind of relationship. He likes to get close, to study the girls and get to know their movements before he makes his own. But murder isn't his primary motive. It might have become necessary with Amelia, but only because things changed once you found Caroline. And that's the other thing. The burials could have a two-fold reasoning for him. One to presumably protect himself, but based on their elaborate nature they could also be a form of protection for the victims too.'

'A strange protection,' O'Connor said. 'You've listed burglary, why do you think that?'

'He calculates risk. He abducted Caroline in broad daylight. If he did something like that, he has already tested the waters, developed confidence in breaking the law and probably getting away with it. With the snooping, it makes sense he's watched people before, broken into places just for the thrill of it, that sort of thing. Anyhow, what I really wanted to talk to you about is that while there's a lot in the report we've already covered, there are a couple of things I've purposely left out.'

'Yeah? What and why?'

'Well, I can only put things in the report that I can back up fully.'

'Sure.'

'What do you think of, O'Connor, when you look at the images?'

O'Connor placed her report on the table between them. 'I think of a lot of things, but mostly that I want to get the bastard.'

'But what do you see when you look at the girls, other than the horror, when you look at the positioning, how would you describe the way they are lying?'

O'Connor's eyes narrowed as he thought about this. 'They're both in the foetal position, so I suppose they remind me of babies.'

'Yes, but what else?'

'The fingers are joined, and I see in your report you think they are in prayer.'

'Don't you?'

'Probably. Could be.' He sighed. 'Nolan really hates that religious stuff.'

'So what else? What words would you use to describe how they look?'

'Asleep? Innocent?'

'I agree. I don't know why, but he is crafting them, O'Connor, trying to create or recreate an image.'

'Meaning, he has history?'

'We all have history, but everything about these crime scenes feels staged. Do you know what I thought of earlier when I looked at both girls?'

'Enlighten me,' he said with a touch of weariness, beginning to tire of the question-and-answer game.

'I thought that they both looked like angels. Don't look so sceptical, O'Connor.'

'Well, I don't know, Kate, it's a big ask. I mean, bloody angels?'

'That's why I didn't include it in the report,' Kate said, shooting him a meaningful glance. 'Look, all I'm saying is that we don't know for sure what this guy sees when he looks at them, but he sees something. And that's not the only thing I've left out.'

'Go on, I'm listening.'

'It's the crucifix.'

'The one Caroline Devine was wearing?'

'Yeah, you see it's been bothering me all along. Our man is neat, organised, almost takes pride in how he buries the girls. The crucifix is an iconic symbol, so if he left it there, he must have been happy to do so.'

'But Amelia didn't have one.'

'Exactly. That was why its significance initially seemed less crucial. Do you remember when I said we have to look at the murder and then the burial of Caroline Devine as two different things – one frenzied, the other calm, planned and careful?'

'Yeah.'

'Well, the same goes for how we look at the two girls. There are the similarities, but there are also differences.'

He was looking at her with more interest now. 'Keep going.'

'We've already looked at the idea that Amelia's killing was different, and certainly the burial area was, as was the speed with which he made his move. If she was a loose end, then in his eyes Amelia could have been less worthy, almost of a lower status. That, in turn, means Caroline was elevated, more deserving.'

'He sure has a funny way of showing it.'

'Listen, O'Connor, if that crucifix was left on her neck, he wanted it there. And that's not all, look at the type.'

'A cheap replica, something you would pick up for a euro.'

'Yes, but a replica of what?'

'A silver cross?'

'It's a corpus crucifix, with the body of Christ on it.'

'So?'

'So supposing he gave it to her, the type was specific to him for a reason. But the only way we can be sure it's part of his signature is …'

'Yeah?'

'… is if there's another victim.'

'Your report, Kate.'

'What about it?'

'"Likelihood of repeat killing – HIGH"?'

'Not something both of us didn't already know,' she said quietly.

'I know that, but it looks much bloody worse seeing it there in black and white. Listen, I'm not sure about the cross thing, but I'll run with it. Nothing has come up on any of the databases to do with the ribbons, so we might as well see where this takes us. Gunning's pushing the enquiries via Interpol, at Nolan's request, not mine, I might add. He's a smarmy bastard, Gunning – says nothing when he knows he's fucked up, and is like a bleeding beacon when it goes his way. Either way, maybe this will shake something more from the mix.'

'I want to talk to Jessica again,' Kate said. 'You said yourself, she's holding something back.'

'Right, but it will have to be tomorrow. By the way, we've had some good news from the canal site. Hanley's got us another boot cast, same size, same markings. It's as common as muck, but it's a connection.'

'Anything on the book yet?'

'Yeah, he's pulled some prints, nothing matching on AFIS, though. If our man has a previous history in burglary, he's keeping it very secret.'

'Okay. I better go. It's late. See you tomorrow, O'Connor.' She stood up.

'Do you want me to drive you back?'

'No, thanks, I'm fine. The fresh air will do me good.'

Walking towards Mervin Road, the streets grew quieter the nearer Kate got to home. Crossing at the traffic lights on the corner, she passed a jogger coming the other way. She had seen him a number of times before while she was out running. He raised his hand in acknowledgement. She smiled back, glad she wasn't the only person pushing herself hard on a Saturday evening.

St Michael's Psychiatric Hospital, Dr Samuel Ebbs' office

AFTER HIS LAST CONSULTATION WITH ELLIE, DR EBBS had many things to reflect on, not least of which was whether Ellie Brady had spoken the truth, or the truth as she believed it.

It would seem reasonable to assume that, after the fire, she had withdrawn into a kind of protective shell, not out of self-preservation from prosecution but out of necessity for survival. The fact that Ellie had been incapable of showing her true emotions could have been responsible, in part, for blame being laid at her door. That possibility was one of the main reasons the file had unsettled him to begin with. There seemed to be very little doubt about her guilt; everyone, including her husband, had believed and accepted that she was guilty.

Nevertheless, if she truly believed in this mystery man who had befriended Amy, why had she accepted the blame so readily? He knew logic and depression by nature didn't go hand in hand, but if what Ellie had told him was true, the past fifteen years had been stolen from her. It took a certain calibre of person to maintain a silence for that length of time, and to remain as steadfast in their thinking as Ellie had.

However Ellie Brady had arrived at the set of circumstances that resulted in her daughter's death, there was no denying she had paid a heavy price.

The writing in the copybook had triggered something, perhaps feelings locked away for a very long time. The sedatives he gave her were strong, but necessary. The right balance was critical, one wrong move and he could end up undoing any progress made. There were never any guarantees, of course; grief always kept its own time.

From his reading of her file and case history, it seemed that it was Ellie's physical condition, rather than her mental one, that had been the chief cause of concern in her early days at St Michael's, especially when she had been force-fed intravenously. Was her decision to eat and drink again based on the realisation that her punishment would be greater alive rather than dead? He felt sure that the surrender of her life and freedom had settled far too easily on Ellie's shoulders.

He considered whether or not he should notify anyone else of Ellie's latest revelations, but he couldn't lose sight of the fact that he was dealing with a long-term patient. At this point, everything had to be assessed slowly. No matter how genuine Ellie might have appeared in her discussion with him, she could simply have been relaying her own version of events, none of which could be validated at this juncture. Whatever happened in Wexford had happened a very long time ago; waiting a little longer wasn't going to hurt anyone.

Meadow View

HE WAS GLAD HE HAD GONE FOR A RUN; HE FELT reinvigorated in both body and mind. The garda car outside Jessica Barry's house was no surprise. He had heard on the news that the police were planning to release a photofit and she was the only one who could supply it. Perhaps he should have taken care of her earlier, but, then, the girl had barely looked at him. Perhaps it was Kate Pearson's involvement that had encouraged the girl to open her big mouth? Kate Pearson was quickly becoming the most interesting aspect of the investigation, and one he intended to study very carefully. If she hoped to get inside his mind, it would prove difficult, but would be well worth watching.

Remembering the young boy huddled over his father's shoulder, he reflected, not for the first time, on how little those who receive love appreciate it. Maybe Amelia and Caroline had been errors of judgement: both had let him down and had been far too immature to appreciate the importance of the situation. Perhaps what he needed now was an equal, someone with both the sensitivity and experience to understand him. As a firm believer in fate, he couldn't deny that Kate crossing his path meant something. Was she sent to test him, question his resolve? Or were there more interesting aspects to be revealed?

The first time he had noticed her wasn't long after he'd moved into Meadow View. He had passed her running in Herbert Park. There was something special about her even then, a certain determination, an alertness that he could see immediately. He recognised her drive, she was pushing herself, her level of concentration, focused, striving, thrusting herself beyond the boundaries of pain, showing her hunger to succeed. His curiosity aroused, he had followed her home, seen her with the child, and then later with that husband of hers. He had been too quick to dismiss her, had not known her full potential. But he had been drawn to her, there was no denying that.

Tomorrow he would go to Cronly Lodge and, if necessary, he would take time off work the day after. He had already taken time out earlier in the week, and considering how little his services were appreciated, it shouldn't prove difficult to do so again.

He had regrets. Not about Amelia. Killing her had been necessary. Caroline was different though. The place he had chosen for her was perfect. The elderberry tree must have been at least twenty feet high. When it had all turned so badly wrong with Caroline, the place had come to mind immediately. In fact, the more he thought about it, the more he knew he couldn't have chosen anywhere better. His mother used to say that berries could grant you a long life. He wanted to remember Caroline the way he'd left her: safe and sound, looking like a perfect angel.

WHEN KATE GOT HOME, SHE WAS NERVOUS IN CASE Declan asked about her plans for the following day. O'Connor would be setting up the next meeting with Jessica Barry, which meant she needed to keep her time free. She knew it would be tricky to discuss not being around again.

She found Declan in the sitting room, watching television, a glass of wine in his hand. When he looked up, his face was softer than earlier. He seemed more approachable, willing to talk.

'You look tired, Kate,' he said as she took the armchair opposite him.

'I am. You look a bit tired yourself. How are you doing?'

'Okay.'

'I hope that was a nice bottle of wine.' Kate looked at the empty bottle on the coffee table.

'It was – I did offer to share.'

'I know you did.'

Declan turned up the volume on the television: the double murder was the top news story. They listened in silence as the newsreader gave an update:

Gardaí from Crumlin and Harcourt Square have now joined forces with detectives from both Rathfarnham and Tallaght garda stations in the hunt for the killer of the two murdered schoolgirls, Caroline Devine and Amelia Spain. Chief Superintendent

Nolan, who is heading up the investigation team, has issued a statement requesting the public to remain calm, and to contact the Helpline number, which is at the bottom of the screen, with any information. A photofit has been released, and the public's help is being sought in relation to identifying this man, who they hope will come forward so he can be eliminated from their inquiries.

'It's bloody awful,' Declan said with a sigh. 'Not a very nice one for you to be involved with.' She was surprised by his show of support. 'Sorry for being grumpy earlier,' he went on, 'I guess I just miss having you around.'

Kate looked over at him. 'I know you do, Declan, and if I could help it, I would.'

'Truce?'

'Sure,' she agreed with a reassuring smile.

'What do you say we all do something tomorrow? We could go see your mom, have lunch out, then take a drive somewhere, spend time together, just the three of us. Charlie missed you today. I did too.'

Kate took a deep breath. 'Declan, I'm really sorry, but I might have to work tomorrow.' She saw the look of disappointment and then hurt register on his face, but she plunged on. 'Look, when this is all over, we can have as much time together as you want. I've already sent Ocean House an email to say I need time off. Once this case is sorted, I won't rush back. We are both well overdue a holiday anyhow.'

'Kate, I don't know.'

'What don't you know?'

'About us.' He stood up.

'What about us?' she said, her voice sounding weaker than she meant it to sound, almost as if it belonged to someone else.

'You don't really need me to spell it out for you, you're not stupid.'

She bit her lip, stung by his tone. 'I know things haven't been great, Declan, but we're not the first couple to go through tough times.'

'Don't psychoanalyse us, Kate. We're not products of some research findings.'

'I'm not saying that. Look, all we need is time.'

'Well, let me know when you have some, and while you're at it, why don't you let Charlie know as well.'

'That's not fair.'

'Isn't it?' He started walking towards the door.

'You know it's not. Where are you going?'

'Out.'

'But it's late.'

'Don't wait up.'

Charlie woke when Declan slammed the front door, appearing suddenly in the doorway of the sitting room. He was in his Batman pyjamas, rubbing his eyes with sleep. Kate hugged him close.

'You okay, honey?'

'Where's Daddy?'

'He'll be back in a minute. Come on, superheroes need their sleep.'

'I don't want to sleep. I want Daddy.'

'Here, I'll read you a story; you pick, any one you like.'

He eyed her suspiciously and looked so earnest, with his black spiky hair and cartoon pyjamas, that in spite of everything, she smiled.

'I want them,' he said, pointing to the comics Declan had bought earlier.

It was a toss between Batman and Superman, so Kate opted for the latter. Superman now had heat vision, which could shoot laser beams, along with x-ray and telescopic abilities. As Kate attempted to get her son to settle down in his bed, it was Superman's powerful breathing skills, knocking over cars and freezing objects on the spot, that kept Charlie blowing at her face, constantly telling her to freeze.

Sensing that he might have pushed her too far, he sheepishly asked for his *Bear* story about the lost bear, the one who is eventually found under the bed. He may have thought superheroes were the best thing ever, but he wasn't ready to let go of his favourite bedtime story yet.

Kate stayed in the room long after he had fallen asleep. She thought about Declan, about how maybe he had a point, that he had only said what she was already thinking but didn't want to admit out loud. She had been tied up with work a lot recently, but work wasn't the problem, and deep down she knew it. Obviously Declan did, too. There was a time when she never doubted that the two of them would always love each other, when everything between them was easy, as if it was simply meant to be. Had her feelings towards him changed so much? Had she stopped loving him? She had no idea what she could do about any of it right now, but whatever she was going to do, it would have to wait until the investigation was over. They'd both have to try and be patient until then.

Incident Room, Tallaght Garda Station
Saturday, 8 October, 10.30 p.m.

O'CONNOR WASN'T THE ONLY ONE WORKING LATE – a couple of the CCTV guys were still going through footage at the back of the Incident Room when he arrived. He nodded to both of them, then phoned Gunning.

'Any more on the Interpol searches?'

'Lots of dead ends, nothing concrete, but I'm pushing hard. You know me, O'Connor, I like to get results.'

'Yeah, well, we all do, but not all for the same reasons.'

'What's that supposed to mean?'

'Never mind, keep me posted, that's all.'

'What about your end, anything fresh in?'

O'Connor was slow to give him too much information, even if they were both on the same side.

'Looks like we might have a match with the boot print at the canal.' O'Connor allowed the last remark to settle, knowing it would irritate Gunning. 'The boss is thinking about whether we should release information on the ribbons and the plaiting.'

'What's holding him back?' Gunning sounded glad with the change of direction.

'You know the way this shit is seen, the media will jump on it – ribbons, plaiting, ritual laying of bodies – could make things a whole lot worse.'

'I hear you. Like a hand grenade going off in the middle of a fire drill.'

'I know. The photofit went out on the late news, so it's a waiting game now to see what that drags in. Nothing concrete by late tomorrow afternoon and my guess is he'll go public with the ribbons. The plaiting, I'm not so sure.'

'So how's your Ms Pearson getting along? She's a real beauty, nice and sweet.'

O'Connor chose to ignore his last remark. There was something about Gunning's voice that irked him, and he wasn't happy about him mentioning Kate. Even over the phone, he came across like a posturing peacock.

'Funny you should mention Kate. I have a job for you.'

'Nolan wants me to keep working on the Interpol searches.'

'I know he does, which is great, because we're going to please both him and Kate with this one.'

'I'm listening.'

'The crucifix Caroline Devine was wearing, it may be nothing, but put it into the mix. Sounds like you have bugger all on the ribbons and positioning, so let's see what comes up with the cross. I'm sending you over a replica photograph now.'

'Right.'

'And Gunning.'

'Yeah?'

'If you get anything, no running to Nolan with it, remember that I'm the Senior Investigating Officer.'

'Wouldn't dream of breaking the chain.'

'Good. One other thing.'

'What's that?'

'Kate isn't *my* Ms Pearson, she's a respected criminal psychologist who is helping to find a killer.'

Before Gunning had the opportunity to answer, O'Connor hung up on him.

WHEN KATE WOKE UP, DECLAN WAS ASLEEP IN THE BED with his back to her. She had no idea what time he had arrived home, but judging by his snoring, he wasn't moving anywhere in a hurry. She walked across the hall to check on Charlie, and he too was out for the count. She knew that the interruption to his sleep last night would mean a lie-in. Normally, she would have relished the chance for longer in bed, but not today. She made her way to the kitchen and sat at the table with her coffee and phone in front of her. She didn't have long to wait.

'Morning, O'Connor.'

'Right, Kate, meeting with Jessica set up. They're expecting you.'

'Great, I'll head straight over.'

'By the way, I gave your report to Nolan and Donoghue and they're not happy.'

'Why not?'

'They were hoping for more. What they want to know is what he'll do next.'

Kate swallowed her annoyance. 'It doesn't work like that. It's been one full day since I've been officially involved. Do they want me to fabricate patterns?'

'I'm just saying—'

'What we have is what we have. I'm going to talk to Jessica, if any more comes out of that, you'll be the first to know. But, O'Connor, there was one other thing I didn't mention last night.'

'What's that?'

'In the report, I've noted that he repeats behaviour.'

'Yeah, I saw that.'

'It goes back to Amelia being perceived as a loose end. Even though she disappointed him, he carried out part of her burial the same way.'

'So?'

'That tells us far more than the details of the burials, the ribbons and positioning being his signature. It tells us about *him*. He likes the familiar, routine, takes comfort in doing things the same way. If the crucifix is an indicator of Caroline's elevated status, the lack of it on Amelia, her disappointment to him, didn't deter him from assigning familiarities, similar behavioural patterns. As I said, he likes routine.'

'Listen, Nolan's thinking about going public with the ribbons and the plaiting, how do you think our guy will react?'

'Depends on how it's presented. He's particular, probably likes the idea of being somewhat elusive, taking pride in how he handles things. If Nolan releases information about the ribbons and plaiting, there'll be a side of him that will feel complimented in some way. He has an ego, O'Connor. By the way, I saw the photofit from Jessica on the news last night, it wasn't very distinctive.'

'I know, sometimes these things work for you, sometimes not – but you never know with photofits, it's all part of flushing him out. They're pushing his link with the swimming pools too, so plenty of phone calls in, the guys are working as fast as they can.'

'All right, I'll ring you after I've spoken to Jessica. Have you the statements in from Amelia's family and friends?'

'Pringle will have them for the morning session. I'm running late. Talk later.'

'Sure.'

As she put down the phone and sipped her coffee, Kate knew well why Nolan and Donoghue weren't happy. She wanted to know what his next move would be too. The killing of both girls formed the beginning of a pattern, one that could be relied upon heavily, if murder was his main motive or if the crimes were sexually driven. His stalking of Caroline, and possibly Amelia, meant he had been looking for something from both of them. The development of a relationship, even non-sexual, all pointed one way: he was looking for emotional closeness. Would he repeat the same pattern soon, or was he reassessing his choices all the time? She would need to consider the statements from Amelia's family and friends, but right now she had Jessica to contend with. If the girl was holding something back, she'd have to get it out of her.

≈

Perhaps it was being under tighter police security that had changed the girl, but this time when Kate met Jessica Barry, the girl looked very different. She wore no make-up and when Kate arrived, she was curled up on the sofa in soft white pyjamas with pink daisies. Kate couldn't make up her mind whether she looked more or less vulnerable without her war paint on, but with it gone, Kate could see how pretty she was. Rather than the overconfident stance of the previous day, Jessica looked anxious. Looking at her, Kate felt that whatever walls she had tried to build up to protect herself had come tumbling down.

Mrs Barry offered to make some tea, but Kate turned it down, knowing that being alone in the room with the girl was never going to be on the cards. Child protection regulations prevented them talking one on one, but Kate didn't mind – she felt that, on this occasion, Mrs Barry's presence in the room was a help rather than a hindrance. Any distance Jessica had originally displayed towards her mother was now gone, along with the make-up and the rest of her adolescent front.

'How have you been, Jessica?' Kate asked gently.

'So-so.'

Mrs Barry nodded in acknowledgement.

'Good. These things are difficult.'

'That's what I've been telling her,' Mrs Barry agreed, appearing more confident.

'Jessica, yesterday when Detective Inspector O'Connor and I spoke to you, we both felt there was something you were holding back.'

'I helped with the sketch, didn't I?'

'I know you did, and I understand they've got lots of calls from the public already. But I'd like to go back to the man, Jessica, the one from the swimming pool. How well did Caroline know him?'

Jessica looked over to her mother, but Kate pressed on. 'Jessica, I'm not trying to say anything bad about Caroline, I just want to see if there was anything else about this man that might be relevant.'

'Jessica, you can trust Kate,' her mother said softly. 'Anything you say will be treated with the strictest confidence. Isn't that right, Kate?'

'Of course. Nobody is setting themselves up as judge and jury here.'

Again Jessica looked over at her mother, who gave her another reassuring look and nodded her head.

Jessica pulled her body into a tighter curl and traced the outline of a daisy on her pyjama leg. 'Caroline met him again afterwards, after that time at the swimming pool.'

'How do you know?'

'She told me. Well, she didn't exactly say they'd met up. She just said in passing that she'd met him, nothing sinister or anything. It was just a chance thing, it wasn't important.'

'Did she meet him more than once?'

'She might have.'

'Jessica?'

Jessica gave a little sigh of frustration. 'They talked, that's all. I think she felt sorry for him. She was really good at swimming, you know, he said lots of encouraging things to her, about never giving up. She said he was a good listener, she liked him, said he was nice, that he was kind to her, sort of like a teacher.'

'And what did you say?'

'Not a lot. She knew I didn't like him. I mean, I'd only seen him once, but when Caroline set her mind to something, that was it. She didn't think he was odd, she thought he was grand.'

'Did she tell you his name?'

'No.'

'Why not?'

'I don't know. Maybe she thought I didn't want to know, maybe she thought I didn't understand, maybe she was right …' Her voice trailed off.

'So how did she talk to him? Was it over the phone?'

'No, I don't think he had one. I don't know, but he lived nearby, she'd see him around when she was out; like I said, nothing planned or anything.'

'Why didn't you say all this before?'

'I dunno,' Jessica said, shrugging her narrow shoulders. 'I guess I felt like I was betraying her or something. She didn't do anything wrong.'

'I know she didn't, Jessica. Listen, what happened to Caroline was an awful thing, but it could happen again, so what you tell us will make a huge difference. You say you think he was local.'

'I'm not sure, like, but he must have been if he was around here all the time.'

'Kate, my daughter is obviously distressed. Perhaps that's enough.'

'I realise that, Mrs Barry, but if this man was with Caroline, we need to know everything Jessica can tell us. I don't like to sound dramatic, but another girl's life could depend on it.'

Mrs Barry looked at her daughter, then gave a tight nod for Kate to continue.

'Jessica, is there anything else? Anything at all?'

'No, not really, except …' she paused.

'Except what?'

'Well, I don't know if it's important.'

'Tell me anyway.'

'Her chain.'

'The one with the crucifix?'

'Yeah.'

'What about it?'

'It was just a cheap thing, but Caroline liked it.'

Kate held her breath as Jessica spoke, feeling they were getting near to something now. 'He gave it to her.'

'Are you sure?' Kate asked.

'Pretty sure.'

'As a present?'

'Yeah, like it was nothing, it wasn't anything.'

'But Caroline liked to wear it?'

'Sometimes.'

'Why do you think that was?'

'I dunno, because it was pretty.'

Kate frowned, knowing there was something else the girl was holding back. She had to be careful here and not spook Jessica into withdrawing again.

'She didn't just wear it because it was pretty, did she, Jessica? You know why she wore it, don't you?'

'It doesn't matter.'

'Well, maybe not, but just say it anyhow.'

'It was what he said about it.'

'What did he say?'

'It's stupid.'

'Go on. Please.'

'He told her it would keep her safe.'

'Safe from what, Jessica? What would it keep her safe from?'

'Weirdos, you know what I'm talking about, guys who mess with young kids.'

'Sexual abuse?'

'Yeah. It's all so stupid now, isn't it? He killed her, didn't he?' Her voice rose and her face went pale as she said the words.

'Jessica, try to stay calm. We don't know for sure who killed Caroline, but it's important we know what this man said to her. Did Caroline feel under any threat in that way from someone in her life?'

'No, I don't think so. I think she just thought it would help her.'

'Now think carefully, Jessica. What did Caroline tell you – what exactly did he tell her about the crucifix keeping her safe?'

'I dunno, religious crap. He said it was a sign of Christ's unconditional love, how in death he wanted to protect the innocent.'

Kate sat back, Jessica's last sentence repeating over and over in her head. She thought of biblical words she had learned at school: 'Suffer little children to come unto me.'

'Is that it, Jessica? You are not holding back on anything else?'

'No,' Jessica replied, shaking her head. 'That's it. That's everything.'

'Thank you so much,' Kate said warmly. 'And thank you, Mrs Barry. You've been really helpful, Jessica. This really will help us.'

Ellie

SINCE COMING TO ST MICHAEL'S, I HAVE NEVER SOUGHT personal possessions, I didn't want anything to remind me of the past. In the beginning, there was no talk of such trivialities. Back then, it was all about punishing me or holding the lunatic back from the edge of madness. It took some time before the undercurrent of anger and pity became more about dealing with the carcass of the person I'd become, rather than the circumstances of its creation.

In here, you're cut off from the outside world, but that doesn't mean it doesn't come in. It comes in through the faces of those who've looked down on me, bearing the imprint of how they viewed and judged my so-called crime. To be fair, some tried to hide it, preferring to cover up how they felt under the guise of their professionalism. Invariably, even the staunchest of them slipped.

Recently, though, the outside world has come in differently. I have my updates from Bridget, snippets from real life as she sees it. There's the radio that plays in Living Room 1 when we have our meals, the television we watch in the evening in Living Room 2. Sometimes, the outside comes in with the new inmates. Some of them are so young – all of them seem younger than me.

At the start, I think us long-termers frighten them. The fear is written across their faces as clear as day. They see us, and get scared we are their future. They're not told about our individual stories or our past. Why would they be? Our past, like their fear, is on our faces too. We are all victims to it.

I think people look at me with pity now. Pity is somewhat easier to take than hate. There are those who still avoid me, still look on me as a child killer, a woman capable of the worst crime imaginable. I know the question a great many of them want to ask when they see me. It is something I would ask myself if the situation were reversed. *Why doesn't she kill herself? Why does she choose to live when her child is dead?* I understand why they think this, because I've thought the very same thing.

At the beginning, or at least when I arrived at St Michael's, no other option seemed open to me. Losing my life was something I would have welcomed. At the very least, it would have taken me away from all the anguish and the pain. I'd even thought about the afterlife – how, if I killed myself, there might be a chance, despite everything, that death would bring me closer to her. I had no fear of death, no fear at all. In many ways, there was no other way forward. What was there for me to live for after Amy was gone? I'd no interest in the sham of a life I'd been living, and despite how I felt about Andrew, what we had would never have been enough. I would have always known that the two of us being together was in some way responsible for what had happened. Even if it wasn't, happiness was something I neither sought nor wanted any more. Happiness would have been impossible to bear.

The decision to stop eating was an easy one. After my failed attempt to kill myself in the fire, they decided I needed to be watched day and night. So there was no other option open to me. It would be slow, but it was an effective way of dying. It was when they moved me from here to the main hospital that Joe visited me. It was the last time I saw him, barely conscious by then, my body tied up with tubes and machines.

I heard the nurse tell him I might not be able to hear anything. That helped him, I think, to clear his mind of things he might otherwise have held back. He displayed all the emotions I'd expected – anger, pain, a complete lack of understanding about how I could have done such a thing. His words were a way of saying goodbye to everything that had gone before, rather than looking for any real answers. I had gone beyond listening to people, but when Joe came into the room, I knew I owed him that. He had lost Amy too.

When he spoke, he sounded different from how I remembered him. A man who has lost everything doesn't speak with the same voice; his grief deepens everything. What I hadn't expected was how his grief had left him with little room for hating me. I think by the time he was able to build up his resolve to come and see me, he had taken on much of the blame too. Just like me, he turned inwards. Perhaps he asked himself questions, ones that ensured his sleepless nights would be filled with waiting for answers, filling the loss.

He spoke about how he didn't understand how sick I was, chided himself for doing nothing. I could have tried to convince him of the truth, I could have made a last-ditch effort for him to understand that it wasn't me who killed our daughter. But then I realised. I realised the truth would hurt him even more. He would have worried about how Amy might have suffered, how afraid she might have been. Either way, when he came into my room that last evening, the only thing I knew for sure was that I owed it to him to listen.

He stopped talking halfway through his visit, as if he had run out of words but could not bring himself to leave. In the corner of my eye, I could see his shape sitting like a large heap on the hospital chair. When he told me he had come to say goodbye, I felt more sadness for him than for myself. He planned to go to Canada, with Andrew. He hadn't wanted to leave, but everywhere he went, every person he met, they all seemed to know who he was. The sadness in their eyes was too much for him. He said he didn't hold out much hope, but at least if he was someplace else, he might be allowed deal with his grief alone, not feel like it belonged to others. In part, I think, I preferred him angry. When he was angry, he had some fight left in him.

Again, he asked me why I had done such a dreadful thing. It was pointless. Even if I thought about denying it, what would it have achieved? How would it have helped him? I guess he thought if he understood, he could move on, but I doubted it. All of us cling to our own desperate methods of survival. I knew the truth, and it was a truth I would not be sharing with Joe.

When I attempted to speak, he didn't hear me at first. I tried my hardest to call out his name. All I heard was a cracked whisper, but it was enough to make him look up. 'I'm sorry' was all I could say. He wanted more, I knew that, but as he took in my words, I sensed a form of closure for him, some faint hope that what had gone before might some day be resigned to memory.

When he stood up to leave, we both knew he was drawing a line in the sand and I was not going to stop him. Unlike me, he had done nothing wrong. If Joe found some small relief in my apology, that was okay by me. The truth was something only I needed to bear. He had lost his daughter, he had suffered enough.

After he left, I made the decision to eat again. I had no desire to get better as they, the hospital staff, had kept jabbering on about. Rather, I decided that death was far too easy an escape for the likes of me. Why should I be released of the burden of guilt, when a man who had no hand or part in being anything other than a good father blamed himself for missing the so-called tell-tale signs of his wife's madness?

When I see Dr Ebbs again, I'll ask him for Amy's photograph. He'll give it to me, I'm sure of it. Maybe it is okay for me to ask for a piece of Amy back. It's not because I feel any more deserving. My punishment is one thing I am absolute about. But I would like to have one small thing to place under my pillow when I go to sleep. After fifteen years, it's not a lot to ask. No matter how bad my next meeting with the doctor is, I know that by the end of it, I will have her picture with me. I might write to her, use my copybook. It doesn't matter what the words are, as they will be our words, and that is a beginning of sorts.

Cronly Lodge

IT WOULDN'T TAKE HIM LONG TO GET TO CRONLY LODGE, traffic was always light on Sunday mornings. He had thought about taking the train, one left Dublin at 7.32 a.m., but the return train wasn't until 14.01 p.m., which would restrict his other plans.

On the drive down, he went over the events of the previous day. He had felt unsettled during the night, and hadn't been able to put his finger on exactly why. It was only when he had the opportunity to reflect, he realised how much the past few days had taken out of him. He didn't like loose ends, untidiness – nor did he like being rushed.

Provided he had no unwelcome visitors to Cronly, he should be able to take care of things quickly. If everything went to plan, he would be back in Dublin by early afternoon. He'd already texted that irritant Daniel about being sick. Bulldog Face loved the limelight; no doubt everyone would think him on his deathbed by the time Daniel filled them in breathlessly.

Today, he chose to wear his charcoal merino turtleneck sweater, finishing off the look with a grey cashmere scarf, the way he'd seen Jude Law wear it in *Alfie*. The day was bright and crisp, so he'd decided on his fitted grey wool blazer as a perfect complement. He had numerous expensive items in his wardrobe. Although careful with money, he always chose items that would withstand the test of time. It was all about balance, a saving here, another one there, affording him the odd indulgence and reward.

The ribbon was safely stowed in the buttoned-down pocket inside his jacket, close to his chest. He hoped it would bring him good luck. Sunday would be busy in the village, but he had no intention of engaging in tedious social interaction. His mother's funeral had been a trial: the obligation to play the loving son, Mrs Flood taking charge, the gardener and handyman, Steve Hughes, prowling around the house like he owned the place. Even that awful man from the caravan park, Oliver Gilmartin, had attended. Still, it was all old news now. Things were moving on.

≈

No matter how many times he walked the pathway to the big house, the magnificent nineteenth-century facade was always pleasing to his eye. The lime-washed walls, imbued with the smell of the sea, and the high sash windows, battling down for the harsh winters of a seaside town, had such a soothing effect on him. Importantly, the once decrepit condition of the house, as it had been in his youth, was no more. Even the gardens looked well. He could hear still his mother's high-pitched voice in his head: 'The thing I've learned about planting Lily of the Valley is that you must pick a place to plant them, and absolutely nothing else.' At first, he had planned to cancel Hughes tending the gardens – he had never liked the man and found him too friendly for his station. On reflection, he had changed his mind. He realised that keeping the gardens looking good might help sell the house, in time. Besides, Mother had been fond of having Hughes there to keep the garden exactly as she liked it. She had her flaws, but the lowering of standards was never one of them.

The last time he'd been to Cronly, Caroline was with him. It seemed like a lifetime ago, although only four days had passed. He pushed open the front door. The house was cold and dark inside, with the curtains drawn tightly. Despite this, it still filled him with a welcome sense of being home.

Wasting no time, he made his way to the kitchen. The back door by the stove was bolted from the inside. He slid back the bolts, unlocking the newly fitted Chubb lock before heading out through the garage and up the pathway to the top of the hill. From there he could see the coastline for miles. Tara Hill stood 800 feet above sea level, formed on molten rock more than 400 million years old. The furze and heathers that flanked the surrounding area had lost their bright summer shade of yellow, but the elderberry trees were still adorned with dark cherry-coloured berries, a sublime delight after their summer of creamy-white clusters.

It was his mother who had told him that the elderberry tree dated back to Roman times, and that it was the tree Judas hanged from after his betrayal of Christ. To William, the trees were magnificent specimens. Ever since his holiday in Tuscany as a boy, he'd grown to compare the view from Cronly Lodge to the view overlooking Costa degli Etruschi.

He inhaled a deep breath. That day, the brilliance of the elderberry trees was surpassed only by the vibrant blue of the ocean, despite it being October. He knew the water would be perishing cold, but he was still tempted to chance a swim, resisting only because time wasn't on his side. The beach was one of his favourite places, even in summer, when it was spoiled by the annual throng of vulgar tourists. It was here, as a child, inhaling the smell of the Atlantic, that he had developed his love of swimming; the beach, like Cronly Lodge, held good memories for him, as well as bad.

Once back inside the house, he checked the doors and windows, turning the Chubb twice on both the front and back doors. Pulling across the bolts he'd recently fitted, he checked his watch. It was just gone ten o'clock, time was speeding against him, but the important thing was to remain calm, a clear head would achieve so much more.

The ticking of the Napoleon clock soothed him with the familiarity of its sound, just as it had when he'd been here with Caroline. Safe and constant, it had guided him with timely patience the night he'd prepared her. He had tried not to think about the blood as he'd cleaned down her face and body. He remembered how her skin had looked so pale, her hair soft and delicate in his fingers, the tease of her lovely curls. He had been surprised by how long her hair was when he'd brushed it out. Plaiting it was very relaxing. Within the rhythm of the clock he'd completed his task, remembering the right positioning. Although her body had become rigid, he fixed her until she was close to perfect.

It had been different after Mother died. He had felt dragged down. At first, he thought it was the tiresome visitors, all that gushy outpouring of sympathy and he having to maintain the pretence of the grieving son. Even the weeks following her death, he had been struck by how much the whole episode had sapped the energy from him. All that time during her illness, despite her frail disposition and restricted movement, she still seemed to be everywhere. Even when she was gone, he could still feel her watching his every move. The walls, the furniture, the creaks within the floorboards, they all reeked of her. He'd burned her walking stick in the fire the night she died, pushed it into the flaming grate as if it were a poker, watching with pleasure as it turned to ash.

He had no expectation of being distraught when she passed, but stupid thoughts came into his head. Within days of her death, he became convinced she was still alive, her and those porcelain dogs of hers, their eyes boring into him no matter which part of her bedroom he stood in.

Walking around the house the night he'd killed her, he had tested everything, checking how they reacted to their new owner. In the downstairs kitchen, he'd lifted the plastic tablecloth from the long wooden table, the one he used to run his toy cars on as a boy. The tablecloth, although changed many times over the years, smelled the same, the stench of old plastic rising, its suction being ripped from the surface. Parts of Cronly became stifling, overpowering. Memories skipped time, as if something that had happened a long time ago had only just occurred. All her talk of Tuscany had precipitated events; his trip to Italy to recapture his fleeting childhood memory of happiness; his accidental meeting with Antonio Peri, in the end, his mother's ultimate damnation. Had it not been for her lapses into the past, he might never have found out the truth, and the thoughts he had laboured under ever since would never have unravelled, making sense of those events from so long ago.

He had displayed a remarkable calmness of spirit through it all. His mother's death, ill for some time, terminal, was no surprise to Dr Matthews. The assumption that she had drifted into a permanent sleep was an easy one to foster. The small spasm her body gave out before the pillow quietened her; a perfect ending and far better than many poor souls suffered. He still remembered the eight Beatitudes: 'Blessed are they who are persecuted for the sake of righteousness, for theirs is the kingdom of heaven.' Yes, in the end, right was done. Another man, a weaker one, might have shirked his responsibilities, but not him. Shirking responsibilities was not something he had ever allowed himself to do.

It hadn't been easy, looking at her afterwards – her dead eyes wide open, her lower lip hanging down, her mouth ugly. To him, mouths said a lot about a person. He had made a study of mouths, and knew the ones to hate: people who spoke with the contents of their lunch a garbled mess on their tongues; old people with wrinkly, sucked up lips, no longer full of lustre; or those wretched women at the street stalls near Newell Design, using their mouths like sirens.

His mother had looked older in death, as if her body had finally been allowed to show its real age. He closed her mouth before the stiffening took hold, along with her eyes, placing a coin on each lid to keep them closed.

Within hours, her remains were removed, taking up residence

at the funeral parlour, safe and sound. He had complimented the undertaker, Hennessy, on how well she looked in the oak coffin with its brass handles. They had both taken such care in choosing it for her.

All of this was necessary to keep up the façade; how one was viewed within one's own community was important. Even now, months later, he could still see her sitting up in the bed, propped by her pillows, giving her the appearance of royalty, ruler of her domain. He had seen many times how she could use her vulnerability, then her fragility, to get attention, but not any more. Like the good looks of her younger days, which had turned men into fools until they tired of her, she was gone, leaving him to forge his new beginnings.

After he had killed Caroline, he'd known he couldn't keep the girl at the big house; the body would spoil. He had only managed to catch the fleeting cherry red of her lips with the Polaroid before they, too, lost their vitality. Catching the shade had pleased him, but the more he'd looked at the photographs, the more different she'd become. She wasn't right – her skin was too pale, her hair lighter than he'd remembered it. There was something about the plaits, too, not finishing in the correct place. And her mouth, the colour of her lips against the cherry of the ribbons, looked maroon, more like the dying berries on the elderberry trees.

He checked his watch again, this time comparing it to the time on the Napoleon clock, both perfect, twenty minutes before eleven. Once he had the fire in the front living room blazing, he dragged in the plastic bag from the garage. It smelled putrid when he untied the string and opened it. The blood-soaked cloth used to wipe Caroline's hair was at the top. Her earrings were already neatly tucked away in the attaché case upstairs – once a magpie, always a magpie. Remembering the ribbon in his pocket, he knew he wanted to spend time upstairs before leaving, but all in good time.

The living room and the garage took longer to clean than he

thought they would; he had forgotten how much blood there had been. The garage was colder than the house, and he'd been forced to put on one of his mother's old furs. When he finally got upstairs, he had barely any time left. It was a spur of the moment decision to take the Polaroid image of Caroline back to Dublin. He would have to keep it at Meadow View and although he wasn't inclined to have visitors there, it irked him a little, never liking to link the past with the present.

By the time the fire in the living room had died down, it was past midday. He was still confident he would be able to make his next couple of social calls, just as he had planned.

Incident Room, Tallaght Garda Station
Sunday, 9 October 2011, 12 noon

AS SHE PULLED OUT FROM JESSICA BARRY'S HOUSE, Kate's phone rang.

'O'Connor.'

'You talked to Jessica Barry?'

'Yeah. Where are you? It might be easier to meet rather than talk on the phone.'

'The Incident Room.'

'Okay, I'll be there shortly.'

On the way to the station, Kate thought about everything Jessica had told her. In one way, it all made sense, but in another it was totally contradictory. The crucifix left with Caroline, the positioning of the bodies, hands joined as if in prayer, even the lengths the killer was prepared to go to bury both girls, all pointed towards a form of protection, crafting how they looked, perhaps an almost spiritual recreation of innocence, something intensely personal to him. The contradiction was that the killer was the persecutor, not the protector.

When Kate entered the station, a young female garda escorted her down to the Incident Room, pushing open the double doors and pointing Kate in the direction of O'Connor's temporary office. Immediately, she got the sense that, even though it had been only four days since the first victim had gone missing, and two days since her body had been found, the room had all the appearance of an investigation that had already run for far too long. She could hear the prioritised calls from the helplines ringing constantly in the background, the hum of computers, printers splurging out information, desks and shelves littered with stained coffee cups. Every person in the room had a frown on his or her face, all looking tired but focused and utterly determined.

When O'Connor spotted her through the glass panels of his makeshift office, he gave her a nod. He looked like a man who wanted information, and wasn't in the mood to wait for it.

'How did your last Incident Room meeting go?' Kate asked him as she took a seat opposite him.

'Not good. Now, fill me in on Jessica.'

'It seems Caroline and this guy got friendly.'

'Friendly?'

'There was more than the interaction at the swimming pool; as we both suspected, Jessica was holding back. They met other times too. According to Jessica, he must be local because he and Caroline kept bumping into each other, but that could have been something he staged. Either way, he befriended her and Caroline looked on him as a kind of teacher, someone she could turn to for support.'

'What else?' O'Connor got up, closing the glass office door behind her and cutting out the noise from the Incident Room.

'He was the one who gave her the crucifix.'

'Jessica is sure of that?' O'Connor sat down again, opposite Kate.

'Absolutely, but that's not all.'

'What?'

'It's what he said to her. He told Caroline it would keep her safe, that the crucifix was a sign of Christ's unconditional love, that through death He wanted to protect the innocent. According to Jessica, he said it was to protect Caroline from people like Innes.'

'Did you ask her why?'

'Why Caroline felt she'd need protection from paedophiles?'

'Yeah.'

'Jessica didn't know. She thought Caroline simply liked the idea of the cross protecting her.'

'And your theory?'

'It's part of the mix. I'm not sure how it fits in yet.'

'Do you think Caroline was being abused?'

'There's no physical evidence to back it up, but that doesn't rule it out either. There is another possibility though.'

'I can't wait to hear it, Kate.' O'Connor leaned back in the chair, hands joined behind his head, the look of intensity never leaving his face.

'Well, the subject obviously came up in conversation, otherwise why would Jessica know about it? But maybe it isn't Caroline's concerns we should be looking at, maybe it's his.'

'You're saying we're dealing with some religious nut with a fear or aversion to paedophiles?'

'Religion is a big part of it.'

'How exactly?'

'Too early to pinpoint, but the symbolism is important to him. The crucifix is a form of religious protection. Then the way he dealt with both girls – the fingers intertwined, the layout of the bodies – maybe he wasn't putting them in the foetal position, maybe he wanted them kneeling. The ribbons, they're different. They aren't religious, but they are equally as important to him.'

'Where do you think they fit in?'

'Could be a memory, something cemented in his mind.'

'So why act now?'

'Something happened, a trigger of some kind. Remember the book we found with Caroline?'

'We can't be sure he gave it to her.'

'I think he did. It fits. The poet's recurring theme around the death of a beautiful woman, the gentle nature of the poem 'Eulalie', all about loss: "Eulalie's most humble and careless curl … her soul shines bright and strong."'

'Talk sense, Kate.' O'Connor, obviously agitated, stood up again, pacing the room, looking out at the team and away from her.

'I *am* talking sense. He's looking for a relationship with them, non-sexual but intimate, a bond, a form of closeness.'

'So why kill them?'

'Put bluntly, they failed him.' She turned around to face him. 'O'Connor, you would make me feel a whole lot more comfortable if you would just sit down.'

'I don't want to sit down.'

'Suit yourself.'

Reluctantly, he sat opposite her again.

Kate continued. 'What did you get on the statements from Amelia's family and friends?'

'Other than physical characteristics and an interest in swimming, Amelia and Caroline seem to be polls apart. Amelia was extremely confident, happy, no underlying weight issues or anything else, quite the extrovert.'

Kate thought for a few seconds before speaking again.

'He's made a progression, O'Connor. Amelia looked right, but wasn't. He got closer to Caroline, believed her more suitable.'

'So when he abducted her, he expected what?'

'Time together, I think, but the girl panicked. He wouldn't have liked that. It explains the frenzied attack, totally at odds with how he killed Amelia.'

'So what's his next move?'

'Depends.'

'On what?'

'Well, on him for a start. He has a pattern, a logic that makes sense to him. But of the two victims, Caroline is the key.'

'Why are you so sure?'

'He gave her elevated status – the choice of location, the crucifix. He wanted it to be perfect.'

'Perfect? Everything is far from fucking perfect. By the way, Nolan's told Rohan to release the stuff about the ribbons and the plaiting to the public; as of now it's live on the public airways.'

'A bit of a risk.'

'We don't have an option. Right. So Kate—'

'I know what you're going to say, O'Connor. You want my next report as of yesterday.'

'You're great at reading minds, I'll give you that. I think it's good that Nolan has released the information on the ribbons and the plaiting. Someone out there knows something. Just because we can't connect the dots doesn't mean someone else can't.'

Cronly Lodge

STEVE HUGHES WAS SURPRISED TO SEE THE OLD CARINA in the drive for the second time in a week. He wondered if the new lord of the manor was planning on calling more frequently. If that was his intention, then he'd better pay one last visit inside; otherwise he might not get another opportunity to look after his unfinished business in there. He was supposed to do the garden maintenance on Tuesdays, but with another job arranged in the town, he'd figured he could get it out of the way early. Still, there was no point in doing it with Cronly there; he didn't want to give him something else to moan about.

Returning a couple of hours later when the coast was clear, Steve wasn't surprised to see the curtains pulled over in all the ground-floor rooms, this being the new owner's way. Cronly had fitted bolts on the inside of the doors downstairs, so entry through the kitchen was a non-runner, but Steve still had his keys to the double locks at the front, compliments of old Mrs Cronly. The old bat was nearly as odd as the son, but she'd been friendly to him over the years. Steve reckoned she had a soft spot for his charm. He heard plenty of stories from Ollie Gilmartin about her, each one better than the last. Apparently, she used to be easy on the eye, and easy with other things as well. Rumour had it that the son was illegitimate, the father a priest who ended up high ranking in the Church.

No doubt at the time it was a right scandal, but Mrs Cronly wasn't a woman to go hiding under a rock. According to Ollie Gilmartin, most reckoned the money came from the Church in the end. The house had been in ruins in the seventies, owned by the bank in all but name. It would have taken a lot to get a debt like that off your back and, according to Mrs Flood, it was when she thought she'd lose the house altogether that she'd packed herself and the boy off to Tuscany with one aim – to get money, any way possible. Whatever the truth behind it all, Mrs Flood told him that after Alison Cronly and her son came back from Italy, money was never a problem again.

Steve knew the son didn't like him, and as far as Steve was concerned, the feeling was mutual. Cronly would have assumed the only key in Steve's possession was for the back kitchen door, which was no doubt the reason he'd put those bolts on and changed the lock. Still, he was insulting his intelligence if he thought a couple of extra locks downstairs would keep him out of the house. Even if he hadn't been given keys by the mother, he'd still have got inside.

The wages due to him for odd jobs and gardening were still being paid into his bank account by the son, but he reckoned that wouldn't last much longer. He wanted to get the rest of the cash hidden in the house before it was too late. Near the end, the mother forgot his money was paid directly into the bank and insisted on paying him all over again. He never refused and, as time went on, she'd become less discreet about where she kept her money – in the sideboard on the landing. There may not have been a whole lot left in there, but whatever there was, Steve figured it was due to him, for all his listening to the old bat in the past.

On reaching the front door, he double checked behind him, conscious that William Cronly wasn't long gone. Relieved when his key still worked, he closed the front door behind him quickly.

Passing the living room on his way to the stairs, his curiosity was aroused when he saw the hot ashes in the fire, some of which had blown out onto the large hearth rug. If there was one thing he knew about William Cronly, it was that he was awful tight when it came to money, and lighting fires in the middle of the day was not something he'd have done unless he had planned to hang around for a while. He was about to go upstairs when he noticed that the ash on the rug looked wet. Kneeling down, he put his hand to it, and discovered that the whole mat was soaked. He looked around more carefully, and it was then that he realised parts of the walls had been washed down too. He thought about checking the garage, to see what cleaning stuff had been used, but then remembered the bolts, and the new lock fitted on the back kitchen door.

His head told him to grab the money and get the hell out of there, but his gut told him Cronly had been up to no good. In the past, when the old bat was asleep, Steve had roamed around the house plenty of times, but he'd never gone into the son's bedroom. Mainly because Cronly gave him the creeps, especially the way he'd crawl around the place. You were never fully sure whether or not the guy was there. He remembered once standing in the kitchen, making himself a cup of tea, when Cronly came right up behind him – nearly killed him with the fright.

Abandoning any further investigation downstairs, he went upstairs to get the last of the money out of the sideboard, deciding that with the house empty there would be no harm having a good last look around.

In a house like Cronly, the place was one nook and cranny after another. He'd been in the mother's bedroom many times, but with this being his last opportunity to check things out, he made up his mind to have a look in at the son's room. He had no idea what to expect, just thought it would be like the rest of the house. In many ways it was, but the thing that struck him most was how much of the stuff looked like it belonged to a kid. There was a painted wooden train set made up in the corner, and to the left of the bed sat stacks of comics. On top of the window seat, a whole bloody toy farm – all the animals set out, like a child had just been playing with them. There were other items on the top of a high wooden dresser: an ornate silver crucifix on a stand, a framed photograph of a man with a husky dog, a folded piece of cream silk cloth, and what looked like an old library book, *A Traveller's Guide to Italy,* to the side, all the items placed like it was some kind of altar, and to the front, on top of the piece of cream silk, a tiny metal key.

It didn't take him long to find the attaché case under the bed, and when he saw the Italian stickers on it, he remembered what Mrs Flood had told him about the family trip to Tuscany. Maybe he could cash in on a whole lot more than the contents of the sideboard. Maybe there was something in this case that might hold the Cronly family secrets. He felt like a kid himself when the tiny key turned in both locks.

At first, the contents of the case were a disappointment. Apart from a Polaroid camera, some spools of ribbons and assorted bits and pieces, there was nothing of value. What finally attracted his attention was a small leather pouch with a tie string, like the kind gold miners might have used to hold nuggets. Pulling open the pouch, he didn't find gold nuggets, just three miniature plastic zip bags, each one containing a lock of hair. He wasn't sure what any of the contents meant, but he reckoned they meant something to William Cronly. Most of the items, including some small earrings, were things you'd expect to see in a girl's suitcase, which made him wonder about the son's sexual predilections – or even perversions. It would certainly explain why the snotty little shit never got married.

He was about to put the suitcase back where he'd found it when he noticed the small crucifix on a chain. It was just a cheap yoke, but under it was a faded pink Polaroid photograph.

WHEN KATE GOT BACK TO MERVIN ROAD, DECLAN and Charlie had made a pretend camp out of bedclothes, with sheets spreading from one couch to the other.

'Come under, Mom, it's cool,' Charlie shouted, his little face red with excitement.

'Is your Dad hiding in there?' Kate tilted her head down and pulled up one of the sheets. Declan crawled out from underneath, looking a bit sheepish. Kate raised her eyebrows in amusement.

'You okay?' she asked

'Let's have coffee, Kate. Charlie, you're now on lookout duty. Let no one pass.'

Declan made two cups of coffee and brought them over to the table in the kitchen, where Kate waited silently until he sat down beside her.

'You didn't get back until late.'

'I needed to clear my head.'

'Want to share your thoughts?' She blew her coffee to cool it down.

'Look, I don't know what exactly, but something is going on here. Things aren't right between us.'

'I know that, Declan. I guess I've known it for a while,' she said, putting her coffee cup down, 'but I just didn't want to admit it.'

Although she didn't know what Declan was thinking, her response seemed to make everything more real. Declan opened his mouth to speak again, but was interrupted by her mobile ringing. She picked it out of her bag and saw O'Connor's name on the screen.

'Let it go, Kate.'

'I'll only be a second. It might be important.'

'And we're not?' Declan looked down into his coffee.

'Of course we are. Look, I'll take this and get it out of the way.'

Kate walked out to the hallway. 'O'Connor?'

'That idiot Gunning has actually got something back from Interpol.'

'What?'

'It's a connection to the crucifix, similar age, but the case is complicated. I have the images here.'

'Can you send them over?'

'You know that stuff is encrypted. You'll have to come back to Tallaght.'

'Now?'

'When would you like to come over, Kate? Yes, bloody now.'

'Okay, okay, I'm on my way.'

Declan had remained seated, waiting for her. He looked up as she walked in and his features, set in a hard line, spoke volumes.

'Don't bother, Kate, I can tell by the look of you you're already on your way out the door.'

'It's just this case, Declan. I can't do anything about it.'

'Wave to your son on your way out,' he replied, his voice cool and unforgiving. 'He's the small guy on lookout.'

SAMUEL WAS LISTENING TO THE RADIO IN HIS KITCHEN, working on a cryptic crossword puzzle he was determined would not get the better of him, when the news reporter on the lunchtime news mentioned the ribbons and the plaiting. He turned the volume up. He had heard about the double murders, of course, who hadn't? But when the newsreader mentioned the red ribbons and the plaiting, he listened more intently.

Was it possible that Ellie Brady had made the whole thing up and he had been taken in by her lies? If she had heard the news bulletins, it would certainly explain why she had decided to come out of her shell all of a sudden. He had not discounted the idea that what she believed she remembered, and what was, in fact, the truth, might be two very different things. Yet if her story was nothing more than a fabrication, then Ellie Brady was some actress. For the first time in a very long time, Samuel felt real anger towards a patient. He'd believed Ellie Brady, had been moved by her story, but right there and then he cared less about her mental condition and more about how he might have been conned, particularly at this late stage in his career.

His next meeting with Ellie wasn't until the following morning. It would give him time to assess this latest development. If Ellie had listened to the coverage on the news, there was another possibility he could not dismiss, one that was easier to accept than believing Ellie had purposely wanted to trick him with a copycat story. He knew only too well that guilt did strange things to people. At this point, it was completely possible that Ellie may not realise that she was making the whole thing up.

KATE'S THOUGHTS WERE ALL OVER THE PLACE AS SHE drove along the roads back to Tallaght Garda Station. She seemed to be doing nothing but apologising lately, particularly to Declan and Charlie. She hated leaving the two of them, especially when the look of disappointment on her son's face equalled the look of annoyance on her husband's. No one was happy. Although Declan probably didn't realise the unhappiness extended to her too.

She retraced her steps from the car park, into the station and back to the Incident Room, this time not waiting to be escorted inside. She was beginning to feel that O'Connor wasn't the only one who needed a temporary office. Everyone looked just as they had done an hour earlier, frenzied and preoccupied, as if time was standing still. She weaved her way through their desks and walked into O'Connor's office.

'What do you have, O'Connor?'

'A missing person case from forty years back. It was reopened five years ago. Skeletal remains of a young girl found buried in the grounds of an old church.'

'Where?'

'Livorno, Tuscany.'

'Do they know who she was?'

'Thirteen-year-old Silvia Vaccaro. The site was owned by the church, but it was subsequently sold to a developer. It was during the excavation that the girl's remains were discovered.'

'Anything more?'

'Yeah. At the time of the girl's disappearance, she was returning from a visit with her uncle, a Bishop Antonio Peri. He lived close to the church grounds. Her parents sent her there in 1972 to spend time with him, mainly because she had aspirations of entering the religious life.'

'A long time back, O'Connor.'

'I know, but what's significant about the case is, firstly, the girl's age, which was similar to that of both our victims, and, secondly, a silver crucifix was buried with her body.' He watched Kate for her reaction.

'Like the one we found with Caroline?'

'Close enough, although Silvia's was the real thing, not some cheap copy. The crucifix was given to Silvia by her parents, both of whom had died before the remains were discovered, but it was one of the first clues to the girl's identification. According to the statements taken from the parents after she went missing, it was supposed to keep her safe while travelling away from home.'

'Any idea how she died?'

'She had multiple fractures, consistent with falling from a height, but the fact that the girl was buried and an attempt was made to keep the body hidden meant someone knew what had happened to her and didn't want anyone else finding out. The Italian police have treated the death as suspicious since the remains were discovered.'

'Do they have any suspects?'

'That's where it gets complicated. The church grounds in Livorno are less than a mile from the uncle's home. The authorities spoke to him. He had moved to Florence not long after the girl's disappearance, but came back to Livorno about a year ago.'

'And?'

'He died a few months back. According to Gunning, and to quote his exact words, "he's a dead-end".'

'Where are the images you mentioned?'

'Here.'

O'Connor turned his computer screen in Kate's direction. The images from the Tuscan burial site formed a boxed pattern across the monitor. Just like both Irish victims, the skeleton remains of Silvia Vaccaro had been photographed from numerous angles. Kate took in everything she saw while O'Connor continued.

'As I said, according to police reports, the fractures were consistent with falling from a height and were the most likely cause of death. What's interesting, though, isn't just the connection you mentioned about the crucifix, but the grave itself.'

'What do you mean?'

'You tell me, Kate. Keep looking.'

She didn't know what O'Connor meant, but Kate kept searching the images. Nothing obvious struck her. It simply looked like a hole with assorted bones in the ground. The remains may have revealed information to a forensic anthropologist, but to the naked eye not so much. It was then she remembered something from the photographs at the first mountain burial site, taken after the remains of Caroline had been removed. The more she studied the images from Tuscany, the more she saw how the stones near the bodies looked similar. At first she had thought they were not unusual, figuring them to be the way stones would naturally form underground, but the more she looked at the remains from Tuscany, the more her eyes were drawn to one particular element. Right at the top end, where the girl's head would have laid, was a large, flat stone. In Caroline's case, Kate had assumed it was too large for the killer to dig out, part of the natural formation, but at the Tuscan grave, a similar large stone was located in the same spot. Her eyes widened as she saw the connection.

'So you see it?' O'Connor asked.

'The large flat stone? It's like the one at Caroline's burial.'

'But this happened forty years ago, Kate. Can it be linked to our cases?'

'If it's connected, our killer must have been a child at the time of this girl's death. If he witnessed it, and that's a big 'if', maybe our victims are some form of copycat burial.'

'Why copy it?'

'I don't know. The bishop, the one the girl went to visit, what do we know about him?'

'There were rumours of him being indiscreet with women, young girls too, nothing concrete, just unsubstantiated accusations.'

'Fits with what Jessica said about the protection from abuse. You said he died?'

'A few months back. And guess what?'

'I can't wait.'

'He fell from a height. It was considered an accident. He'd gone out walking near a dangerous spot. They reckon he slipped.'

'But you don't think so?'

'I don't like coincidences, Kate, never have.'

Kate's mind was racing, trying to make the links that would make sense of all she was seeing and hearing. 'Maybe that was the catalyst.'

'What do you mean?'

'Something has brought our guy out of the woodwork; you said the death of the bishop was only a few months back?'

'March this year.'

'I'd hoped we'd find history, but I never thought it would be as old as this.'

'So what's your opinion on the flat stone?'

'For what it's worth, O'Connor, I think the stone is a pillow.'

'A pillow?' he said, surprised.

'You heard me. Do you have a spare desk I can use? I'll need to work here for a while. Home isn't an option right now.'

'Take that one in the corner,' he said, nodding to the far end of his office. 'Kate, I don't like how this investigation it filtering out. I know clear cut cases are rare, but this one is like a bloody maze.'

'There is a core O'Connor, and our killer is right in the middle of it. All we have to do is figure out where.'

'And bloody fast, Kate. Look at the room out there, once those calls start flooding in about the ribbons, plaiting and talk of ritualistic burials, we'll be so far under we might all as well be buried up in that bloody mountain.'

Meadow View

BACK AT MEADOW VIEW, HIS FORM COULDN'T HAVE BEEN better, having made excellent time returning from Wexford. The stroll from the garage in Terenure had pleased him too – nothing like fresh air to get a better perspective on things. Looking out the kitchen window, he reflected again on how the days were getting shorter. Despite enjoying his outdoor recreational pursuits, a part of him didn't mind the reduction in daylight hours, believing one should always go with the seasons.

He regretted his neglect of reading material over the past few days, something he would put right very shortly. Making himself a cup of Mokalbari tea, he reviewed the books he hadn't yet read and some he planned to read again. Shortly after he moved to Meadow View, he'd arranged for wooden bookshelves to be fitted either side of the fireplace. He liked rearranging the books, placing his new favourites on the top, giving them the status of importance they deserved. To him, books were precious, they were fuel for the imagination. He remembered his summers as a child, reading on the beach, and how in winter, when he needed to avoid his mother's male friends, they were his greatest ally.

If he wanted to, he could convince himself he was one of the characters in whatever novel he was reading, imagining places he had never been. As a boy, he had read comics too, many of which were still in the big house. He was fond of most of the superheroes and even when he progressed to older reading material, he had always kept some old comics at hand.

The year his mother told him about Tuscany, it had sounded like the biggest adventure ever. He plagued her for days with questions: how they would get there, who they would see, why they were going, how long they would stay. She told him very little. All he knew was that they would take the train to Dublin and then fly from Dublin airport; their final destination was a place called Suvereto, in Livorno. He couldn't wait to visit the mobile library at the end of the month, like a scavenger, to read everything he could find on Italy. Although the holiday had come out of the blue, he had embraced the idea of such a wonderful adventure, even if his mother didn't explain why they were going there to begin with. He wasn't to know then that the trip was going to change everything. Even in that second blissful week, he did not have any inkling about how his life would turn out at the end of it.

He remembered the place so clearly: the extreme heat, how his clothes stuck to his body, how the shade was a blessed relief, how the midday sun made the air hard to breathe. There wasn't even a hint of a breeze in those hours between midday and three o'clock, nothing like the winds that flanked the beach at home. The people were different too. At first, he liked listening to them speaking Italian and moving in ways that were so different from people at home – the heat made them move slower, made them happier to stop and sit and spend endless hours seemingly doing very little. At Ciampino airport he had listened to the announcements over the speaker system, the voices sounding strange with their accents and also loud, like people shouting. The airport unsettled him. Almost immediately, he felt people were staring at him, as if he was something odd, something that needed to be worked out. When they looked at his mother, it was different. The women checked her from head to toe, as if she were a mannequin in a shop window; the men smiled, following her movements by turning their heads.

Irrespective of how people looked at them, he had no intention of letting it interfere with the most exciting time of his life. It was his first holiday and the small attaché case he'd carried with him on the train from Gorey to Dublin and on the flight to Rome was filled with comics, books on Italy and the spool of red ribbon he'd taken from the upstairs sideboard. The attaché case felt like his last connection to home, and although home was not where he wanted to be, he kept it close to his chest as he and his mother travelled by train to Livorno, and then on to Suvereto.

Sipping his tea, he thought again about the Italian countryside, and how different it was from the Irish landscape. Although there were vast fields of green, in Tuscany especially, some of the land appeared scorched, and often more rugged than the Irish sunny southeast. The vineyards seemed to run for miles, and you could pass by vast spaces without seeing anyone in the fields. He was amazed by the buildings, both big and small, with their orange rooftops and their precarious positions, stuck into the side of the mountain or valley.

When the train had reached Livorno it was past noon, the worst time for the heat. His mother had displayed more than her usual share of displeasure and annoyance as they'd waited at the station. Whoever had been supposed to meet them was late. Up until that point, she'd been elated by the trip and at some moments had even been kind, as if she cared about him. He had wondered if, like the people, she too would be different outside of Ireland, but still he held back from asking her too much. Soon she'd reverted to blaming him for everything, annoyed when he needed desperately to go to the toilet, complaining about him leaving her alone in a strange country, but eventually she had let him go inside the station.

When he'd returned, she was like a different woman. Even before he'd got to the platform, he'd heard her high-pitched voice sounding excited – the unmistakable way she spoke around men. The man she'd been talking to wasn't like any priest or religious person he'd seen before. His garments, despite the heat of the day, had been intricate and ornate, in vibrant reds and purples, but very much at odds with the large straw hat he was wearing, like the men in the pictures with the gondolas. He'd escorted them to the front of the station, where his car was waiting. When he'd taken off the hat in the car, the man had revealed a fat, bald head, sweating with the remaining strands of his hair. William had disliked him instantly.

He'd kept his silence in the back of the car all the way to Suvereto. The drive had been hot and clammy, with only a small breeze coming in from the windows at the front. He remembered feeling pleased he'd changed his clothes at Ciampino airport, putting on a new white shirt and navy shorts. The only thing that had bothered him was his milk-bottle-white legs, which had looked odd next to the tanned complexion of the man his mother referred to as 'the bishop'. His mother hadn't changed her clothes and was still wearing the heavy ones from home. She had discarded her jacket on the back seat beside him. Little by little she had pulled her skirt up well past her knees, undoing the top buttons of her blouse. Bishop Antonio had reacted the same way most men did. When she placed his hand on her right knee, he left it there. Applying her bright red lipstick, looking into the dusty vanity mirror on the passenger's side, his mother had sat back, satisfied.

He left his memories and turned his mind back to his reading and research, while almost automatically switching on the afternoon news on the radio to keep up with events. The main coverage was still about the murdered girls. There was one difference, however: it was the first time they had mentioned the ribbons or the plaiting. Taking out the Polaroid image of Caroline from his jacket pocket, all he felt now was sadness. The similarities to Silvia were undeniable. His mind began drifting again, thinking about the room with the windows, the heat of the Italian sun beaming through the stained glass. He could still see, in the corner of the room, the rocking horse, its brown mane brought over to one side, swaying back and forth as if the rider had just left the room, the horse carrying on, believing someone was still sitting in the saddle.

THE MORE KATE LOOKED AT THE IMAGES FROM THE Tuscan burial site, the more convinced she became that if the killer was linked to this death forty years ago, either directly or indirectly, he had carried the memory of it with him all his adult life. Something had acted as the catalyst, prompting him to take action now, but the impetus, although important, wasn't the key. The answer lay somewhere between this young Italian girl's death and the death of Caroline Devine, and Amelia Spain, forty years later.

O'Connor, who was talking into his phone, something which had seemed permanently attached to his ear since she'd got there, looked up when she stood in front of him. She waited for him to finish his call.

'What was it you said, O'Connor, about Caroline and Amelia being polls apart?'

'Amelia was extrovert, confident. Other than the swimming and her looks, she was a very different girl from Caroline Devine.'

'So we can deduce that his attraction to Caroline became stronger because of the type of girl she was. Like Amelia, she was athletic. The assailant was physically fit, which makes sense, similar attributes. He was looking for someone not unlike himself. But unlike Amelia, who may have come across as overconfident, Caroline appeared vulnerable and sensitive. She was a listener, wanted to help others, and her appreciation for books could have given her more depth in his eyes.'

'Where's this leading, Kate?'

'Well, if the killings are linked to the Tuscan burial, it means the key to our killer's motivational needs began early, sometime in childhood.'

'So?'

'So we now have a possible third victim, Silvia Vaccaro.'

'You're not saying he killed her too? As you said, he could only have been a child.'

'It doesn't matter right now who killed her, what matters is that if I'm right, irrespective of the catalyst behind his current killing spree, he may well be seeking to turn back time, and Silvia is the key to all of this.'

'Keep going, Kate.'

'We know Caroline was driven, an excellent student according to her mother, ambitious, wanting to prove herself.'

'I'm still not getting you.'

'His progression, O'Connor – all the time, he is looking for the ideal girl. If he is recreating the Tuscan burial, he could well be trying to replace Silvia, or his memory of her – but we must study the victim's behaviour too, it is just as important as studying the killer's. He befriended Amelia, was drawn to her physically, but soon lost interest, her personality was unsuitable. Then there was Caroline; the more he got to know her, the more he studied her, the more emotionally connected to her he became, the more her behaviour convinced him it was the right time to make his move. It was a calculated risk, but one he was prepared to take. When Caroline reacted badly, he would have blamed her because he believed she'd failed him. He had taken risks for her, and she had let him down.'

'It still doesn't answer who will be next.'

'No, it doesn't, but he will move on. Whatever the reason for him crossing the line, he is not going to stop now, but next time he will change things, just like he changed from Amelia to Caroline.'

'Change how?'

'It could be someone older.'

'Older?'

'Well think about it. His selection process is adapting. Initially it was looks and general interests, and then the girl's personality traits became the decision-maker. Things turning out badly with Caroline means he won't make the same mistake again. You have to remember, O'Connor, in this man's eyes everything he is doing makes absolute sense. The girls are failing him, not the other way around. If he's looking for a Silvia replacement, then it would explain the age of both victims, but as you said, he would have been a child himself forty years ago. If Caroline was close to perfect, but her behaviour disappointed him, he could well attribute it to her age and adapt his mindset. None of us can reinvent the past, at least not exactly.'

'So what happens when he chooses his next victim?'

'He may have chosen her already.'

'Why do you say that?'

'He repeats, takes comfort in the familiar. Remember the locations of both girls. He didn't move far. He's a creature of habit, likes to stay within set territories, doesn't want to move far away from home. Jessica may be right about him being local, but he uses a car. Statistically, serial killers with vehicles travel six times as far as those who get to their victims on foot. He's working out of Dublin, but he could be anywhere in that geographical area. The point is, his scope is nevertheless restricted. As I say, he stays close to home. His next victim will already be known to him. She might have slipped under the radar before this, but now his needs are changing, she'll become more important to him.'

'And his selection process?'

'She'll have done something to get his attention, a reason for his admiration.'

'When will he make his move?'

'When he is good and ready, or when he is pushed.'

'What then?'

'Assuming she doesn't play ball, he will lose it. His temper will flare up again, only the next time, his disappointment will be even greater, because next time, he has nowhere else to turn.'

'And?'

'And it will be everyone else's fault except his; he won't internalise blame, he isn't capable of it. The victim, whoever she turns out to be, will suffer, as will anyone unlucky enough to be with her.'

Ollie Gilmartin wasn't the type of man to display excessive emotion, but giving the grass at Beachfield Caravan Park its final cut for the year always pleased him. It was part of his caretaker job, but he never liked doing it; still, whether he liked it or not, it needed to be done. When he did the last cut before winter, he thoroughly enjoyed the satisfaction of knowing it was over and done with for another year.

The weather over the past few days had been dry, so that in itself was a blessing. Not that Ollie cared much about how neat the grass would look at the end of it, but dry grass was a hell of a lot easier to cut than the wet stuff. He had got most of the end-of-season jobs done, even with the stragglers still on site up until the day before. There were always a couple of occupants who insisted on hanging on until the arse end of the season, usually those without kids, the 'DIY enthusiasts' who did their own fair share of battening down the hatches for the winter months.

He had switched off the mains power yesterday, and the water supply, as soon as the last of them had left. It was with a certain kind of satisfaction that he pulled over the large blots on the entrance gates for the end of the season, glad that it was over. After nearly twenty years of working there, he was well used to closing up and looked forward to the colder months. Ollie wasn't a sun or beach lover, which was why his mobile home was located well beneath the trees, ensuring that even on the brightest of days, he was shaded. He had his own private water and electricity supply too. All in all he had managed to set things up at Beachfield to his own liking. His pigeon loft was a little farther out, seeing as the birds needed a clear view of the loft for their return, but the winter was a quiet time for the pigeons. That meant he could treat the cold season as a time for peaceful hibernation, which suited him perfectly.

Being the caretaker of a caravan park didn't pay well, but the place was dry and he could do most things his own way, and in his own good time. Some of the kids could prove to be a nuisance during the summer, but a good roar usually sent the little feckers running. Ollie liked the feeling of being the master of his small kingdom. Throughout the season, nothing happened unless he gave it the okay and, even then, he set about doing his odd jobs in accordance with how the mood took him. He got most of his tips at the height of the season when things were at their busiest, and the size of the tip generally had a positive effect on both his mood and co-operation.

He made his mind up pretty quickly about people. Many of the visitors to Beachfield were regular punters, returning year on year. But all of the visitors quickly learned the fastest way to Ollie's heart was by sending something extra his way. If you were a 'regular' and a 'regular tipper', you earned the privilege of calling him 'Ollie'; if not, you called him Oliver. He knew the ones to mind on site and the ones who were best ignored. They all went through the same vetting process. Before he'd let any of them past the gate, they underwent his specific form of 'welcome meeting'. With the newer ones, he made a special point of chatting as soon as they arrived. He wasn't much of a talker, but it was important to set down your mark, make an impression, and even more important to gauge their worth. There was no point being rude at the beginning, never knowing which ones would turn out to be the better tippers.

His mobile home was positioned at the main entrance gates, giving him a clear view of arrivals, no matter what time of day or night they came. He wasn't happy if they arrived after dark, unless they were a regular tipper, of course. For those who dared to arrive late at night, disturbing him, Ollie wasn't backward about coming forward with his mood. Anyone who arrived after midnight was simply ignored. They could sit there until morning for all he cared. He'd hung a large sign on the front gate: 'No admittance after midnight.' Those who chanced their arms on that one soon found out that Ollie Gilmartin could be a very hard man to deal with.

The outgoing season had been busy. The recession certainly hadn't damaged business, if anything it was the very opposite, with all them jetsetters staying at home. There had been no end of new arrivals once the schools had closed for the summer. As was the case since the beginning of Ollie's reign, everyone who came to the holiday park was taken note of in his Registration Book. Even if you were only a day-tripper, the fact remained that if you walked and breathed at Beachfield Holiday Park, you were put in that large navy register book, whether you liked it or not. Every single visitor had to go into Ollie's mobile home and sign in. If nothing else, the registration system Ollie had in place gave him the additional benefit of letting him know who would be responsible for the tipping. Filling in the registrar was one of the first caretaker jobs that had been explained to him, and it appealed to his sense of being the main man, the one in control.

He had lived alone most of his adult life and now, at the age of sixty-two, he'd gathered belongings the same way he'd gathered people around him – enough to get by, but never any more. Anything of value, other than his secret stash of whiskey, was locked in the old chest he'd bought at auction in Gorey ten years earlier. At the end of his mobile home, he'd removed one of the sofa beds and put in a makeshift desk. On the desk was a cup with a broken handle that held his pens, and a small plastic statue of the Virgin Mary, which sat on top of a black leather Bible, one he'd inherited when he'd taken over. He was fond of having the Bible there, adding an air of authority to his role and influence; he let people jump to their own conclusions about it.

The coming of winter meant the return of poker nights – his only passion after the pigeons. After the clocks went back, he and the lads played every Friday night, spending hours winning and losing their meagre sums of money. There had been the same four players for the past ten years. The only change had been when Jimmy snuffed it two years ago. It wasn't the same with just three of them, which was why they had allowed Steven Hughes to start playing. He had a right mouth on him, Hughes, so as far as Ollie was concerned, he was okay as a poker player, but nothing more.

No, Ollie liked his own company best. Not that it came without a price. He made sure to keep his shotgun handy at night, by the side of the bed. Living alone made you an easy target, if you allowed it to. They had tried to break into his place a few years back, a right pair of hard men they were. But they'd gone running like hyenas by the time he'd finished with them, two shots from his Lanber had sorted them right enough.

He returned to his mobile home after finishing the grass-cutting, and as a reward poured himself a large whiskey. Ollie's mouth salivated at the thought of that first kick of alcohol, the beginning of his peace and quiet for another year. A strong wind was starting to build up outside, but that only made the whiskey taste sweeter.

The last thing he expected to hear was a car horn honking.

'Fuck this,' he said out loud, taking a quick swig from the glass. 'This better be bleeding important.'

Mervin Road

HE STOOD ON THE OPPOSITE SIDE OF THE ROAD, looking across at the house divided into apartments. The yellow door of 34 Mervin Road was bright, the side gate easy to jump, getting into the rear of the building wouldn't be a problem. There was a fire escape fitted, which made things even easier. If it were night-time, he would have to smash the glass on the light sensor on the tree opposite, but that wasn't a problem at this hour. Experience had taught him that what was needed most was speed, and to be able to pick the right moment, to wait until another sound – a neighbour closing a bin, heavy traffic – camouflaged any noise.

He moved quickly and climbed the fire escape. The husband and the child had arrived back from a visit to the shops ten minutes earlier. If Kate came home unexpectedly, he would have to deal with that. The open bedroom window helped things considerably. He was inside in less than a minute. The noise of the television blared from the living room, a football match from the sound of it. The first door in the hallway was locked, so he tried the next one. It was Kate's bedroom, he was sure of it, as neat as a pin. He liked neat people.

When he stepped back out into the hallway, he noticed the door at the very end of the corridor was ajar. He walked down to it without a sound and looked inside.

The child was deep in sleep. Just as well, he thought, considering how loud the father had the television on. Other than the sounds coming from the living room, the place was as good as an empty house. He made his way back down into the bedroom he'd just left and closed the door behind him, placing a chair against the handle to give him ample warning of anyone heading his way.

Having no real expectations about what he was going to find didn't deter him. He had learned over time that the things people kept, and the way they kept them, could give some very interesting insights. The first thing he noticed was a postcard by the bed from Sweetmount Nursing Home. It was addressed to Kate Pearson, and had a very nice message from staff at the home. They wanted to thank her for the beautiful flowers she had brought on her last visit. Four of them had signed their names at the back. The picture on the front was of a very fine-looking building. In small letters on the bottom right of the card was the address of the nursing home, in Greystones. He put it into his jacket pocket.

The bedroom was divided between male and female things: wardrobe space, bedside lockers, everything, including the under-sink cabinet in the en-suite, had a separate section for the joint occupiers of the room. The upper shelves in the wardrobes had the more interesting items, such as photo albums, jewellery, odd bags, various books and magazines. Ms Pearson had an intelligent selection of reading material, another pleasant surprise, especially when he saw her small green copy of *Palgrave's Golden Treasury*. It was dated 1931 and had been a present from her late father: 'To Kate, with love always, Dad.' It had all the classics, Shakespeare, Wordsworth, Keats, but no Blake, something that always annoyed him, such a shame that he had been left out.

Pulling open the drawer in the dressing table, he found it jammed with papers and other smaller items. Instinctively, he was intrigued. When things were jam-packed in that manner, it was generally a good sign that something of value might be found. His instincts didn't let him down. The drawer was full of the usual mishmash of personal items, such as old cheque book stubs, prescriptions, letters, receipts, loose photographs. He noted the random manner of the drawer's contents and put his first black mark against Kate. He examined each item in detail, having found in the past that if you rushed this type of thing, you could miss something important. His patience paid off when his search turned up an item that exceeded even his expectations.

At first, he wasn't sure what the contents of the A4 brown envelope were. It was addressed to Kate's mother, Gabriel Pearson. The report inside was very thorough and, judging by the date, it was completed when Kate was quite young. He knew that psychological assessments of children were not an uncommon occurrence; one of his clients from Newell Design, an ex-principal, had said they were now ten a penny.

This was different, though. The report on Kate Pearson had been done over twenty years before, which would have been unusual enough for the time. She did come from an educated family of course, a privileged family, but still, he felt this discovery might turn out to be extremely relevant. Closer examination of the report didn't reveal the usual suspects his ex-principal friend had alluded to, dyslexia, dyspraxia, ADD. Certainly, Kate's intelligence was not in any doubt. She had received a rating in the 99 percentile, meaning she was top amongst her peers, a fact that increased his admiration for her. According to the report, what Ms Pearson suffered from was something the child psychologist referred to as a thin psychological skin. It would seem the younger Kate had extreme sensitivity to the ways others dealt with her; he could relate to this sort of sensitivity. An incident had occurred when she had been twelve, an attack while out with her friends. The girl had got away unharmed, but the event had left its scars nonetheless. It was noted that her mother had found the event difficult to cope with as well, a factor that the report concluded added to the girl's feelings of being vulnerable. Other than a series of exercises to help Kate gain back her confidence, there seemed to be little else mentioned as a way of moving forward.

To William, it was obvious that the principal problem was her mother. He could see immediately that, like him, Kate had suffered from a lack of attention. Oh yes, he knew her mother's type, full of her own importance. Although ill-equipped to cope at that tender age, Kate had managed her survival alone.

As the envelope was addressed to Kate's mother, more than likely it had only come into Kate's possession after her mother began to reside at Sweetmount Nursing Home.

A further search through the drawer brought very little else by way of value, apart from a small pearl earring, missing its match. This he put in his pocket along with the postcard, as a token from his visit.

When he went back out into the hall, he noticed the travel suitcase by the front door. Maybe the husband was planning a small trip away. The door from the living room was still ajar, but the man inside stared straight at the square box, oblivious.

He went back up the corridor again and pushed open the door of the child's bedroom. This time, he slipped inside the room. An afternoon nap was good for a boy. The child looked happy asleep, not likely to waken any time soon, so he set about familiarising himself with the contents of the boy's room. There were a couple of Superman and Batman comic books, which naturally grabbed his attention, and a painting of what looked like Batman, no doubt done by the child. A book on the locker told the story of a missing bear – perhaps the reason why the child was holding his teddy bear so tightly.

Turning his attention to the sleeping boy, he stood over the bed, gazing down at him, like a large shadow. The boy looked so vulnerable, so alone. He bent down close to him and gently worked the teddy bear free of his arms. He watched as the boy turned into his pillow, as if trying to locate the missing bear in his sleep. He smiled, and dropped the toy to the floor, kicking it far enough away to ensure it was out of the child's reach.

As things turned out, he had calculated his visit perfectly. Not long after climbing back onto the fire escape, he heard the front gate opening, then Kate calling out a hello as she opened the front door. It all felt like it was meant to be.

O'CONNOR HEARD NOLAN ARRIVE BEFORE HE SAW HIM, his voice bellowing through the Incident Room, addressing Donoghue first before marching in to see him. The next full squad meeting was set for 4.00 p.m., but it was customary for Nolan to arrive early. Out of habit, O'Connor fixed his tie and removed the empty coffee cups from the desk. When Nolan flung open the door, without knocking, he was sitting tall, with a straight back, ready.

'I hear Gunning's got a lead from Tuscany.'

'Young female, similar age, suspicious death, a silver crucifix buried with her, plus—'

'Plus what?' He sat down heavily opposite O'Connor.

'There was a flat stone present at the head of the burial area, not unlike what we found at the first Dublin burial. Kate Pearson thinks it could be significant, but the death happened forty years ago.'

'I see.'

'It could be nothing, Boss.'

'I know that, but you think it's something?'

'Yeah, I do.'

'I want Gunning to go over there. He can shake information out of people like a KGB agent, nothing like being in a place to get a proper grip on things. Mulcahy's in charge of the purse strings, but cutbacks or no cutbacks, if a trip abroad is necessary, I'll turn him on his head myself and shake the money out of him.'

'Right, I'll organise it.' O'Connor waited. Nolan looked far too comfortable in the chair to be finished yet.

'We're setting up a reconstruction for broadcast tomorrow, last movements of the girls and all that. The public need to feel we are active on this one, O'Connor.'

'We *are* active.'

'There's one thing being active, there's another thing the public believing it. Anyway, it's a good idea at this point. We have the photofit, albeit limited, a car, year and model. It may not be connected, but we'll put it out there. The information about the plaiting and the ribbons is now public. We'll push the swimming connection too. The public seeing the girl's last movements might spur something. If someone has information, guilt has a habit of opening people up.'

'What about the crucifix?'

'We'll include it, but keep the Tuscan thing to ourselves for now – too vague, no point feeding those international journalists extra lines when we have enough trouble with our own lot. I'll get Rohan to put something in the next press briefing, along the lines that it may or may not be significant – that right now, we're not ruling anything out.'

Nolan looked up at the wall clock behind O'Connor's desk.

'Right, I'll see you outside in five. Do you want to tell Gunning about his little trip, or will I?'

'That's up to you, Boss.'

'I'll send him in to you so.'

'There's one other thing.'

'What's that, O'Connor?'

'Kate thinks our killer could decide on someone older next time.'

Nolan raised an eyebrow. 'Great. Why is there nothing about this case that ever sounds like good news?'

OLLIE PULLED BACK THE CURTAINS ON HIS MOBILE home like he was taking a swing at them, and damned the man to hell when he realised it was Steve Hughes who was making all the racket with his car horn. They weren't even due to play poker. He dropped the curtain again and looked around. No matter what brought Steve to his door, Ollie wasn't of the mind to be sharing any of his best bottles of whiskey with the man. By the time he opened the door of the mobile to let Hughes in, he'd safely hidden it away.

'Some afternoon, Ollie, what?' Steve Hughes rubbed his hands together to get a bit of warmth.

'What the hell are you at, frightening the life out of man, jumping on that bleeding horn of yours?'

'Not feeling too sociable are we, Ollie?'

'Less of your smart mouth. I'm not in the mood for visitors. Most decent folk would be of the mind to leave a man alone when he wants some peace.'

'It's just as well I'm not decent, isn't it then?' Hughes joked.

'You said it, not me.'

Steve looked over at Ollie's whiskey glass. 'Any of that whiskey left? I could do with something to calm my nerves.'

'There's an end of a bottle over there by the sink. Go easy on it, mind, it's the last drop I have.'

'Sure, I can bring you back one tomorrow.'

'Right so. Go on then, if you are going to replace it with a full bottle.'

Steve poured what was left of the cheap whiskey into a glass drying by the sink. He took two large gulps out of it before sitting down opposite Ollie on one of the sofa beds.

'Yer man's been down again.'

'Who?'

'Who do you think, the fucking king himself.'

'Well, it's his house.'

'You don't have to tell me that, Ollie. Cronly made that only too clear the last time we had the pleasure of each other's company. Put more bolts on, so he did.'

'Probably down getting it ready so he can put it up for sale. I heard he'd called into Moriarty Auctioneers in the village not long back. The man couldn't wait to high-tail out of there after the old one died. He's barely been down since.'

'Made a couple of house calls lately, though.'

'As I said, Steve, it's his house.'

'He's been doing a bit of spring cleaning too.'

Ollie's ears caught the inflection in Hughes' voice and he was interested, in spite of himself. 'Spring cleaning?'

'Yeah, he had his cleaning stuff out all right. The place stunk to high heaven of bleach everywhere. Didn't pay much mind to it at the start, but then I noticed how he'd taken to washing the carpet in the living room, even some of the walls. You could tell right away they'd been given the once over.'

Ollie wasn't going to enter any conspiracy contest with Steve Hughes. 'So what? Nothing wrong with a man giving the place a bit of a tidy up.'

'That's what I thought, and sure I know well how he is always tidying stuff up and all. But it was a bit fishy, all the same.'

'What do you mean, "fishy"?'

'Well, like, there were bits that got attention and other bits that didn't.'

'You're not making any sense, man, what the hell are you on about?'

'I'm just saying, it wasn't like the way he'd normally go about things, you know, doing one thing at a time. Like you'd have thought he'd have cleaned the whole carpet.'

Ollie felt his head starting to throb. He'd already had enough of Hughes' voice and everything else about the man. 'Hughes, don't you go drinking any more of that whiskey, cause as it is, I can't make any sense out of what you're saying.'

'The carpet in the living room, there was some of it cleaned and some of it not. Why would he have done that now, tell me that?'

'I don't know. Maybe the man spilled something, for God's sake. It seems to me like you are making a whole lot of something out of nothing.'

'That might be right, but I haven't told you the best bit.'

'And what would that be?' Ollie said wearily.

'When I went upstairs—'

'Hold on a minute, what were you doing in the house in the first place?'

'I'd forgotten something, needed to get my hands on it before yer man did.'

'I'd call that breaking and entering.'

'I'd call it getting what was rightfully owed to you.'

'Get on with it, I'm listening.'

'Well, when I went upstairs, my curiosity got the better of me.'

'That's not like you at all,' Ollie said sarcastically.

'Less of that, Ollie. People in glass houses and all.'

'It's my whiskey you're drinking, which gives me rights. Keep talking.'

'When I got upstairs, right, I started to wonder what yer man's bedroom was like. It wasn't a room that ever had the door open, even when the mother was alive. I was a bit reluctant at first, like he might have been watching me somehow, but I went in and I couldn't believe what I saw.'

'What?'

'The room hadn't changed from when he was a boy. I mean, everything in it was like something a kid would have, comics, trains, toy cars, nothing but that kind of shit. Oh yeah and on a tall dresser, the guy had a huge silver crucifix, on a stand and all.'

'Nothing wrong with a bit of religion, plus maybe he's someone who likes to keep things, some people can be sentimental.'

'More like fucking mental, if you ask me.'

'Well anyhow, you were there in the room with his majesty's toys …'

'Yeah, and it was then that I saw the case.'

'The case?'

'Yeah, under the bed. It was one of those old yokes, you know, with the locks that snap.'

'An attaché case?'

'Whatever. Anyhow, I pulled it out and opened the thing up.'

'And?'

'And that's when I got the biggest surprise of all.'

Ollie kept his face neutral, but he felt like rattling Hughes to get him to spit it out. He clenched his fists and kept his eyes on Hughes, eager now to know what Cronly could have hidden away in his room.

Hughes leaned forward and took great delight in drawing out the story. 'The case, it was filled with all girls' stuff. You know, ribbons, earrings, even a small chain, all that kind of shit.'

'So maybe it belonged to someone else?'

'Who the fuck else would put that kind of stuff under yer man's bed?'

'I don't know, nothing as queer as folk, as they say.'

'Exactly, you've put your finger on what I was thinking. I reckon yer man's a fag. The kind that likes to dress up as well.'

Ollie sighed deeply. 'So you came all the way over here to disturb me just to tell me that? I don't give a flying feck if the man is gay. I couldn't care less.'

'Nah, you haven't heard everything.'

'Jaysus, Hughes, less of the bleeding drip feed, will you.'

'Stop interrupting me then.'

'Oh I see, the man drinks my whiskey and I can't even talk. Is that it?'

'Shut up, Ollie, I'm trying to tell you about the photo.'

'The photo?'

'Yeah. And do you know who was in the photo?'

'Obviously I haven't a fecking clue,' Ollie said through gritted teeth.

'Well I'm not one hundred per cent sure, which is why I came over here with it.'

'You took it with you? You stole it out of his house?'

'I can bring it back as easy as I took it away.'

'Christ, Hughes, you don't make things easy for yourself. Go on, so, give me a look at it.'

Ollie had one long look at the image. Even though it was faded, he had no doubt who was in the photograph. There were some faces you couldn't forget.

'Well, is it who I think it is?' Hughes asked eagerly. 'That girl who got burned in the fire here?'

'You might well be right there, Steve, but it's a long time ago. I reckon the best thing you can do is put that photograph right back where you found it, and fast. You don't want yer man on your case about breaking and entering now do you?'

'Yeah, I know all that crap. But why do you think he has a photo of a dead girl? It's weird, isn't it?'

'She isn't dead in the photograph. Maybe he just came across it, maybe there's any number of explanations. But either way it's not your property, so there's no call for you to be taking up my hospitality.'

Steve kept staring at the Polaroid. 'I think it's fishy.'

'Yeah, I heard you the first time.'

'Come on, Ollie. You must have a theory. Why do you think he has it?'

There was no way Ollie Gilmartin was going to sit and discuss the dead girl with the likes of Steve Hughes. He wanted him gone so he could think this through. 'It beats the hell out of me, Hughes, but it's none of our business. Now off home with ya, while I have some patience left.'

Meadow View

HE HAD ALMOST FORGOTTEN ABOUT THE PEARL earring he'd taken from Kate's bedroom until he noticed it on the hall table. The postcard was still safe inside his jacket pocket, but in his excitement he'd omitted to put away his small treasure. On impulse, he put it back in his pocket, beside the card. He headed out into the late afternoon feeling more upbeat than ever. His mind returned to Kate's house and the packed suitcase, which he felt sure belonged to the husband. Did it represent an opportunity he should act upon?

Things couldn't have turned out better with his little trip earlier that day. A tiny bit of luck and good planning could generate extraordinarily wonderful results. The more he thought about Kate Pearson, the more he realised how interesting she was. They had so much in common – intelligence, integrity and, of course, a less than appreciative mother. He had believed Kate to be an adversary initially, but the more he learned about her, the more he liked her. She had suffered as a child for sure. The attack, no matter what that report suggested, must have affected her. She would have had to overcome enormous difficulties to patch her life back together afterwards – something only those who have truly suffered could understand. Kate's mother hadn't had the sensitivities required to be a good parent, demonstrating the sort of character traits that are very disabling for a child. It would seem Kate had managed to withstand some very difficult beginnings, not an easy thing for anyone to do, and certainly admirable.

He realised now that visiting the nursing home in Greystones was essential. He needed to know if Kate was worthy of further attention. There was no better way to study a person than by getting close to their family. Taking a few days off work made everything much easier. He was glad he'd texted Bulldog Face. There would be no questions asked on his return. It would be just like his leave of absence. His boss had simply looked at him uncomfortably when he'd told him he needed time off due to personal circumstances. The fool hadn't asked one question, not even when he told him about his ailing mother, and he would be exactly the same about his sudden sick leave.

The more he thought about it, the happier he was that Kate was looking after things. It was strange the way certain things turned out. It was her role to put together a profile of the killer, which in this case meant she was studying him as closely as he was studying her. There was a delicious mutuality in their situation that pleased him.

As he walked to the garage in Terenure, he wondered what she would think if she knew just how clever Mr Invisible had been. A trip to her mother was precisely the next course of action. Also, older people do so love their visitors. Indeed, the more he considered the task in hand, the more he was determined to relish every moment of it.

≈

He arrived at Sweetmount at 4.15 p.m. with a box of chocolates under his arm and a large bunch of white lilies, which had been his own mother's favourite. If he were the kind of man who whistled, he would have done so, but he decided a dignified entrance was best on this occasion. He turned the handle gently on the front door, unsure if it would grant him access, but to his delight it was open, so he walked straight into the hallway.

The home looked exactly as he had expected it to look. There were mismatched chairs with old women sitting in small scatterings around the room. Most of them looked up and smiled at him the way they would smile at any other visitor. He waited with his chocolates and flowers, knowing someone in authority would soon arrive. He wasn't disappointed.

'Hello,' said a woman with a voice sounding like she'd overdosed on an extra portion of cheeriness.

'Oh hello,' he replied as cheerily as the greeting he'd received.

'Mr ...'

'William, please.'

The woman with the excess of cheer put her hand out to shake his.

'William, it's very nice to meet you.'

'And you, I assume, must be Joan?'

'Well yes.'

'Kate has told me so much about you, and all the other girls. These are for them.'

Relieved to get rid of the chocolates, he offered them to the well-endowed chest of Joan Keegan, knowing full well she was delighted at being referred to as a girl.

'Why thank you, William, they'll be delighted.'

'Kate has nothing but praise for you, and indeed Niamh, Ali and Caitriona. We are all most grateful.'

'She's very kind. Are you related to Kate, William?'

'I'm an old family friend. My apologies, Joan, I know so much about you, I forget that you know so little about me.'

'So you're here to visit Gabriel?'

'Yes, if that's okay. I wanted to surprise her, you see, and again, I apologise, I probably should have given some notice.'

'Well it's outside normal visiting times, but we're easy about these things here. We want our ladies to feel they are in a "home away from home".'

'I'm sure they do. Kate couldn't speak more highly of the place.'

'Again, she's most generous. William, has it been long since you've seen Gabriel?'

'Yes, a couple of years. I was away working, you see, just back in Ireland a little over a month.'

'You picked a bad time to come back here. The place is in an awful mess.'

'Yes, I know, dreadful altogether.'

'You know about Gabriel's condition then?'

'You mean about her being a little forgetful?'

'Well, I'm afraid it's more than being a little forgetful. I'm sure Kate has told you that Gabriel is in the advanced stages of Alzheimer's. It's a very disabling disease and such a tragedy for a woman as young as Gabriel.'

'Indeed, it's extremely tragic. My own mother suffered from it, you know. I minded her myself in her later years.'

Joan smiled delightedly at this shining example of a good son. 'Then Gabriel will be in safe hands. I'll leave these in the kitchen for the girls and get her for you. Unfortunately, we need to keep Gabriel in the more restricted area of the nursing home because of her condition, I'm sure you understand. She's in great form today, what with the bit of sunshine outside, she loves a little bit of sunshine. I'm sure she'll be absolutely delighted to see you.'

'Thank you, Joan. I'll wait here, shall I?'

'Certainly. Kathleen there will keep you company. She loves to chat, don't you, Kathleen?'

As he waited for Joan to come back, he took his seat beside Kathleen, who indeed was very keen on a chat. He was very pleased with how things were turning out. It had been so easy, looking up the nursing home online. The website had lots of helpful details, including a picture of Joan Keegan, the proprietor. He noted she'd gained a few pounds and a few years since her web photo had been taken. Joan had only written her first name on the postcard, as had Niamh, Ali and Caitriona. The prescription receipts stuffed in the back of the dressing table drawer might not have meant anything to most people, but the medication was something he had given to his own mother. The more he thought about Kate and all the things they had in common, the more he realised his worries about how badly things had gone with Caroline and Amelia were ill-founded. Had it not been for them, he and Kate Pearson might never have met. Really, he couldn't deny that everything was falling into place as part of a delightful pattern.

As he waited, Kathleen told him all about the nursing home – what time they had dinner, how to get to the gardens out back. She even introduced him to the other ladies who sat in the large hallway. They all liked sitting there because of the open fire, Kathleen told him; she herself just loved open fires. He was extremely attentive. By the time Joan Keegan wheeled Gabriel Pearson out to greet him, he knew more than enough about Sweetmount Nursing Home, and the lovely ladies in it.

The first thing he noticed about Gabriel, as her wheelchair moved closer to him, was the way her mouth hung open, her lower lip dry, incapable of joining the upper one any more. It must be disgusting to watch her eat. No doubt she would have to be aided. His mother had been like that for a while, after one of her turns, the food continually collapsing out of her mouth like a sloppy child.

'Lovely to see you, Gabriel. You look absolutely splendid.'

'Look, Gabriel, William is here to visit you, and he's brought you such beautiful flowers.'

Gabriel attempted a smile at both William and Joan, taking the lilies, smelling them automatically. When she looked up at him, she kept pushing her hair behind her ear, a form of repeat comfort, thanking him over and over. The woman had good manners at least.

It must have been difficult for Kate lately, what with the boy and all, both of them being such a draw on her attention. A sickly parent with a selfish disposition could wear a person down. He understood this more than most.

Two cups of tea later, and Gabriel was very happy to allow him to take her for a visit to the back garden. He knew exactly where to go. Kathleen had been very precise: a small area around the back that gave lots of sun and was away from the noise of traffic. It was like being in a secret garden, Kathleen had told him.

He asked Joan for a blanket to keep out the October chill, insisting loudly that Gabriel must be wrapped up well before venturing out. Caitriona had been most obliging, running upstairs to fetch one. A number of the ladies gave them a wave as they departed for the garden.

'It's lovely out here, is it not, Gabriel?'

'I love gardens.'

'I know you do. Most of the flowering is gone now though. Shall we explore the secret garden at the back?'

'Secret garden? I don't know any secret garden.'

'Well, it's a secret, isn't it?'

Attempting to turn her head backwards to look up at him, she said, 'I don't think I know you.'

'I'm William, Gabriel. Forgetful are we?'

'I don't think I know you.'

'You will, Gabriel, you will.'

'I want to go back. I'm cold. Take me back,' her voice was loud but hoarse.

'Don't get angry, Gabriel. It isn't ladylike.'

'I want to go back. Nurse, nurse.' Her voice sounding pathetically weaker.

'They can't hear you, Gabriel. Look, we are here now. I'll put the brakes on the wheelchair and sit beside you. Plenty of room on the bench now we're alone.'

'I want to go back, do you hear me? I want to go back. My daughter—'

'Kate?'

'Kate, yes Kate.'

'Kate and I are very close, Gabriel. She's a little busy right now.'

He looked round to check that they were indeed out of view from any of the windows. He smiled to himself. Good old Kathleen had been spot on about this place.

'Shall I move your blanket up, Gabriel? You said you were cold.'

'Can I go back? Please, I don't want to be here.'

'But you love gardens.'

'Who are you? I don't think I know you. My daughter will be worried. My daughter …'

'You put a strain on her, you know. Kate finds it very tough right now.'

'I don't mean to be a bother.'

'Maybe not, Gabriel, but you are.'

'Did she say that?'

'She didn't have to.'

'I just want to go back inside. Can I go back?'

'Shush now, no need to get upset. I need time to think a little. Why don't you go for a nap like a good girl?'

'I don't want to. I want to go back.'

'It's not all about what you want, Gabriel. Close your eyes, that's the girl. Everything is going to be just fine.'

He noticed saliva dripping down one side of her mouth, just like his own mother. It wasn't fair, she was being a selfish bitch. The woman was blind to what she was doing to poor Kate. Standing behind the wheelchair, he moved his fingers through her thin hair, the pink of her grained scalp more obvious now. She hadn't expected him to yank her by it, there was barely enough for him to get a decent hold.

'Ahhh, you're hurting me.'

'It's supposed to hurt, Gabriel.'

'Please, please. I don't know who you are. Please take me back.'

'Now, now, Gabriel. Not so loud. Nobody can hear you here, so less snivelling, please. It's not very ladylike, now, is it?'

Putting his hand over her mouth, he listened as the trees swayed, the breeze getting stronger all the time. In the distance, he heard the hum of traffic and within it, the faint sound of the birds.

'You are a disappointment, Gabriel, a distraction for Kate. You understand that, don't you? I need to take care of you. While you're here, she can't be free. She doesn't know it, of course. Just like Kate, I had to mind my mother. But was she grateful? It took me a while to understand just how selfish she was. Are you listening to me, Gabriel?'

He took his hand away from her mouth.

'Please, I don't know who you are. I want to go back. I'm cold, I need to go back.'

'Cold, are you? Thinking of yourself again? It's always about you, isn't it? It's not right. Yes, my mother was the same, utterly selfish. You only know these things afterwards, of course. Afterwards, everything becomes much clearer. Are you still listening, Gabriel?'

He leaned in closer.

'What's that, Gabriel? Not so melodramatic now, are we? Dear, dear, muttering is terribly rude.'

'I want to go home … please. I don't know you. I'm cold. I want to go inside.'

'A little patience, Gabriel, I need to contemplate our next move.'

It would be easy to close his hands tight around her neck and snap it. Shut her up once and for all. Some might think it a relief. But how would Kate feel? Would it distract her? The beginning of a relationship was tricky. She had only just begun her work in understanding him. One wrong move and he could ruin everything. No, he decided on reflection, now wasn't the right time. There was no need to rush. Gabriel wasn't going anywhere.

Tidying her hair, he pulled her blanket further up over her knees, listened to her mumbling her prayers, soothed her by rubbing her forehead until she dozed off.

He didn't hear Caitriona coming around the corner. 'Gabriel, it's time for your tea. We can't keep the other ladies waiting.'

'What perfect timing, Caitriona,' he gave her one of his biggest smiles. 'Gabriel must be famished by now with all this fresh air.'

He had no doubt Gabriel would forget about him by the time she was back inside. She barely even turned to watch him walk away. Alzheimer's was such a convenient disease in so many ways.

Ellie

I WON'T SEE DR EBBS UNTIL TOMORROW. EVER SINCE I made up my mind to ask him for Amy's photograph, time seems to be turning more slowly.

By late afternoon, most of the weekend visitors have gone and all the weekend's top television programmes, recorded since Friday night, are being rerun in Living Room 2. The days of the week don't matter to me, but to others, those who are lucky or unlucky enough to have visitors, they are very important. Even when I was a normal person I never liked Sundays, and I've had no reason to change my feeling towards them now. All I care about is that when I see Dr Ebbs, I will get a piece of Amy back.

There are the usual suspects gathered for our afternoon TV viewing. The 'inmates' of our wing are all women. There's Lizzie, a chain smoker. She sits in the corner, in her 'special place', for lighting up. It's been five years since the smoking ban, but they still put her there. Underneath her chair is a decade of burned tobacco stains. Like me, she is a long-term patient. So too is Emily. Emily tells everyone she suffers with her nerves, whatever that means. Unlike Lizzie and me, she still gets visitors, mainly her son. According to Emily, he owns St Michael's and she believes it's very good of him to allow us lunatics to stay here. Then there is Margaret. She and I have something in common: she too has tried to kill herself. She doesn't believe anyone loves her. Her family tell her they do, but she doesn't believe them.

The *Late Late Show* is on Friday nights, but most of us see it on

Sunday. I'm not a fan of the programme. Mary loves it. On Fridays she says, 'Fridays wouldn't be Fridays without the *Late Late Show*.' When she gets to see it all over again, she says, 'Great. Sundays wouldn't be Sundays without the *Late Late Show*.' Mary has been here longer than any of us; she came in when she was eighteen. A man did badly by her, got her put away because she was 'trouble'. According to Mary, that was a lie because 'my mother, God rest her, brought me up proper'. Mary is fifty, which means she has been here for thirty-two years. That's a long time. Most people think Mary is slow, soft in the head and kind of stupid with it. I don't see it that way. I just think of her as different.

I've no interest in any of the programmes really, but I usually sit with them on Sunday. I hate the day either way, so I might as well pass the time somehow. I want the time to go faster now, so that I'm with Dr Ebbs sooner. We settle ourselves in armchairs and the theme tune blares out, making Mary very happy.

The first item is about the murder of the young girl. I've heard about it on the radio. Since Friday, they say another girl has been found. As part of the segment, they are showing pictures of children murdered over the past twenty years. They do this whenever there's a news story about bad things happening to children. I often think about the other families, wonder if, like me, they hate it too, seeing the frozen images put out for public consumption over and over. I'm not surprised to see Amy's picture nor am I surprised when no one looks at me. Either they've forgotten the reason I'm here or they're new and don't know my story. Perhaps no one cares any more.

The discussion is about whether society has become more dangerous for our children. Lots of people want to speak. The show is having what they call a heated debate. This type of thing pumps up the viewer ratings, so it happens often. Mary is transfixed by the screen. I've stopped listening to their arguments. After a time, it all becomes nothing more than a mishmash of words. Fear gets people upset, but despite their heated debate, none of them thinks anything like that will ever happen to them.

When Dr Ebbs asked me what it was that I was afraid of, I told him it was change. Change upsets the routine, the cocoon I've created for myself. Is that cheating? If I'm being honest, if the only reason I exist is because death would be too easy an option, then I shouldn't take the protected path.

Like those people on the television, I'm afraid, but I'm afraid of different things. In here, physically I'm safe. I can live out my protected existence, continuing my life of nothingness. But I can never escape from me. I can't go back and change all the things I want to change. No matter how long I'm on this earth, nothing will ever undo what has happened; nothing will ever bring her back.

Seeing Amy's picture on the television reminds me again that I will ask Dr Ebbs for her photograph. It's a big step, and I fear perhaps I'm starting to forgive myself. There can never be any talk of that. I just want to look at her before I go to sleep. I think Dr Ebbs believes in me and, for some reason, that means something. Maybe Bridget is right, maybe the good doctor is just that: good.

It's only when the programme shows images of the first young girl murdered that I take a closer look. She is wearing her school uniform. She looks so young, so full of life. Maybe that's why I'm thinking the way I am, because when I look at the girl, it's as if I'm seeing a different version of Amy staring back at me. As they continue the debate, they leave the image up on the screen, so I have plenty of time to make my own comparisons. The more I look at the image, the more I wonder if I've gone completely mad, because the longer the picture is up there, the more convinced I am that I am right.

If I were to ask someone a question about the murdered girls, one of the nurses, say, they wouldn't like it. They would think I had a sick mind. Not that they don't think that already, but even so, considering my history, a question from me about murdered girls would be taken badly. Bridget is my best hope, but that means waiting until the morning. I can ask her about both girls then, find out what she knows. It wouldn't be a good idea to say anything to anyone else now. There is no point. I'll just sit here and go to my room when I'm allowed.

≈

Back in my room, I pace the floor. I don't have a large room, so I don't have far to go, back and forth. I wonder if my curiosity about the girls is a good or a bad sign. Why do I care? After all, they aren't Amy. It's daft thinking this way. What can I possibly achieve by finding out more about them? Did I imagine the similarities in the first girl's looks? Is it of any importance? Maybe I'm trying to bring Amy back. Maybe I want to relive all of it again so that, somehow, it will make sense.

Ever since I made the decision to ask Dr Ebbs for the photograph, I've started to think and feel things I haven't thought or felt for a very long time. To a great many people, the photograph of Amy would have been something I should have asked for from the beginning. But for me, asking for it, even now, feels undeserving. Feeling undeserving is something I'm well used to, but what I'm not used to is how my heart and my head feel. It's as if they're opening up in ways I've long since forgotten. All the remembering, thinking back about Joe and Amy, and Andrew, it's forced me to think about the person I used to be. I know I can never be her again. I wouldn't want to be. She's a stranger, a woman no longer of relevance. Or maybe I'm wrong. Maybe that woman is what this is all about. Maybe all these years I've fooled myself into thinking my punishment was to live out this nothing existence, when really it should have been about facing that woman again, my old self, and really looking at who she was and why, other than self-punishment, she should still be here.

I don't understand any of it clearly, but somewhere inside of me something is shifting, like an enormous tidal wave moving inland, slow, quiet, but devastatingly forceful. Before the fire, like most other people, I thought I understood death. That having lost others – parents, grandparents, friends – I had an insight into it. I was wrong. That kind of grieving tells you nothing about losing a child, because the loss of your child isn't like anything else.

When I think about the murdered girls, I think about how their parents are feeling, the hell they must be going through. Nothing will ever bring their daughters back. They won't ever hear them laugh or cry, or argue or sing, or any of the things they used to do. All they will feel will be the aching sadness and emptiness in their hearts. It will eat away at them until what is left is worn down, no longer fit for purpose. They will know the only thing worse than looking forward is looking back. I've lived that life for the past fifteen years. I know it as well as anyone can. I know the hellish silence that comes with death, when the only sound is the sound of your own madness.

Bridget will give me answers to everything I ask her. I'll explain that I don't fully understand why I need to know about these girls – perhaps it's because of the similarities to Amy. I'll tell her that I don't mean the girls or their families any harm. She won't think badly of me, she doesn't think about people that way.

I get into bed and pull the bedcovers over my head. I feel cold. Maybe the shaking will help me sleep. Anything is easier than thinking.

KATE SAT ALONE IN THE DARK, HER MOBILE PHONE
switched off. She thought about phoning her mother, about checking
with O'Connor, she even considered ringing Declan, but somehow
nothing seemed right any more.

She had allowed Charlie to stay up late, taking her time getting him
ready for bed, not minding when he'd insisted on a million stories. He
had asked her why she looked sad, and instantly she'd regretted not
hiding her feelings better. They'd played Snap and she'd let him win,
enjoying his laughter when his hand had snapped down on top of
hers. But with Charlie now asleep, it was as if somehow everything
had stopped. The investigation would have to stay on hold for another
while; all her rushing around, all the things that had seemed so
important for so long, didn't seem quite so important any more.

Had she been running away from things? Had she not cared about
saving their marriage? Had she neglected both Declan and Charlie?
Declan had obviously decided that she had done those things. Kate
was not so sure. Nonetheless, it had taken the packing of his suitcase
for her to realise there was no running away from feelings. They
always catch up with you. He'd packed his suitcase and left them,
without even telling her where he was going, probably a hotel room,
an empty hotel room, anywhere other than being with her. At least
she had taken some action and cancelled work at Ocean House for
the next few days. She needed time to think, time to work it all out.

The wind outside was building up. Her mind felt blank, tired. Then a sound from out back stirred her, a noise like smashing glass, and something falling. Kate walked over to the back window. A black cat was on the fire escape, the sensor light was broken again. She stood at the window, thinking about how even the apartment sounded different now it was just the two of them.

Huddled on the couch, the darkness and the wind reflected her mood, like she was out in the wilderness, the howl of nature the only thing making any sense. If it rained now, it would be a relief. She wasn't in the mood for tears. Tears were for long after. Right now, she needed to stop running, to stop everything. It's a funny thing, loneliness, the way it creeps up on you. One minute everything is such a rush, people are everywhere, and then you are right back to just you. Kate had no desire for morning, nor any wish to set a clock, or be anywhere other than where she was. Tonight was all about being still. Tomorrow would bring its own answers.

OLLIE HAD NO IDEA WHY WILLIAM CRONLY HAD A photograph of the girl who was killed in the fire, or why he had any of the other stuff either, but he was pretty sure that whatever the answer was, he wasn't going to like it.

Standing at the gateway of the Lodge, looking up at the old building with its curtains drawn, his mind went back again to that summer.

≈

Ollie hadn't been working at Beachfield long when the fire happened. A bloody awful affair. The girl's mother was a right lunatic. He had caught her roaming about the caravan site a couple of nights before it happened. Up to no good she was, parading around the place when all other decent folk were in their beds. He hadn't had a good night poaching, so his mood wasn't good when he came upon her. Cheeky as anything, she even questioned him about his gun, like he was the one requiring interrogation.

The day the blaze took hold, at first he thought it was vandals, and he had cursed his bad luck. If that blaze had really got going, it could have taken the whole bloody caravan park with it. He raised the alarm as best he could, banging his fists on caravans and mobile homes on his way. Within seconds there were men running for the water hose, looking for anything to fill up with water.

When he reached the caravan, the door was locked, so he went back for the main set of keys. Although it was a bit of a struggle, he got the door open. The smoke caught him in the chest, forcing him to stand back in an effort to clear his lungs. He knew the caravan was occupied. The family had already been there for nearly a week. Covering his nose and mouth with his jacket, he crawled on his hands and knees under the smoke in the living area. When he pushed through to the back room, he saw the woman and the girl. The mother was the nearest one to him. He grabbed her, managing to get out before the flames went shooting through from the bedroom. By the time he'd got out with the woman, others, including her husband, had arrived. It didn't take long for the man to work out that his daughter was still trapped inside.

Everything happened so fast. Within seconds of Ollie getting the wife out, the thing turned into an inferno. The heat was intense, forcing them all back. The roar of the fire was like nothing Ollie had ever heard, like an angry beast that kept on exploding with rage. The water hose wasn't much use either. Some of the men did their best to pour water on the thing, but their efforts fast became useless. The father of the girl went mental. It took all Ollie's strength to hold him back. Ollie was a big man, but the girl's father was having none of it and he managed to get loose seconds before the fire cracked out the glass. As the flames roared into the black smoke, there was an explosion, knocking the father off his feet. When the gas cylinder at the back blew, Ollie grabbed hold of him again. By then, the man must have known his daughter was beyond saving. He could still see that look of blind acceptance on the father's face, looking over at his wife, and then back to the flames. There was something about how the woman stood, her skin blackened by the smoke, her eyes wild, that made her look as guilty as hell.

≈

The fact that Steve Hughes had found a photograph of the girl up at the Lodge didn't make sense. But if the photograph proved one thing, it proved that William Cronly was connected to her, and it was a connection that Ollie wasn't happy about. The fire may have happened a long time back, but if William Cronly did know the girl, then things were more than 'fishy', as Hughes had put it. Things were a whole lot worse than that.

Ollie had only visited Cronly on two occasions in the past. The last time was two days after the death of Alison Cronly, when he had been forced out of duty to pay his respects. It was a small parish, and folks felt it was necessary to give the impression of a close community, especially in death. The first occasion, fifteen years earlier, wasn't long after the fire.

Up until that point, he'd only heard about Alison Cronly from Fitzsimons, the owner of Beachfield, and from what he'd heard about the woman, and the airs and graces about her, she was someone who insisted on being treated in high regard, even if you didn't take kindly to her reputation. It was for that very reason that Ollie had avoided her, not wanting to kowtow like everybody else. After the fire, there was a right fuss about the place. Everyone was talking, everyone had a different story about what they thought had happened and who was to blame. There seemed to be no credit given to the fact that he had risked his life to save the mother. If anything, it was the very opposite. If his suspicions at the time were correct, from the looks he was getting, the question everyone was asking was why had he saved the madwoman and not the child. The whole bloody thing had pissed him off to high heaven. He had no idea when he had dragged the woman out that he wouldn't get a chance to go back in. After all, she had been the nearest one to him. How was he to know she'd set fire to the blasted thing?

Ollie had no intention, before or after the fire, of having any call to meet Alison Cronly in person. When he did meet her, at first he didn't have a notion who the hell she was. Feelings were running high after the child's death, what with the garda presence and all the bloody questions they had. Fitzsimons had been on edge, too, worried about how it would all affect his insurance. There had certainly been a whole different approach to fire precautions after that episode.

It was late in the evening, nearly a month after the fire, when he'd stumbled on Alison Cronly. He'd spotted a woman down at the seafront from where he'd been standing on the grassy area overlooking the strand. At first, he hadn't been able to make out what it was that he was looking at. He'd thought that maybe something had been washed in from the sea, but the closer he'd got to it, the clearer it had become that the curled-up heap on the shore was a woman. He had no idea how long she'd been there, but it was a couple of hours at least since most folk had left the beach for the evening. He'd known straight up that she wasn't a resident from Beachfield.

When he'd got close and called her, Alison Cronly had looked more startled to see him than the other way around. Another half hour and the woman wouldn't have been seen. Apart from the darkness, the tide had been on its way in. When he got to her, the water was no more than a foot away from her. Ollie knew he could be a bit gruff, especially when it came to conversations with women, so he'd been somewhat lost for words when he'd stood looking down at Alison Cronly, kneeling on the sand. To make matters worse, she'd looked like some religious freak, bowing her head as if she'd wanted to offer herself as a sacrifice to the ocean. Despite her position and obvious shock at seeing him, when he had asked her who she was, she hadn't been backward about coming forward with her name. She'd said 'Alison Cronly' like it was supposed to mean something.

Even if he'd never heard of her before, the one thing obvious to Ollie was that the woman wasn't in any normal state. He hadn't planned to be putting his rescuing skills to use again so quickly but, knowing it wouldn't take him long to get her back to Cronly Lodge, he'd done just that. As far as he'd known, she lived on her own, with Mrs Flood the housekeeper going in and out during the week. As it was a Saturday, he hadn't been sure if anyone would be at the house when he got there, but one thing had been certain, if he hadn't got her off the beach, he'd have had another death on his hands, and Fitzsimons would be having even more of a canary about things.

Walking to the Lodge, there hadn't been a whole lot of words between them; being friendly was the last thing on his mind. What he'd wanted was to get the crazy woman somewhere she could be someone else's problem. She hadn't got her keys, or a bag, nothing other than what she was wearing, so when they got to the drive, he was relieved when someone opened the front door. The guy had been a stranger to him, but he'd turned out to be her son, or at least had introduced himself as such when they'd got within shouting distance. Ollie had got the distinct impression that he wasn't particularly pleased to see either him or the old woman. When he'd introduced himself to Ollie, it was in as uppity a voice as Ollie had heard tell about the mother. It hadn't been a particular surprise – like mother, like son and all – but still, it had been clear enough to Ollie that the woman wasn't in her right mind. The look of emptiness on her face down at the beach and all the way back to the house hadn't changed.

The young master hadn't taken too kindly to Ollie passing remarks about her needing a doctor; the only thing that had been clear was that he was very keen to get rid of him, like an unwanted piece of shit on your shoes.

From what he'd found out after, head wise, that was the start of the woman going downhill, and if what Hughes had said to him was true, Alison Cronly had been missing a few marbles ever since.

The conversation with Steve Hughes the previous day was still bothering him, and had done so non-stop from the beginning. At the time of the fire, there had been no talk of the son at the house, and even though Ollie had seen him the night he took Alison Cronly home, that was a while after the fire all the same. He had no good reason to think anything other than the son had arrived afterwards.

But then, he had a photograph of the girl. There was no denying that. Ollie knew that if the man had such a photo, there must have been a bloody good reason for it.

He thought about walking up to the Lodge, as if the house itself might have answers, but he had no intention of following in the footsteps of Steve Hughes and breaking into the place. He just wanted to give his head a chance to work things out. If William Cronly had been visiting his mother at the time of the fire, he couldn't have been there for long. Mrs Flood would have told the neighbourhood about the prodigal son returning, unless, of course, the guy had kept himself out of the way. But sure, what would have been the point in that?

The more he thought about things, the more he didn't like the answers he was coming up with. The fire had happened a long time back, but with Steve Hughes' interfering, Ollie needed to work out the best course of action. If Steve was of the mind to call to Ollie about what he'd found, then he would be of the mind to talk to a whole lot of other people as well. He'd been right to tell him to put the photograph back. Even if it proved to be nothing important, he was happy that at the very least he'd told Steve to do that.

Ellie

DR EBBS LOOKS MORE AGITATED THAN USUAL, OR maybe I'm thinking this because of how I feel.

'Good morning, Ellie. How are you?'

'I don't know.'

'Did you not sleep well?'

'No.'

'Do you want to talk about that?'

'No.'

'You look pale, are you unwell?'

'I'm fine.'

'Are you upset?'

'No. I've heard stuff, seen stuff.'

'Like what?'

'It's to do with what I told you the other day, about what really happened to Amy.'

'I'm listening.'

'It's about the girls who got killed.'

'The girls from Dublin?'

'Yes, I think … I think whoever killed Amy killed them as well.'

'You're talking about this man you saw in Wexford again?'

Why isn't he shocked? He looks strained, puzzled, but not shocked, definitely not shocked.

'Yes.'

'And what makes you so sure?'

He's staring at me, talking at me, like I'm some form of idiot, his tone almost patronising.

'Everything, the ribbons, the plaiting, the crucifix.'

'What about the crucifix?'

'Amy had one. She had it in Wexford.' My voice sounds fast, desperate. 'They said in the reports this morning that one of the girls was still wearing her crucifix when she was found.'

'You didn't mention anything about a crucifix before.'

'I didn't think it was important before.'

'Ellie, lots of people wear crosses.' He sighs.

'I tell you it's him. I know it.'

'Okay, let's just calm down, shall we. It's very understandable that you're thinking this way.'

'What way?'

'The case is so similar to Amy's.'

'Did you see the images of the first girl? Do you think she looks like Amy too?' Maybe he understands after all.

'No, Ellie. I haven't seen any images, just what I heard on the radio, but I understand how it could confuse you, cause you to think all sorts of things.'

'You don't understand. I know it's the same man.'

'How can you know?'

'Because of what Bridget said.'

'Bridget?'

'Yes, Bridget. She told me this morning about the first girl they found in the mountains, that she was wearing a crucifix. I saw a picture of her on the television yesterday and she looked just like Amy. They could have been sisters.'

'Ellie, please understand me when I say this, it is very possible that the incident of these girls' deaths, and the memory from all those years ago, could be getting mixed up inside your head.'

'You don't believe me.'

'It's not that, Ellie.'

'Well what is it then?' I want to stand up, walk away, but I have to make him believe me.

'Look, I'm just saying that we need to be careful. The mind is capable of tricking us at times.'

'You are just like the rest of them.'

'Who?'

'All of them, all of the others, they didn't believe me either.'

'Calm down, Ellie.'

'I am calm.'

'You say you heard all this from Bridget this morning?'

'Yes.'

'But that you had already heard some stuff, seen some stuff?'

'Yes, on the television.'

'When?'

'Yesterday. It was a repeat of the *Late Late Show* from Friday night.'

'And you hadn't seen it before?'

'No, not before. Why do you ask? What difference does it make?'

'I was just wondering about it, perhaps something you heard or saw could have upset you the other day?'

'I hadn't seen anything the other day. Look, I want to go.'

'Ellie.'

'I want to go. NOW.'

'Perhaps it's best if we talk later, when you're less anxious.'

'Will you believe me then?'

'Ellie, you are obviously upset. I can see that. You look pale. I will give you something that will help you relax. Then, if you're up to it, we can talk later.'

'Give me whatever you like, but I want the picture of me and Amy.'

He reacts to the defiance in my voice by breathing inwards and pausing, then, without question, he hands me the photograph from the file. 'I'll get someone to take you down to your room.'

I don't answer him.

'Ellie, are you okay?'

'Couldn't be better.' Walking to the door, I don't look back at him, but turn the handle as if I'm a free woman, like everybody else.

Meadow View

EVEN THOUGH IT HAD BEEN WELL PAST MIDNIGHT BY THE time he'd returned to Meadow View, he rose early on Monday morning and followed the same routine as if it had been a work day. Kate's light had stayed on until late. It had taken everything within him to resist going to her. She looked so fragile on the couch. He'd watched her from the fire escape, understanding fully what it's like when someone you care about lets you down. She was well rid of that husband, though. It took a special kind of person to understand someone like Kate. She needed someone like him, someone who would appreciate her. Of course, timing in these matters was crucial.

He made breakfast – two poached eggs and wheat bread – and decided to fill the kitchen with music in celebration of not having to go into Newell Design. Taking the music centre down from the bedroom, he chose one of his favourites, Vivaldi's *Le Quattro Stagioni,* 'La Primavera'. There was something uplifting about new beginnings. Raising the volume to the highest, he blocked out all other sounds, marvelling at how great music could raise you from the mundane, could lift spirit and soul, in such an extraordinary way. It was precisely what he needed.

His suffering had made him a stronger man, and he had no intention of engaging in any outpouring of emotion, indulging in melodrama like Gabriel and his mother had done. He didn't approve of such heightened performances, he'd even disliked it as a boy; drama had always been his mother's speciality.

In Livorno, it had been the same. They had only arrived at Castello de Luca when it became evident that each time his mother spoke, she would assume a raised tone, a ploy she'd used to illustrate that she meant business. Despite his young age, he had sensed that Bishop Antonio Peri wasn't a man who would be distracted easily. From the very first day, the bishop had given the distinct impression that, despite his mother's sense of importance, neither she nor her son had been wanted there.

Suvereto had been unlike anywhere he'd seen before, up so high on the slopes of the hills overlooking Costa degli Etruschi, with its wonderful paved streets and stone buildings. He had been enthralled the first time he'd passed through the ancient wall surrounding the town, the streets narrow, the buildings tall, so high they'd blocked out the sun, keeping the inhabitants cool and enclosed whilst moving within them. The sounds too had been different, voices bouncing along the streets like ghost rumblings.

Despite his early enchantment, within a couple of days he had become disappointed with his Tuscan adventure. Other than when they visited the town of Suvereto, they'd stayed mostly at Castello de Luca, and although it overlooked the coast, he'd been restricted in his movements and not allowed to travel far. He had quickly begun to feel that his new adventure was becoming nothing more than a repeat of things at Cronly, only worse, because at least at Cronly he could escape to the familiarity of his room or his secret hideaway.

It was only when he met Silvia that things had changed.

Silvia was a year older than him and, unlike others, she'd showed no hesitation in becoming his friend. She'd been such fun to be with. It was as if the world had taken on a whole new meaning because of her infectious enthusiasm for life. She'd told him all about her plans to follow the Lord, and had trusted him with her most intimate thoughts. To Silvia, her beliefs had been wondrous. It had seemed so alien to how people from home thought about God. To them, He had been something to be feared but, to Silvia, He had been someone to be loved. Together they had explored the castello with far more fun than he would have had alone. His mother had seemed relieved he had found someone to keep him company, which had given her more time to concentrate on getting what she'd wanted from the bishop. He was a man, after all, and Mother had been accomplished in getting what she wanted out of men.

It was Silvia who'd explained to him how the dead dreamed. When people died, she had told him, they dreamed about the living, some becoming guardian angels to protect souls from birth and through life. She'd said that, when she died, she wanted to become a guardian angel. He had listened to her so intently, believing every word she had told him. She even looked like a guardian angel with her strawberry-blonde hair, making her stand out from her fellow Italians with darker hair. She'd told him this while they sat at the cliff edge. From that vantage point they had been able to see the trees all the way down to the coast. At the time, he had not known what he felt for her was love, being unfamiliar with such emotion.

Perhaps if they hadn't been so consumed with each other's company, they would have noticed certain things about the castello that they'd overlooked. A lesson learned when young stays with you forever. He had no intention of falling victim to that weakness again: not noticing important contradictions that could turn out to be significant in the end. At the time, neither of them had thought it strange that, despite the fact that no children lived at the cleric's castello, there had been items there for them to enjoy. They had never thought to wonder why the rocking horse was in the room with all the windows, or why the bishop kept the best toys in his private rooms. Instead, they had accepted these toys and arrangements at face value, which had made their stay at the castello a bigger adventure than it would otherwise have been.

He had prayed with Silvia in the tiny church down in the basement, a room that was a smaller version of The Cloisters in Suvereto, with its curved walls and arches. He remembered the iron banisters on the stone staircase heading down, cold to the touch, and the steps, steep and narrow. Sometimes they'd giggled, hands over their mouths, trying to keep their silence all the way to the bottom. At first he had liked being down there with Silvia. Away from the intense heat of the afternoons, the air had been cooler there, more welcoming. He'd liked to listen to her pray, watch her go deep inside herself, kneeling below Jesus on the crucifix, at peace with her creator. Looking back, he knew even then how special she was.

At first, when he went on his night prowls, he'd gone alone, not wanting to expose Silvia to the sins of the flesh he had witnessed, the way Mother and men had behaved. He wanted to protect her from that. It was only when he'd thought it was safe that he'd brought her with him, when the attention of the bishop to his mother had decreased, and his mother's mood had deteriorated with it. In the dark, they'd crept through the corridors like shadows, both of them enjoying the secrecy and the heady sense of disobeying the rules. He had not known she would take to wandering alone. If he had, he would have insisted on following her.

Yesterday at Cronly, he had had very little time to spend in his old bedroom, but he had taken out the lock of her hair. He still felt such disappointment thinking about Caroline. She had been exactly how he remembered Silvia. Perhaps Kate would have enjoyed the Castello de Luca. People with sensitivity are so much better equipped to appreciate the delights of the imagination. Silvia, too, had that gift. When he had laid out Caroline, she had looked just like Silvia at first, as beautiful as the last time he'd seen her. He had made a point of everything being perfect, right down to the last detail, from her hair to the ribbons, then laying her body exactly right and resting her head just as he remembered.

KATE LEFT HER FIFTH MESSAGE ON DECLAN'S MOBILE.
She knew he was due at work in less than half an hour, and the chances
of getting him there were slim after he started his Monday morning
meetings. Frustrated, the next call she made was to Sophie, confirming
that she would pick up Charlie from school, with instructions to put
him down for a nap if Kate was still out when the two of them got
back home. Kate wasn't the only one leaving messages. She had already
received half a dozen calls from O'Connor, but she wasn't ready to talk
to him yet.

'Charlie, hurry up in that bedroom. We're going to be late.'

Kate brushed her hair, tying it back in a tight ponytail. Her eyes
looked as if she had spent the previous night lowering double vodkas.

'Charlie, I'm warning you. Come on.'

'I can't find my shoes.'

She flung open the bedroom door, full of tiredness and frustration,
but when she saw her son standing there alone, he suddenly looked so
small in his blue school uniform that it stopped her in her tracks. She
smiled at him.

'Okay buster, let's look together.'

Kate took him by the hand. His grip was tight, fingers stretched to
hold on to hers. It didn't take long to find the shoes. She sat him on
her knee and pulled up his socks, before putting the shoes on.

'I'm tying the laces, Mom. I can do it.'

'Okay – you do the first knot, and I'll do the second.'

'But that's cheating.'

'No it isn't, Charlie. It's sharing.'

Kate checked her phone again – still no messages from Declan.

'Mom, I can't find my schoolbag.'

'It's in the hall, Charlie, come on, we're late. You don't want to upset Mrs Evans.'

'Pooh to Mrs Evans.'

'You don't mean that! Now come on, monkey.'

≈

Kate waved to Charlie through the school gates. The noise and mayhem of a Monday morning in the yard was just one step above organised chaos. It didn't take long for Mrs Evans to get Charlie's class together in a line, huddled tight; they looked like a rope in danger of unravelling at any moment. Before Kate walked away, Charlie turned to her again, waving as if he'd just remembered she was still standing there. He gave her one of his biggest smiles before turning away and leaving his home life temporarily behind him.

There was no point putting off phoning O'Connor any longer. He picked up her call, again before it got to the second ring.

'About time too, Kate.'

'Good morning, Detective.'

'I've been trying to get through to you all morning.'

'Hardly, seeing as it's only 9.30.'

'Nolan has sent Gunning to Tuscany. He wants him to apply pressure to the Italian police, inject more speed into the answers we're getting. As of now, he's landing on Italian soil.'

'So Nolan is taking the connection seriously?'

'Call it having a nose for these things, or bloody desperation, but, yeah, he thinks there's something in it – or if there isn't, he wants it ruled out before any more time is wasted.'

'He's right.'

'Kate, where are you now?'

'At Charlie's school, I'm just leaving.'

'I've been thinking about your theory, about our killer's progression.'

'What about it?'

'Well, I told Nolan about it. He wasn't exactly jumping up and down with joy.'

'It's all about mindset, O'Connor. We're dealing with psychotic behaviour here. Our killer is driven, probably more driven than you or I.'

'Speak for yourself, Kate. I'm more than bloody driven right now.'

'But you're not delusional, at least not yet. Our guy is fixated on the task in hand. Everything he does, he believes it is utterly necessary. In his perception of things, he may feel that he's been driven to look for someone else to fulfil his emotional needs. Either way, he is looking forward. There is no other option for him at this point.'

'Kate, where are you going to now?'

'They don't expect me at Ocean House, so I'll be working from home today. I want to go over all the images and notes again. Something else might just raise its head.'

'There's a televised reconstruction going out later, they're filming part of it now. Is there anything you want to throw into the mix?'

'What about the Tuscany connection?'

'Nolan thinks it's too early, and I agree with him, but Rohan has released details on the crucifix. At the moment we are playing it low key, stating it may be significant or it may not.'

'It will still have an impact. The media is a powerful tool, O'Connor, you know that. My advice is to get everything you possibly can in there without instilling panic, but the visuals of both girls' last movements is going to hit home. You can be sure of that.'

'Leave that one with me.'

'Okay, but one other thing, O'Connor?'

'What?'

'The photographs from Tuscany, they're only of the burial site. Did you get any of Silvia Vaccaro before she died?'

'I've asked for them – I should have them this morning. Either way, once Gunning gets to Livorno, he'll use his charm, but I know what you're thinking.'

'Similar features to our victims.'

'It would certainly make things nice and tidy, Kate.'

'Let me know when you hear back.'

'You'll be one of the first people I call.'

Ellie

I EXPECTED MORE FROM DR EBBS. I GUESS I EXPECTED him to believe me. When he didn't, it felt like the way it was before, when things like that mattered to me. Not being believed is of no consequence when you don't care – but when you do, it disables you, like losing your voice, the ability to speak. Some piece of you dies inside. It has to, otherwise you'd go completely mad.

At first, when I was with the good doctor, I was so angry I wanted to fly into a rage. But then I remembered. It's when you are most frustrated, when you are struggling to make people listen to you, that they want to listen the least. They start to look at you as if you are insane. The more hopeless it becomes, the more desperate you are to be believed, and the more they begin to doubt every word you say.

It didn't take long for my anger to turn inside. I scolded myself for my foolish eagerness, for telling him everything I'd learned from Bridget. He should have sensed how it had turned my world upside-down. How could I have been so stupid? It was like I was right back to the time after the fire, when I knew the truth, when I knew someone had killed Amy. Now my head wants to explode, knowing he has killed again.

Blast Dr Ebbs to hell, what does he know? All his fancy talk, all his promises. 'I'm with you all the way,' he said, wanting to help me, worried about how everyone else had let me down. He even had the gall to question my silence. I should have known he would be no different to the others. I know well enough that I'm speaking the truth.

When Bridget came this morning, she was taken aback by my questions. Her surprise was to be expected I suppose, what with me not normally being the talkative type. Even if I had enquired about the weather, she would have been surprised. But afterwards, she at least listened. I explained to her what I'd heard, that I'd only got bits of it and that I needed to know the rest. Without telling her all the reasons why, she told me everything she knew. Bridget being Bridget, she had the whole story.

The more I heard about the murders, the more I felt like someone had slapped me in the face, roaring at me to do something, anything, other than nothing. I was afraid, for sure, remembering things from before, like some awful dream I was being forced to live again, with all its vivid horror. Only it was worse now because at the back of my mind, the silent roar was gaining voice, telling me that I had allowed it to happen.

I had not known where my questions would lead me. Maybe I thought it would turn out to be nothing. Maybe I thought I'd imagined all the similarities with Amy. But hearing Bridget recount the details, the pieces of the jigsaw fell into place and I felt more convinced than ever that what I was hearing was exactly what had happened to Amy. That realisation, that conviction, scared the living daylights out of me.

When Amy died, I had no fight left in me to argue, but after listening to Bridget I realised that if what she said was true, it meant this time, more than ever, I had to make people listen. This time it had to be different.

I was careful with Bridget, but then I didn't want to burden her with the truth. I didn't want to scare her. She would have wanted to help in her own way, but I knew Bridget wasn't going to be able to make things happen. Dr Ebbs had believed me the first time, so there was no reason for me to think he wouldn't believe me again. I got that one badly wrong.

Now it's as if everything trapped inside me since Amy's death has been stirred up again, like a demon that has been there all along, waiting for someone to unlock the door. I don't know what to do with this demon, but I know he won't go away.

Bridget was kind this morning. She could tell how upset I was and asked if I wanted her to tell Dr Ebbs that I was unwell. I said no. She put me back into bed after my nausea, told me she'd bring me down a light breakfast on a tray. She washed my face with a cold face cloth, giving me instructions to stay underneath the covers. I lay there as she cleaned the sink of vomit. She did her best to rid the place of the stench. I felt the closest to being loved I've felt for a very long time. In a funny way, knowing that Bridget cared helped me before the anger came.

Arriving to see Dr Ebbs, I was determined. The wave of anger that had spread through me after Bridget left had put fire back in my soul. It was the kind of anger I remembered feeling before, the kind that consumes you, but at least tells you you're alive. I held back at first, not sure which way to go about telling Dr Ebbs. I was afraid of blurting out the whole thing. I recalled how that tack had backfired on me last time around. People had looked at me as if I was mad. Well, I guess I had been. So I knew that today, I needed to be calm. I tried to judge the situation as best I could. But from the moment I opened my mouth, I knew he didn't believe me. I recognised that look from the get-go. Whenever they ask stupid questions, you know you're in trouble because you know what they're thinking: *Let the lunatic have her say, and then ignore her.*

When he tried to placate me, something else changed inside. I wanted to scream. I knew he wasn't listening. The hope that you can change someone's mind fades quickly. I saw exactly how it was going to play out, and I was damned if I was going to go through all that disbelief and frustration again. I wanted out of there, and quick.

So I swallowed the tablets he gave me. I knew I had no choice. The nurse checked I had swallowed them, as she was instructed to do. I waited until she was out of earshot. It didn't take much to force the tablets back up. Bridget had left some of the cleaning stuff with me in case I was sick again. I cleaned everything up, even though I was weak. But whatever weakness my body felt, my head felt strong, stronger than it had felt for a very long time.

By the time I was finished, the place looked and smelled as perfect as when the nurse had left. I sat looking at Amy's photograph for a long time before I finally put it under my pillow. When I did, I thought long and hard about how I was going to make things different.

This time around, I have to succeed – with or without the good doctor's help.

GARDA ADELE BURLINGTON HAD BEEN ANSWERING calls on the helplines since the start of her shift at ten that morning. It was her third day doing the same thing: recording details received from the public, and rating the calls for passing further up the line.

'Public Information Line.'

'My name is Dr Samuel Ebbs.'

'How can I help you, Dr Ebbs?'

'I'm phoning in connection with the murders of the young girls in Dublin.'

'Where are you calling from, Dr Ebbs?'

'St Michael's Institution. I'm the senior psychiatric consultant here.'

'And what information do you have?'

'Well, it's to do with a patient under my supervision, Ellie Brady. She's been remembering information about the murder of her own daughter, something that happened fifteen years ago. You do understand why I am hesitant about making this call?'

'Dr Ebbs, any information you give me will be treated confidentially, I assure you. You can talk freely.'

'Okay. Ellie Brady is a long-term patient here, and is believed to have been responsible for the death of her daughter fifteen years ago.'

'Her daughter's name?'

'Amy. Amy Brady. She would have been of similar age to the victims in Dublin.'

'And what has Ellie told you?'

'She believes the person who has committed the current murders killed her daughter as well.'

'You sound hesitant, doctor?'

'Ellie is under psychiatric care for a reason. I have no way of validating any of the information she has given me, but according to her, the way the girls were found, with the plaiting, the ribbons and the crucifix, was exactly how she found her daughter. It was a long time ago, but she is adamant.'

'Will we be able to speak to Ellie Brady if that proves necessary?'

'That is the problem. At the moment she is under sedation because of her heightened anxiety. As I said, I don't know if any of this is true. My main concern is that if it isn't true, interviewing Ellie would only serve to elevate whatever medical difficulties exist.'

'Could you give me your telephone number, Dr Ebbs? I will need to call you back to validate the contact source.'

'Certainly.'

Waiting for the return call, Samuel was still unsure if he had done the right thing, but either way, he had made the decision, and all he could do now was manage things from there. When the officer finally rang in through the main switchboard, she assured him she would pass the information on to the investigation team. He gave his mobile phone number should they need to contact him outside office hours.

He hung up feeling unsettled about the call and his divulging of patient information. It was up to the police now how they chose to proceed. He had done everything he could do.

Meadow View

HE THOUGHT ABOUT KATE. HER EYES HAD LOOKED TIRED this morning. She must have spent the night crying, poor thing. She had tried to hide it, of course, for the sake of the boy. Not that he'd appreciated it, mind you. He had barely waved to his mother at the school gates. He would have done anything to have had a mother like Kate, but most people don't get that lucky. Most people have to play the hand they're given. Silvia had understood that. She'd looked on difficulties as challenges, not knowing how cruel real evil could be. He should have protected her, he knew that now. It was no excuse, being only a boy. Learning about his mother's meddling had brought clarity, but it hadn't lessoned his guilt. That would be his burden to bear.

He fed Tabs, then took his time walking back up the stairs. He felt relief once he closed the bedroom door and pulled the curtains closed to darken the room. Lying on the bed, he allowed his mind drift, just like he had taught himself to do as a boy.

Events over the past while had taken their toll on him. Certain aspects – Mother, dealing with that other business in Tuscany – were inevitable necessities, but that didn't lessen their impact. Justice had waited far too long to be done. He still remembered returning from Suvereto, how lonely and lost he had felt, no longer interested in all the things that used to enthral him. Silvia was perfectly safe now. She was in a place where no one could hurt her. Mother's instruction had been clear: there would be no mention of what had happened in Italy; he was to keep his big mouth shut. Nothing, she had warned him, would be achieved by bringing up that awful mess again. Besides, the bishop had given his word that he would look after them. Their money worries were gone, their future independence guaranteed. Things would be different from now on. She could buy him all the comics and toys he wanted; all he had to do was ask. Two weeks earlier, her words would have meant everything to him. Two weeks earlier, he hadn't known Silvia.

He had kept his side of the bargain and had never mentioned it to a living soul. Over time, he had accepted it for what it was. We all have burdens. Had it not been for her ailing health and the painkillers, her evil brain wouldn't have been tricked into telling him what had really happened. Once he knew the truth, events had to take their own course.

It had been at the beginning of his third week at Castello de Luca that he'd realised how much Silvia meant to him. They had been acting out a play about Joan of Arc. Silvia was Joan, while he'd imitated the angry crowd, kneeling on a pile of straw to burn her at the stake. When he'd cried, he thought she would laugh at him, think him stupid, but she hadn't.

'Don't cry, William. I hate it when people cry.'

'I'm okay.'

'You're not. You're sad. Don't be sad.'

'I can't help it.'

'Did I upset you?'

'No.'

'Well then, why are you crying? Is it the play? We can do something else. We can pretend we're going on a great adventure, the way we do when the castello gets dark.'

'It's not that.'

'What is it then?'

'I don't want to go home.'

'Why not?'

'I have no friends there.'

'But everyone has friends.'

'I don't. They all hate me.'

'Why do they hate you?'

'I don't know. Mother says they're jealous.'

'Are they?'

'Maybe. I don't know. They just do, that's all.'

'It won't be so bad. We can write. You love stamps and stickers. I'll put a different one on every time I send you a letter.'

'But I won't see you. You'll forget about me.'

'Friendship isn't like that, William. It stays even when people are apart.'

She had been right. He had never lost her. She was far too important. Years later, when his mother had become convinced that Silvia was haunting her, a part of him had wanted to believe it. Despite her hysterical blubbering, he had been excited by the idea. Of course, he'd spoken to the young girl fifteen years earlier. He befriended her. He'd even taken her to his hideout and given her one of the tiny crucifixes to keep her safe. But he'd known she wasn't right.

Mother had never been the same afterwards.

Caroline had been the only one who ever came close, and just like Silvia, she had no idea how special she was.

He was older now, his needs had changed. Like him, Kate had suffered and known vulnerability, had overcome it on her own. She was his intellectual equal, forever striving. If Silvia had lived, she would have been just like Kate. Fate had played its final hand. All this sorry mess now required was for Kate to get inside his head, to understand him. But she could only see part of the picture. He needed to explain things properly to her. She was upset over that husband of hers – he was Charlie's father, after all – but he wasn't good enough for Kate. She didn't realise it yet. But she would. She was a very clever girl.

OLLIE COULDN'T FIND STEVE IN ANY OF THE USUAL spots and he wasn't answering his mobile phone. If it hadn't been for his meddling, Ollie could be relaxing at Beachfield instead of playing a modern-day Sherlock Holmes. He wished Steve Hughes had never come near him with that damn photograph.

Smyth's bar was the only pub in the town where he drank. As it was lunchtime, he decided to give up looking for Hughes until he had a full belly for the job. It was quiet in the pub; October was a bit of a slow month, which suited Ollie just fine. He took a seat at the bar, in front of the large television screen, and called for his usual. As he savoured his first pint, he ordered bacon, cabbage and potatoes; none of that curry crap for him.

No sooner had the plate of food arrived in front of him than the horse racing was switched over to the news. He had heard about the murdered girls, you couldn't avoid it, but when the photographs of the two girls appeared on the big screen, he thought he had gone a bit mad. He told himself it was just Steve Hughes and his wild talk getting under his skin, but the more he looked at the girls' pictures, the more uneasy he felt. When the reporter mentioned a Toyota Carina car, it put paid to any enjoyment his dinner offered him.

If he couldn't get Steve Hughes on the phone in the next half hour, whether he'd put that Polaroid photograph back or not, Ollie was going to have to take things into his own hands. Those girls may have been killed in Dublin, but last he'd heard that's where William Cronly was living. He didn't relish the prospect of what lay ahead, but then, the only thing worse than having to drag up old history was getting himself into more shit.

Ellie

MORE THAN MOST, I UNDERSTAND THE CONCEPT OF loneliness. I've lived it since the day I came into this place. When you're institutionalised, you forget the way people in the outside world think. You're no longer able to understand normality. I've seen it happen to other women too, some of those I've shared my life with for the past fifteen years. I've seen how the day to day of doing nothing defies the logic of the human race outside these walls. Days soaked in routine: the time you wake, the time you sleep, mornings and evenings made up of breakfast, dinner and tea, your room, your bed, the half-people you all become. It's often the complete absence of anything new or different that sends you really mad. Without realising, I've become that way myself.

For days now, I've had the sense that things were shifting, changing. It was in the little things, like how I stood at the mirror down from Living Room 2, looking at it like I was trying to see something, find someone. How I thought that that someone might have been my old self, even though I knew she was nowhere to be found. When I opened up to Dr Ebbs about Amy, she seemed real again, as if somehow, even after fifteen years, I could find her more quickly than I could find myself. I'd cried for her, something I had not allowed myself to do before. I've questioned myself every day I've been here, watched the sun creep into my room each morning, witnessed the seasons change outside, year in, year out. I kept on going in order to punish myself for not seeing all the things I should have seen. I failed to pay attention to the little things and, the worst sin of all, I became so focused on myself I let my daughter slip away from me.

I know who her killer is. I've seen his face in here many times, it comes back to me in fleeting pieces of memory. I see him talking to Amy, although I can't be sure the face I remember is true or imagined. He laughs at me before I go to sleep. He tells me he has Amy instead of me. Looking at my copybook, I hold the pen tightly, like I want to crush it, feeling the sweat build up in my palm. There are so many things I remember about that summer and yet even now there are parts I still struggle with. It's hard to get it right. It's like looking for the story behind the story, catching shadows you missed first time around. Things you didn't realise were important – a look Amy might have given, words dismissed without really listening because you believed them trivial – have now become weighted down with significance and meaning.

The memories are circling inside my head. Ever since I wrote those three words in the copybook, the voices are going around and around, like a carousel moving too fast. All I can catch is the fusion of coloured lights, words jumbled into their repeated rhythms, unable to be slowed down and deciphered.

I realised something this morning, something I should have realised long ago. It's just me now. Since Amy, it has always been just me. What I need to do is think, to remember anything that could make a difference. Doing nothing is no longer an option, even though I'm not completely sure why that is the case.

My hand is shaking on the page as I try to remember. I see the dirt road, the one off the main pathway to the beach. I walked it one of the days with Amy. She wanted to show it to me. I remember hearing people's voices from the beach, but I couldn't see them. They seemed distant, the sand dunes on our right blocking out the view. On the left, there were flattened fields with bales of rolled-up hay and on either side of the path, the wild grasses. Amy pulled some up and made a pretend fan.

We walked along the road until the sand dunes disappeared and the hay fields went out of view, and we saw the woodlands. The clearing wasn't far, just past some trees with blossoms of white sprays. I didn't know what kind of trees they were, but Amy knew, she said they were elderberry, that they bloom with white flowers, but after summer red berries grow, berries the colour of cherries. She'd explored the path before with him. I paid no mind to her.

When she asked me to walk farther, I told her I was tired. I wasn't tired. All I wanted was to go back. Amy was so keen to show me something. What was it? It was something about a hideout. What else can I remember? Every detail is important.

I start to write it all down, beginning with the elderberry trees, and our last walk at the back of the sand dunes.

Gorey Garda Station
Monday, 10 October 2011, 1.45 p.m.

THE LAST TIME OLLIE GILMARTIN HAD SPOKEN TO Garda Damian Murray had been four months earlier. Some busybody made noises about a bit of alleged poaching, and Garda Murray had called him in for a little chat. He'd been nice enough about it – just laying out the lie of the land, so to speak. Ollie had time for the man, thought him a fair copper, so he was relieved to see him behind the front desk when he walked into the station.

'You sure about these registration details, Ollie?'

'What kind of a question is that? Of course I'm sure.'

'Just asking before I ring it in. Don't want to be sending the boys in Dublin on a wild goose chase, do we?'

Ollie winced at the reference to poultry. 'I'm absolutely sure. It was off the road for a while, but he started to drive it again lately.'

'And you say Steve Hughes has a photograph that might be helpful.'

'Could be, is all I'm saying.'

'And how do you reckon our Mr Hughes came upon this photograph?'

'You'll have to ask him that. I'm only saying what I know.'

'Right, hang on so, Ollie. I'll ring in this registration number, then you can give me Steve Hughes' mobile and we'll all have a chat.'

'Always happy to oblige.'

'Indeed.' Murray grunted before leaving Ollie alone in the room.

Ollie tried Steve again. This time he got an answer. 'Where are you, you bastard?'

'Steady on, Ollie. I'm a busy man, you know.'

'Yeah, right. You still got that photograph?'

'Was planning on putting it back later.'

'Well don't bother. I'm at Gorey station. Murray will be ringing you in a minute.'

'What the fuck for?'

'That photograph. He'll need to see it. I've given him the registration number of the Carina. Those murders in Dublin, the ones with the two girls, they think the killer might have driven the same type of car.'

There was a silence as Steve Hughes obviously tried to grasp what Ollie was saying to him. 'Are you for fucking real?'

'No, I'm making it up. Of course I'm for fucking real. Murray's on his way back. When he phones, act surprised.'

'That'll be easy.'

Incident Room, Tallaght Garda Station
Monday, 10 October 2011, 2.00 p.m.

'O'CONNOR, MAKE YOUR WAY OUT OF THAT GLASS house of yours, something's raised its head, and it might be worth looking at.'

When Donoghue thought something was worth looking at, it usually was. As the bookman, he was forever on the lookout for connections. O'Connor wondered if the stories he'd heard about him were true. According to some of the others, Donoghue could crack a crime in a novel within the first twenty pages. Apparently it was something of an obsession with him. True or not, in real life he was not a man to be messed with.'

'Skipper.'

'Sit down, O'Connor.'

'Right.'

'Something's turned up. We got a call from a Dr Ebbs at St Michael's Psychiatric Hospital. He claims one of his patients, an Ellie Brady, thinks our man killed her daughter.'

'One of his patients?'

'Yeah, Adele Burlington took the call. It came in on the priority helpline.'

'You're kidding me, right?'

'I don't kid about murder, Detective.'

'Sorry, I didn't mean that ... go on.'

'I remember the case myself, happened fifteen years ago. The murdered girl was the same age as our victims. Different MO though. Filicide by arson'

'This woman, Ellie Brady, you say she's a psychiatric patient.'

'Yeah, and I know what you're thinking.'

'What does the doctor say?'

'Says he's not sure. She could be making it up, copycat type of thing. Not unusual. But here's the thing, O'Connor. The killing happened in Wexford, the mother set fire to a holiday caravan, she was dragged out, but the child perished.'

'Go on.'

'You know how I love connections. Well, we got a call in from the station in Gorey ten minutes ago. A guy just walked in there, an Oliver Gilmartin, says he knows the possible owner of the Carina. He's being interviewed now.'

'The same area as the Brady murder?'

'Wexford is a big place, but Ellie Brady's daughter was killed there. I'll run the plates. Why don't you and your psychologist friend have a chat with Ellie Brady.'

'Right, keep me posted.'

'Will do, and I'll start the paperwork for pulling that old murder file, just in case.'

KATE'S MOBILE PHONE SANG OUT WITH THE ALL-TOO-
familiar piano riff ringtone she'd allocated to O'Connor.

'Kate.'

'Detective.'

'We're taking a trip.'

'Where?'

'The northside. I'll do the driving. I'm on my way to pick you up.'

'Any chance you could tell me why?'

'I'll fill you in on the way. You at home?'

'Yeah, I'll be ready.'

Looking out the tiny window of her study, Kate watched a young
mother pass by with her baby wrapped snugly in a buggy. At the
newsagent's, two men chatted as a woman in a smart grey suit walked
past them. Ordinary people getting on with ordinary lives, a luxury
Caroline's and Amelia's families no longer had. She thought about
Declan, how if there was going to be any hope for them remaining
as a family, things would have to change. She tried him one last time.
This time he picked up.

'Declan.'

'Kate, sorry, I can't talk now.'

'That's okay. When?'

'I should finish up around five. I can ring you then.'

'Okay. And, Declan?'

'What?'

'I'm sorry.'

'We'll talk later. I have to go, Kate.'

Turning to the photographs of the murdered girls on the study wall, Kate thought again about the Tuscan burial site. If Silvia Vaccaro's death and the killing of the two girls were connected and the flat stone was a place for them to rest their heads, it was another indicator of his affection for his victims. His perceived relationships with Amelia and, more importantly, with Caroline may have been delusional, but to him they felt utterly real. Eighty per cent of female victims know their killer – a frightening statistic. The one thing Kate knew for sure was that whoever the killer was, he knew his next victim in some way and could be watching her right now. They needed to find him before he could make his move.

≈

Kate sat in the passenger seat beside O'Connor, who seemed more hell bent on getting wherever it was they were going than filling her in on the details.

'I'm waiting, Detective. Where are we heading?'

'We're going to see an Ellie Brady. I've squared it with her doctor.'

'Doctor?'

'Yeah, she's a patient at St Michael's, a psychiatric hospital. It's a lead we got via the public information lines. Ellie Brady's daughter was killed fifteen years back, a case of filicide. The mother set fire to the caravan with both her and her daughter in it. Ellie survived. According to the doctor, Ellie now claims the person who killed the two girls also murdered her daughter.'

'I'm not sure I like the sound of this, it's hardly reliable testimony.'

'Donoghue thinks there might be something in it, and he has an uncanny knack of being right about these things.'

'Did you get the image of Silvia from the Italian police?'

'Not yet. Wait a second, Kate, I need to take this.' O'Connor answered a call on his hands-free set.

Kate couldn't help but think that they might be wasting their time interviewing a psychiatric patient, but she was willing to go with it for now.

Listening to O'Connor's side of the conversation, she reckoned he must be talking to DI Gunning. She found their animosity fascinating – two men, both of high intelligence, equal ranking in the force, same age, both with an active interest in solving crime – on the face of it, they had a lot in common. But that was where their similarities ended, other than their desire to be the dominant alpha male. It was the latter similarity which was at the root of their rivalry. Given the choice, though, she'd work with O'Connor over Gunning any day.

When O'Connor ended the call, he smiled at her.

'That was our travel guide from Tuscany.'

'So I gathered. What did he have to say?'

'He went to the site where the bishop supposedly slipped.'

'And?'

'It was a steep drop all right. According to Gunning, it was less than a quarter of a mile from where Silvia had been buried. Meaning she could well have fallen from the same place, which is a bit coincidental. And that's not all.'

'What?'

'Gunning had a look at the case file. He says there is a resemblance in facial features to our victims, as we suspected. Nolan was right. Sometimes you just have to get the hell over there to check things out.'

'If the bishop's death wasn't accidental and our guy was involved, it meant he returned to Tuscany for a reason, and there is only one which is springing to mind.'

'Revenge?'

'It makes sense. Also, the bishop's death, accident or otherwise, was six months before the current murders – sufficient time for him to stalk both girls and follow through on making his move.'

'He certainly took his time turning into an avenging angel.'

'Think about it, O'Connor. Assuming our killer was a child at the time and that the rumours about the bishop were true, if Antonio Peri was responsible for Silvia's death, our guy would have looked on Antonio as the hand of evil – time may have passed, but his emotions would not necessarily have faded.'

'Yeah, but that doesn't answer the question, why wait? It's forty years since the girl's death, Kate. Five years since her remains were discovered.'

'Something else must have happened, something current. Crimes don't always fit into sequential patterns. It just takes something fired into the mix to send ricochets all over the place. If our killer was a child at the time of Silvia's death, he didn't go to Tuscany alone. We know from Jessica that his voice didn't have an accent, at least not to her. He's not from outside Ireland, which means he travelled to Tuscany, both as a child and as an adult.'

'Okay. We'll start trawling flight passenger lists around the time of the bishop's death, starting with flights into Florence.'

'He wouldn't have taken a direct flight. He'll play clever. This guy does nothing without meticulous planning. I know it's not what you want to hear, O'Connor, but all means of getting there will have to be looked at, including flights to Pisa and Rome.'

'Jesus, that's some task, Kate.'

She smiled wryly at him. 'Our guy wouldn't want it any other way.'

O'Connor rang Donoghue and gave him instructions to get listings of all flights into Italy, along with passenger details for ferries from Ireland and the UK to mainland Europe for the weeks surrounding Antonio Peri's death.

As they drove through the large entrance gates of St Michael's, Kate and O'Connor looked at the building in front of them in silence.

The large, grey, rundown structure loomed on the landscape like something from a Hitchcock movie.

'I suppose you're wondering if Ellie Brady will turn out to be another ricochet? I know I am.'

'Maybe, O'Connor,' she said without too much belief in her voice. 'Convince me – what else do we know about her case?'

'The files are archived. All original documents and exhibits are kept in vaults at HQ in the Phoenix Park. You can't go pulling old case files without good reason. Donoghue is doing the prep work. He'll push for opening the file as soon as he hears how we get on.'

'Right, let's get in there so and see what Ellie Brady has to say for herself.'

Meadow View

HE HAD CHECKED THE FINISHING TIME FOR JUNIOR INFANTS at the school earlier that morning, and arrived in plenty of time. When the bell rang, all three classes filed out, monitored by their teachers, each of the little ones collected by the dispersing group of mothers, nannies and some token fathers. When he hadn't seen Kate, he'd thought the boy would be kept waiting, but instead the boy was led away by someone else. Charlie had called out her name. Sophie. He heard Sophie tell Charlie that they were going to the park and afterwards, if he was good, they would make pizza for tea.

Things weren't going exactly to plan, but no matter. Intelligent improvisation was all that was required. He had already packed the car with hiking boots, backpack, torch and a rope. The duct tape was in the boot too, along with provisions, should they be required.

Turning the delay to his advantage, he bought some comics for the child – something to keep him occupied on the way down. Having made the decision to postpone everything for at least another hour, it gave him ample time to have a late lunch at Meadow View.

He set up the laptop on the table in the kitchen to catch up with events. They had that horrid photofit on again – not a bit like him, the face looking like that of an old man. Zero out of ten to Jessica if she was the one responsible. He allowed himself a moment of smug satisfaction.

When the doorbell rang, it made him jump. No one would be able to see him in the kitchen from the front of the house, but if he wanted to look out without being seen, he would have to go upstairs, which was impossible. Turning off the laptop, he did his best to listen, but the only thing he heard was another ring on the doorbell.

It might not be anyone important, but, still, he stayed where he was until they stopped ringing. He didn't make it out of the kitchen in time to see who it was. It was ridiculous to think it had anything to do with the investigation. They had absolutely no way of connecting things to him.

He checked the clock in the kitchen, then pulled all the curtains closed before heading off to pick up Charlie. The child had looked so innocent last night, hugging his teddy. Not quite the superhero after all.

Interview Room, Gorey Garda Station
Monday, 10 October 2011, 3.00 p.m.

'RIGHT, MR HUGHES, TAKE A SEAT. JUST GIVE ME A second to get organised here.'

Steve did exactly as he was told while Garda Murray pulled out a statement pad and pen, ready to write down everything he was about to say. Sitting opposite Steve at a small, square, formica table, Murray filled in the upper section of the sheet. 'Interview with Mr Steve Hughes of 25 Edmond Street, Gorey, conducted by Garda Damian Murray, Monday, 10 October, 3.00 p.m., Gorey Garda Station.'

'Now I'm going to ask you some questions, Steve, and in your own words you can let me know the answers. Is that okay with you?'

'Sure.'

'I understand you work at Cronly Lodge.'

'Yeah, gardening and a bit of handiwork.'

'And the owner, you say he drives a Carina?'

'That's right.'

'Ollie has given us the registration number.' Murray paused to write the registration number down again.

'Right.'

'Which brings us to the matter of the photograph. The one Ollie says you found.'

'I went straight to Ollie with it, I did.'

'And why would that be?'

'I said to myself, if anyone knows what this is all about, it'll be Ollie Gilmartin.'

'And he had an opinion on it, did he?'

'Not exactly.'

'Go on.'

'He told me I should put it back.'

'Back where?'

'At Cronly. I found it in his lordship's, I mean in Cronly's bedroom.'

'You have a habit of sharing a bedroom with Mr Cronly, do you?'

'No.'

'Why were you in it, so?'

'Well, it's like this. Your man, Cronly, he's been acting strange lately, putting extra bolts on the doors.'

'Bolts?'

'Yeah, large yokes.'

'To keep people out, do you think, Mr Hughes?' Murray gave him a sarcastic grin.

'Maybe, but the thing is, I had a load of stuff there, tools and the like. I needed to get them, and, well, let's just say Cronly wasn't overly fond of my company.'

'So you thought it was okay to break in uninvited?' Murray asked, as he wrote down Steve's answer about the tools.

'Not exactly. The auld one, Alison Cronly, she was the one who employed me, she gave me a key, told me I could use it anytime I wanted.'

'I understand Mrs Cronly passed away a few months ago. Talking to the dead are we now?' Murray's look of disbelief left Steve in no doubt as to how this was going.

'Look, I needed my tools. I had only one way to get them. That's when I thought things were a bit suspicious.'

'Suspicious?'

'Yeah, with all the cleaning and that.'

'Cleaning?'

'Well his lord— I mean Cronly was down yesterday. Lit a fire in the house, though he could only have been there for a couple of hours.'

'No law against lighting a fire in your own home.'

'I know that, but he'd washed down the wall and the carpet. I thought it was odd, coming all the way down to do some spring cleaning.'

'The photograph?'

'I came across it upstairs, when I was checking things out.'

'You still have it?'

'Right here.'

Garda Murray studied the photograph.

'I thought Ollie might know about it, him being around at the time the girl was killed, like.'

'Wait there, Mr Hughes. Myself and Ollie Gilmartin are about to get reacquainted.'

ON THEIR WAY TO DR EBBS' OFFICE, KATE AND
O'Connor passed through long corridors that had long since lost
their freshness. Tall sash windows dominated the structure, chipped
high ornate ceilings, walls that were a collage of pale pink emulsion
and hard laminated floors – everything about the building echoed
abandonment. Kate wondered if the residents would consider that
an apt description for themselves too. In the hallway, just before they
reached the doctor's door, a gold ornate mirror with black spotting on
the glass reflected the two of them. Its intricate frame looked like the
rest of St Michael's, like something left behind.

'Detective O'Connor, Ms Pearson, good to meet you.'

Dr Ebbs was tall and slim, his black hair balding from the centre,
his face tanned. He wore a crisp white shirt and pink tie. He was
handsome, Kate thought, and moved with the gentle elegance of a
man who was self-confident, though not arrogant. O'Connor got
straight to the point.

'Doctor, Ms Pearson and I don't have a whole lot of time here. We
need to find out, and as quickly as possible, what, if anything, Ellie
Brady's disclosures have to do with our current investigation.'

'I appreciate your frankness, Detective, but before I bring Ellie in
here, I need to make a couple of things clear. Ellie is a long-term
patient. I am relatively new to this institution, but as Ellie's psychiatrist
I took the decision to alter her medication a little over a week ago,
reducing the level of benzodiazepines in an effort to bring Ellie out

of her entrenched mindset – one she has maintained for a number of years. But what I must stress is that it is still too early to tell if Ellie's emerging cognitive state can be relied on. She claims she saw the man who killed her daughter, but she is fragile, and I will monitor your questioning with one aim and one aim only, to protect my patient.'

'Understood, Doctor. Ms Pearson and I will handle the questioning with due care.'

'Thank you, Detective. Just give me a moment and I'll go ask Ellie to join us.'

≈

Ellie Brady looked cautiously at both Kate and O'Connor as she and Dr Ebbs entered the office. Kate watched Ellie, taking in everything about her. Next to Dr Ebbs, Ellie looked drab. She was thin, with short brown hair tucked behind her ears, dressed in a grey shirt and faded jeans, both two sizes too big for her. Despite her shadowy appearance, Ellie held her shoulders back, like a woman who meant business, or at the very least like a woman trying to give the illusion of such. Dr Ebbs did the introductions. As Ellie sat down, she placed what looked like a child's green copybook on her lap, both her hands rested on it.

'Ellie, my name is Detective O'Connor. This is Kate Pearson. Dr Ebbs will be remaining with us while we conduct this interview, and Kate will be asking a few questions. Is that okay with you?'

'Certainly.'

'Good. Now Kate, would you like to take it from here.'

'Ellie, hello.'

'Hello.' Ellie cleared some phlegm from her throat with a small cough, covering her mouth. Her voice sounded strong, but with the demeanour of someone who hadn't spoken with strangers for a very long time.

'I understand, Ellie, that you believe the person who killed your daughter may be the man we are looking for.'

'There is no maybe about it. I'm sure.'

'And what makes you so sure?'

'Do you have children, Ms Pearson?'

'I do, a son. He's four.'

'How would you feel if you lost him?'

'Devastated.'

'That's how I was, Ms Pearson.'

'Kate, please.'

Ellie kept her gaze on Kate, as if they were the only two people in the room.

'I was devastated for a very long time, Kate. I still am in a way, but my thinking is clearer now.'

'Ellie, why don't you tell us about how you found Amy?'

'It was early morning, before most people at the caravan site had woken. I had come back from visiting Andrew. Did Dr Ebbs tell you about Andrew?'

'No.'

'He was the man I thought I was in love with, my husband's brother. I had come back after being with him. I checked in on Amy, and that's when I realised.'

'What did you realise?'

'At first, I thought she was sleeping. She was in her bed, her hair plaited with two red ribbons.'

'Like the girls in Dublin, Ellie?'

'That's right. She was wearing a silver crucifix. I had no idea where she'd got it from, but I think she'd had it for a couple of days. The ribbons, they were wrong. She didn't have red ribbons like that. She usually wore bobbins in her hair. They looked odd too.'

'How do you mean, odd?

'I don't know, old-fashioned. She lay above the covers, still in her nightdress. That was when I noticed how strangely she was lying.'

'What way was that?'

'Curled up like a baby in the womb. But when I looked closer, I realised that wasn't right either. It was because of her hands, you see. They were closed together, the fingers intermingled.' Ellie's eyelids opened wider, holding her stare, and her fingers replicated the way her daughter's hands had looked. 'It was as if she was praying. And that was when I realised that she wasn't sleeping. She was kneeling. When I got closer, I recognised that grey colour of death. The skin on her face was cold, but her body wasn't, although it was losing its warmth. I knew she was dead.'

Even though Ellie maintained eye contact with Kate throughout, Kate could see O'Connor's shift in body movements out of the corner of her eye, hearing Ellie's mention of Amy's hands joined in prayer, and the positioning of the body. A lot of details were public knowledge, including the plaiting, ribbons and the crucifix, but nothing had been mentioned about how the girls' bodies or hands were found. O'Connor coughed as if to signal for Kate to continue.

'What did you do then, Ellie?'

'I stayed with her until Joe, my husband, woke up. I told him Amy was sleeping. When he left, I went back in to her, spoke to her. I knew what had to be done.'

'Is that when you set fire to the caravan?'

'Yes, soon after that. I remember feeling calm. I was content you see, once I'd decided to go with her.'

'What happened then?'

'The fire took hold quickly. I remember the caravan filled with black smoke, the heat, the crackle. Then that Gilmartin man saved me.' Ellie shook her head, as if to pull herself out of her reverie.

'Oliver Gilmartin?' O'Connor broke in, remembering the name from Donoghue's conversation about the Carina.

'Yes, he was caretaker of the caravan park.'

O'Connor shot a look to Kate, who nodded slightly and continued.

'You seem very clear on things, Ellie?'

'After fifteen years, Kate, you can get a lot of clarity.'

'I can imagine.'

'Can you? I doubt it. There are some things you have to live through. You might think you can imagine it, but you haven't walked in my shoes. I hope you never do.'

Kate didn't reply immediately, taking in Ellie's last words.

'Ellie, you told Dr Ebbs you saw a man, a man who you believe killed Amy; can you tell us about him?'

'He was nothing out of the ordinary. I thought he was one of the fathers of the other kids at the park.'

'What age, do you think?'

'My age I guess, or a little older. I only saw him a couple of times.'

'But you are sure he killed Amy?'

'Someone killed her, and it wasn't me. I loved her more than life. I just didn't show it.'

'Your copybook, Ellie, may I ask what's in it?'

'Things I remembered.'

'Can DI O'Connor and I take a look at it?'

'Sure.'

Opening the first page, Kate saw the words 'Amy', 'Dead' and 'Wexford' written in large block letters. On the second page, Ellie's handwriting changed. It was smaller, joined, slanting to the right, obeying the rules of the page. The first words to catch Kate's attention were 'elderberry trees'.

'MR GILMARTIN, COULD YOU STEP BACK IN, PLEASE?'

'No bother.'

'Mr Hughes tells me you might know the girl in the photograph.'

'A lot of people would know her, at least those here at the time would remember her. It happened a long time ago, can't see how it's important now.'

'You said nothing earlier.'

'Nothing to say. Steve found the photograph, figured he was the one with the information.'

'But you think she's the girl killed at Beachfield?'

'It looks like her. I can't be sure, though, but there's a resemblance all right. The mother was a right lunatic.'

Murray gave him a look, as if to remind Ollie he hadn't forgotten about their last poaching conversation.

'I don't want either of you two clowns going anywhere. Do you hear me?'

Both of them nodded in response.

Ollie thought about telling Murray about the day he found Alison Cronly down on the beach, but decided to play it careful. If he wasn't sure what to say, saying nothing was a whole lot better than doing anything else.

O'CONNOR WAS THE FIRST TO STAND UP AND SHAKE Ellie's hand and then Dr Ebbs'. Kate did the same, only in reverse. Ellie's hand lingered in her grasp a little longer.

'Goodbye, Ellie,' Kate said softly, 'and thank you.'

O'Connor almost bounded up the corridors, switching back on his mobile phone as he walked. Kate said nothing and let him make the call he had been eager to make from the time Ellie Brady had mentioned how the girl's hands had been joined and the name of Gilmartin.

'Donoghue, we'll need to get that file. Ellie Brady's case is connected.' He put his phone on speaker for Kate to hear.

'I'm already on it.'

'And another thing, Donoghue, the guy the boys down in Gorey are talking to, Gilmartin, he was the one who pulled Ellie out of the fire.'

'I know.'

'How do you know?'

'Murray's been on. Gilmartin has confirmed a photograph of Amy Brady was in the possession of the owner of the Carina, a William Cronly.'

'You ran the registration plates?'

'Yeah, it was registered to the late Alison Cronly of Cronly Lodge. Then it changed ownership to her son, William Cronly with an address at Meadow View, Rathmines. I sent a squad car around to the address earlier, but they didn't get an answer. I'm sending another one there now.'

'We'll need a search warrant.'

'We'll need two. The guy still owns a house in Wexford too. It means pulling a judge at the courts in both locations.'

'Donoghue, I want to know everything we can find on him. Social security number, where he works, what he had for breakfast, everything. Who do you have checking the travel details to Italy?'

'A half dozen of the guys from Harcourt Square.'

'You've given them Cronly's name?'

'They're running with it now. I'll come back to you when I know more.'

'Right, let me know when either of those search warrants comes through. I should be back there shortly.'

By the time O'Connor hung up the phone on Donoghue, both he and Kate were in the car on their way back across the city.

'I don't want to rain on your parade, O'Connor, but something isn't adding up here.'

'What do you mean? It all makes perfect sense to me. The Carina, lives local, the guy had a photograph of Amy Brady and an identical MO.'

'Not quite identical.'

'Well it's as near to fucking hell identical to me. The plaiting, the ribbons, the crucifix, positioning of the body, it all adds up. You said yourself, our man likes to repeat.'

'He abducts them first. Then he buries them.'

'Maybe, but perhaps he didn't have a shovel handy, Kate?'

'I'm not saying to rule him out, but it is different. He does repeat, but we're looking at the end result here, people do similar things for different reasons. With Caroline, her death wasn't his intention. It was a frenzied attack that ended in a ritualistic burial. With Amelia, it was premeditated. He went prepared to kill her. But he still abducted both of them.'

'I'm not disagreeing with you there.'

'The burials are two-fold for him, O'Connor – one to protect him, the other to protect his victims. If he planned to kill Amy Brady, he would have taken her, like the other girls. He's a risk-taker, but he would have lured her into going with him. If he did break into the caravan and the girl either refused to go with him or didn't react the way he wanted her to, the killing would have been brutal, frenzied, like Caroline's. Ellie Brady didn't mention any injuries to the girl's body, no blood, no external signs other than the girl looking as if she was sleeping.'

'Yeah but—'

'And why wait?'

'You said it yourself, Kate, it only takes a trigger. Something else coming into the mix to set the whole bloody thing off.'

'I know I did. But once started, these things don't stay dormant. Emotions can remain pent up for decades, but when they unravel, they can't be put on hold.'

'Let's agree to disagree, shall we?' O'Connor pulled up outside her apartment.

'Look, keep me in the picture. Something isn't adding up. I just haven't worked it out yet.' Kate closed the car door behind her.

'Okay,' O'Connor lowered the window on the passenger side.

'Oh, and another thing, O'Connor.' She leaned in. 'If William Cronly did go to Tuscany as a boy, he didn't travel alone. Find out when the mother, Alison Cronly, died. She's part of all this. Nothing happens in isolation.'

'Sure, Kate. Will do. I'll keep you in the picture.'

'Talk to you later.'

O'Connor turned the car with a squeal of tyres, speeding off down the road. Kate watched him leave, then turned to look up at the first-floor window. She hoped Sophie and Charlie were back from the park. Hearing Ellie Brady speak of her devastation had made Kate desperate to hug Charlie. Then in a little over an hour she would get to talk to Declan, and maybe, finally, they could set about rebuilding their life together.

Mervin Road

HE STOOD BACK FROM THE WINDOW IN THE LIVING ROOM, watching Kate say her goodbyes to the driver of the car. He had waited until the babysitter had sent Charlie into the bathroom to wash his hands before grabbing her from behind.

'Shush, now, don't struggle. We don't want to upset Charlie, do we?'

Sophie hadn't listened. He had taught her a lesson, the stupid bitch.

He turned back from the window, happy in the knowledge that Kate was on her way. He looked at Charlie, now sitting on a kitchen chair, facing the doorway from the living room to the hall, ready to greet his mommy.

'Mommy will be here in a second, Charlie. I told you she wouldn't be long.'

He hadn't wanted to tie the boy up or put the duct tape across his mouth, but Charlie had to learn a lesson too. Not everything in life is nice. The sooner he understood that, the better for everyone.

William put his fingers through the boy's hair with his left hand and, kneeling down in front of him, held his Swiss Army knife in the other. 'It's time for you to be the superhero, Charlie.' He wiped the tears from the boy's cheek. 'You are going to be a very good boy. We don't want to upset Mommy, do we?'

He left the living room door open, ensuring Kate would see Charlie from the hallway the moment she arrived home. He smiled at the boy again, skipping into the hall and pressing the flat of his back tight against the wall to the left-hand side of the front door. He heard Kate walk up the communal hallway, then rummage in her bag for her keys. He heard the key going in, turning in the lock. 'Tick tock' went the clock.

The front door half ajar, Kate saw Charlie, feet tied to the chair with a narrow rope, hands behind his back, duct tape across his mouth. She gasped and ran straight over to him, the door closing shut behind her.

'Come in, Kate,' he said. 'Welcome home. Charlie and I have been waiting for you.' He stepped closer, positioning himself between the mother and son, and the front door. This was all going swimmingly.

Kate wrapped her arms around Charlie and gave him a reassuring look before whispering quickly, 'It will be okay, Charlie, I promise.'

William moved towards them. Kate saw the glint of the blade as she knelt by Charlie's side.

'That's a good girl, Kate. We'll all be going for a little drive in a minute – one big happy family. Isn't that right, Charlie?'

'Where's Sophie?' Kate asked.

'Don't worry about Sophie. She's been taken care of. But my apologies, I'm being rude. I forgot to tell you my name, Kate. It's William Cronly, by the way.'

She didn't need an introduction. 'Hello, William.'

'Pick up those comics for Charlie, will you, Kate?' He pointed to a pile of Batman comics on the coffee table to her right. 'He'll need something to read on the way down.'

Kate picked up the pile of comics, as William moved nearer to Charlie. He held the knife to Charlie's throat and she could feel her heart constrict in her chest. Adrenaline pumped around her body, making her feel sick.

'I'll carry him to the car, shall I? It's only around the corner. Now, remember what I told you, Charlie, about being close to sharp blades. They are very dangerous. Isn't that right, Kate?'

O'CONNOR WASN'T LONG BACK AT THE INCIDENT Room when the second squad car reported from Meadow View. There was still no answer at the house.

'Stay there. DI Byrne is on his way, as are Hanley and his crew. I'm expecting the search warrant to come through shortly. Keep me posted.'

He looked up as Donoghue walked into his office.

'Our man works at Newell Design. Rang in sick over the weekend. They haven't seen him since Friday afternoon.'

'Anything on the travel details?'

'The week Antonio Peri died, William Cronly took a Dutch airline flight from Dublin to Paris, and a connecting flight to Galileo Galilei airport at Pisa.'

'What about—'

'Before you even ask, yes, we checked car hire. He picked up a car at Pisa airport. He has an immaculate credit card rating by the way.' Neither of them smiled.

'And the mother?'

'Are you ready for this?' Donoghue raised both eyebrows.

'Tell me.'

'She died two days after the bishop jumped. She was terminally ill for some time – cancer, and accelerated dementia.'

'So Kate was right – the trigger.'

'The what?'

'Nothing. It doesn't matter. What's the story with pulling that old case file?'

'We should have clearance later today.'

'Right, all we have to do now is find the bastard. Let me know when those search warrants are in.'

When Donoghue left, O'Connor picked up Ellie Brady's copybook, reading again her description of the road at the back of the sand dunes. Standing up from his desk, he opened the door and shouted over at Donoghue.

'We'll need another tech team on hand for Wexford. There's a pathway in the vicinity of Cronly Lodge that might need checking.'

'Where?'

'Not sure as yet, but I know someone who has a good idea. Just put it in place.'

'The Dublin warrant is in.'

'Good. Let's see if all these dots join up.'

Before he left, he tried Kate's mobile. It rang out.

Mervin Road

KATE COULD SEE THE TOP OF CHARLIE'S SPIKY BLACK HAIR in the rear-view mirror, but she could also see William Cronly's face. O'Connor had been right; Amy Brady's killing was connected to the Dublin murders. She needed to work this out. She needed time.

'Where are we going, William?'

'Pull out nicely, Kate and head for the N11. We're going on a little trip to Wexford.'

She could hear Charlie whimpering in the back. Her heart was thumping, a passing car blared her out of it as she tried to pull out too fast.

'Relax, Kate. Charlie is going to be just fine.' He smiled.

She drew breath. If he touched or harmed Charlie, she would kill him with her bare hands. She knew that. But she also knew she had to remain calm, for Charlie's sake as much as her own. She couldn't lose it now. What did he want with them? Despite the knife, he was behaving as if they were just going on any old day trip, as if the most pressing concern to him was all of them being nice to each other.

'Why don't you drive, William? You know where we're going. You must know the way better than I do.'

'No, no. I'll stay back here with Charlie. It's very straightforward Kate, just take the same road you use to visit your lovely mother, Gabriel.'

'My mother?' She made her voice remain calm, while her hands gripped the steering wheel, her heart pounding. She clicked on the indicator, ready to pull out from the kerb, this time checking more carefully for traffic, finding it hard to focus, willing herself to be calm.

'It's fine, Kate. Don't fret. Gabriel is doing okay.'

He knew her mother's name. She had no way of knowing if her mother was okay. But Charlie's whimpering in the back was getting louder. He was crying and scared. If the two of them were going to get out of there, no matter how the hell she was going to do it, she needed to concentrate and stop panicking.

'That's the girl. You're doing great. I knew you would be marvellous.'

'Charlie, it's okay. Mommy is just going to drive for a little while.'

'Charlie understands, don't you, Charlie?' Kate watched as Charlie shook his head, frantic, the way he did when he was overtired or distressed. Shit, shit, shit, she thought.

'Now, Charlie, you don't want to make me cross. It's not nice to disagree, a little boy like you, so lucky having such a loving mommy. Although we can't forget Daddy, can we? Where is Daddy, Kate?'

She had to think.

'He's at work.'

'He wasn't at work last night. You don't have to lie to me, Kate. I know he's gone. I saw the suitcase.'

Kate caught his stare in the rear-view mirror. This was worse than she thought. How the hell did William Cronly know so much about her?

'Don't look like that, Kate. You're better off without him. He was never going to be good enough for someone of your calibre.'

She needed to establish a rapport. Right now, all she could do was keep talking and keep using his name. 'Why do you say that, William?'

'Don't be modest, Kate. Your drive, your dedication to your work, your intelligence, the way you applied yourself to finding out so much about me. I've seen you out running. I can recognise someone with discipline and determination. Every fibre of your body, every expression on your face tells me how hard you push yourself. It is a good thing

Declan has gone. It gives us time to work things out together. You do understand, I hope, that I couldn't help what happened to Caroline or Amelia?'

Running, he'd seen her out running. His face had looked familiar, but she couldn't place where she had seen him. Eighty per cent of women know their killer. He'd been with her mother. He knew Declan had left. He knew she was upset. He had watched her. In her head, she could hear her own voice talking to O'Connor: 'He'll latch on to someone, someone familiar to him, someone who got his attention, someone he admires.'

'I understand, William.'

'Good. That pleases me.'

Everything was shooting around in her head, what he knew about her, what she knew about him, and the full extent of her situation – and Charlie's – became clearer by the second. She was the progression. She was the next choice, and the process was already well in motion. She knew that if she let him doubt her, he would kill them both. What could she use to manipulate him? His intelligence? He had mentioned her running – should she talk about physical dexterity, his planning, boost his ego? He took comfort in routine and repeat behaviour. He was looking for friendship, someone to be close to.

'William, why don't you tell me about Silvia?'

'Ah, Silvia,' the words sounded like something delicious had just landed on his tongue. She wanted to scream. 'You know about Silvia? That surprises me.' Sitting forward, the knife still in Charlie's side, he touched her shoulder, resting his fingers lightly, like an insect, his hand lingering. She felt her skin crawl.

He smiled at her. 'But then again, Kate, I'm forgetting how clever you are.'

THEY TRIED THE DOORBELL OF 15 MEADOW VIEW one last time, then put in the door. O'Connor and a couple of the detectives from Harcourt Square entered first and checked that the premises were safe, before stepping back to let Hanley and his crew take over.

The inside of the house was tidy and immaculately clean. It didn't take long for one of Hanley's crew to discover that the shoes and boots in the under-stair storage area were all size nine, with a slight wearing down on the left side. Not a lot on its own, but another piece of the jigsaw as far as O'Connor was concerned.

There were books stacked neatly on the bookshelves either side of the fireplace. On one of the top shelves they found newspaper cuttings of the recent murders, placed in the sleeve of a large hardback book by someone called Pascal.

O'Connor's phone rang. It was Donoghue.

'We have the Wexford warrant. The second tech team and the squad cars are only twenty minutes away.'

'Good. We're doing well here, have matching size nine footwear, and looks like William Cronly liked to collect newspaper clippings of our victims.'

'Nothing conclusive?'

'It's still early days. He's careful, but nobody's perfect.'

'You'd like to think so. I'll let you know when the crew arrives in Wexford.'

'Thanks.'

O'Connor texted Kate – 'Ring me when you can' – before turning, hearing Hanley call him from upstairs.

'You might like to see this, O'Connor.' Hanley held up a clear Ziplock bag with a Polaroid photograph inside. O'Connor stepped over to the bedside locker to stand beside Hanley and took the sealed evidence bag from him. He looked at the photograph of Caroline Devine. Despite O'Connor's overriding desire to nail William Cronly, he was still taken aback by the image of the dead girl.

'Right, Hanley, keep searching. I've a few calls to make.'

Walking back down the stairs, the first call he made was to Samuel Ebbs at St Michael's, the second to the crew on the way to Wexford, speaking to DI Carey, the supervising officer, and the third was to Donoghue. He had only hung up the phone on Donoghue when he got another call back from him.

'O'Connor.'

'Yeah.'

'Declan Cassidy has put a call in.'

'Kate's husband?' O'Connor did a double take, wondering why Kate's husband would have made contact.

'He'd arranged to meet Kate at 5 p.m., but he went home early, wanted to surprise her. Are you sitting down, O'Connor?'

O'Connor felt a sudden coldness rush through him. 'I don't need to fucking sit down. Jesus. What is it?'

'We think our man has taken Kate, and the boy. Cassidy found the babysitter tied up in the child's bedroom, lacerations to the neck, bruising to face and arms. She told him a guy broke in and was carrying a knife.'

'Fuck, fuck, FUCK.'

'He took her over an hour ago, O'Connor.'

'Shit, if he's taken them to Wexford, he could be nearly there by now. Have you pinged Kate's phone?'

'Doing it now.'

O'Connor rang Carey. 'Carey, this is now high risk, category 1 – woman and child kidnapped. I'm sending more men down. Get there fast, but take it easy when you get there. As far as we know, our man is armed with a knife, nothing more. But we can't take any chances. He has Kate Pearson and her child. Nothing can go wrong here. Are you listening to me, Carey? ' His voice rose the further into the call he went.

'I'm hearing you.'

'Good, how long until you get there?'

'Ten minutes at the most.'

'Ring me.'

O'Connor wanted to do anything rather than stand still, but he forced himself to stop and think. What had Kate said? Murder wasn't his motivation with Caroline. He had to have taken her some place he felt safe. Where? It wasn't Meadow View, they'd found nothing there to indicate a primary crime scene. It had to be Cronly Lodge. It was the only thing that made sense.

Getting into the car, his instincts told him to drive straight to Wexford, now, but something else was bothering him. It was the words from Ellie Brady's copybook. Changing the direction of the car, turning it towards St Michael's, the words 'his hideout' repeated themselves over and over in his head, moving from a quite whisper to a loud, relentless scream.

Gorey, County Wexford

KATE HAD TAKEN A GAMBLE ASKING HIM ABOUT Silvia, but she needed to know as much about the man sitting in the back of her car as possible. The more she knew, the more she would be able to understand his motives, and the more ammunition she would have to use against him. She had to pit her wits against his, but it was already a game of catch-up because he knew so much more about her.

'Silvia suffered, you see, Kate. She was an innocent, someone believing in goodness, not clouded the way others are.'

'Silvia was your friend, William?'

'Oh, yes. But I let her down.'

'William, you shouldn't blame yourself.' Was he the reason Silvia fell? Did he cause her accident? Was it an accident? She needed to know who else was there. The bishop, Antonio Peri, certainly, but who else? William must have been just a boy, so he hadn't travelled alone.

'Thank you, Kate, but don't worry about me on that score. It's a burden I've borne for a very long time. I've learned to live with it. I'm not afraid of suffering.'

'You were very young, William. Did you have to travel alone?'

'No, no. Mother and I travelled together. She had a mission, you see.'

'A mission?'

'Yes, an end game. Mother thought she was being very clever. I hate to talk about all this in front of the boy, Kate.'

'It's okay.' She glanced at Charlie in the rear-view, but she needed William to talk. It was the only way she could get her head around what to do next.

'Are you sure, Kate? I'll be discreet, but I do want you to know as much as possible about me.'

'I want to know all about you too, William.'

'I know you do,' his tone soft. 'Well if you're sure.' He paused. 'Sadly, Kate, I was the result of a cleric's indiscretion, at least that was Mother's story. I was illegitimate, a bastard.' He looked over at Charlie. 'Someone to be whispered about. It's not nice when people talk behind your back, Kate.'

Kate tried to maintain her focus on the motorway, taking in each time William Cronly lowered his voice.

'I used to think my father was an explorer. There was a picture of a man on the piano in the music room. An attractive silver frame, you'd have liked it, Kate.'

'Would I, William?'

'Oh, yes. It was very classy. But, of course, my father wasn't an explorer at all. It was just another lie, another fabrication, all cloak and mirrors. Mother was very good at that.'

'What happened when you went to Tuscany, William?'

He didn't answer straight away. He looked out the window, as if his mind had suddenly become distracted. Kate needed to use the time well. If Silvia had died when he was a boy, the event would have traumatised him, tied him into the past, perhaps rendering him incapable of moving on.

'Take the next exit, Kate. We're nearly there.'

'Okay.'

What had been the trigger? Why had he come out of the woodwork? What had changed things? She needed to keep him talking.

'How's Charlie doing in the back?' She had to keep using Charlie's name, too. He needed to look on her son as a person. If she emphasised William's suffering as a boy, maybe he would look on Charlie in the same light.

'He's doing fine. But he's not interested in his comics. Maybe he's tired?'

'He could be. He usually likes comics.'

'I do too.'

'Do you?'

'Oh, yes. Still do. Superheroes, like Charlie.'

Kate smiled thinly. 'You two have a lot in common.'

'Do you think?'

'Definitely.'

'I was hesitant about bringing Charlie with us, Kate.'

'Perhaps we should take him back.'

'Oh, no. But I did worry about the trauma. I'm a very understanding man when it comes to how children feel.'

'I know you are, William.'

'But then I realised something.'

'What was that?'

'Well, it's very simple, Kate. Things like this can make a boy stronger. He's been spoiled, Kate. You must see that. You have to suffer to realise how lucky you are. Don't you agree?'

Kate's knuckles were white, her hands gripping the steering wheel so hard it hurt. 'I guess it depends on the suffering, William.' She could hear the quiver in her voice. But at least, whatever William Cronly's feelings were towards her son, he saw a future for him, no matter how warped it might be.

'William, why don't you tell me about Tuscany?'

'It was beautiful, Kate. The view from Castello de Luca was remarkably similar to home.'

'Home?'

'Cronly Lodge. Don't worry, you will see it soon. It even had some elderberry trees. It was in Tuscany that I met Silvia.'

'What happened to her, William? What happened to Silvia?'

Kate watched his expression in the mirror. She needed to pick up even the slightest change in demeanour. Again, his mind seemed to drift. But this time, she didn't have long to wait.

'It was dreadful, Kate. I loved her, you see. I didn't know it then, far too young to understand. She trusted me, she was my friend.'

'Go on, William. This is important to me too.'

'Is it? I do hope so, Kate. Your feelings matter a great deal to me.'

Again she held her silence, smiling in response, alert to the faintest whimper from Charlie, knowing how terrified he must be.

'When it got dark, Silvia and I would go exploring. It was something I taught her, Kate. I was used to roaming around the house at night, listening to the floorboards creaking, learning to be light of foot. We'd take a kerosene lamp with us because the passages of the castello were dark at night, except for the room with the windows, of course.'

'The room with the windows?'

'Yes. It was our favourite room. Six tall, stained-glass windows in a semi-circle. At night, the moon shone through them, a beam of light exploding into the room. During the day, we would play there together. The rocking horse was there too. In the dark, his eyes reflected the light of the moon, dark red they were, sometimes they looked like large rubies. I went looking for her one night. I wanted to give her a present before I left. But I couldn't find her. She wasn't in her room, and she wasn't in the room with the windows either. It was then that I heard it. The scream, echoing through the walls and the corridors, just like the way the sound travelled in the old town of Suvereto, sending vibrations everywhere. At first I thought it was an animal screaming, the screech was high-pitched, like a wild cat.'

Looking at him in the rear-view mirror, Kate could see his eyes glaze over, as if he were back there, in those rooms, hearing the sound again. He was completely caught up in the memory. She could see that the present had fallen away from him and he was in the past – trapped by the memories, as she'd suspected.

'I followed the sound. I knew the way to the bishop's rooms. He let us play there sometimes. I held the hurricane lamp up high, making sure I could see as much as possible, following the sounds. The closer I got, the more I knew it was her. I called out, wanting her to hear my voice, but I could barely hear my own. The echoes were too strong. When I got to his door, I could hear him, goading, laughing. At first I couldn't open the door, but I used my penknife and fiddled open the lock. I saw him lying on her, pushing into her, her legs spread open. When he turned and saw me, the fat pig didn't care. I ran at him. She screamed, her eyes were wild, lost.'

Again he paused.

'When I flung myself at Antonio, he wrestled with me, throwing me to the ground, and that was when she got free of him. Even when she ran, it was as if she was blind, as if she was looking inside herself instead of ahead. When I called after her, she didn't turn. I followed her, so did Antonio, out to the cliff edge. He was shouting after both of us, his voice vile like the vermin he was. She ran so fast. Her white nightdress made her look like a ghost, a brilliant white against the moon. And then she fell. Her scream lowering in sound the farther down she went. Until all I heard was the silence.'

'Did you help bury her, William?'

'We all did. Antonio, Mother. But I fixed her.'

'In the grave?'

'Yes. I plaited her hair the way she liked to wear it. I went back to the castello to get her crucifix. She wasn't wearing it that night. She had had nothing to protect her. Then I gave her my present.'

'The ribbons?'

'They were red, with a perforated edge, a herringbone pattern. I knew she would like the feel of them. I had taken them in my attaché case. I tied both her plaits, resting them on her shoulders after I positioned her, fixed her nightdress, placed her head on the stone pillow, joined her hands, bent both her knees. She looked as if she was praying. She wanted to be a guardian angel, Kate. Even in death, she wanted to help others.'

'And your mother, William. What did she do?'

Kate watched his face change, anger and a look of defiance returning to it.

'Mother was happy. She got more than she bargained for. It takes a lot of money to keep a mouth shut, especially one as big as hers. It was only a few months ago that I found out the real truth.'

'And what was that, William?'

'She had encouraged him to do what he did. My mother was a whore, Kate. She slept with dogs. Antonio entertained her for a while, but she soon realised he had other interests, interests of the younger variety. Nobody mattered to her, you see, nobody other than herself. I had to take action. I had done nothing for far too long.'

'So what did you do?'

'I killed Antonio of course, pushed him off the cliff edge, the snivelling coward. Begged like a baby, his scream all the better for it.'

'And your mother?'

'I gave her the same death as Amy Brady, smothered her with a pillow. An eye for an eye, Kate.'

'Did you kill Amy Brady, William?'

'No, no. That was Mother. She thought Silvia had come back to haunt her.' He snorted. 'I heard Mother coming back to the house that night. I knew she had been up to no good. She told me she had taken care of everything.'

'So you went back to Amy's caravan?'

'Yes. The girl was still warm. I thought about taking her out of the caravan, looking after her the way I'd looked after Silvia.'

'What happened?'

'I fixed her hair, made sure she was wearing the crucifix. Then I heard that woman's footsteps, the girl's mother, another little whore.'

'Ellie Brady?'

'It was easy to hear her, even from a distance. I heard the crunch of the gravel under her feet. So I did what I could for the girl – joined her hands, prepared her.'

'And what about your mother, William? After the fire, you protected her? You let Ellie Brady take the blame?'

'She hadn't cared for her daughter either. Barely knew she existed.'

'But your mother—' Kate stopped herself.

'What?'

'It doesn't matter.'

'Of course it matters, Kate. I owe you an explanation. I can see that now.' Kate felt the anger rise in his voice as he continued. 'Mother used to say blood is thicker than water, but it wasn't that.'

'No?' Kate wanted to cry, to be anywhere with Charlie other than where they were now.

He laughed loudly. 'I foolishly thought it was madness, you see, brought on by belated guilt. But I was wrong. The only person my mother ever cared about was herself. When she finally told me the truth, I saw that crystal clear.'

'I see.'

'I knew you would, Kate, because you're a very understanding person. Slow down here. We're taking the next right turn.'

Kate slowed down. On taking the turn, she caught a glimpse of the squad cars down the long drive out of the corner of her eye – at exactly the same time as her abductor. He instructed her to keep on going. She thought about stopping the car, screaming out the window for help, but just as she thought this, he pushed the knife closer to Charlie's face.

'Do you like going to the beach, Charlie?'

Charlie had a blank look, as if his mind had reached overload with fear. Kate felt like crying as she looked at her son, his little face white, his eyes blankly staring, all the fight and life gone out of him. His head didn't move this time, he had no response to their abductor's question.

When William directed her towards the beach road, Kate did exactly as she was told.

DONOGHUE TRACED KATE'S MOBILE PHONE TO HER
apartment at Mervin Road. It was not the news O'Connor wanted to
hear. As he pulled into the grounds of St Michael's for the second time
that day, he knew Dr Ebbs would be reluctant to release Ellie Brady
into his care, even if she was accompanied by a nurse – but none of
that mattered. As far as O'Connor was concerned, two lives were in
immediate danger and everything else would have to come second to
that.

When he arrived, he was relieved to see Ellie standing with Dr
Ebbs and a young nurse at the front entrance. The nurse introduced
herself as Sinead. O'Connor opened the back door of the car for the
two of them, ushering them in as fast as he could. All the while, Dr
Ebbs was in his ear, talking constantly about what to do and not to
do, but he was only half-listening. His mind was on Kate. All going
well, he could reach Cronly Lodge in a little over half an hour with
the sirens on.

He was speeding down the N11 when he got the call from Carey.

'Carey, fill me in.'

'No sign of Cronly, Kate or her son down here. I've cordoned off the
surrounding area. It's a detached house, set on about an acre. I think
we have our primary crime scene. Tech team have picked up residue
markings of elongated blood splatters on the wall near the fireplace

in the main living area, then smaller blood-splatter traces farther out. They've bagged and tagged a number of items already, including a metal fireside poker. We have traces of blood pooling in the living room, and also in the garage out the back. Area one, the living room, most likely place of initial attack. Area two, the garage, was probably where body or bodies were brought before or after death.'

'How old are the blood markings?'

'They're not from today, if that's what you're asking. Preliminary feedback from techies is that it looks like an attempt was made to clean the scene, but they're picking up enough trace evidence to keep them busy for some time.'

'Okay. Anything else?'

'We bagged a lot from upstairs too, especially in what looks like a kid's bedroom. We found an attaché case with a number of items, including a silver crucifix and a spool of red ribbon. Plus three small plastic zip bags, each with a lock of hair.'

'Well you have plenty of support down there, so I want eyes and ears everywhere.'

'I'm about to set up checkpoints in and out of the town.'

'No, don't. No uniforms. Keep it plain-clothed and low key. If Cronly is heading in that direction, I don't want to spook him. We'll need some DIs down at the beach too. That's where I'm heading. I should be there shortly. '

'Right, I'll pull the marked cars away from the front of the house. But O'Connor, he's going to know he has visitors.'

'He might know that already. Even so, I don't want to push him out of the area entirely. Any change, phone me.'

O'Connor almost forgot about Ellie and Sinead in the back of the car, until Ellie spoke, quietly, but assured.

'What's his name, Detective?'

'The man we're looking for?'

'Yes.'

'William. His name is William Cronly.'

O'Connor waited for her response. When it came, Ellie's voice remained slow, as if the speed of his car and the need to get to Wexford fast were completely at odds with her thinking.

'Detective, you think he killed those girls from Dublin?'

'I do.'

'And what about Amy?'

O'Connor needed to control his voice, keep it gentle, especially now he knew Kate and Charlie weren't at Cronly. Ellie was his only means of finding this guy's hideout and he wasn't taking any chances.

'A photograph of Amy was found, Ellie, at William Cronly's house in Wexford.'

'What kind of photograph?'

O'Connor knew Ellie's question was loaded. What she really wanted to know was whether or not her daughter was alive in it. From what he'd heard from Donoghue, the photograph was taken while the girl was very much alive.

'I haven't seen it myself, Ellie, but it's a Polaroid image taken of Amy probably while you were holidaying that year.'

'Holidaying?' Ellie said it in a tone that contradicted every common understanding of the term. 'How are you so sure it's a photograph of Amy?'

'I don't have the full details, but I understand Gilmartin, the man who dragged you from the fire, has identified her in it. Ellie,' O'Connor's voice was almost pleading, 'we'll be there shortly. I need your help. You do understand that, don't you?'

'I understand you're telling me that William Cronly is the one who killed my daughter.'

'Yes, Ellie, we believe so.' Ellie kept her silence. O'Connor continued. 'We also believe he killed Caroline Devine and Amelia Spain.' Ellie did not respond. O'Connor knew he needed her onside.

'Ellie?'

'Yes?'

'I don't want Kate or her son added to that list.'

'Nor do I, Detective O'Connor, nor do I.'

For the first time since his passengers got into the car at St Michael's, he breathed a sigh of relief for that at least.

DRIVING DOWN THE BEACH ROAD, HE TOLD KATE TO PARK the car at the back of the closed-down amusement arcade, instructing her to get out and wait while he unbuckled Charlie from the back seat.

Kate thought about making a grab for Charlie and running as far away as she could, but she knew that with Charlie in her arms, he'd outrun her. She still had the car keys, so if she overpowered him, she might have a chance to get away, but he was fit, strong enough to win the physical battle against her. She couldn't risk it. If she crossed him, he'd know all the trust-building in the car was nothing more than a pretence, and Charlie would be in even more danger. If she had any hope of getting herself and Charlie out alive, she had to keep playing his game, wait for her chance to get her hands on that knife, use her head, and hope that the opportunity would come soon.

Standing with her back to the deserted amusement arcade, her legs felt like jelly, the sharp October breeze blowing her hair in every direction. She was shivering, more from fear for Charlie than from the cold, but still she smiled at their abductor, as if they were a normal family out on a day trip.

When she heard Charlie moaning from behind the duct tape and saw him struggling in William Cronly's arms, it took every ounce of self-discipline she had not to make a grab for him.

'Now, now, Charlie, you don't want to make me angry.'

Kate moved forward. 'Shush, Charlie. It's okay, don't worry. Maybe I should carry him, William? He'll be less of a handful with me.'

'I don't think so, Kate. The track we're taking is steep and you're not used to it. You might let him fall.'

'I'll be careful.'

'Trust me, I know these things. Now, Charlie, don't get me annoyed.'

'Honestly. I'll take him, William. It'll be better.'

'Okay,' he relented, 'but I'll keep close behind you, that way I can take him quickly if you stumble. We don't want anything happening to him Kate, do we?'

Charlie grabbed hold of her, tight, like a wild baby chimp. He buried his face into her neck. Kate felt his tears on her skin. She put a hand under his jacket, wanting him to feel her close. She felt his skin soaked with sweat through his T-shirt, heard his heart thumping, remembered her own feeling of terror all those years before. He had grabbed her from behind, a knife to her throat, her screams loud but unheard, knowing the only thing between her and death was the most fleeting of chances.

'Shush, Charlie don't cry, it's okay. Mommy is here.'

THE DISCOVERY OF CAROLINE DEVINE'S PHOTOGRAPH at Meadow View was conclusive evidence as far as O'Connor was concerned. He had no doubt that the blood and hair samples taken from the Lodge would link William Cronly to Caroline's murder, and ultimately to that of Amelia Spain. Coupled with the knowledge that he had taken a flight to Italy the week Antonio Peri died, and had in his possession a photograph of Ellie's daughter, O'Connor was certain that the man who had taken Kate and Charlie was the same man who had committed all four murders.

In five minutes he would be at the beach front. O'Connor again went over in his mind everything Kate had told him about the killer. The high level of intimacy he perceived with his victims, a risk-taker within controlled parameters, leaned towards the familiar, repeat behaviour, watched his victims before making contact and believed he was developing a relationship with them. O'Connor cursed under his breath. All this time they had been looking for the killer, the killer had been watching Kate.

He thought back to earlier that afternoon, when he had dropped Kate off at her apartment. He had been the one who had left her there. He was the one who had driven away, when the man he most wanted to have by the throat was lying in wait for her. O'Connor struggled to stay focused on the road opening up in front of him, knowing that if everything Kate had said about the killer was true, he had taken her somewhere he felt safe, a place that had to be so close now. It took everything in O'Connor's power to stay focused. He phoned Donoghue.

'Donoghue, is everything in place?'

'DIs are there, all armed.'

'And they know to hold out until I get there?'

'They're on the ready, waiting for you. Nolan's been informed. We have dog teams there too. They've a woollen hat belonging to the boy and a scarf belonging to Kate. Helicopters on standby for wide sweep of the area should we need them.'

'I don't want to spook him.'

'I know that, O'Connor. The DIs have called in a Carina with matching plates parked at the back of the amusement arcade. It was found empty.'

'I can see it now, Donoghue. I'm pulling in.'

'Take it easy, O'Connor.'

'I will.'

The tyres of his car screeched to a stop on the gravel. He turned to his back-seat passengers and said as calmly as he could, 'Okay, Ellie, it's time.'

The Hideout

KATE CARRIED CHARLIE IN HER ARMS, REASSURING HIM, constantly whispering in his ear as she walked the dirt track, the back of the sand dunes on her right. It was bitterly cold now and almost dark. The breeze coming in from the sea was biting and without mercy. William Cronly followed closely behind her, like a shadow. Her old fears ever present, only this time her fears were not for herself but for the little boy frightened and crying in her arms.

Charlie wanted to pull the duct tape off his mouth, but she told him to leave it. She couldn't risk him screaming and upsetting their abductor. She remembered her response to O'Connor's question about what would happen if his next victim didn't play ball: 'He will lose it, his temper will flare up again, only next time, his disappointment will be greater because next time, he has nowhere else to turn. It will be everyone else's fault except his own. He won't internalise blame, he isn't capable of that. The victim, whoever she is, will suffer, as will anyone else unlucky enough to be with her.'

Farther down the track, to their left, the land opened up to harvested fields, while the dirt track continued to skirt the back of the sand dunes. When the track narrowed, she saw the trees up ahead. They were elderberry trees, just as Ellie Brady had written in her copybook. He was taking them to his 'hideout'. This meant that, in his eyes, she was still within his trust. She knew she must not do anything to risk breaking that trust. Right now, his fragile sense of connection was all that was keeping them alive.

Declan would have tried to phone her after five o'clock, as

promised. Would he keep trying to call, or wait for her to call him back? Would he go to the apartment? At what point would someone raise the alarm about Sophie? She had no way of knowing if anyone would miss either of them. She felt so alone, with Charlie in her arms and William Cronly at her back. It was all down to her. She knew her son's life was in her hands, and she wasn't altogether sure she was equal to the task of protecting him.

At the end of the path, they met a steep incline and, beyond it, she could see the woods. Dark twigs and fallen leaves from the last few weeks felt slippery and wet underfoot. When she lost her footing, Cronly touched her right arm.

'We're okay,' she assured him.

'Not long now, Kate.' After the incline, Kate could see a steep drop to her right into more woodland, stone boulders covered in moss, the air filled with forest smells, creaking branches, birds and insects buzzing. It was like everything was in high definition as she tried to remember the way, tried to take in any detail that might prove helpful.

When they reached the edge, she put Charlie down, telling him to wait while she made her way to the ledge below. He whimpered, his eyes bloodshot. Cronly lifted him into her waiting arms, then followed them, jumping with the agility of a man half his age. The way down got steeper the farther they went. All the time William Cronly stayed close behind them. When they came to another clearing, the ground levelled off, and William stepped past her, walking on ahead for another twenty metres. He stopped suddenly, pulling back branches and all manner of natural camouflage, to reveal what could only be described as a cave.

Kate felt the panic rising in her, facing the prospect of going inside this hidden place, a place that if you didn't know existed, you would never find. As soon as she stepped inside with Charlie, they would be trapped in a whole other way. A feeling of sickness swept over her again. How could she get them out of this?

Once inside the cave, he lit a hurricane lamp. The light revealed a small camp burner for cooking, comics, and books covered with clear plastic sitting on a flat-topped trunk to her left. All manner of tins and boxes were lined up on metal shelves in the corner. She saw an oval mirror with steel grips hanging on a silver chain, supported by a masonry nail hammered into a groove in the granite wall. She thought about pulling it down and wrapping the chain around his neck. It was a chance, but she hesitated a second too long and the chance was gone. She had to be ready. If she got any kind of an opportunity, she would have to take it.

As Kate's eyes adjusted to the lamp light, other items gradually became clear. There was a basin on a stand. To the left of it, some soap and a towel, it too covered in clear plastic. Against one wall stood a toy soldier wearing a red uniform, half a metre tall, dressed like a sentry with a toy gun held high on his shoulder. Many of the tins on the shelves had stickers: Tea, Coffee, Marbles, Matches, Nails. The place smelled of paraffin and moss and damp, the ground a mix of clay and grit.

'Sit down.' He pointed to a grey stone boulder to the right of the cave opening, one big enough for both Kate and Charlie to sit on together. Kate sat down first. Charlie wanted to sit on her lap, but she placed him to her side so she would be ready to leap forward at the faintest glimmer of opportunity. She put her arms around him, rubbing her fingers through his hair, trying to keep him calm. Lowering her head, she whispered, 'Shush, shush,' over and over into his ear, until his body eased and his crying settled.

'Is this your place, William?' she asked, already knowing the answer.

'Yes, it's brilliant, isn't' it?' His voice now more enthusiastic than before.

'Yes.' She kept looking around her. 'How long have you had it?'

'Since I was a boy. I found it one day purely by accident. I was on a treasure hunt.'

Suddenly it all made sense – the comics, the toys, the secret hideaway. He was stuck. Part of William Cronly had never moved on into adulthood. In his mind, he still craved being that small boy. What happened to Silvia had never left him. He was trapped, caught in a time before whatever guilt or loss had got mixed into the whole sorry mess that was his life.

'I have a present for you, Kate.' He took a small silver crucifix out of his inside pocket.

'You shouldn't have.' She reached out, took it and opened the clasp, then fixed it around her neck, before pulling Charlie back in tight beside her.

'Oh, but I had to, Kate. I have a confession to make, you see.'

She looked up at him. The height of his body above her felt oppressive. Again, he reached into his jacket pocket. He took out a length of red ribbon, the same colour and size as he had used to plait Caroline and Amelia's hair. She said nothing as he placed it on the shelf behind him. Then he showed her a pearl earring – one she recognised as her own.

'I'm a bit of a magpie, Kate. I hope you don't mind.'

'I don't mind at all, William.'

He took a torch out of his backpack and switched it on, sending the light to the ceiling of the cave. She heard a flapping noise. He stuck the base of the torch into the part-mud, part-grit floor and sat down opposite her on another boulder.

'Now we're here, Kate, I have a question for you.'

She waited.

Ellie

DETECTIVE O'CONNOR IS TELLING SINEAD THAT under no circumstances is she to leave the car, assuring her that he will stay close to me. Another police officer gets in beside her. I can tell young Sinead is out of her depth.

I hear O'Connor issue instructions into his walkie-talkie. 'Everyone is to take it nice and easy. We don't want him knowing we're here.'

There are police dressed in SWAT gear, dogs, German shepherds, and men who I assume are plain-clothes detectives. I feel the breeze coming in from the sea. I shiver. O'Connor puts his jacket around me and for the first time, I can see his gun.

The shutters on the amusement arcade are all down, but I can hear the whiz of the slot machines, the ping of the pinball, see the silver coins moving back and forth on trays, everyone trying to win a prize.

I walk down the pathway I went down with Amy.

'Try to remember everything,' O'Connor says.

I want to turn back time. To be with her again, instead of stopping the way I did all those years before, not doing as she asked. I want to follow her this time.

'Are you sure this is the way, Ellie?'

'I'm sure.'

I taste the wet salt air, sand blows into my eyes from the sand dunes, the fields to my left are flat. I can see Amy; she is running ahead of me. She turns and smiles, pulling some wild grasses from the side of the dirt track, making a pretend fan. I hear the sounds of strangers, families playing on the beach, ghosts in her world. The road narrows ahead of me, and I see the elderberry trees. Their berries are dark red, shrivelled, limp. Out of season.

O'Connor is telling his people to spread out. They move like silent whippets, quieter than the creaking trees. We reach the point where the ground drops down into the woodland. I can no longer see the sand dunes.

'Where did you go next, Ellie?'

I can hear Amy's voice, begging me to follow her. I look all around me.

'Where Ellie, you have to remember? Where did you go next?'

I wish I could turn back the clock, change everything, take Amy by the hand, go with her.

'Ellie?' His voice rises for the first time.

'I'm so sorry.'

'Ellie, you need to remember. Where did you go next?'

I look at him, wanting to give him the answer. I hate myself all over again.

'I didn't go any farther with Amy.' I shake my head from side to side. 'I told her we needed to go back.'

The Hideout

KATE WAITED FOR HIM TO ASK HIS QUESTION, ALL THE time wondering how she should handle her next move. He still had the knife in his right hand. Somehow, she had to persuade him to put it down. If she had the knife, she and Charlie had a chance, however small. She needed him to relax more. She had to encourage his belief that she could give him everything he wanted – trust, loyalty, friendship. If she could do that, it was her best chance of getting that knife away from him.

'Yes, Kate. It's a rather difficult question to ask.'

The words 'trust, loyalty, friendship' repeated in her head. He had to believe her.

'I don't mind, William. Go right ahead. We're all friends here.'

He smiled back at her, but Kate could tell he still wasn't sure if he should believe her just yet.

'I do hope so, Kate. I value friendship enormously.'

'I know you do, and so do I.'

'Kate, I know about the attack. The one when you were twelve. I read the report.'

She was furious at herself. She should have worked this out. He had been in her apartment, had waited for her, but he could have been there before, taken her earring then. He had noticed her out running, admired her determination. The investigation had brought her directly into his focus. If he had read the report, he knew all about her vulnerability, had already likened it to his own – a common bond.

'These things make us who we are, William.'

'I know they do, Kate. But the report, it wasn't specific. It lacked detail. The truth of everything is in the detail, don't you agree?'

Kate thought before answering. She needed this man to trust her fully, even if he was the last person on earth she wanted to share her fears with. She had no choice. Trusting someone with a secret, sharing a piece of yourself, was the quickest way to establish a higher level of friendship, parting with information normally given to those you cared about, people you believed would understand.

'I feel I can trust you, William.'

'You can, Kate.'

She sensed him softening, his shoulders relaxing. The grip on the knife, was it less tight? Was she imagining it?

'I was very frightened.' She wrapped her right arm tighter around Charlie, holding his hands in her left hand.

'Go on, Kate.'

'I'd gone out with friends. We got separated. I could still hear them talking up ahead, but I knew someone was following me.'

'How did you know?'

'I'd seen him earlier, out of the corner of my eye. It was just a fleeting movement. I'd forgotten about it instantly. But then I knew something wasn't right. I got a kind of sense.'

'What kind of sense?'

'I don't know, as if I'd heard him, a feeling that someone was closing in. I told myself not to be stupid. I kept on walking, as fast as I could, trying to catch up with the others. It was then that he grabbed me from behind.'

Kate looked to check any change in his reaction. There didn't seem to be any.

'He held a knife to my throat.'

He looked down at the knife in his hand, but kept holding it.

'I started to scream. I kept on screaming. It must have been loud, but I could barely hear it. It was as if it was inside of my head instead of being outside. As if the sound only existed in my mind, loud and silent at the same time. I was sure no one would hear it.'

'What did you do?'

'At first, nothing. He pulled me farther into the woods. He wasn't speaking, but I could hear him breathing, heavy breaths, the stench of alcohol, his panting on my neck. It felt wet from him, and the sweat, his arms locked around me, the knife cutting into my throat. It was then I saw them. Two men – they seemed so far away. They were my only hope. I kept screaming, even though I knew they couldn't hear me, but it panicked him. He loosened his grip ever so slightly. It was only for a split second, but it was enough. I pulled away from him and ran and ran and ran, until I could no longer hear him, feel him, smell him.'

'What happened then?'

'Nothing.'

'Nothing?'

'I was safe. At least at first I thought I was. I thought I'd got away from him, but in my mind I never did. In my mind, he never left me.'

'Did they ever find him, Kate?'

'No. I still don't know who he was. He's a stranger, a man without a face.'

'Do you dream about him, Kate?'

'All the time.'

He believed her. She was sure of it. The truth isn't an easy thing to falsify. He looked at the knife again, this time as if he felt guilt about it being there. She was so close to getting him to release it. She had to continue.

'Sometimes at night, I can still feel him close to me again, his breath wet on my neck, the tinge of the blade. Even now, I can't bear to have someone walk close behind me.'

'I'm sorry about earlier. I hadn't realised.' His eyes softened. 'Is that why you run, Kate?'

'I run, William, because I feel it gives me control. If I run, if I keep on running, all the time getting faster, pushing myself hard, I believe I can outrun him.'

Kate glanced down at his left hand; his grip was definitely loosening. He pulled down the zipper of his jacket with his right hand, undid the top button of his shirt. She would only get one more chance.

'I see,' he said, exhaling a deep breath.

Kate looked away, seeing again the pile of comics and books. Under the clear plastic, she could make out the name – Blake, William Blake.

'William, you read Blake I see.' She pointed to the books.

'Oh, yes.' He pulled himself out of his reverie, smiling. 'I forgot all about your interest in literature. Your copy of *Palgrave's Golden Treasury*, a present from your father, I understand.'

She wanted to scream again.

'Such a shame, Kate, that they left Blake out of that collection. Shakespeare, Wordsworth, Keats, all included, but no Blake. *Songs of Innocence* – are you familiar with his poem, 'Night'?'

'No, William. I'm afraid I'm not.'

Would he want to show her the poem? It was a chance.

'Oh, it's wonderful, Kate.' He stood up. 'It speaks of an innocent world protected by angels.'

'Can I read it?'

'Of course you can.' He still had the knife in his hand. He bent down beside her, leaning in to open the plastic covering on the books. 'You see, Kate, the angels thought they had the power to protect, that they could prevent the slaughter of lambs by wolves and tigers. Silvia thought so, too.'

The plastic is difficult to prise open. He puts down the knife.

Kate leapt with a decisiveness she didn't even know she was capable of. She lunged for the knife where it lay on the ground, using the split-second of his surprise to get to it first. She didn't hesitate for a second – sticking the blade deep into his neck and shoulder, close to his throat. She pulled it back, then pushed it down again, harder, deeper, until she saw the blood. When he fell back to the ground, she grabbed Charlie and ran. She ran faster than she had ever run, faster than she thought possible, holding Charlie in a vice grip across her chest, only looking forward, even though she could hear him closing in behind her.

The Woodlands

O'CONNOR LOOKED ALL AROUND HIM, TAKING IN everything he saw, everything he could hear, knowing it was like looking for a needle in a haystack. If this was it, he would have to send in the tracker dogs, even though it risked alerting Cronly to their presence. He divided the SWAT teams up further, spreading out the search area, putting the tracker teams on alert. Ellie was standing beside him, quiet and watchful.

He looked up to the sky. The light was fading fast. This would become almost impossible once they were working in darkness. *Where are you, Kate?*

It was then that he heard it, the first noise. It sounded like an animal in the undergrowth, branches breaking, scuffling. He looked sharply in the direction from where the noise was coming. He felt Ellie's body tense up beside him, she had heard it too.

Then it came – a scream from deep in the woodlands. Above him, the jackdaws took flight from the trees.

He heard someone call out. A man's voice. The man was roaring in a rage, 'Kate. Kate. Kate.'

O'Connor gave the signal and the teams moved immediately and in unison, closing the net on the area. As they worked forward, there was a flash of colour through the trees. The noise of scampering increased – like a fox running away from a pack of hounds. The teams raised their weapons, at the ready.

'Hold fire. Wait. Hold back,' O'Connor called.

Then he saw her: it was Kate, crashing down through a pathway in the woods, her hair streaming behind her, her eyes wild, her son clutched across her chest. She wasn't thinking, wasn't looking – she was just running blindly, running for her life.

O'Connor moved quickly, Kate and her son were still a good way down, a steep drop separated them. He ran towards the incline, closing the gap, leaving Ellie behind him. When he saw Cronly emerging from the trees, he could see he was gaining pace on her. O'Connor saw the blood coming from his neck. He had a bloodied knife in his right hand, holding it up high, his face a mask of anger and hatred.

O'Connor bellowed into the walkie-talkie. 'Suspect armed with knife. Cronly's injured.'

O'Connor jumped down to the ledge and Kate finally saw him. Her eyes registered disbelief before her face clamped down with a determined look – she ran even faster, straight towards him.

He shouted to his teams again. 'Victims close. Get ready to make your move.'

'O'Connor,' she screamed. Cronly was almost in touching distance of her.

O'Connor lunged for her, pushing her to one side and throwing himself on top of her and the boy. He roared into the walkie-talkie. 'I have them. Get him. Now!'

≈

O'Connor let DI Carey carry out the arrest of William Cronly, once they had taken him back to where the cars were parked by the amusement arcade. As far as O'Connor was concerned, he wanted to put as much distance as he could between him and the man he had wanted to track down from the moment they discovered Caroline Devine's tiny body. His concern now was Kate, Kate and her son.

'You two okay?'

Kate was bent over Charlie's rigid body, cradling him like a baby, a broken silver chain with a crucifix discarded at her side. She looked completely done in. Gently, she removed the duct tape from Charlie's mouth and massaged his face, whispering to him all the while. O'Connor stood awkwardly beside them, watching. Slowly, the boy's body relaxed somewhat and he fell against his mother, holding her hand tightly and crying into her shoulder.

'Now, now, there's a good boy. It's all over. The man is gone. The police have him. It's okay.'

O'Connor knelt down beside them. 'Charlie,' he said, rubbing the boy's arm, 'I'm Detective Inspector O'Connor.' The boy sniffed and looked at him. 'I'm the policeman who was in charge of catching that bad man. He's safely in the back of the squad car now – you know, the one with the blue flashing light. He's going straight to jail, Charlie. He can't get at you or your mum ever again. Okay?'

Kate smiled gratefully at him. Her heart was still pounding, but she attempted to speak as normally as possible – for Charlie's sake.

'What was that thing you did back there, some kind of combat manoeuvre?'

O'Connor smiled at her. He wanted to touch her face, but he didn't let himself. 'I needed to get you both down quickly.'

Her smile faltered. 'I know you did. Thanks.' She pulled Charlie's face in close to her chest. 'Can I borrow your phone, O'Connor?'

'Sure.'

O'Connor issued instructions to the tech team that was examining the hideaway. 'Take your time down there, guys, we can't miss a beat on this one.'

Declan's phone rang once before he answered it.

'It's Kate … Yes, we're fine. Don't worry, we're okay. We're both here. Charlie is right here with me.'

O'Connor turned away.

'I know,' Kate continued. 'We love you, too.' She handed the phone to Charlie. 'It's Daddy.'

O'Connor turned back to them. He saw the tears streaming down Kate's face as she knelt beside her son, still holding him close to her. O'Connor nodded to himself; things like this make people stronger as a family.

He looked away again and snapped into the walkie-talkie, 'Carey, have you got him in the car?'

The cracking sound of gunfire blocked out Carey's response.

Ellie

'WHEN DETECTIVE O'CONNOR LEFT ME TO HELP KATE and her son, I slipped away unnoticed. During the mayhem, everyone thought I was with someone else. It was a risk, going to the caravan park. There was no guarantee that Ollie Gilmartin would still have his gun.'

'How did you know he had one?'

'I couldn't be sure, Dr Ebbs, that he still had it, but I remembered the night he caught me sneaking out of the caravan. I was trying to get to Andrew. I think Gilmartin was out poaching.'

'The night before the fire?'

'No, no, it was a couple of nights before that. I recognised the type of gun, a Lanber. He was all mouth about it, talking about its reliability or some such nonsense. He was trying to distract me from asking too many questions. I guess I was doing the same thing.'

'I see.'

'His place wasn't far, positioned right at the front of the caravan site. I had only been there once, with Joe. It's funny the things you remember.'

'So what happened when you got there?'

'I can still see myself walking towards it, then thumping the front window of his caravan, hard, the noise reverberating, as if it was knocking on the doors of memory. I stood back when he opened the door. I watched him walk down the steps from his caravan, wanting to get a handle on what was going on. The police cars and officers at the amusement arcade hadn't made a sound, but when he stood forward, he could see their blue lights flashing behind me.'

'You were calm during all this, Ellie?'

'Fifteen years is a long time to wait, Dr Ebbs. At first, when he saw it was me, Gilmartin looked like he'd seen a real ghost. He was speechless. But I could tell his curiosity was aroused when he noticed the squad cars in the distance. It didn't take a lot to get him going. Even if I hadn't told him the police wanted him, he'd have looked for any excuse to hightail it out of there.'

'Away from you?'

'Yes. I recognised the guilt on his face. The truth isn't an easy thing to handle. I know that more than anyone. A guilty conscience, Dr Ebbs, is a mighty powerful thing.'

'What did you say to him exactly?'

'Not a lot.'

Dr Ebbs looks surprised.

'He went to go back inside, to grab his coat or whatever, but I stopped him. I told him he needed to hurry, that Detective O'Connor wanted him now. They had Cronly. He had to hurry. He was hardly going to argue with me.'

'So you went inside his caravan?'

'Memory, Dr Ebbs, it's a strange thing, isn't it?'

'I guess it is, Ellie.'

'When I stepped inside that caravan, it was like I was back to the day I stood there with Joe, Amy waiting for us outside in the car. Gilmartin, he had a small plastic statue of the Virgin Mary. It had caught my eye that first day, sitting on top of a black leather Bible. They were both still there, in exactly the same spot. Incredible, isn't it, Dr Ebbs, how some people are such creatures of habit?'

'So you looked for his gun?'

'I ransacked the place, found his tools in the corner. There was a locked cabinet, a makeshift thing, barely keeping itself together. I used his crowbar to prise it open.'

'And the bullets?'

'They were in a cardboard box in the kitchen drawer, handy in case of unwanted visitors.' I let out a short laugh. I can tell Dr Ebbs isn't amused, but he doesn't interrupt.

'I broke open the barrel of the Lanber, put in two cartridges, closed the gun, pulled the safety button back, the way my father had shown me, ready to take aim. I was more sure about what I was about to do than I had been about anything in my entire life.'

'Go on, Ellie.'

'I walked back to the amusement arcade. It wasn't far. When I got there, one of the detectives had William Cronly. There was blood on his neck, and his hands were cuffed at the front.'

'You fired?'

'Yes. I felt the gun bolt, jolting me, the sound of both bullets, louder than anything I had ever heard.'

'So what stopped you, Ellie?'

'What stopped me shooting William Cronly?'

'Yes.'

'When I looked at him, Dr Ebbs, I believed I would kill him. The choice, at long last, was mine to make. For what it's worth, after I called out his name, before I pulled back the trigger, when he stared back at me, I think he knew exactly who I was.'

'But you fired the bullets into the air instead?'

'I used to think, Dr Ebbs, that the hardest thing about loss was the remembering, because within it, the true enormity of things becomes fully realised. It is strange the way the mind can trick you into believing one thing. To be so sure of something, you never doubt it. You keep failing to ask the right questions. The truth hides, you see. It can stay hidden from you for a very long time, if you let it. I know I did. Right up until the moment I realised I needed to grasp the one thing I was trying hardest to run away from.'

'And what was that, Ellie?'

'The very thing that mattered most of all. When I walked that dirt track, the one at the back of the sand dunes, I felt Amy there with me, walking ahead, willing me to follow her, as if the past fifteen years hadn't mattered. She called to me, Dr Ebbs. She was there, waiting for me. She always has been.

'When the choice was mine to make, I thought of Amy and me, and not of him. Evil had visited the two of us. We had not asked for it or wanted it to enter our lives. When I looked at William Cronly, I understood. All the evil belonged to him, or whatever rotten life had made him who he was. It did not belong to Amy, or to me. The evil wasn't part of us. I think, in the end, I decided there had already been far too much killing.'

'So what now, Ellie?'

'Have you ever been on a carousel, Dr Ebbs?'

'Yes, Ellie, as a boy.'

'It turns around and around for so long, you think it is never going to stop. The coloured lights can be blinding, its music playing over and over, until you feel almost part of it, as if the world beyond the carousel is a world you are no longer ready for, or belonged to.'

'And are you ready now, Ellie?'

'No, not quite, but I will be.'

ACKNOWLEDGEMENTS

The creation of a novel is a journey which begins well before the first word is written and continues long after the last full stop. I owe a huge debt of thanks to many people who I have been lucky enough to meet along the way, and I will try to thank as many of them as possible here.

Firstly, I would like to thank the members of An Garda Síochána who assisted in the research for this novel, specifically, Tom Doyle of Rathfarnham Garda Station and Paul Smith, Bookman at Tallaght Garda Station and Incident Room, who helped me with a wide variety of questions regarding police procedure. Any inaccuracies within the manuscript are mine and not theirs.

The publication of this story would not have happened without the hard work and belief of a number of key people: Ger Nichol, my agent, who has been a trail blazer from the outset; the team at Hachette Books Ireland, especially Ciara Doorley, commissioning editor, and thanks also to Rachel Pierce, editor extraordinaire, who made the whole editorial process such a positively creative experience.

I returned to writing in 2006 after a twenty-year gap, taking small steps at first but learning and making great friends within the writing community. I would like to thank Eileen Casey, who facilitated my first creative-writing class, and who rekindled in me the wonder of the written word. Also, Dermot Bolger, who took myself and a small group of emerging writers from South County Dublin under his wing, helping each of us to follow this wonderful creative process. Shortly after returning to writing, I joined Lucan Creative Writers Group, and words cannot express the debt I owe to my fellow writers and lifelong friends within this group, people who I feel privileged to know, and who will always be close to my heart. I would like to say a particular thanks to the late Joan O'Flynn, a writer, a friend and a woman who made an enormous difference to my life.

My thanks to Vanessa O'Loughlin from Inkwell and Writing.ie, a wonderfully energetic lady who has stepped forward and channelled a vibrant, writing and reading community. Also thanks to the amazing team at the Irish Writers' Centre, who do enormous work supporting writers within this fantastic writing sanctuary.

I would also like to thank Triona Walsh, who gave me the impetus necessary to take this brave step; Mary Lavelle, who kindly and diligently read the first draft of this manuscript, and Valerie Sirr, who suggested *Palgrave's Golden Treasury*.

Social media has changed the way we communicate with each other and in the main I have found this to be a hugely positive experience, gaining many friends through Twitter, Blogger, Facebook and other media links. The list of people I have met, and who have helped me along the way, is far too extensive to mention individually here, but you know who you are, and I thank you from the bottom of my heart.

Thanks to all my friends, writers and non-writers, for believing in me and being such a support throughout this wonderful experience. My deepest and heartfelt thanks to my family, especially my husband, Robert, to whom this book is dedicated, my wonderful daughters, Jennifer and Lorraine, and my equally wonderful son, Graham, and a very special thanks to my beautiful first grandchild, Caitriona, who waited patiently in the wings while the last edits to this manuscript were put in place.